Burying The Shadow

The line to the feasting table is drawn:
At its head the amorphic stand of permanence,
Withering strands of sun.
Absent are the sectarians;
Their places home now to dust and scorn.
Here seasons ride through on fire,
Swollen for this spring of blood.
At prayer-tide the reflection must die:
Shadow lingers in the mind, exciting inquisition.
Enter the colonnade, soul-thorns blossom as fell garlands,
Petulent and lewd.
The unjust are abroad,
Fulcrum shifting through translucent ground.

Caught between moon and eye, lies Man;
Existent as waves curious of the shore,
Scavenging in truant shadows for flesh to clothe dreams.
Some, drunk on the elixir of thought,
Beckon for sweet violation amongst threads of chanted rain;
Purging impurity with rhythm-wine,
Earth noise, without language to break its back.
From cloudless iris the outcasts gaze, masked by overfall;
Solace seeking for souls grown ripe;
Veiled of ash, adorning arms of the ancient
Witness to immaculate union.

A splintered table, encircled
By convergent fingers of reparation,
Ascending inward
Through convoluted time: eternity smiles.
Suffer the Eloim. . .

Sek-eh-zoad Ess-keh-reh-eh-tah

BURYING THE SHADOW

Storm Constantine

HEADLINE

First published in 1992
by HEADLINE BOOK PUBLISHING PLC

10 9 8 7 6 5 4 3 2 1

British Cataloguing in Publication Data
Constantine, Storm
Burying the shadow.
I. Title
813.54[F]

ISBN 0–7472–0404–7

Royal paperback ISBN 0 7472 7951 9

Photoset by Intype, London

Printed and bound in Great Britain by
Richard Clay Ltd, Bungay, Suffolk

HEADLINE BOOK PUBLISHING PLC
Headline House
79 Great Titchfield Street
London W1P 7FN

To Jay Summers
Sometimes, our life together is like a war in heaven,
but our paradise is never lost.

ACKNOWLEDGEMENTS

With thanks to my editor Caroline Oakley for her shaping talent; Lynn and Carl McCoy for the jacket portrait; Skez for the introductory poem; Sal Bryant for her assistance with the 'Shadow' illustrations; Ruth Oakley for helping me polish up the final draft, and all the other ways, large and small in which she supports and assists me; Pat Cadigan for her valued friendship via the air mail service; Vikki Lee France and Steve Jeffery who dedicate so much of their free time to the running and expansion of the information service and its magazine 'Inception', and all the people who have helped them over the past year. Also, to those whose special friendship and encouragement sustains the author through the light and the dark: Deborah Howlett, Michelle Nelson, Dr Shep, Ashley Smith and Paula Wakefield.

Prolegomenon

'Lift your head to me. . . .' His is the kiss of the timorous lover. Feel his inhuman lips on the throat, the heat of it. The bite, when it comes, is cold. Begin to sink as the blood flows into his mouth; it is almost soothing. No pain. No pain at all. His teeth grind into the muscles; ecstasy and torment. Life, the very being, is flowing out. Unholy nourishment. Holy nourishment. Drained slowly.

The trauma of it feels like being torn, but it is no more than suddenly having the ability to experience reality in a different way. Waiting for the end . . . for what? Cannot foretell. No longer flesh, no longer blood. Soul. Free.

CANTO ONE

'. . . And this dire change, hateful to utter . . .'
Paradise Lost, Book I

A renegade burned out among the stars last night.

I and my brother were visiting the open-air theatre in the Avellan
zuko with the Di Corboran family, for the opening night of the
new Zamzummim production. The play, as is usually the case with
Zamzummim confections, was the light in the centre of a jewel;
coruscant. As well as the noble families of Sacramante – humans
all – many members of the artisan eloim throngs were present,
including Miahel Shahakim who was being brought out by his elders
for a second cycle. This inevitably caused a stir among the patrons.
Miahel had been confined to the atelier courts for over forty years;
now he emerged, fresh as a dew-heavy bud, sleekly fed and quivering with unspent energy. His presence was almost as gratifying as
the Zamzummim play. Almost. Beth and myself were alone in
representing the Metatronim throng that night; our father was incubating a new epic lyrica at the time and needed the support of his
kin around him. We had always been somewhat estranged from
our family throng; Metatron's creative parturitions barely touched
us nowadays.

During the interval, all artisans present in the audience, together
with their patrons from the great families of the city, repaired to
the salon above the stage for refreshment. Here, long windows
were thrown open to the night, and the balconies were festooned
with heavy swags of woven flowers, oozing a frenzied perfume. The
night was alive, as only a late summer night can be. Below us, in
the zuko square, the rank and file of the city milled in a great
crowd, queuing at the essence-blenders' stalls to buy their cocktail
cordials. They were not permitted within the theatre itself (indeed
could not afford it), but dressed up in their best clothes to celebrate,
in their own way, outside. Occasionally, they'd be brave enough to
glance up at the balconies, hoping for a glimpse of a famous eloim
artisan. For several minutes I leaned upon the rail, gazing out
across the city of Sacramante, breathing in its riot of scents: the
hot flesh-smell beneath me, the flower haze above. In the room
behind, Oriel Zamzummim was bashfully courting praise for the
first half of his production, nervously pointing out that, as yet,
the praise was undeserved. What if no one liked the second act?

5

Nevertheless, he accepted the congratulations and kisses of his admirers; none of it was undeserved, in my opinion. I had no fears for the second act.

Spreading out my arms along the balcony rail and leaning backwards, I showed off the precise lines of my new velvets while just inside the room, my brother, Beth – as ever a potent charm in black and gold lace – grilled Oriel for information about his current work in progress. Beth is an artist; I knew he did not really care what Oriel was doing. Exhibiting interest was simply a political move. I raised my head and watched him with a faint smile on my face, waiting to catch his eye. So beautiful, my brother Beth – I love no other more. Just as our glances collided through the throngs, our glasses raised in delicious complicity, a terrible sound came from outside: a cry, a wordless shout.

At that moment everything went utterly still, but for the light shooting from jewelled throat to jewelled throat, from candelabra to chandelier. Nobody spoke, because the sound, so immediate in its intensity, told the artisans present all we needed to know. We *felt* it too, felt it deep and hard beneath our skins. As one, the silent gathering slid out on to the balcony, human patrons in quick pursuit. Below us, all the eyes of the crowd were raised in the direction of the atelier courts. The high, dark tower of the campanile could clearly be seen, with its baroque crown of stone lace, so intricately worked. Something moved there, something that generated a hiss within each throat and sent fingers flying to open mouths. A figure clawed at the fragile lace of the bell tower; a tiny, stick-like figure at this distance. I saw the gleam of cloth of gold, of golden hair; white hands and face like little marble stones.

I felt Beth behind me as he entered my mind through the door that is his alone and asked me, 'Who? Who!'

I felt for his hand, clutched it until my fingernails bit flesh. 'They have closed all doors,' I informed him. 'I cannot tell.'

Another play was being enacted on the campanile, but we were too far from it to discern the details of its drama. There was movement, jerky movement, and time hung suspended like an iron sword. Then the wind of flight was in my blood, in the blood of all of us, and the figure fell. For a brief instant we were permitted ingress through the splintered doors of a ruined mind; I felt the body arch, felt the hurricane of impending destruction in my flesh, felt . . . nothing.

Moments later a scream shattered the balmy night air: again and again.

I gasped and buried my head in the supple fall of my brother's hair. His arm curled around me. It was over.

We were in the centre of a numbed ganglion of scratched nerves. Nobody spoke, but the breathing was loud. Then, quite nearby, the proprietor of the theatre summoned one of his people through the stunned silence. There was a whispered inquiry and the servant departed. There was no more fuss than this.

'Perhaps it was a stunt,' a Di Corboran woman said, brightly, fracturing the hush.

Beth's arm tightened around me. 'Perhaps,' he answered, though I saw reflected in his eyes the same bitter-cold dread that was in his heart. In both our hearts. We knew that cry: it was the lament of a soul's death, yet at that distance we could not identify the source, or put a name to it. We, the eloim throngs, for whom death is but a far threat (as is rare disease to men and women), were having to face the Dark Brother with increasing regularity. Death was not occurring through decay or sickness, but through suicide: the ultimate, unbelievable obscenity. At first, we had thought the self-destructions a bizarre coincidence – freak events – or else a natural culling of defective spirits, but now . . . How many dead? Five, six? And in the space of only seven months. Was this condition confined to the city; or were other eloim, abroad in the world, suffering the same decline? Would it pass? Would the sardonic brother furl his wings once more and leave us be? What was engendering this terrible despair, causing eloim to seek the kingdom of their most feared enemy? So far, our elders, the Parzupheim, had refused to view these events with importance. Now, concern was growing among the throngs. Soon, surely, investigation must be made and action taken.

The theatre-master's servant returned and whispered in his master's ear. People were beginning to move back into the theatre for the second half of the play, discreetly holding on to each other – men, women and eloim alike – and trying to recapture the heady pleasure of the early evening. There was little point in letting whatever tragedy had occurred blight the performance. The performance is the life of the city, *our* life, and beyond all considerations of personal grief. Whatever information the servant had imparted to the theatre-master would not be discussed until the performance was concluded; it would be improper to do so before, and disrespectful to Oriel. Poor Zamzummim; I am sure he saw acute omens in what had happened. Yet the performers, as if driven to excellence by the shade of calamity, sailed through the rest of the play with exuberance and zest, clawing back the cowering spirits of the audience into the moment, and making them soar and ache with passion.

After the performers had left the boards, I made a point of visiting the eloim's private balconies high above the stage, in order to applaud Oriel Zamzummim warmly for his efforts. He was an appealing figure, dark and intense of countenance, yet dwarfed by his overwhelming brethren of greater height and stature. I accorded them a brief, cordial glance. 'Gimel,' Oriel said, half rising from his seat as I approached. 'Gimel.' Just my name, so softly. I leaned forward and briefly touched his hand.

'Come to the house soon,' I said. 'And when are you going to create a part for me in one of your successes, hmm?'

He smiled vaguely. 'I wouldn't presume, sweet lady,' he said, pressing the ends of my fingers to his brow.

'Well, I request it!'

That cheered him up a little. 'You honour me.'

I accompanied him to the astral dome above the balconies, where everybody was heading, for liqueurs. I felt quite light-headed, and somehow drained, as if I had been weeping for hours. Leone Di Corboran, the special patron of the Metatronim throng, sought me out and plucked me from Oriel's arm. He had the news, of course, and it was only right my patron should tell me.

Leone had never denied himself any of life's pleasures; he was a large and solid man, but for all his size not without his attractions. 'Where is Beth?' I asked him, as he opened his mouth to speak. Around us, everyone had gone into huddles and they were speaking quickly, in low voices.

'He begged me to give you his apologies,' Leone said. 'He has retired to the inner salon for a few moments alone.'

'Without me?' I was astounded.

'Listen to what I have to say, Lady Gimel, listen. Then, you may understand why your brother needs a brief privacy.' Calmly, he imparted the information that the figure we had discerned on the campanile tower had been none other than the celebrated sculptor, Tasha Rephaim. I was appalled. Rephaim, not yet in the full flowering of his first cycle, had been on the cusp of enormous popularity within the city. I could not understand why he should seek extinction. Leone spoke crisply, sensitive to my feelings yet eager to rid himself of the burden of how Tasha had wailed into the bell – the sound that had alerted us – and then opened his throat to the wind. He had bled himself down over the stone, until weakness had caused him to slip and fall, to smash upon the rounded, well-trodden stones of the northern atelier court. It was not his scream we had heard after that, however, but that of his mistress, who had found him lying there. She was one of us, an eloim poetess. I knew her well, and her pain misted my eyes despite the golden brandy Leone slipped into my hand. I could tell that the lady's pain was condensing hard within every eloim heart as we smiled and nodded at our friends, talking in voices that barely shook of the capricious bent of the artistic soul.

A well-padded patron lady who was eavesdropping, said to Leone, 'Perhaps this hysterical temperament is only to be expected amongst these creative souls.' Then, she smiled at me. 'But then you, my dear, are not like that,' she added, patting my hand.

'Indeed not,' I replied, lightly.

'Of course not!' Leone said. 'Yet maybe my bright goddess of the awning is sickened, nonetheless.' He put a proprietorial hand beneath my elbow. 'See, she is white, white as milk-ice.' He leaned close to my ear and whispered, 'Perhaps you would like some air, my dear.'

'That is most thoughtful of you, sir. I am indeed feeling a little distressed.'

As we left the lady's company, he added, 'He was a friend of your brother's, of course, this Rephaim.'

I nodded, speechless.

My patron took me out on to the star terrace that poked perilously out above the city, and proceeded to woo me under the cover of concern. A light drizzle had begun to fall: the sky's response to Rephaim's death, rinsing the evidence of his atrocious act from the stonework of the campanile. My heart was bursting with his spilled blood; again and again, it tugged within my breast as I relived the sculptor's last flight. I could barely fend Leone off.

Beth did not speak at all on the way home, and I laid my fingers over his own in silence. Our carriage flew like a black prayer over the cobbles; Beth had ordered the flanking lamps to be doused as a mark of lament. The great walls of the atelier courts were also unlit, and the gates opened in silence to let us pass. The narrow streets and modest plazas were empty of life and slick with rain, while above them the soaring ateliers brooded, their dark windows as blank as weary eyes.

Once in the house, Beth wept for a few minutes, and then walked like a sleeper into the brush-court, where he painted furiously for the rest of the night. In the morning, I found him there, slumped beside his easel, an empty philtre of bitter-oak in his hand. Oblivion then, I thought, and looked at the canvas. Madness there, little other than I had expected. Grief and love, too, but mainly madness. I made a sound – without inflection – but a sound nonetheless. Beth raised his head and looked at me through red eyes.

'It has come, then, to the steps of our home,' he said. 'We are not safe.'

'You and I are quite safe,' I replied, though unsure of him.

He shook his head. 'No. The evidence can no longer be ignored; it will not simply go away. We have contracted a sickness from the blood of our patrons. We must have!'

I opened my mouth to protest, but Beth would not let me speak.

'Gimel, listen to me.' He looked up at me with feverish eyes, urging me to remember a conversation we had had the last time one of our people had died. 'It is obvious that the eloim have contracted a soulscape malady. There is only one cure. We both know, no matter how much the elders want to deny it, that we are prone to such afflictions. Perhaps we are not as different from humankind as we like to think.' Beth had been incubating this

9

theory for some weeks. I had indulged it to begin with, believing he simply needed some kind of frame on which to hang his fears. I did not want to believe he might be right in his assumptions.

'You talk of evidence,' I said, carefully, 'But there is none to support your theory, Beth. I understand how the suicides make you feel – I too am horrified by them – but still think you should control your fantasies as to their cause.'

Beth ignored the criticism. 'The only evidence I need is what my instinct tells me! I know I am not alone in reaching this deduction, Gimel. We cannot wait any longer. The time for debate and discussion is past. We must travel, sister; it is up to us.'

I turned away from him, lacing my fingers into a constricted knot. 'I don't think so, Beth. We are too insignificant, too young. Let others take the lead.'

He scrambled to his feet, roughly pulling my shoulder so that I had to face him again. 'No. I trust only myself – ourselves. We must travel and we must find a soulscaper, Gimel, one who is suited to our needs. It has gone on too long, come too close. The sickness breathes upon our necks. I, for one, can wait no longer for others to act.'

His vehemence shocked me. 'Perhaps you *are* right,' I said, 'but do you really think a human can help us? I am not convinced of it. Rephaim was your lover, Beth. Naturally, you are distressed by his death, but I still think we should wait.' In truth, I did not cherish the thought of travel. I prefer to laze rather than move.

'Then wait here without me,' he said and left the court.

I sighed and sat down among the paints and canvases, sullying my skirts with pigment, grease and chalk. Later, I would go and pack. He knew I could not bear my life without him near me.

'. . . thou from the first was present, and with mighty wings outspread dove-like sat'st brooding on the vast abyss . . .'
Paradise Lost, Book I

Above the continent of Lansaal is an inland sea, which the Lannish people call the Womb of the Land; its northern shore is flanked by the lands of Atruriey and Southern Khalt. A short sea-journey north of the famous Lannish port of Toinis, lies an island – a relic of some past sub-terran flexing. It is but a vast table mountain, whose sheer sides rise up out of the water without blemish. No person can scale these cliffs; the only way up is through the heart of the mountain, by way of the wide shafts and scramble routes. The mountain is named Tapar. On its wide, flat summit lies an immense petrified forest, and within this natural construction rears the city of Taparak, home of the soulscapers. Taparak is a city of silicon and stone, shaped as if by an artist's hands. It was my home too, in the beginning.

Listen then, for I am a soulscaper and have the gift of the story tongue. I am Rayojini, daughter of Ushas, daughter of a skilled line. I have the way of it; into the mind like a bat, I go, and out again, dragging Fear in a net, for that is my profession. I was born in Taparak and, for a long time, could imagine nowhere different. It is a hot, dry place, but the Taps milk the sky-cloud of moisture, channelling it down through the mummified claws of the forest's hands. Inside the mountain, below the city, there are lakes of icy water, clear and fragrant with the cloud-spirits' soul-scent, and close to the lakes are the sponge-root farms: terraces of pale, phosphorescent fungus.

As a child, I ran through the bough-streets of Taparak, my imagination used only for play. I, like my playmates, had heard our elders speak of the soulscape, but to us it was a distant country. We visualised it as a land of monsters and fabulous people – our childish ideas not too far from the truth – and once, in our games, I was crowned queen of this place. Pretty Heromin, son of Sarcander the Wanderer, became my slave for a day. Our soulscape was a place that shimmered with the inchoate buds of later carnal blossoming. As such, it was instrumental in our development.

Sometimes Ushas, my mother, would call me to her side from

11

play, and I would go clambering like a moth-grub from branch to branch, among the higher reaches of the city, helping her to gather the sweet-clay of scraper bugs – insects that live within the ossified bark – which we took home to make into bread and cakes. Then a client might come and blow upon our door-chimes, and my mother would send me outside again, lighting the resin-bowl before I'd even left the hollow.

Until the age of eight years, I was a simple girl, with no more thought in my head than the sun-gilded notions of a child at play. I was not insular, having many friends. I was also imaginative (though not excessively so) – as was required of a budding soulscaper – and certainly not prey to any sons of the Fear. All this changed on my eighth birthday. I remember it clearly even now. Ushas and I had home-hollows root-vicinity at that time; it was long before my mother gained ascension within her guild. We often talked of the day when her soulscaping accomplishments would secure us a more prestigious high drey among the clouds, although our discussions were a game of wishes rather than a real desire to move home. The hollow was more than enough for our needs and, though a long way from the sky, convenient for ground-level amenities and dew-gathering. We lived alone because my mother had never wanted to marry particularly – I did not know who my father was – and for her, one child was enough.

Ushas roused me early and I stretched into the morning knowing that today was the day I would at last learn something of my mother's professional secrets. Today, I would step off the narrow, twisty path of childhood, with all its secret haunts, and put one foot upon the wide road of womanhood. It would be a long time, I knew, before I advanced more than a few paces up this exciting, new road, but at least it was a beginning. All potential soulscapers underwent a ceremony when they reached a certain age. It was a confirmation of our parents' desires for us to follow in their footsteps, although it was not irrevocable. However, because of the nature of the rite, changes of heart in later life were rare.

I was to be chanted into the future, by no less than my mother's guild-scryer, Vasni. Vasni was an extremely powerful individual and, even while he still lived among us, a legend among the Taps. At fourteen, he had castrated himself and had consequently experienced extraordinary visions – most of which had prophesied specific events, all of which had come to pass. He was not only a scryer but a superlative soulscaper in his own right. Now he was getting old, his travelling days were over. In Taparak, work is slim for a soulscaper – there being so many of us – which is why we travel so widely. Since his retirement from active range-guild service, Vasni had had to content himself with scrying, but he still held a high position within the guild as a mark of respect for his talents.

Ushas dressed me in new trousers and shirt for the occasion, neatly embroidered with the symbols of our family and of the family profession. I was allowed to rinse out my mouth with bitters-root solution – a terrible taste, but it dyed my teeth and tongue a beautiful cyclamen-pink colour with indigo shadows. This was the ceremonial mouth decoration of the soulscapers in our trunk-community and when I smiled, everyone was sure to know that I, too, shared this honoured occupation. I had known for some time that my life would begin to change after this event, and had begun to prepare myself for it. The days of play would be past, and I must discipline myself to a deep, and often incomprehensible, education. Naturally, even though I was aware of the hard work required of me, I looked forward with pleasure to the new status I could enjoy. Even trainees in the craft were accorded respect in Taparak – from those outside the soulscape, as well as from those within. Because most of the city's population had some connection with soulscaping, (even if they were not fully fledged scapers), I did not expect instant elevation to a higher position within the community, but I would no longer be treated as a simple child. Also, I would have access once more to companions who had already undergone this rite of passage. The lovely Heromin, for example, had recently knelt to the scry, and I missed his company.

Ushas marched me out into the main root thoroughfare, striding along in her brightly dyed, layered skirts, telling anyone who paused in greeting that she was taking her daughter, Rayojini, to Vasni the scryer. 'Her distance is to be endowed this morning,' she said, a ritual phrase. As a response, people pinned shards of polished bark into my hair.

Our beliefs may seem strange to those who hale from other lands, where it is understood that no person has one future alone. It may seem primitive or wayward that in our society a person's life is chosen for them at the age of eight, when an infinity of possible futures might otherwise await them. Much later in life, one man was to say to me (a lover, so he was frank) that it is as if the Taps cut away all but a sliver of their children's lives, and that to condemn them to one future alone was a torment worse than slow murder. He was a foreigner, of course, and what he said may have been true in the mindscapes of foreign folk; but this is our way, and no scryer ever blew out a future that caused a parent to break down in despair. Vasni and his kind are compassionate as well as wise. I and my mother were happy enough, swinging along through the morning; me with my bright, beautiful smile, and Ushas with her news for everyone.

Vasni lived high in the city, on the seventh of the central trunks, no less, and two tiers down from the aesthetes. Ushas and I walked the thoroughfare from Great Root to Spiral, where we entered a pulley carriage and were drawn aloft. The young man tending the pulley made bright and hopeful remarks to my mother, but she just

13

smiled and said, 'I promise you my daughter instead, when she's a mind.' I was flattered but didn't remotely believe either of them would remember the message for that long. Ushas was always very lovely – right until the day she died, which was from a poisoning she picked up somewhere off-continent, long after I'd climbed my own bough. That day, she was radiant; her long black hair twisted into ropes and greased in place, with sparkling metal pins threaded through the lobes of her ears. She leaned back over the side of the pulley-cart, her hair-ropes swinging free, and hung on to the cables. She had strong, bony features, muscled limbs. Her skin had the matt, silky sheen of black plums. How she loved life in that body. In later years, I was glad she had died before she lost her beauty; it would have distressed her so.

We jumped out on to Vasni's platform and Ushas blew heartily on his wind-chimes to tell him we were there. A boy, wearing a ceremonial robe of russet cloth, came out from the hollow to answer us, and took us into the smoky chamber where Vasni worked. All the light-boles were curtained with yellow sacking, round which the most vigorous beams of sunlight streamed in penetrating spears. What with the smoke and the sharp rays, and the row of elderly scry-women mumbling in the corner, it was a strange place for a child to find herself. Only two of my relatives, apart from my mother, had been able to attend the ceremony. Brothers of my mother and older men, they seemed to me of vast experience and therefore intimidating as they squatted silently near the scry-women at the back of the chamber, still dressed in travelling coats as if they'd had to hurry to arrive on time. They were practically strangers to me.

Vasni rocked in front of his smoky embers, legs crossed, palms on each knee. Even as an old man he was handsome, run to forest-thinness rather than the matronly fat carried by many of the castrati scryers. He wore a loose robe of stained orange; the symbols of his family and guild burned into the cloth. His arms were covered in fading tattoos, his brown-skinned skull shaved but for the liana-braids hanging from the back of his head. It was said that he had been stunning in appearance as a youth. One of my friends, a girl named Aishar, had once told me Vasni kept his genitalia, mummified, in a wrap of bark and silk, just to remind himself how much he had given up. I had also heard that he was scorned for ending his line in that way; beauty is appreciated among our people, and the most favoured are expected to breed and thus continue their blood-line. I had seen Vasni before on ceremonial occasions and he had once blessed me by touching my face, but he seemed a strange and awesome figure to me this day, and I shrank back behind my mother. She gently put her hand on my shoulder, and murmured a few words of encouragement. Vasni leaned over the embers of his fire and inhaled the smoke deeply, before raising his

14

head and saying, 'Ushas, my child, let me greet you.'

My mother gently pushed me from her skirts and went to lean over the fire. She inhaled the smoke and then put out her tongue, on to which Vasni smeared a fingerprint of ash, or what looked like ash. Then he pressed his thumb on to her forehead and chanted a line or two. My mother responded with a soft murmur of notes, and then sank down into a cross-legged sitting position opposite him. He nodded in satisfaction and slowly raised his head again, fixing me with his steady stare. He beckoned.

'You, child of the child, approach!'

Cautiously, I went towards the embers. Behind Vasni, the row of scryers started to chant, swaying from side to side. Vasni's boy began to beat out a simple rhythm on a carapace drum. My uncles began to hum softly: a low, deep, masculine sound. Slowly, the sense of ritual stole around the smoky chamber and entered my mind and body. The outside world was eclipsed from my mindscape; rarely have I experienced such moments of total reality. My mother sat with bowed head, intoxicated by the fumes, although I did not know that then. I went around to where Vasni was sitting and, at his direction, sat down by his side. He smiled at me and, in the dim light, the indigo dye on his teeth looked as brown and tarnished as old blood. For a while he spoke to me of soulscaping, the history of our people, our responsibilities and vocations.

The Tappish are descendants of the great Deltan Kings of ancient times, a guild of healers who colonised the island. Being scholars and mystics, as well as healers, our ancestors had sought to probe the secrets of the human mind. They discerned two areas within the psyche, which are very closely linked; the mindscape, which is the realm of conscious thought and decision-making, and the soulscape – a deeper, more inaccessible area – in which the hidden desires and compulsions, the most esoteric symbols of the entire human race, reside. 'Within the soulscape,' Vasni said, 'dwell all the gods that ever lived, all the thoughts that have ever been thought, all the memories of the human race.'

Perceiving an interconnection between all living things, the ancient Taps believed that every individual was somehow linked through the abstract country of the soulscape. By understanding the soulscape, it might be possible to understand human motivation. The fortunate discovery of the properties of certain herbs and their parasites was instrumental in developing the soulscaping craft. By prudent use of the mind-altering substances they found – through burning the crushed wings of scaper beetles – our ancestors were able to prove their theories. They learned how to expand their awareness and actually enter the soulscape themselves. By doing this, they found they were able to have a direct effect upon the soulscape's reality: they could *change* it.

'The soulscape,' Vasni told me, 'can be visualised exactly like a

15

vast city.' 'Your personal scape,' he said, 'can be seen as a many-roomed house within this city. Each of us has our own house there, and most people never open their doors to look outside. They do not know how to. Yet we Taps cannot only go outside our personal dwellings in the soulscape, but can enter other people's dwellings too. We can travel wherever we wish on the streets and in the parks of this place, always aware of each house's relation to the city, perceiving the greater picture. And because we can see the houses from the outside as it were, it is easy for us to discern where they are damaged and how to repair them. Through soulscaping, we can heal the human mind of most hurts and, because the majority of illnesses are connected with the mind, we can often cure the body of physical ailments as well.

'But healing is not our only task,' Vasni continued, raising a stern finger. 'No. We are hunters too.' He spoke to me then of the great Fear that haunts the minds of humankind, always lurking in the shadows, seeking weaknesses that are doors into the soulscape. Finding ingress, the Fear breeds madness, hysteria and weird moon-cycle delusions. While soulscapers travelled abroad, plying their trade, it was also their duty to be alert for the Fear, to pursue it into the soulscape, corner it and slay it.

The alarm I felt at this news made me confident enough to ask questions. 'What is the Fear? What does it look like?'

'Nobody but a soulscaper can see the Fear,' Vasni answered, leaning towards me. 'And they look for it in the eyes of their fellow creatures. A good soulscaper can always see the Fear looking out, if they have trained themselves to recognise it. As to what it is, I can only say this: it is a very old thing, perhaps a renegade fragment of the soulscape itself that has escaped into the world. Once a person is infected with it, only a soulscaper can drive it away.'

'Is it ever dangerous for us?'

Vasni pondered my query. 'If there are dangers, they are those of ill-discipline, carelessness and pomposity. A dedicated, well-schooled soulscaper would rarely accost something they could not handle. But . . . there are always exceptions. It is important for you to apply yourself diligently to your training.'

How exciting my future sounded! I would be trained to enter this subconscious realm and work with the creatures found there. I would be a healer and huntress. It seemed as if, one day, I would tread the soil of my invented playtime worlds, for they existed within the soulscape. All imaginative creations lived in this place, where myth was tangible and could be experienced through all the senses. I listened earnestly to everything Vasni said, wanting to please him, to show him I was capable of following my mother's path.

He finished his narrative with a closing gesture; hands spread out, palm downwards, extended from breast to arm's length. 'Now,

16

we shall see,' he said. 'Lean forward, child.'

His long, hard fingers curled around the back of my neck. I was puzzled for a moment and then, with unexpected force, he pushed my head down towards the glowing embers at our feet. I remember I struggled. I remember the glow of the charcoals suddenly becoming large and livid in my eyes, looming towards me like fiery boulders. My mother, still slumped with her head upon her breast, didn't even look up. 'Relax, child,' Vasni said, behind me, in a sibilant voice. 'Trust me and breathe. Breathe deep.'

Close to, the smell of the embers was bitter and stifling; the heat scorched my throat. My eyes began to sting, and I blinked them furiously, hot tears falling down on to the charcoal and no doubt turned to steam even before they met the heat. I coughed and it seemed that my whole body convulsed; the cough came from somewhere very deep inside me. It was terrible. I was afraid that Vasni was going to burn my face, that my ritual was to be one of scarring and torment. Vasni was pinching the nerves in my neck so tightly, I could not move at all. The only sounds I could make were insignificant mews, barely audible.

Just when I was sure I was about to pass out, if not lose my eyes and skin to the heat, Vasni yanked me backwards, and thumped me in the centre of my chest with his free fist. I gulped air, so disorientated, I tried to swallow it like food. Vasni pressed me gently on to the floor, into the rough, gritty folds of his perfumed sacking-mats. 'Lie still!' he commanded. I lay on my back, trying to remember how to breathe properly. Vasni inhaled loudly, and I could visualise great columns of smoke being sucked off the fire and into his nostrils. When he spoke, his voice was full of the power of the fire, and the women nearby bleated affirmatives between each slowly intoned word. 'Now,' he boomed, 'I will scry for the child's future and as part of this ceremony I invoke those who will watch over her in this life: the guardian-pursuers.'

The scryers behind him began to keen in high, warbling voices and I lay there with eyes squeezed tight, my fists clenched across my belly. My head was full of the potent smoke; I had never felt so dizzy, and my limbs ached in a strange way that was at the same time uncomfortable and pleasant. What would happen now? Who were the guardian-pursuers? I had not heard of such people before.

Vasni chanted in ancient Tappish for a while and then slipped into the modern tongue. His voice was perfectly pitched: no crack of age, no falter of lips and tongue. 'Heed us, unseen ones,' he began, his voice sonorous above the crooning of the women. 'We bring to you a fledgling soulscaper. May one of your number assign their soul to hers. May they urge her to excellence in life, protect her from the Fear, drive her ever to inquiry, fill her dark corners with their shadow, be with her from this moment until she leaves the flesh and crosses to the soulscape in body and mind. Hear us

17

and approach! Reveal yourselves in this one instant to the child Rayojini, daughter of Ushas! Make yourselves known, oh unseen ones. This I, your servant, Vasni, request; I, who gave you my manhood for eternity. Hear me and approach!'

Instantly, there was silence. I could hear the women breathing, but the drumbeat and the chanting had ceased. Vasni's presence filled the room, even behind my clenched eyelids. I could feel his life-force beating like a slow, smoky wing across my soul.

It was then that I opened my eyes. Perhaps they were still full of smoke, or the effects of it, but it seemed as if the whole chamber was in utter darkness, but for the shape of Vasni and the dull glow of the embers. I could not see the walls, the light-boles, or even any of the other people whom I knew were sitting there with me. All was Vasni: Vasni like a living tree, his roots of spirit dipping down into the petrified heart of our city, down into the mountain and down into the fertile ooze far below. I could almost see the living essence of the world rising up through his spine, fountaining out of his head, falling to the ground, sinking back into the deep shadows of the earth. And then it seemed as if Vasni, too, was fading from my sight, as if I was being drawn far away until Vasni and his embers were like little dim pictures in the distance. Gradually, a formless darkness came between me and this image. It was winged, or cloaked, this darkness, and billowing like an enormous black wind-sail. I was filled with a dreadful terror: had the Fear itself come for me? But I could not escape. Closing my eyes made no difference, for I could still see and I could not move my head at all. My tongue seemed to have swollen to fill my mouth; I could not call for my mother. The roiling shape loomed over me and I screamed in my head. Was this the guardian-pursuer Vasni had summoned? It was a dreadful thing – so alien to the light and space of Taparak. I could not believe the soulscapers had access to, or affinity with, such creatures. It appeared to lean over me and, for a second, the darkness parted, like a veil being drawn aside. Within, I saw the most astounding thing: two beings, two auras of pale light, giving off a perfume as beautiful as spirit-scent. They looked like male and female, but even as a child I knew the unseen ones could have no real gender as we understood it. The female seeming shape smiled at me and reached towards me with a glowing, white hand. Her nails were like bright red almonds. I tried to reach out in return, but even though she seemed so close, it was as if I tried to reach across an infinity, a universe. We never touched. She looked at the male, and they nodded at one another. Then they took a step forward as if crossing from one tree-platform to another. It was not difficult for them. Both of them leaned down, and I felt as if my flesh were alight with their radiance. The female kissed my brow, followed by the male. My flesh began to burn there: a delicious, cold burning. I wanted to make a sound, any sound, but

18

I could not. And then they were gone. In an instant. The chamber rushed back in to fill their space, ringing with the sound of women chanting and the low, steady call of Vasni the scryer.

I had met my guardian-pursuers, and that day I loved them as benevolent spirits. Later, I learned otherwise.

'In the day we eat of this fair fruit, our doom is, we shall die. How dies The Serpent? For us alone was death invented?'
Paradise Lost, Book IX

Thirteen dead. Thirteen: the number of all things fatal and dark.

We had been away too long, caught up in the wine of the world, drinking ourselves into heady euphoria. Thirteen had died in our absence. Yet, despite these tragedies, the world had continued to turn unheeding, dragging its aging tide across the land. Our house in the eastern atelier court was filmed with dust, so the first thing Beth did upon our return was to scold the servants. Four years we had been away. Too long. Out there, once our task of finding a suitable soulscaper had been successfully completed, we had almost forgotten the point of our travels. That is the allure of travelling; all eloim succumb to it eventually, if only for a short span.

We had crossed the inland sea from Sacramante, landing in the Lansaal port of Zhijelih. This was a central point, and we could take our time, travelling across the land towards Taparak. We had taken the precaution of bringing our own transport with us from Bochanegra – one of the fleeter Metatronim carriages, accompanied by members of our human domestic staff from home; a driver, his boy, and a body servant for each of us. These people were trusted individuals, to whom our safety and comfort were of fundamental importance. While it is impossible for eloim to make humans exactly like themselves, it is possible to grant them longevity. Our immortal blood, while not so potent as to grant immortality to humankind can, if imbibed on a regular basis, at least double their lifespan. All humans in eloim employ were subject to this practice. A rapid turnover of domestic staff would be inconvenient to the throngs; just as the servants learned to do their jobs properly, they would wither and die. If their ichor intake were monitored carefully, a human might well enjoy the bloom of youth for a hundred and fifty years. After that, unfortunately, their own metabolism seemed to take over, and they succumbed to a natural fading towards death. For reasons of security, there was a strict rule among the throngs that longevity should be bestowed solely upon the most loyal servants.

We assumed that many soulscapers would be wandering about Lansaal, which might save us having to enter Taparak itself. Aware

21

of the scrying strength of the Taps, both Beth and myself were anxious to avoid the city, if at all possible. While there were no recorded incidences of soulscapers recognising the eloim for what they were, we still harboured a basic unease about the Taps. If anyone could penetrate our disguise in the world, they could. And the concentration of soulscaping ability to be found in Taparak was something neither Beth nor myself was eager to confront. What would happen if someone suspected we were not like ordinary travellers? I dared not think about it. All my people knew that the phenomenon soulscapers called the Fear was eloim-born: ghost fragments of memories of despair from the time of the Expulsion and Devastation – tragic events in our history, of which we were forbidden to speak. It would be catastrophic if this fact were discovered; old hatreds might rise to destroy us. The Taps were a constant threat to eloim-kind because of this. However, we respected the soulscapers because they were the guardians of humanity's health and sanity. And yet, because of their penetrating insight into the minds of others, every time we approached a soulscaper we risked exposure. Beth and I stalked them because we had to, even though we feared them – but we feared their city more.

Beth, needing action and spontaneity, husked more than a pretty soul or two on the journey east. I myself had no desire to sup – anxiety about our business crushed my appetite – and I took only a modest refreshment from my maid, when hunger became too pressing to ignore. As we had anticipated, soulscapers were plentiful in Lansaal, so there was no reason to delay our mission. I confess that I was not entirely happy about that. From the first, this idea had been Beth's rather than mine, and I still questioned the wisdom of it. I feared discovery and was unsure whether we would emerge victorious from any direct confrontation with a soulscaper. What if they were stronger than us? Beth sneered at my fears, although I was sure he was anxious about this himself. He refused to discuss it, though. I told him we would have to be circumspect in our approach to these people – men and women alike – and yet the very nature of our mission meant we would have to be more open with them than I felt was wise.

'Don't fret, Gimel,' Beth said, as we travelled towards the town where he had decided our search would begin in earnest. 'I have devised a strategy.'

I stared glumly out of the carriage window, watching our man-servant Ramiz's booted foot swinging from the side of the driver's seat. We followed the coast road and although the sunset flinging colour across the sea was breathtaking, I could take little pleasure in it.

'A strategy? Don't be absurd,' I said. My maid, Tamaris, sitting beside me, reached out timidly to touch my hand, seeking to bestow reassurance. I uncurled my fingers from beneath the sleeves of my black lace-and-velvet travelling coat and squeezed back gently. Tamaris is such a loyal girl.

Beth laughed. 'It is very simple,' he said. 'After we have secured lodgings in Lumeza, Tamaris and Ramiz can scout around for lone soulscapers. They can arrange meetings in discreet locations. There will be very little risk.'

'I feel you have no grasp of the reality of the situation,' I replied. 'What happens when we meet these people? Do we tell them everything and trust they are sympathetic? It is a stupid plan!'

'Of course we don't tell them everything!' Beth said scornfully, idly unravelling one of the tassels hanging from the window curtain. 'We will induce them to enter our soulscape. Once they have bonded with us in that way, we can employ our usual methods for subjection. It can't fail.'

'Really? Why do you speak of "they", in that case? Surely we shouldn't have to do this more than once.' Tamaris pressed against me more firmly; she hated it when Beth and I had cross words.

'Gimel, be sensible,' Beth said. 'Soulscapers are familiar only with the human soulscape, and we are not human. I am convinced it will take an especially puissant individual to withstand the inner landscape of an eloim! This might take several meetings, but don't worry, if we are lucky, the first may well be suitable.'

His optimism and cheerful anticipation did not reassure me.

Lumeza was a small, untidy community. We took accommodation in a fohndahk, at the edge of town, where chickens ran about in a yard outside, gossiping noisily, and dust from the coast road furred all the appointments in the guest-rooms. I stood dejectedly in the middle of my room, which was barely furnished, while Tamaris made soft sounds of outrage, and dusted the spotted mirror with her sleeve. The windowsill was cluttered with dead insects and the air smelled fusty, like decaying corn. The floor, the door and window-frame, the wooden beams of the ceiling, all looked dried out and splintery. From this miserable base, my brother and I would begin our vital quest.

Tamaris and Ramiz went out into the night, while Beth and I sat out in the dusty yard of the fohndahk to await their return. We drank orange wine in the heavy dusk, and did not speak. I was aware of the beating of my heart; I was nervous. Perhaps our servants would not find a soulscaper. Perhaps some unseen agency would save me at this final moment, and we could go home.

The moon sailed up the star-shot sky and the air cooled towards the graveyard hours beyond the midnight, chilling my skin through my lace stole. 'To bed, I think,' I said, putting down my glass, rubbing my fingers together, for the sweet wine had made them sticky. I stood up, and pulled my wrap tightly around my shoulders.

Beth was a pale shape before me, slumped back in his chair, dappled by moonlight coming down through the ilex trees in the yard. I could tell he was annoyed. Somehow, I had achieved a minor victory. And then there were low noises coming towards us through the night, and I recognised the bubbling sound of Tamaris' laughter.

'Why don't you sit down?' Beth said quietly, but I remained standing.

The soulscaper's eyes and his teeth flashed whitely in the darkness; astounding against his matt black skin. His laughter was deep and genuine. He accepted our offer of wine, begged by Tamaris from the sleepy fohndahk matron, whom she'd had to call from her bed. He had a name, of course, this first soulscaper brought for our inspection, but I cannot recall it now. He was a mature man, lean from hard travelling.

'I'm told there is work for me here,' he said, looking at me. I raised a hand without replying and gestured towards my brother. Let him do it. At that moment, I wanted no part of this business.

Beth smiled. 'There might be. But it is a tricky matter. I am loath to discuss it here.'

The soulscaper's smile seemed to freeze on his face, but I'm sure no one else noticed, perhaps because I was the only one looking for it.

'Sounds sinister!' he said, and put down his glass of wine. He did not touch it again. 'Where, then, would you like to discuss this *tricky matter?*'

Beth extended his hands. 'Please, bear with me. Perhaps we could take a walk together.'

The soulscaper eyed our gathering: tall, muscular Ramiz, with his gypsy looks; minx-eyed Tamaris in her witch's gown of red and wreathed in ebony hair; and Beth and myself – how did he see us? Forbidding, aloof? Or just conniving rich children from the far opulence of Bochanegra? Then he smiled, and I swallowed reflexively, gulping the cold air. In that smile, I saw the certainty that he could take us on – all of us – if necessary.

'A cool night for a walk,' he said, standing up, 'but perhaps bracing.' He indicated for Beth to lead the way. Tamaris and Ramiz paused to let me precede them – however informal our relationship could be at times, they were aware of their place – but I gestured for them to overtake me. I followed last, numbed with cold and dread.

We walked along a lane overshadowed by spreading trees. Tamaris murmured softly to Ramiz, looking back over her shoulder occasionally, perhaps to check I was still with them. Beth was talking rapidly, I could see his hands moving, but could not hear his voice, and the soulscaper strolled with slow dignity beside him,

24

paying attention but apparently adding no comments, asking no questions. We climbed a stile into a tree-bordered field, far enough from Lumeza for any sounds we might make to be unheard by anyone else.

'Gimel?' Beth directed a challenging look at me, perhaps wondering whether I would shrink from this summons. I approached the soulscaper, dragging my skirts through the dew-damp grass. Tamaris and Ramiz lolled against the fence behind us; they were not to be included in this part of the proceedings but – as our dependent humans often are – were eager to spectate.

'He will examine your soulscape,' Beth said.

'Mine?' What had Beth told him?

'Only if you want me to,' said the man gently. I dared not look at him, sure my eyes would betray everything.

I nodded. 'Very well. Will it . . . take long?'

The soulscaper had squatted down in the grass and was rummaging through the bag he'd been carrying. 'No, I must ignite the fume. Perhaps your companions could move back. There is no breeze, I know, but the smoke can travel. . . .'

Beth smiled at me tightly and sauntered back to the fence. For a few moments, the soulscaper prepared his materials in silence. Then, as he applied tinder to a charcoal, he said, 'Are you sure you feel comfortable with this?'

I stared at the grass. 'Yes. It's quite all right.'

'You don't have to feel ashamed,' he continued, blowing on the flame. 'Your illness is not your fault.'

I remained silent.

'We could have done this at the fohndahk, you know. No one would have thought anything of it. I've treated people there before.'

Beth must have told him I was sick, and an invented skittish temperament was the excuse to get us to this isolated spot. Why couldn't he see we were deceiving him? I should tell him now; raise my eyes, look at him. My limbs felt frozen, a paralysis not caused by cold. The soulscaper took off his coat and spread it on the grass.

'Lie on this,' he said. 'Relax, close your eyes, breathe deeply. . . .'

Numbly, I obeyed, telling myself I was undertaking necessary action. Later, I could rebuke Beth in the strongest manner for making me do this. Later, it wouldn't matter. I thought of Rephaim falling from the campanile. I steadied my breathing. I let this kind stranger look inside my mind.

I was aware of distant noise, floating in a pleasant haze, where summer clouds scudded across a cornflower sky. I awoke to activity, anguished voices, violent movement. Someone trampled on my arm. I cried out and rolled off the soulscaper's coat on to the wet grass. Tamaris was shouting, and there was a mêlée of floundering limbs beside me. I heard the dull thump of flesh against flesh, then silence, but for panting breath. I scraped my hair from my face and saw Ramiz standing nearby, bent over, his hands on his knees. Beside him, Beth stood upright, wiping his mouth. There was a dark, huddled shape on the grass between them. It did not move at all. The air was full of the intoxicating perfume of fresh blood. I found myself salivating, both nauseated and hungry.

Tamaris hurried towards me, put her arms around my shoulders.

'Get up,' Beth said. 'Quickly!'

'What happened?' Tamaris helped me to my feet. I could not look at what lay on the grass.

'He couldn't take it,' Beth said sharply. 'I thought this might happen.'

'It killed him?'

My brother shook his head. 'No . . . but he saw . . . he knew.' He sucked his upper lip, staring down at the motionless shape. Then he glanced at me. 'Are you all right?'

I did not answer, but struggled, light-headedly, towards the stile. Tamaris scurried after me.

'He went crazy,' she said, 'flinging himself about. Lord Beth ended it for him . . . in a civilised way. We could do nothing else.'

I could not bring myself to speak, painfully aware that we had contravened an unspoken law. We had killed; not through the sup, but in cold blood. Nothing felt completely real; the night around me seemed like an illusion. I could remember nothing of the man being in my mind. Beth came up behind me, reached to touch me. I shook him off.

'Don't speak. Don't touch.' I said.

'Get her to bed,' Beth said to Tamaris. 'Ramiz and I will remove the remains.'

As I walked unsteadily back to the fohndahk, leaning on Tamaris' arm, I was thinking how wrong the soulscaper had been in his assessment of his ability to protect himself. So wrong. His own madness was the last thing he'd feared.

He was the first, the first of many.

I forced myself to develop a shield of passionless dedication, rather than ponder the possible consequences of our quest. It helped to think that we were engaged on a holy mission and that each soulscaper we encountered was simply expanding the knowledge we needed to save our people. A kind of unreality took hold of me. Coolly, I did what had to be done, feeling nothing. Tamaris and Ramiz became quite adept at sniffing out lone soulscapers, although after the first occasion we were more discerning about who we actually let into our soulscape. We used the same story of my fictional illness, which allowed me to sit quietly and uninvolved while Beth did the talking. I felt queerly detached during these interviews, as if I really were mentally ill. Beth was pleased. My demeanour added conviction to his claims. I did not realise that a change was coming over me.

Both Beth and myself could speak Lannish, but we used only the Bochanegran tongue for our transactions. The soulscapers, all of whom it is said, speak every language in the world, were as we suspected shrewd creatures to a fault. Several of them were keen enough to be acutely suspicious of us, despite our convincing fabrications and superbly delivered performances. I remember one or two of them actually believed my brother and I to be victims of the Fear. One man told me he did not like what looked out of my eyes. How could I respond to that? He was clearly seeing the truth of me; for all my pious motives, a dangerous killer.

Once we had approached an individual, and allowed them access to our own soulscape, we could not simply leave them in possession of this knowledge and pass on. Only the patron families in Sacramante were aware of our more intimate needs, as predators – for obvious reasons. To other humans, any creatures needing to feed on their ichor for survival were simply legends; no more real to them than fairies or ghosts. However, it seemed that no soulscaper was strong enough to endure the weirdness of our inner landscapes; in short, it tended to drive them mad. We could not risk these pathetic casualties blurting something out to their colleagues, and so had to cull them in order to cover our tracks. At first I was sickened by the necessity of having to dispose of these people, although Beth appeared to relish it; his sensuality had run riot since we left Bochanegra. Until that time in Lansaal, the only murder of humans by eloim I had witnessed had been the rare and regulated ritual of sacrifice, part of the agreement we had with the patrons. At home, regular supping was nothing more than honouring the holy trade; sustenance for pleasure. Except for the occasional sacred sacrifices, which were always confined to significant festivals or events, death was not part of our relationship with humanity. But as time went on, my heart seemed to harden to the culling. Looking back, I feel that a beast was loosed in me in Lansaal – it was certainly loosed in Beth – an ancient beast from ancient times, which still lurks within the hearts of our people, waiting for the scent of terrified blood to wake it from sleep. This beast led me, let me stand by while Beth killed, let me – eventually – bend to the unwilling sup myself. May the Old Ones forgive me, but as the leagues rolled past our carriage windows, the pleasures of the hunt came over me too and I reverted to a forgotten, former wildness. Eventually, I no longer had to force myself to kill. And yet, at the time, I could not find the will to be ashamed of it, which means I must accept that this cruel greed is a part of me, thankfully hidden in the regulated, civilised world of Sacramante, but always present in the deepest corners of my soul.

Our kills became cleaner; there was little mess. And what remained of the victims, after Beth and I had taken any sustenance we desired, was buried by Tamaris and Ramiz. We found no one capable of withstanding the eloim soulscape. It was as if some higher power of the world condemned us for our actions. Every day brought us nearer to Taparak with our quest unfulfilled.

Eloim living in Lansaal were few and far between, and tended to be very unapproachable. Most were enclosed family groups, who were nervous of outsiders because of the need to keep their identities secret. Their virtual immortality caused them problems, and meant they had to move accommodation quite regularly, so that suspicion was not aroused among the local people as to their longevity. As it was, the majority of these families were either feared or viewed with scorn by their closest neighbours, because of the distance they maintained from the local community. Shrouded carriages, securely walled demesnes, and tribes of in-bred servants who would occasionally roam outside the walls, were fuel for gossip and speculation. Because the eloim were so careful, they made themselves weirdly visible. In Sacramante, we had evolved very complex and painstaking methods for camouflaging our differences from humanity. We could not have maintained these precautions without the cooperation of our patrons, but the provincial eloim did not have recourse to human supporters. Their lives were often fraught with danger.

Beth and I did manage to secure lodgings in one or two eloim redoubts – we missed the company of our own kind, but I found the Lannish eloim oppressive; their paranoia is infectious. Discreet inquiry assured us no one but Sacramantan artisans appeared to be suffering from the sickness of despair. Perhaps their consistent anxiety about being discovered left no room in the hearts of Lannish artisans for yet darker pressures. Because eloim outside Bochanegra have no human patrons, they really do have a much harder time than their Sacramantan peers; there are, for example, no willing offerings for the sup from outside their own staff. Beth and I wondered how they ever managed to find time to express their creativity, and it was true all works of art we saw in these houses were frantic, doom-laden affairs. Their reluctance to seek sanctuary in Bochanegra mystified both Beth and myself. We concluded they must have a proud and defiant streak within them, and must, in some ways, enjoy their precarious existence.

We discussed our intentions with no one; as far as the Lannish eloim were concerned, we were simply the spoiled scions of a noble Sacramantan house, idly exploring the continent. Most advised us to return home as soon as we could. They thought we were too innocent to be roaming Lansaal, that in our ignorance we might betray their existence to humanity, although they disguised their self-concern as being worried about our safety.

As we approached Toinis, we stayed for two days with a venerable eloim diva, a sweet and incredibly ancient lady who, in order to protect herself, had resorted to supping only on the blood of chickens. Her name was Favariel Eshahim, and she claimed to be the last remaining daughter of a lost eloim throng. Her skin was in a disgraceful condition – only to be expected, considering her meagre sustenance. She lived in an area plagued by a particularly stringent religious code – implemented by a particularly stringent local priest – so was forced to be meticulously careful in her behaviour. A myriad of diverse cults thrived in Lansaal, and a group of rich mystics had formed the Church of Pure Soul in Favariel's area about sixty years ago. Any eccentrics were regarded as heretics by the infuriatingly active high priest, especially those who did not attend the church on a regular basis. Favariel tried to appease this quick-tempered zealot by sending yearly offerings of gold to the church – an act which allowed her a precarious security – and pleading a frailty of age which precluded church worship. 'I fear he will live for ever!' she declared, when telling us of her difficulties with the man. 'I only hope my gold lasts longer than he does! Whoever comes after him just cannot be as bad!'

She lived in a wonderful old house, which was falling badly into decay. And yet, with its rose-garlanded, crumbling walls, its ancient stone embellishments, the house only appeared more beautiful because of its dissolution. There was but one servant left in the house, an elderly peasant woman who had been with Favariel for eighty years or more. At one time, she had provided her mistress with sustenance, but now Favariel refused to sup from the woman; she was too old, her blood was thin, and the strain placed on her heart by being supped might easily kill her. Favariel feared being left alone. She, more than any of the Lannish eloim we had previously encountered, was delighted to meet us, and laid the amenities of her household at our feet, insisting on showering both Tamaris and myself with gifts. Our luggage cases were stuffed with exquisite antique jewellery and elaborate gowns of pale, powdery silk. In return, Beth quickly painted a flattering portrait of her, and our servants insisted on letting her sup from their veins to her fill. By the time we left her, she looked much healthier, and a youthful bloom had come back into her flesh. We also arranged to send her a couple of human retainers from Sacramante, once we returned home. I thought it disgraceful that no other Lannish eloim clan had done anything to help her before now.

On our last night in her house, as we talked together after supping, she mentioned that she thought a lone artisan was wandering around the countryside, who behaved eccentrically to her mind. Eccentric, by eloim standards, presaged something extremely odd indeed. I pressed her for information, worried she might be referring to the business Beth and I were involved in, but she seemed

29

reluctant to expand on her theory. 'They leave signs, that is all,' she said. 'It has been going on for some years.' After that, Beth and I were alert for the phenomenon, but came across nothing out of the ordinary.

Our experiments with soulscapers had continued to be depressingly unsuccessful. It got to the point where we had taken so many victims, the urge to sup was lost. Even Beth was sated, and we had to resort to outright murder; precious blood spilling untasted over the Lannish fields. The beast in both of us was exhausted, and a dim perception of the foulness of our behaviour began to clarify, once more, in my mind. In the end, I called a halt to the procedure; it was pointless and wasteful.

We had reached the lively port of Toinis and, as usual, had taken lodgings in a secluded fohndahk. I was tired, disillusioned with our quest, disappointed with myself, and wanted only to return home. The encounter with poor Favariel had especially depressed me. Beth was still eager to continue, as he was enjoying our travels immensely. I think this was because his creative soul had opened up like a sunflower, away from Sacramante. As he feasted on the sweet ichor of the Taps, it seemed their mystic lifeblood flowed into his fingers, summoning marvellous scenes from the soulscape. Gone were the precise and mannered portraits he was famous for at home, which hung on the walls of patron galleries. Now, his paintings were undisciplined and fierce: no demure maidens in limpid bowers, but powerful sorceresses depicted against violent skies, cowering souls dismembered at their feet, soulscape monsters wheeling round their heads. He painted beautiful demons that smiled with frightening realism from the canvas; demons that – even though only representations in paint – promised pain and pleasure in equal measure. Beth had sold many of these savage, lustful canvases as we travelled; they intrigued the Lannish art dealers and commanded a high price.

One evening, we sat out on the fohndahk terrace, lazily drinking our way through a carafe of orange wine. Tamaris and Ramiz had ventured out into the night, intent on secret adventures of their own, the mysteries of humans closely allied to eloim households, into which we were too polite to pry. Beth was in such a lively mood it was difficult for me to broach the subject on my mind, but eventually I forced him to listen to me. 'We cannot keep destroying soulscapers,' I said. 'They are too precious.'

Beth resented my sharp tone. 'Then what do you suggest we do? I have no intention of returning to Sacramante until we have accomplished our task.'

'But, Beth, they are too old, all of them, in spite of their smooth skin and silky eyes.' My remarks were loaded with insinuations. 'Their experience works against them. We need someone who has the Tappish ability, but who lacks the preconceptions of a mature scaper. You must know this, too, in your heart.'

Beth gave me a keen look; I saw his fingers twitch around the stem of his goblet. 'So, the answer is simple. We find a young soulscaper; a *very* young one. Someone who is out on their first scaping-range.'

I shook my head. 'No, still too old. If you insist we continue in this madness, there is only one recourse. We must go to Taparak, and find ourselves a child. Someone who is yet untrained, and whose mind is more malleable. We have no choice. It is either this, or else we go home and wait for the sickness to find us.'

Beth sneered at me. 'Gimel, you talk nonsense. We don't have the time. A child has to grow. It will take years.'

'All seeds of potential require a protracted growth period. You know I'm right, Beth.' The truth was, he derived so much pleasure from our experiences with the soulscapers that he was disinclined to abandon them. Eventually, his hunger for the sup would return and, when it did, the blood of scapers would fuel the power of his heart. A child would not endow him with such delights; eloim code forbade the supping of children.

He took a silence upon himself at my remarks, which I would not caress away. For all his tendency towards physical self-indulgence, Beth was not stupid. I knew I only had to wait.

Two days later, he relented. 'Very well, we'll take a boat to Taparak and find your child, Gimel,' he said. Content, I allowed him to kiss me.

Very swiftly, I proved myself correct on all counts; we stayed in Taparak no longer than a single night. I was so twitchy while we were there that I could not take pleasure in sight-seeing, which was a shame, because Taparak is an astounding place. It seemed to me as if a crazed artist had carved the whole city out of petrified wood; walkways swept dizzily from massive trunk to massive trunk. Bird-catchers killed their prey by squatting in the higher tiers of the city and throwing missiles *down* on to the birds. This could prove dangerous for people below should the hunters miss their targets, which was fortunately rare. The narrow, root-patterned streets were full of people, most of whom seemed to be visitors from Lansaal, Khalt and the Delta Lands. Native Taps were recognisable through their colourful clothing and artfully braided hair. Carts rumbled over the uneven ground, drawn by small, determined asses that paused for no one. We'd left our bulky carriage behind with the driver and his assistant at the Lannish coastal town of Cozca and, after having ascended to Taparak itself, we'd hired a cart to take us to the visitors' district where accommodation was plentiful. We installed ourselves in a ground level hostelry, while Tamaris went off to ingratiate herself with the local traders and ask a few cautious

31

questions. We supposed that many visitors would be curious about local customs and that inquiries concerning scaper training would not be too unusual.

Tamaris was absent for several hours and was quite drunk when she returned. Still, she had accomplished what she'd set out to do, having forced herself upon a group of Taps in a taverna, in a manner only Tamaris can get away with. Charmed by her open friendliness, the Taps had teased her with stories, unaware that an astute mind was hidden behind the fluttering lashes and girlish smiles. Between us, Tamaris and I extracted the truthful aspects of all she'd heard, discarding the more obvious elements of tale-spinning. The Taps were clever – especially the women – and had given little away, but we still had enough information to help us. It was clear that Tappish children underwent a ceremony at eight years of age, when they were introduced to their future vocation. This must be some form of initiation – perhaps an ideal time, for our purposes, to make contact with a Tappish child. I knew that the soulscapers' abilities to influence the minds of others was far superior to any eloim's – which was why we needed a soulscaper – but it was also true that the Taps relied on their mind-altering substances to change their level of awareness, whereas an eloim could achieve a similar, if weaker, effect through concentration alone. I reasoned that this might mean Beth and I would possess a greater clarity of mind if we established psychic contact with a Tap. Of course, we could not be physically present during one of these initiation ceremonies, which meant we would have to project ourselves – always an enervating experience. After our experiences in Lansaal, we were quite familiar with the procedure of soulscaping, but had not accomplished contact with a Tap from a distance before.

For once, Beth was happy to follow my lead. If hunting was his province, mind-seeking was mine. Tamaris' most precious snippet of information was that initiation ceremonies took place early in the morning. I did not know how long we would have to stay in Taparak, and doubted whether we'd be lucky on our first attempt at finding a suitable child, but there was little point in wasting any time. The following morning, Beth and I composed ourselves in my room at the taverna, lying down on the bed and breathing together, forging a link between ourselves. We had suffered many differences of opinion, even heated arguments, during our journey east, but once our minds touched, all hostility melted away.

'You have hated me,' Beth observed.

'True,' I replied, 'but we knew this journey would be difficult.'

'I'm sorry . . .'

'I know that. Rise!'

We could not enter the soulscape, but we could move, disembodied, through the real world. The combined essence of our minds

32

soared up through the tiers of Taparak, the ancient trunks shadowy to our altered awareness.

'What do you see, sister?'

'Many bright sparks, many souls . . .'

'A child?'

'There are hundreds of children. They are the brightest flickers. Look!'

'Must we examine them all?' The tone of his thought echoed his reluctance for so much tiring work.

'Wait . . . Don't strain yourself, Beth. Conserve your energy. I will search.'

My prowess for mind-travelling had always been stronger than Beth's. I knew I could not keep him away from his body for too long. The shortest journey was exhausting; making contact with another individual could actually be painful.

I released myself to the flow of the world's rhythm, not struggling to search, but simply letting my instincts guide me. Lightly, taking Beth with me, I danced from spark to spark, pausing for the briefest of touches. The children sensed me, but I moved so swiftly that the sensation was too fleeting to cause them alarm. I felt my strength begin to falter and told Beth we would examine only two more souls, when my attention was attracted by a condensed node of energy. Within it gleamed the radiance of a child, but the diffuse glow around it indicated minds expanded beyond normal consciousness. Could we be so fortunate as to discover what we were looking for this soon?

'Beth!'

'I see it!'

Together, we streaked towards the brightness.

There is an old man, and it seems he summons us. He invokes beings that he calls the guardian-pursuers. Surely, he can only mean ourselves. What are we, Beth and I, if not that? We guard. We pursue. . . . There: the child, her lovely gleam, her bright innocence, so trusting. And she too reaches out to us. 'Be with her in life,' says the old man, 'drive her to excellence.' Lead her. Guide her. Oh, it will be our privilege, sweet child. I am breathless before the beauty of her naked soul. We touch, and the link is forged. Clawing the residue of Beth's failing strength into my grasp, I align our souls with the child's. I can even see her name, as if it marks every cell of her body. Rayojini. Rayo. Daughter. She has been waiting for us. She is the one: the only possible one.

Back in the taverna, I blinked into the morning light, my body filmed with sweat, my chest heaving, as if I had been running hard. Beth coughed beside me. I sensed him shiver.

'It is done,' I said, in barely more than a whisper.

33

Beth rolled painfully towards me, and put his damp brow on my shoulder. 'I should never have doubted you,' he said. 'Forgive me.'

'Beth, there is nothing to forgive. The journey brought us here . . . Everything that has happened . . . inevitable. . .'

He nodded weakly, and presently fell asleep. I was drained beyond the point where I could comfortably sleep myself, and lay quietly, in a deep relaxation, listening to the morning sounds of Taparak outside. A great burden had been lifted from my soul. I had divested its weight on to the child Rayojini, and I knew she would not feel it there. It could not harm her. Not yet. Not for a long time. The child was my little seed. As had been promised in the ritual, I would haunt her to womanhood, I would nurture and strengthen her powers from afar. She would flourish within the caul of my benevolence.

Leaving the island, I was quite happy to let Beth lead us further east. We ended up in Atruriey: a marvellous land. The people there reminded me strongly of our patrons, and we were welcomed as artists most warmly. I even think one or two of them suspected there was something different about us – beyond what might be excused as an artistic temperament and aristocratic feyness – but nothing was said. Bloated with our actions in Lansaal, we had little need to feed for several months, and took only wine and water. I got involved with a travelling eloim theatre-company, for whom Beth was happy to paint scenery and, accompanied by Tamaris and Ramiz, we stayed with this group for several years. During this time, I maintained a subtle contact with Rayojini, watching her grow from a distance. Sometimes when she had girlish problems which she found difficult to solve, I prodded her a little with an idea or a feeling, although I shrank from making my presence too obvious. I thought it unlikely that guardian-pursuers were, under normal circumstances, real beings. After having spoken to so many soulscapers in Lansaal, I thought these creatures were probably metaphorical images for the child's own conscience. Therefore, it was vital that Rayojini didn't seem to be more in tune with the idea of her guardian-pursuers than other children. If her mother or her tutors became suspicious, they might undertake a deep soulscaping on the child, and destroy my link with her. Still, it was pleasurable when I could help her. I liked to feel her earnest little mind praying to Beth and myself, thanking us, as her guardian-pursuers, for our guidance. The fact that she addressed both of us did needle me a little though, because Beth had scant interest in the child, leaving it to me to keep an eye on her progress. He never communicated with her at all and yet, in her prayers, I could see him through her eyes: beautiful, shining, powerful. When she grew up, would she start desiring this handsome image in her head? What then?

Then, one evening as we were sitting round a camp-fire in deepest

34

Atruriey, a twitching started up in my fibres. Beth caught my eye and a feeling passed between us. We knew it was time to return home. Absurdly, I felt I would be leaving Rayojini behind, but I did not speak of this to Beth. I kept it secret, how fond I'd become of the child.

The city was in a hectic mood when we returned. Invitations to the Di Corborans, the Vielkorekhs, and the Mougadis littered the welcome-table in the hall of our house, some of them quite eaten away by mice. Our especial patron, Leone Di Corboran, dispatched two of his daughters, Leda and Vicretia, to our domain once the servants had gossiped in the zuko, and news of our homecoming spread.

Although we had been back for two days, Beth feigned tiredness and shut himself in his room, so I had to entertain the creatures alone. I had intended to visit the Metatronim family-stronghold that afternoon, for news had come to us from a friend of dreadful occurrences during our absence; the sickness had not abated. In all honesty, I needed to see my family, just to make a head count and reassure myself that they were all in good health. Therefore, I felt extremely indignant when Tamaris informed me Leone's daughters had arrived. Still, without our patrons, our lives would be very difficult indeed, so I pasted a welcoming smile across my face, and bid Tamaris show them up to my solar.

Vicretia was the sweeter of the two Di Corboran girls, although Leda possessed the greater wit. The last time I had seen them, Leda had just been married to her second cousin, whereas Vicretia had been a silent and delicate girl of thirteen. Vicretia had now blossomed into a very attractive young woman; Leda, on the other hand, had just blossomed. I assumed she now had a brood of her own. 'Fashaw, Gimel,' Leda told me, breezing into my solar, trailing limp gloves like filleted limbs, 'but you haven't changed a bit! Four years you've been away too! Wild air suits you, truly. Look at me!' She twirled before my dark mirror. 'A pound for each year of your absence!' I suspected it was slightly more than 'that. She bustled towards where I lounged, in artistic composure, on the divan. Her lips pursed in anticipation. 'Oh, but you've been missed.' I deflected the kiss by turning my head. She caught me on the ear.

'Don't lick me, Lee!' I laughed sweetly, to sugar the sting. 'You lie to me anyhow. What of your other favourites, hmm?'

'None as lush as you!' she quipped, admitting to nothing.

I peered over her white, plump shoulder. 'Hello Vee, how lovely you look! It's been so long. Come, sit by me.' I patted the divan, protecting the place with my hand, so that Leda could not stuff herself into it and had to fit herself into a chair opposite instead. 'So, are you ready for news?' Leda could hardly contain herself.

Silent Vicretia, dear little thing, eased down beside me like a

35

floating feather. I curled my fingers over her own, but addressed her sister. 'Always, Lee, always. So, tell me.'

'There has been a riot of suicides among the artisans.'

Yara Sarim, whose family was in some ways connected with ours, had communicated with us directly on our return and had told us everything. So, this was not news, but I feigned interest. 'Indeed?'

Leda nodded eagerly. 'Quite so.' She counted off on her fingers. 'Camiel, Murek, Sasleel – it's like a disease. And that's not the worst. Two years ago – oh, it seems like history now – Lilthia Emim took a knife to both her parents, her brother and, finally, herself. You have been wise to keep your distance. Father says it must be an evil taint from the Strangeling, blowing over the city in the wind, that affects the sensitively composed. Personally, I think it's a result of hedonistic excesses and you, dear Gimel, are not prone to such; neither you nor your brother.' She frowned. 'Where is Beth, incidentally?'

I considered it politic, under the circumstances, to reinvent his excuse. 'Oh, he's working. Feels guilty being away from the courts for so long, I expect. He sends his regrets, but may join us for refreshment later. You will stay for refreshment, of course.'

'Persuade me otherwise!' Leda rolled her eyes. 'Now, you must tell me of your travels. It must have been so exciting.'

I pulled a rueful face. 'Hardly such. Beth was researching and spent most of his time sketching. I simply mooched around waiting for him.'

'But all those exotic people!'

'They are not that exotic beyond civilisation, dear Leda. I found very little to attract me, I must confess.'

'You are a connoisseuse,' Leda declared, patting herself in congratulation. 'Nothing but the best for Lady Gimel!'

I could not help but flinch at that.

After half an hour or so of further pointless exchanges, I summoned Beth with the mind-chime, and ordered him to join us. He remonstrated, but I kept up the chord until he gave in. He could have plump Leda; she would enjoy it. Beth had been too picky recently, refreshing himself far too meagrely. I wondered whether he'd damaged himself by all the gorging he'd indulged in when we'd first arrived in Lansaal, four years ago. However, sustenance from Leda should restore him utterly. Me, a sensible refresher, and able to pace my supping, would lick an aperitif from the sweet flesh of little Vicretia. Being sensitive, she knew this already, and trembled beneath the light, cool touch of my hand.

Beth was magnificent when he came to the solar; his tawny hair polished like sun-burnished fur, his dark-yellow eyes full of shadow-promise. Leda gurgled in greed. 'You are so thin!' she exclaimed to him. He flexed his darling paws in her direction, lacing the fingers.

36

'While you, Mistress Di Corboran, are fat as a festival chicken!'
he said.

Cooing, she began to unlace her bodice. Slightly nauseated, I
turned to Vicretia and leaned towards her ear. 'Your first?' I whispered. She nodded, fearfully, eyes like a doe with one foot bound
in a twine-trap. 'Would you prefer to retire?' Again, after a brief
hesitation, during which her eyes flicked to the pouting Leda and
back again, she nodded. I rose and held out my hand. Leda was
spread out in her chair, exposing her large, blue-veined breasts into
which my beloved brother had buried his head. She had her hand
in his hair, mewing ecstatically as his teeth broke the skin above
one nipple. As his tongue licked her, his lips began to suck and I
felt a twinge of jealousy; I hoped he would not give in to her
demands for copulation, which were sure to follow. Perhaps leaving
them alone gave her an advantage concerning that, but I had a
mind for Vicretia's comfort, and the sight of her sister writhing
beneath my brother was not pleasant.

'Come,' I said, and led the bewildered girl from the room.

We sat down in the conservatory of eager vines, that greened the
sunlight from above. Poor Vicretia was as pale as a forest flower,
trembling uncontrollably. Yet even in her fear, there was anticipation, excitement. Not wanting to scare her unduly, I supped
delicately at her wrist – no more than a gnat bite. She lay back
against the trellis, her eyes turned up in her head, moaning softly.
I took my time, but supped little. It was important she should find
it pleasurable, this first time.

Afterwards, I brought her a cordial of summer fruits, lightly laced
with brandy, for which she was grateful. The intimacy had unlocked
her tongue. 'So strange it felt,' she said, 'like floating away.'

'Is that all?' I smiled at her.

'Beautiful,' she said. 'I'm flattered you chose me.'

In truth, it was not me who had chosen her, but her father. He
had sent her to us after all, but I did not mention this. A homecoming gift, a new flavour. Leone always kept his children long from
the sup in order to make them more intriguing, – sometimes until
they were sixteen – but I was surprised he had kept Vicretia untasted this long. She must have been at least seventeen years old,
and a year is a long time when your relatives are all satisfied
participants of the sup.

'I prefer a finer vintage, more delicately flavoured, than Beth,' I
said, to please her.

'You did not hurt me.'

'No, we never do. None of us. I'd have thought you knew this.'
She shrugged. 'The tasted keep their secrets.'

Unable to face Leda's flushed bloatedness, I requested her sister
to make my excuses and sent her back to the solar alone. For a
while, I relaxed among the greenery, digesting my refreshment,

rolling my tongue around my mouth to catch the last sweet nuances of Vee's flavour. Although at peace, I was full of the awareness that our lives were changing. The atmosphere in Sacramante, on our return, had been reminiscent of the paranoia haunting the eloim in Lansaal. The Sacramantan artisans were scared, and no doubt would expect us to produce an instant solution.

On the journey home, I had kept up the contact with our little soulscaper. Distance did not seem to lessen our link. She interested me acutely; I was in awe of her active, inventive mind. She had certainly come to regard Beth and myself in different ways. Beth was a pleasurable fantasy, but I liked to think she looked upon me as an imaginary friend. Often, when I looked into her life, I could hear her speaking to me. She liked to talk about her thoughts and feelings aloud. I still had not interfered overtly with her development – there was no need; I just observed. She must be all of twelve years old by now, but it would still be some time before she was ready to fulfil the destiny I had planned for her. Some part of me was resigned to the fact that our designs might yet fail; some part of me did not care. I was content; the sickness could not touch me, for contentment was its bane, I'm sure. Beth though, I worried for. He, like dead Rephaim, was one of those bright blooms that grow quickly flaccid on the vine, eaten by decay in an evening's rain. I thought about the diminished throng of Favariel Eshahim; it seemed incomprehensible to me that such a decline could be allowed to occur. Perhaps it signalled that the time of the eloim was drawing to a close; we had lived upon the world too long. Perhaps the sickness of despair was an inevitable symptom of this wasting, and no soulscaper, however well-suited to our needs, could ever save us. I knew this was an attitude I would have to shed quickly, because it was not one that could be presented to the eloim elders. Notice had come to us or, more accurately, had been waiting for us, that a gathering of the throngs had been called for by the Parzupheim, the most ancient and exalted of our kind. They were anxious to discover what Beth and I had achieved in Lansaal and Taparak. Our father, Metatron, had been ominously silent since our return. I had expected us to be summoned to the family strong-hold in the eastern atelier court even before we shed our travelling cloaks, but no word had come from him. His ignorance could only mean he disapproved of our journey; we had not, after all, con-sulted with him about it before we left Sacramante. I knew he would be present at the gathering, and wondered whether we could expect public criticism from him.

I sighed into the vines. It was time I stopped worrying about greater issues, and applied myself to my personal well-being. I needed to organise myself, emerge from the seclusion of the atelier courts and seek employment; I needed to perform. What I needed more precisely, of course, was the adulation I commanded as my fee. As soon as the throng-gathering was over, I would see about securing a part in a theatrical production. The house of Zamzummim might be a good place to start looking. Indolence was ejected from my body by a wild spear of energy; I wanted to leap up immediately and hurry to Oriel Zamzummim's court. The feeling was to be savoured, but not indulged just yet. First, I would wait here for my brother in the conservatory. Then I would lead him upstairs to bathe away the stains of florid Leda, and make him pure again. After that, we would sleep in each other's arms. Tomorrow I would resume the normal pattern of my life.

'Subtle he needs must be, who could seduce
angels . . .'
Paradise Lost, Book IX

Beth and I walked lazily through the cool, evening air, on our way
to the gathering of throngs; two of our house stewards following
discreetly behind. Sacramante was in a summer flush, the night
thick with heavy perfume squeezed from the tight flesh of the rose-
vines along the walls. We paused to listen to a travelling trovadero,
keening in one of the piazzas. I was recognised there and presented
with a corymbus bloom. In truth, I was glad to be back.

The Castile Edificia had been built, centuries back, on the apex
of a gentle hill, whose toes gripped the slow-moving river to the
East. It was a pale, many-towered building that dominated the
skyline of the atelier courts, constructed of pale stone and hugged
by flowering creepers. Like ourselves, others had chosen to take
the walk that evening and, on the approachway, we came upon a
silken clutch of Hyperachii, strolling arm in arm ahead of us. I was
friendly with one of the males, Jevanael, and released my grip on
Beth – who was trembling with nerves – to go and walk beside him.

'Avirzah'e Tartaruchi just drove past,' he told me, eyes aglow.
The Tartaruchis were, perhaps, the most infamous of eloim throngs,
and undeniably the most compelling. They had a reputation for
wildness, indiscreet supping, and general over-indulgence. They
were also incredibly talented; all their projects were maverick successes. Consequently, the Tartaruchi throng was one of the most
affluent. Avirzah'e was the favoured scion of this House, a playwright, who courted heresy between the lines of his works. It was
said he kept twenty lovers satisfied at one time, but I believed this
to be propaganda he'd put about himself. He was, undeniably,
supremely attractive, with all the irresistible allure of a dangerous
animal. I also had no doubt he had been keenly interested in Beth
and myself for a long time, a point which we had purposefully not
pursued. Naturally such selfish reticence angered Avirzah'e, who
was used to all his whims being gratified. The extent of this anger
was beautifully illustrated by the fact that he ignored both Beth
and myself with a chill that verged on the offensive. Everyone else
in our community – eloim and human alike – adored Avirzah'e.
Beth and I liked to be different, though I suppose in some ways
we were jealous of the Tartaruch prince. As we approached the

41

main entrance to the Castile, I felt my blood quicken at the thought that I would see Avirzah'e soon. This reaction galled me immensely, and I attempted to banish my excitement. Comfort was to be found only in thinking he must feel the same way about us, and resent it as much.

In the courtyard of the Castile, we passed the sleek carriage of the Tartaruchis; horses steaming and stamping in their traces. The air was still full of Avirzah'e's perfume: an eastern, exotic scent. I noticed Beth sniff and grimace.

'Stench of effluent,' he commented, which made Jevanael laugh.

'Be prepared for interrogation,' he said.

Beth pulled a face. 'I wouldn't have thought Tartaruchi had much interest in this dilemma. They are undoubtedly immune to the sickness.'

Jevanael shook his head. 'You are wrong. A Tartaruch infant burned itself to death three months back. Taken so young; a terror.'

'Or an accident,' I added. I did not believe a child could yearn for extinction, let alone grasp the concept of it, but I could understand the scare it had caused. Because of eloim longevity, and the scant need to reproduce ourselves, children are rare creatures among the throngs, and therefore cherished.

As I had expected and dreaded, our great father, the Metatron, was waiting for us in the foyer of the Castile. I'm sure my heart actually stopped beating for a second or two when I first saw him, even though I had prepared myself for this meeting. Beth reached for my arm again, as we made a sedate approach. Metatron stood, like a statue clothed in deep green velvet, among the polished red-marble columns of the entrance hall, other families giving him a wide berth. That alone signified he was not in the best of humours. His glamour never fails to surprise me; it is always as if we are meeting for the first time. Our human allies claim that eloim grow only more lovely as they age; Metatron is a testament to that supposition. An incredibly ancient creature, albeit not so much as to qualify for a position in the Parzupheim, (although it was no secret that he did much of their work for them), he looked as beautiful as raw light, that night. His dark hair was confined in a fillet of titanium; his fingers heavy with old silver rings. At his side, drooped the languid, sleepy-eyed Tatriel, a consort of his, but not our parent. Our mother had been travelling away for many years; we expected not to see her for centuries. As usual when he encountered us – which was generally by chance – Metatron clawed us with a penetrating glance and inclined his head. We bowed in respect. Beth and I had left the family courts many years before; we'd had no yen for family life, although it had been me who'd instigated the move to private court. The reason for this was because Metatron had made it known he wanted another child, and had taken me to his bed several times. I had no doubt, although it was never mentioned, that he had chosen me to carry his spawn. Among our family, there is a facetious legend that Metatron's children eat their way out of the womb from within. Having no desire to spawn at that stage of my life, and even less to be gnawed at in such a grotesque way, I discreetly removed myself from his attention, taking Beth with me. Sometimes, though, I still regretted my decision. The Parzupheim decreed who might be allowed to have children, and eloim of high stature, such as my father, were generally the ones granted the privilege. Sometimes – and especially since becoming involved with Rayojini – I fancied the idea of having a daughter myself. Also, whatever ambivalent feelings I might have about Metatron, I respected and admired him greatly for his beauty and his intelligence.

'Are you prepared, children, to give account?' he asked us formally. There was no greeting to be had from him, no sign of warmth, neither was any mention made of the lack of contact since our return. I had always suspected he still harboured a fury concerning our departure from the family stronghold, although he would never admit to it.

'In all manner,' Beth replied.

'Good. You may both kiss me,' Metatron ordered. Tatriel stepped back, with a serpent gaze. She had always seemed sly to me. Metatron took Beth first. He would nip the inside of the lower lip, and take a tiny licking of ichor. Such was his due; we could do nothing but submit. The nipping kiss was a pantomime of an ancient, forbidden custom, a custom which was never discussed in polite company. I waited patiently, dreading the promise of my father's taste. 'You have matured,' he said to Beth, pinching my brother's throat. 'Present yourself at the Metatronim courts tomorrow eve. And you. . . .' He released my brother and turned to me. He smiled. It was terrifying. I delivered myself into his arms, awash with desire, sick with helplessness; I felt his power over me. 'Gimel, you are such a fighter,' he said gently, and touched my brow with his lips. I had closed my eyes. Only a sudden coldness alerted me to the fact that he had let me go.

We walked slowly to the inner hall, joined by two other Metatronim, far cousins, whom our father had brought with him as entourage. Our stewards remained in the foyer, where they would be fed by the Castile chatelaine. I noticed that, on a cloth-covered table, a small, votive lamp had been kindled near the back of the entrance hall. Beyond its light a tall, dark statue brooded in a web of shadows. Warmed oil was provided in a dish by the lamp. Beth and I anointed ourselves and bowed into the darkness. I shuddered and moved away quickly; the statue discomfited me, even though I could hardly see it. It was an image of one of the original eloim, who had not come to this Earth. His name was Mikha'il, and he was brother to Sammael, who had once been the eloim lord.

43

Mikha'il was regarded as a traitor, although eloim repugnance was obviously tempered by grudging respect, otherwise there would have been no statue. Discussion of our history was not encouraged among younger eloim. Our elders wanted to forget the past, and relatively youthful people, like myself, complied with their wishes; we had been trained to fear our own history.

At the portico to the hall, the Sangariah himself was seated to record the proceedings, his staff present only to supply his utensils. The Sangariah was effectively the governor of the Castile, and handled day-to-day administration for the Parzupheim. Normally, one of his lesser scribes would take notes during meetings; his presence symbolised the importance of the gathering.

The current Kaliph of Bochanegra, Izobella, must have been informed there was to be a gathering of throngs, because she had courteously sent gifts to us. Just outside the hall, a bevy of youths and maidens sat waiting demurely for the serious business of the gathering to be concluded. They were garlanded in rose-vines, the thorns of which had provocatively pricked their faultless skins, conjuring aromatic gems that beaded redly upon the surface. As we passed them, Beth and I made a sacred genuflection, because we knew the significance of their presence. The crowning with thorns and roses, the piercing of flesh by thorns, was a traditional message to signify that Izobella did not expect to have these morsels returned to her. They were sacrifices. Because of this, the supping, the draining of their flesh, would be of holy intention. But refreshment would not come until later. First, we must attend to business.

The hall was oblong in shape, with tiered seating around the edges. Most of these seats were already occupied. I supposed that every eloim throng in Sacramante was represented there that night. The Parzupheim had taken their places upon the platform at one end of the chamber and, as we entered, their amanuensis signalled that Beth and I should place ourselves nearby. The Parzupheim are antique beings of an almost ethereal appearance and, to those of us in our first cycle, seem distinctly alien. History lives in their eyes; it is said they can remember the birth of the world, and the occasion of their coming through from the other place. Looking into their translucent faces, I could believe that easily.

The Partsuf Oriukh Kadishah, a Metatronim like ourselves, raised his hands for silence, although there was very little noise within the hall. Everyone sat down. There was a moment's silence as the Oriukh composed himself for the speech.

'I am gratified to behold so many of our brethren beneath this roof,' he began, 'and wish only that our gathering could be to discuss a happier subject. However, I will address the business succinctly. As you are all no doubt aware, we have lost thirteen souls to self-extinction. It is unprecedented in our history. Death is a trickster whose sleeves we thought we had shaken free of fatal cards, and yet now he comes to trespass in our courts. Our immortality has become a curse. Curiosity has become ennui; anticipation – despair. Our kin throw themselves into the face of Lilit's cup-bearers, spurning life, desecrating our existence. We were born immortal; to extinguish that light voluntarily is an abomination, and one which affects us all. So, the madness takes us; so, we die. The question is: why? As you know, humanity, who are close friends of the Dark Brother, are plagued by a condition they refer to as the Fear. Eloim have never been prey to such sickness, but strong voices within our community have suggested the tragedies we have recently endured may be caused by this unseen thing. This was a controversial suggestion, I know, and even I am unconvinced of its veracity, but certain individuals took it upon themselves to investigate the possibility, and concluded that we should find for ourselves a person who could treat the sickness and expunge it from our midst.' He leaned forward, resting his chin on a clenched fist, his sleeve falling back to reveal a sinuous, tawny arm embraced by golden serpents.

'There are, among humanity, special people. They are known as soulscapers. Doubtless all of you have heard this term before. Humanity, being a younger race, compelled by hotter and more dangerous fires than we, are often prey to madness in all its forms. Soulscapers not only know how to eradicate the condition known as the Fear, but can hunt down all manner of defects in the mind and drive them out.' Here, he paused again and directed a glance at Beth and myself. I lowered my eyes, although I could feel the attention of everyone present riveted on our heads.

'Two of the Metatronim throng,' the Oriukh continued, dryly, 'took it upon themselves, four years back, to seek out a soulscaper of superlative prowess, a soulscaper who might be strong enough to face our sickness and purge it from the soulscape of eloim. My beloved siblings, I give you the Lady Gimel and the Lord Beth of Metatronim. I feel we should now hear them speak.' He extended his hand to indicate the podium to the left of the platform. 'If you would grant us your knowledge, my children.'

It was not an easy thing to stand and make our way to the podium. We were conscious of the scepticism among the eloim concerning our actions. I dared not stare into the seated crowd, afraid I would find the eyes of Metatron looking back at me. Did he intend to humiliate us now?

Both Beth and myself – ever the performers – genuflected towards our audience and took our places, close together. We had previously decided that I would be the one to begin our report, so in my clearest voice I spoke of the child we had found among the soulscapers and how we had been so fortunate as to be able to commune with her at such a suggestive time in her life. I did not mention all the failures we had suffered prior to that discovery.

45

Warming to my subject, I spoke long of our opinions of the Tappish child: her potential, her reservoir of scaping strength. In order to provide an entertaining narrative deserving of my people, I described the strange city of Taparak, and revealed to my listeners the petrified limbs of that ancient forest, the exotic insects that nudged through the hollow warrens, their nectars and juices. Then I went on to recount the ritual we had observed. The throngs were all entranced at this point; I was half-tempted to turn it into a song.

Then someone stood up and raised a hand to speak. I stopped my delivery immediately; not out of politeness but out of apprehension, because I thought that person was Metatron. But it was not. Avirzah'e Tartaruchi had risen to his feet. He was almost directly opposite to where we stood, quite near the podium, and I could see that Metatron was only a few seats away from him. Most people had turned to look at Avirzah'e in attitudes of inquiry, but Metatron looked straight at us. I could not read his face. Beside me, Beth huffed in affront.

'You have reason to interrupt this account?' the Oriukh asked.

The Tartaruch bowed. 'Forgive me. I crave your permission to speak.'

The Oriukh turned to me. 'Well, Lady Gimel, would you object to interruption?'

'If the Tartaruchi throng wish to make an observation, I have no objection,' I replied, graciously. In truth, I was furious.

Avirzah'e bowed in my direction, perhaps a little too extravagantly to be sincere. 'I thank you,' he said, touching his brow, and then straightening up. 'The Lady Gimel speaks beautifully of life beyond Bochanegra. Perhaps we should all make this journey, for our education.' His voice was sweet; an appeasement. It was the beginning of a tournament. I responded as was expected, just as sweetly, with an inclination of the head.

'I would not presume to direct your education.'

The Tartaruch sucked in his cheeks and manipulated his mobile brows into a quizzical expression. 'No? But that is not the issue, stimulating though it might be to discuss. The issue, my kin, is this: the Metatronim speak of children, pretty quick-wits, still budded on the stem. Conversely, our affliction waxes swift. Brave though their plan might be, and perhaps effective in time, I must emphasise that our problems are immediate. We do not possess the luxury of being able to wait patiently for the bud to flower.' Here, he paused, spiked lizard that he is, and stood there showing off his physical power. His argument was indeed relevant; damn him. Such a persistent thorn is this Tartaruch princeling, I thought. Beth was not so philosophical. He made a response, speaking bluntly, and ignoring the protocol for formal construction.

'Have you a better idea then, Tartaruchi?'

The black beast enjoyed impaling my brother with his scornful gaze, almost as much, I'm sure, as he would have enjoyed a more tactile impaling. 'There are thoughts I have in mind, as it happens,' he said.

'Such as?' inquired the Oriukh.

'Well, I, and others too, believe it is an emanation from the distant past of our race which is responsible for our current afflictions,' Avirzah'e replied, frowning earnestly. 'I feel there has been a weakness incubating in our consensual soul, which has grown over the centuries and is now manifesting itself as a form of psychic malady. I know there are certain taboos within our society that forbid examination of the past, but I really feel I have to be quite explicit in this instance and put to you my suggestion that, via past events, the affliction we are suffering derives from humanity itself.' As he had no doubt anticipated, this caused a stir.

The Oriukh raised his hand for quiet. 'A radical suggestion, Tartaruchi. But your terms are vague. Please be more lucid. I am unclear as to whether you are implying that the sickness derives from ourselves, or from humanity. Feel free to expand upon your theory. At such a time as this, there are no taboos concerning discussion.'

Avirzah'e bowed again. 'Thank you. Consider this, my reverend brethren. Humanity, without our presence in their midst, would be like the world without sun or moon. We are their light; we bring them gifts immeasurable. However, should we peruse the reverse condition, it is another matter entirely. What light do we gain from them?'

'Don't be a fool!' Beth interrupted loudly, perhaps more to stem the heresy of Avirzah'e's words than to make so obvious a point. 'Humanity is our sustenance! Without them, we have no immortality. Without them, we all die. Humanity and eloim need each other. You know this. We know this. Only humanity is unaware of the precise nature of the relationship, which makes us the wiser!'

There was a moment's silence, which the Oriukh broke, in a gentle voice. 'Perhaps you should tell us exactly what you are suggesting, Tartaruchi.'

Avirzah'e was glacially cool in the face of my darling brother's fiery upset. 'You are a passionate individual, Metatronim, so I shall forgive the insult,' he said, piously. 'What I suggest is this: we take back the balance of power. In plain terms, I believe we should subjugate humanity and reclaim what is ours by right of superiority. Then, when we are once again all-powerful and not subjugating any natural urges, I truly believe all manifestations of the sickness will disappear.'

There was a shocked murmur which threaded through the hall from end to end. How could the Tartaruch suggest such a thing? A sour taste came into my mouth (the taste of soulscaper blood?). Did Avirzah'e really think we could comfortably become cold-

47

blooded killers? If he did, he was a fool – and had obviously never killed anyone himself. To unleash the beast in every eloim would turn our people into monsters. Our invisibility would disappear. We would be hunted down and destroyed. In the past, some eloim had trangressed the code of honour that forbade us taking unwilling victims for the sup. Because of them, our race had nearly been exterminated by angry humans. We could not chance such a thing happening again. Beth and I were aware how serious a risk we had taken in Lansaal. I did not believe Tartaruch, pampered creature that he was, could even begin to understand the implications of what he was suggesting. It was fortunate Avirzah'e's father was absent from the meeting, for I was convinced Tartarus himself would have chastened his son most severely for such heresy, had he heard it. Avirzah'e, perhaps realising he had been a little too liberal in voicing his thoughts, added, 'Once we were supreme as a race. Now, we huddle among the gutters like rats avoiding the poisoner's rag; hiding among the simpering beau monde, making our pretty pictures, pretty speeches, pretty music. No wonder we are sickening! Our spirits are repressed! I feel we should face ourselves squarely. Once, we were warrior princes, puissant and vital. Now, we languish, and our essence is impoverished. We should harvest our sustenance, not beg for it!'

Amid a thunderous grumbling, Sandalphon, the prince of Sarim, and a close colleague of our father, rose to his feet. 'Your ingratitude makes me feel ashamed!' he said. 'Our patrons excel themselves in generosity. How can you talk of subjugation and conquest? Are we not a civilised race, above such primitive carnage? I am outraged! It is fortunate the lady Kaliph is not present to bear witness to your odious outpourings!'

'Be at rest, Sandalphon, we have our privacy here!' Avirzah'e said. 'The only human lips within earshot are soon to be sealed for eternity.' He glanced at the door at the back of the hall, outside which the Kaliph's offerings were trembling in divine anticipation. 'I understand your squeamishness, however, and beg your indulgence for my plain speech, but I still feel my suggestions are more suitable than that of trusting a human soulscaper to solve our problems.'

'Your unconventional opinions are indeed interesting,' the Oriukh said, 'but impractical. You are young, Tartaruchi, and full of zeal. I appreciate your intentions are voiced in the interests of eloim, as do all of us here, I'm sure, but I cannot empathise with your suggestions. Please, take your seat. Thank you for your contribution.' Thus, the Tartaruchi prince was silenced.

Because of the historical events, when the majority of humanity turned on eloimkind, we need the patronage of sympathetic humans in order to exist; we depend upon their cooperation. However, these same historical events necessitate that only a very few, trusted humans, who have pledged to support us, can be aware of our true nature. Creatures that feed upon blood are abhorred and feared by the majority of humans. There are many myths concerning our previous, more visible existence in the world, but these are now only stories with which to frighten children. But for the most ignorant and superstitous of individuals – who will believe all manner of improbable nonsense – humanity no longer believes that blood-stealers really exist. We do not have the power of soulscapers, but through persistent and concerted effort, we have managed to affect human consciousness to the degree where non-patrons do not question our sequestered lifestyle and our feeding requirements are concealed. However, without the protection of the patrons, and their willingness to provide our nourishment, we would undoubtedly have been discovered by the populace, driven out and killed. Apart from the patrons, we have to maintain a strict distance between ourselves and humanity. Obviously, isolation alone is not sufficient precaution and, over the centuries, we have developed further camouflaging techniques, but there can be no doubt of the debt we owe to the patrons. To express ungratitude was to risk taunting fate; we were all afraid of that, aware of the delicacy of our disguise.

Avirzah'e Tartaruchi very much wished to leave the hall after the Oriukh had silenced him; I could feel it strongly. Used as he was to commanding attention, it did not rest well with him to be contradicted. No doubt, he'd been sure his ideas would have been greeted warmly by the throngs. It was unfortunate for him that he had not prepared his speech more carefully, that he had not avoided emotive terms. I even felt a moment of pity for him, dashed prince. Still, he was foolish to have dragged the reeking past into our midst in that way; it was something all had expelled from their minds. There was so much unsaid about our history; so much pain contained there. Even as I smugly enjoyed the Oriukh's put-down of Avirzah'e I did find myself wondering whether there was not more than a grain of good sense in the Tartaruch's words. His solutions were outlandish, of course, but perhaps the secret to the root of the sickness did lie in the time of which he spoke. I saw his sister offer him a comforting hand, which he shrugged off like a petulant man-child. Beth caught my eye and smiled; he had seen it too.

The Oriukh had dismissed Avirzah'e entirely from his attention. 'How long till your flower blooms?' he asked us.

'Impossible to specify,' Beth replied, 'but we shall be vigilant.'

Then, a new voice interrupted. Finally, Metatron had risen from his seat. 'I find myself praying, my son, that you will not be among the casualties that will doubtlessly occur before this soulscaper is ready for whatever you have in mind.' His words were almost like

49

a threat. I felt Beth flinch against me, and longed to reach for his hand, but I wanted to betray no sign of weakness. 'I would like a question answered,' Metatron continued, facing the Oriukh. 'If we concede to my children's plan, how do we cope with the sickness in the meantime?'

The Oriukh nodded. 'A good point, Metatron. All I can suggest is this: we must stretch our time to accommodate the period of waiting. We must observe each other closely, succour if we can, and trust the sickness cannot accelerate. If anyone manifests the urge to self-destruction, perhaps they should be persuaded to take retreat-slumber until a cure is found. I also recommend that all those of your families currently in retreat-slumber should remain so; again, until the problem is resolved. I feel we should use this time to investigate the condition further; perhaps other solutions will be revealed. When Beth and Gimel's soulscaper is ready to be brought to Sacramante, we will discuss their plan again. Is everyone in accord?'

As the Oriukh was psychically in tune with all eloim, voicing the question was merely a courtesy. The lords of each family rose and gave assent. We descended from the podium; Avirzah'e was the only black maggot amid the nectar of empathy. He had done more to sway eloim opinion in our favour than we could ever have hoped possible.

The throngs had begun to move out of the hall, to take refreshment. The Kaliph's offerings would be conducted to the ceremony room nearby. Beth and I linked arms and walked towards the door. 'Should we attempt reparation with the Tartaruchis?' I asked Beth. It would be humiliating, but perhaps necessary for eloim well-being. My brother shook his head.

'Never. Let him steam to a husk.' He put his arm around my waist. 'Lilit's Lip, am I glad that's over! I need refreshment now, most urgently. May we pair for the sup?'

I inclined my head. 'My pleasure.'

The Kaliph's offerings had been escorted to a large function room, where they milled nervously in the centre, their faces coloured along the bones, illustrating their contained frenzy. In deference, we would make their sacrifice an ecstasy. Many eloim had elected to depart at this point, perhaps having recently nourished themselves, or else hastening to sweeter suppings elsewhere, in more secluded surroundings. Beth and I considered it would be impolite not to partake of the feast. We were honoured guests, after all.

Beth asked me to choose a soul to sup, and I picked a radiant bloom, one whose eyes had followed us across the room, one who wanted us to have him. He was a lovely boy, his flesh petals yellow-brown as lion fur, with pony eyes and the hair of a precious mare. He was exquisite: almost too good to husk, and yet, someone,

50

somewhere, had surrendered him, this lovely son, for our refreshment. I could have wept at the gesture.

He seemed dazed, unaware of his surroundings, and I had to take hold of his arm to lead him into one of the many curtained alcoves that lined the room. Within it, a bed of cushions and recently cut petals were provided for comfort. Beth drew the night-dark curtain around us and we were alone with our willing sacrifice, bright stars in an infinity of blackness. We stripped the flower of its foliage and purred and rubbed our faces across its flesh. The excitement of knowing we would utterly drain this boy kindled frantic desire. He, too, was aroused by the prospect of his sacrifice; the intimacy of this knowledge we shared was more holy than any physical sensations we might soon enjoy. I could not even wait to disrobe myself, but hitched up my skirts and settled on his body, gripping him within, giving myself up to the tide of sensations that began to roll and crest and crash inside me. He bucked me like the precious mare; he bit his lips and made the blood flow. Beth kissed it all away, sucking the juice from the torn flesh, and proffering me a heady mouthful of it in a kiss. The taste made me explode within. I swallowed greedily and bent to take more from the wound itself. My physical desires utterly sated, I rolled to the side, intent on refreshing myself more thoroughly. Beth took my place in one fluid motion. I nipped the boy's throat-flesh, my stomach contracting in need. Such sweet sacrifice. I told him I loved him, covered him with kisses, from brow to breast. I felt his hand in my hair. The fingers convulsed. He reached the moment of release, and in that moment, spoke. He pulled up my head by the hair, brought my face close to his own. His voice was pained, husky.

'Do not kill me,' he said. His breath smelled of blood.

'It speaks! An omen!' Beth cried. Normally, they make no sound at all, having been trained that way, or drugged.

'What did you say?' I asked. We had all become still, the only motion that of trickling sweat and blood. The boy's fingers were still entangled in my hair, quite painfully, in fact. I tried to pull away.

'Don't kill me,' he said again.

Beth and I looked at each other. My brother's face was a mask of blood, his naked chest striped with red. In that moment, reality came crashing in, and the holiness fled. It seemed obscene, what we were doing. Where was the propriety of the sup in this?

'Don't; don't kill him,' said Beth.

Later, we crept out beneath the curtains. We wrapped the boy in Beth's cloak, having licked his wounds clean, and took him home. The way he had reached out to us, denied his holy fate, was a significant part of all that happened later. The name his people had

51

given him was forgotten. We called him Amelakiveh, and he was useful to us, sometimes.

'. . . if there be cure or charm to respite or deceive, or slack the pain of this ill mansion . . .'
Paradise Lost, Book II

When I was sixteen, Ushas was summoned to the city of Sacramante. Lansaal had little truck with the Bochanegran empire; the boundary was a shivery place where realities crossed, and strained to overtake each other. Taparak, situated so close to Lansaal, was more or less considered a state of that realm. Once a year, the Shah of Lansaal and his family visited our city to take a holiday among the high dreys, and spend the time with the most celebrated members of our community. Popular legend suggested that the royal family would sometimes don common clothing and walk in disguise among the people. This was undoubtedly untrue; I am sure the Shah never ventured from his holiday palace near the sky when he was in Taparak. However, other than this royal favour, Taparak itself had very little to do with the government of Lansaal; the Taps were independent creatures, roaming far. Racially, the Taps and the Lans were far apart. Tapar mountain had been colonised, centuries ago, by the black-skinned people of the Delta Lands, who were our ancestors. The Lans were tawny-skinned, and not so tall as us. We considered their culture to be rather primitive in comparison to our own, and discouraged its eccentric religious influences invading the mountain. Our city, however, was a favourite resort with foreign travellers and there was a thriving tourist trade. As many travellers had to cross Lansaal to reach us, pausing at Lannish coastal towns along the way, and using Lannish transport to traverse the water, the Taps enjoyed an easy relationship with the Lans. We brought them revenue; they brought us clients in their slim, turquoise-prowed boats.

It was in one of these boats that my mother and I crossed the sea to Lansaal.

I had only been down the mountain twice before in my life – does this sound strange? Well, there was no reason for me to do so. I had scampered through the phosphorous-lit terraces of the fungus farms and dipped my toes in the icy underground lakes, which shivered with the memory of starlight, but I had never ventured further down the mountain than the third tier, where I would sometimes wave my mother off on her travels. Now, the thought of travelling made me feel uneasy; I was afraid of the world outside. Still, there was no use getting flustered about it; my future lay upon the open road. I was to be a soulscaper and soulscapers were away from home for most of the time.

There was one part of the descent which I particularly hated: at the third-level platform we had to enter the air-raft on its creaking, swaying ropes and be lowered down the wide shaft, known as the Throat, to the ninth level. There were many smaller shafts leading downwards, twisting this way and that, but the Throat was the largest and straightest, being, as its name implies, a yawning maw right down the centre of the mountain, passing through half a dozen levels. I was already twitchy by the time Ushas had bundled me into the basket of the raft, while it was still tethered to the passenger platform. It was like stepping out into infinite space, supported only by a dust-mote, and I was horribly conscious of the enormous gulf beneath us. Ushas mocked my nervousness, bantered lightly with the raft conductor, and settled herself for the ride. Then, the anchors were hauled in and the raft swung out with sickening swiftness into the centre of the shaft. I huddled by my mother's feet and clamped my hands over my mouth, in order to prevent cries of terror coming out and embarrassing us. It was pitch-dark in the shaft, but for the dim orange glow of the conductor's lamp. The conductor was, in fact, the only pleasurable aspect of the journey; a handsome man. Negligent of any danger, he leaned over the safety rail – too flimsy by far – and stared up at the diminishing light above or else down into the threatening dark. Eerie calls floated by us from the pulley-men at the top and bottom. 'Ai-yeee-aaah! Ai-yeee-aah!' and the chittering reply like the call of a desert jackal, 'Yip, yip-yip, yiii-ip!' Once, after a visit to the passenger platform to see my mother off on a journey, I had imagined these adepts of the shafts might be weighing the souls of their passengers; if found wanting, the pulley ropes would snap – clack! – and the unworthy would zoom into the darkness below, their requiem the jackal-calls of the pulley-men. By the age of sixteen, I was proud enough to deny such fantasies, and merely flared my nostrils at the conductor.

Ushas had received a commission from one of the merchant families in Sacramante; a minor problem, they avowed, and hardly urgent, but one which they felt merited arrest at the hands of the most celebrated of soulscapers. Ushas was not the most celebrated of soulscapers, but she was one of the most glamorous, and also the only glamorous soulscaper currently available for commission. Her guild had apportioned her the job.

'I feel it's about time you got off the mountain,' Ushas had said to me, just after we'd finished the celebratory meal following her official commission. For a few moments, I had been intensely irritated, having been looking forward to being left to my own devices

54

at home. Ushas did not fuss or place strictures on my behaviour, but I had already learned the singularly precious joy of having the hollow to myself. Sometimes she had to present herself for further training at the guild dreys, when she would return exhausted after a week or so, and sleep for several days. Other times, she'd get itchy feet, and make small forays into Lansaal on shopping expeditions for luxuries we could not buy in Taparak. While I was still a young child, the guild did not send her away on long 'scaping jobs, but as I grew older, she had started disappearing for weeks at a time. Both of us, I think, were grateful for the space that gave us. By this time, we had risen in the Taparak stratum, and occupied a drey only three levels below that of the scryers. When we'd first moved home, I had missed the ground bustle, but had since fallen in love with the feeling of open air around us, the play of winds among the thinner branches, the illusion that one could be all alone.

I had applied myself earnestly to my studies – being an earnest young woman all round – and would soon be considered capable enough to ply the Tappish trade abroad in the land. Training had had its ups and downs; sometimes I had sunk into despair, thinking I'd never develop the necessary skills. But now, I was beginning to feel more confident and could slip with ease into the scaping trance.

The first time I had experimented with the fumes had been terrifying. No matter how much my tutor reassured me she would remain with me as a guide, I had still feared losing myself in the soulscape. The basis of the scaping-mixes is a strange substance, a resin derived from a hardy mountain plant which can be harvested in two ways. The first is to produce a blend simply for scrying, which is the superficial examination of the soulscape – rather than truly entering it. For this mix, the plants are milked through a small cut and the resulting milk-ooze is allowed to harden and dry. The second method is the one by which we produce a strong scaping-fume that truly alters conscious awareness and allows ingress to the soulscape. Scry bugs feed upon the plant, absorbing huge amounts for their body weight of the active substance in the sap. If the bugs themselves are harvested, crushed and dried, incorporated into a fume mix with raw plant resin, a far more potent fume is produced. Quite how it works upon the human frame, we do not know. The effect is this: two or more people breathing in enough of the fume can enter each other's mindscape and from there, should they be familiar with the path, the soulscape. Gradually, as the fume is ingested into the lungs, outer reality fades. At first, there is a confusion of colours and sensations – impossible to describe – but if regular breathing and tranquillity of thought are maintained, the inner landscapes of each individual are allowed to touch, and the consciousness of everyone present may wander at will in the new territory. Naturally, the technique has its dangers, which is why we

55

soulscapers undergo such protracted training. An inexperienced or untrained person should never attempt to use the scry-bug fume. Without proper control, the individual can become lost in an alien scape, and remain there as an unwanted and disruptive presence, eventually driving the host insane. More than a few soulscaping cases have involved unravelling such amateurish attempts at scape-sharing. Lamentably, unscrupulous individuals in Taparak are willing to purloin and sell the fume-mix off-mountain for a high profit. Many thrill-seekers indulge in illicit scape-sharing, and most of that number end up in trouble. Fortunately, perhaps, it is rare that anybody rescued from such a traumatic condition attempts to repeat the experiment. In fact there are individuals who, once led back to reality, have made it their life's-work to travel around warning others about the practice. They are usually rather demented in their approach, however, and generally end up joining the priesthood of some religion or another.

As trainees, I and my peers were taught not only how to enter the soulscape and wander in it at will, but also to manipulate the information and symbolism we might find there. Initially, all trainees were closely monitored and our tutor, Tiji, would always accompany us. Later, we were allowed to burn the resin in pairs, but it was a long time before we were ever let near someone whose soulscape was less than healthy. The first experience of the inner realm is impossible to describe, but the feelings it invokes are those of terror, wonder and sheer disbelief. There are landscapes there, but they are like nothing seen on Earth; gone are the restrictions of natural order; these are the kingdoms of the imagination, where nothing is impossible or too bizarre to exist. Naturally, not everyone is sturdy enough to withstand the soulscape, and several of my classmates had to drop out of the training. This was not regarded as a failure, because the Taps believe everyone has a skill for something. Those who could not work within the soulscape were encouraged to find a vocation in another craft. Secretly, though, those of us who had the strength to carry on were very proud of ourselves. Only a week before Ushas and I left the mountain, I had completed my first scaping task.

People from Lansaal who could not afford the statutory fee of the soulscapers would send their mindsick relatives to the city, in order to take advantage of guild offers, which promised free healing for those who volunteered to let trainees work on them. My first case involved a young girl, who had been paralysed by a fragment of the Fear. It had taken place in my tutor's residence, all the light boles sealed from light and air. Even now, I can remember how nervous I'd been as I'd mixed the fume in Tiji's watchful, but unobtrusive, presence. She had sat close enough to partake of the fume but did not assume an active rôle in the work. The girl lay, open-eyed, on a pallet at my feet, her breathing shallow. As I

56

breathed in the potent fume, I silently invoked my guardian-pursuers, instinctively addressing the more female aspect, with whom I felt secure. What would the Fear look like? Would it attack me? It seemed a soft, sweet voice was in my head, murmuring reassurance. 'I am with you, Rayo. I will keep you safe.' Gradually the shapes and colours of the outside world began to fade, and I closed my eyes. The soulscape can be seen whether one is physically looking at it or not. In effect, you cannot close your eyes on it. The inner landscape of the sick girl was a silent town, its street unpeopled and littered with rubbish. I recognised the building that symbolised her own mind, because it was covered with a dark, poisonous-looking lichen. All the doors and windows were covered with it. My first instinct was to call to Tiji and ask her what to do, but I thought better of it. I knew what she would say: use your imagination. Fight symbol with symbol. I approached the building and hesitantly picked at the lichen with my fingernails. It was crumbly and dusty and I soon cleared a patch of window, which allowed me to look inside the house. The girl's soul sat upon the floor of an empty room, her face devoid of features: no eyes, no nose, no mouth. She had truly shut herself away from the Fear that had crept up upon her mind and enclosed her. I banged on the window and said, 'Wake up!' The girl shivered but did not change her position or appearance. I scraped frantically at the powdery lichen, all the time talking loudly, hoping to reach the frightened scrap of consciousness inside the room. 'Look how easily it comes away. Why don't you come and help me? This stuff is nothing really. . . . Come on, wake up. Help me clean your house.'

As more light came into the room, it seemed the girl came into focus. I could discern the shape of her face more easily, features were becoming prominent. Eventually, she opened her eyes, got up and walked to the window.

'What are you doing out there?' she asked. 'Who are you?'

I wanted to smash through the panes and hug her. 'I am a soulscaper,' I said proudly. 'And I'm here to clean your house.'

'It doesn't need cleaning!' The girl had a distinctly accusatory tone.

I was about to argue, but one glance up at the walls convinced me to shut my mouth. The Fear had gone. It was that simple. Joyfully, I stepped back and concentrated on returning to normal consciousness. Tiji was there to greet me, her arms around the girl on the pallet, who was trying to sit up, making small sounds of distress.

'Don't let this success go to your head, girl,' Tiji said, her wide mouth pulled into a grin. 'This was an easy one.' Then, because I must have looked a little crestfallen, she leaned forward to squeeze my arm. 'But well done, all the same.'

Soon afterwards, I realised just how easy that job had been. The

Fear was usually inclined to assume forms of a more aggressive or elusive nature. Sometimes, it would take more than one session to root it out, never mind dispel it. But that first job is the one I remember best. It confirmed for me that I was firmly on the soul-scaping path. Within a year or so, I would be ready to pass from the guild college and be sent on my first scaping-range abroad. That did not mean I would be given a commission; I would simply travel from town to town seeking work on my own. After two years, I would have to return to Taparak, and pay the set earnings figure to the guild; what I made over that amount would be mine to keep, although I was already aware that most soulscapers existed by bartering their talents for food and shelter on the road. This first journey, with my mother, would help prepare me for the future.

After alighting with unsteady feet on to the eighth level, my mother led the way on foot down the curling, wide ramp which would open out on the shore. The ramp was busy that day, traders coming and going, a mountebank performing in a recess of the rock, earning oriels for his excesses. Voices shouted, animals brayed and huffed, carts creaked and groaned. Soon, the raft we had travelled down on would be raised aloft once more, carrying passengers and trading goods up to Taparak. All these new stimuli quickly expelled the shakes of the journey down. We came to a place where the sea thrashed into a vast underground cave, and boats were moored to great iron rings in the rock. The ramp turned a corner and there was the splendid vista of the Womb of the Land ahead of us, crammed with the bright masts and sails of Lannish vessels. Carrying our bags, I followed Ushas to the quayside. There was a small community hugging the narrow strip of land between the mountain and the sea at this point; a perilous position. In winter it was flogged by angry waves, and the marketeers and boatmen retreated into deep caves above tide level, where they lived together until the spring. Come that time, the stone town-strip would be repaired, and the Womb would be thronged with boats once more.

The quay was a forest of masts and rigging; boats of all sizes jostling together. Skinny boys in ragged trousers, torn off at the knees, leapt from deck to deck, carrying messages, cargo and luggage, or else selling whatever was portable to boatmen from the mainland and their passengers. Groups of girls, arms linked, wearing marvellous tiered gowns of dark green, indigo and sulky, dull gold, strolled up and down the promenade, singing of stars and crystal; they were scryers of a lesser nature, who had never belonged to a guild and whose talents, my mother told me, were negligible.

I happily basked in all the colour and noise as Ushas secured us passage on one of the ferries. Once on the mainland, we would join a mule-train to Toinis – just a day's journey – where a Bochanegran vessel awaited us. I had begun to wonder what Sacramante would be like, having forgotten how annoyed I'd been when Ushas had first suggested I accompany her there.

We boarded a small boat, along with about half a dozen other passengers. Once we were out upon the waves, all my youthful zest began to soar. I leaned into the wind, against the edge of the boat, and let the wind take hold of my hair, closing my eyes against the scent and spray. Ushas sat cross-legged with the boatman's boy and played Conquer, with a patterned gaming-board and men of different colours. She always won at this game so, when he shouted out in triumph, I knew she must have a soft spot for the boy. I turned and caught her eye, narrowing my own, smiling. She nodded back, with the kind of smile on her face where the mouth turned down at the corners. I had been practising that expression for years and still couldn't manage to do it as well as she did. Today, we were women travelling together, soulscapers on the road, and we could conserve our power by cheating fate to others' advantage. It is a strange code we live by.

Landfall came at Cozca, a relatively small town stuck out on a promontory, north-east of Toinis. We sat down outside a tavern, in the shade of an ilex tree, and sipped at steaming tankards of bitter myrrh-broth, whose perfume clawed the throat like a drug. The land seemed so flat to me, the town so sprawling. And how wide the streets were. Soon, even before the shadows had lengthened into evening, a muleteer came to pin her schedule to the tree. Ushas lost no time in appending our mark. Tomorrow, we would ride to Toinis. A night was spent in relative comfort in a Cozcan fohndahk near the tavern, where we took a room overlooking the ilex tree. After dining, we sat out on the fohndahk patio and watched the funeral line of a local man sway past; the casket drawn on a sledge by two oxen festooned in purple ribbons. The mourners came behind, singing of holy sacrifice, by which we understood the deceased had died the Holy Death, pale as winter orchids on his last bed.

Part of my initial training had included a brief examination of the condition referred to as the 'Holy Death'. Trainees were taught nothing more than how to recognise Holy victims and, having ascertained that a person has died from the condition, to leave well alone. The Holy, or Sacred, Death is a phenomenon found in Khalt and Lansaal, which had begun to occur – or had at least been recognised – a year or so before I underwent my scrying rite. Its origins, however, are indistinct, although the Lans and Khalts swiftly attached religious meaning to it. Strangely, analytical discussion of the subject was never encouraged among soulscaping trainees, which naturally provoked many of us to raise it with our tutors. The Taps are renowned for their rather iconoclastic tendencies regarding other people's beliefs, so it seemed very odd indeed that we should be discouraged from debating something that should surely be analysed in detail and understood. Some of us put forward the suggestion that the Holy Death was caused by a disease and could, therefore, be eradicated if time were spent on studying the phenomenon. Others, myself among them, thought the Deaths were the result of a state of mind, a willingness to die. Tiji reluctantly conceded that in her opinion it could be both of these things, and more. But she stressed that humanity needed certain, inexplicable things to maintain the health of its mindscape; the most experienced of soulscapers believed the Holy Death to be one of these things. The only place in the known world which does not produce cases of the Holy Death is Taparak itself, which surely suggests that the mind-training of the Taps is responsible for their immunity. After all, even a flower-seller in Taparak can be called upon to scry, if necessary.

However, because the condition is so deeply steeped in mystic import, it is not easy to study it rationally, and Tiji urged most strongly that we never try to investigate the Holy Deaths abroad. 'Remember,' she said, 'that, for some, the idea of a virgin being impregnated by a ray of light and consequently delivering a god-child is a given, incontrovertible fact. You also know what can happen to those who contest this belief! If people believe that the gods have taken one of their loved ones, they strongly resent scientific interference. *Never* ask to examine a Holy corpse.'

I had this in mind as the funeral party swayed past. Ushas made no comment to me, but uttered a benison and flicked a few drops of the orange wine we were drinking out on to the dust. One of the mourners noticed this and, seeing our attire and our skin colour, which shrieked Taparak loudly, came to present us with a purple lily. Ushas accepted this gracefully and thumbed the woman's forehead. We were invited to the wake, but Ushas declined, speaking of early starts in the morning and fatigue. I was disappointed; some riotous fun might be had among the pyre trees of Cozca.

Before dawn, my mother pitched me from my bed. She was already dressed and had daubed her cheekbones with gold-green pigment to signify her rank and also that her services were engaged. I had to wear a stripe of turquoise down my nose to show I was still in training and not to be petitioned. This irked me. I had wanted to pretend and put on airs. Still, the day was sweet, made fragrant by the fumes of the resin farms down-wind, the sky clear and limpid. The mules were big animals, well-muscled and fresh; much more impressive than the skinny and cantankerous beasts found in Taparak. The journey began at a brisk trot, the muleteer chanting the rhythm to the mules as the passengers jounced up and down in their saddles; those of them untrained in the art of mulemanship jounced painfully from side to side as well. By mid-morning, we were halfway down the coast road. To the right, yellow beaches tressed with weed sloped away to the wrinkling sea. In a hazy distance the dragon shapes of Bochanegran vessels, carrying merchandise east, could be seen: their masts festooned with flags bearing the heraldic devices of the merchants.

Toinis was chaos. Being a major port, a religious sanctuary for several of the most prominent cults, and home of the Trine Colleges of Alchemy, Astronomy and Word, it was always crammed with people of many different races. I saw sallow-skinned Bochanegrans, who were mostly tourists or students; tall, proud, incredibly black Deltan traders and magi; and even the occasional tow-headed Khalt, who always looked rather lost and far from home. Ushas, after paying the muleteer and, upon entreaty, blessing the mules, dragged me straight to the docks. We spent quite a time wandering up and down, looking for the Bochanegran vessel, *Swift Sprite Windheel*, on which the guild had arranged our passage to Sacramante.

'I hope there has been no misunderstanding,' Ushas muttered, her patience fraying, as we began our third circuit of the quayside. Eventually, we resigned ourselves to queuing at the harbourmaster's booth, where we might inquire as to the *Windheel*'s whereabouts. I wanted to wander off and explore, but knew Ushas wouldn't take it well. She got bored easily and needed someone to complain to as we stood in line. Luckily, there was a Lannish family ahead of us, who had been waiting for three days for passage east to Craienic, and therefore had more to moan about. Ushas listened attentively to their complaints, offering advice.

When our turn came, my mother puffed herself up to a commanding stance and said, 'Good man, tell me please where I may locate the Bochanegran vessel, *Swift Sprite Windheel*. She is expecting us.'

The harbourmaster barely looked up, but pointed over our shoulders. We turned. Through the window, we could see a stately, disdainful, high-prowed vessel nosing aside lesser boats as she cruised slowly into dock. The *Windheel*. Perhaps we'd arrived early.

For some esoteric reason, my body decided it had had enough of sea travel and adopted nausea for the last stage of our journey. True, a late spring hastening had risen in the winds, chopping up the sea beneath the ship into chunks, so that it seemed she bounced through the waves rather than cleaved through them. Ushas doped me up with goldpoppy elixir and virtually strapped me into a bunk in our cabin, while she repaired to the saloon and drank with the other passengers, or else played Conquer. I had never felt so ill in my life and guzzled more goldpoppy as soon as signs of alertness illumined the fuzz in my brain. Thus, by the time we docked at Sacramante, I was more in the soulscape than reality, and my addled senses had become so used to the chop of waves, I couldn't stand on land and vomited as soon as I tried to walk. Ushas was

61

annoyed by this, because she didn't want me to embarrass her. I was deposited, rather roughly, in a dockside orberja, where I sought once more the temporary sanctuary of sleep, while Ushas hired a spindly open carriage to take her to the Carmen Tricante, residence of her employers.

Later, I was sent for. A message came from Ushas to inform me that the Tricantes would not hear of us staying in an oberja during our visit, and that they had offered us the hospitality of their family home. I sat on the edge of my bed while the oberja mistress told me all this, and wondered how on Earth I was going to control my rebellious stomach in the presence of Sacramantan aristocrats. But by the time the Tricante conveyance, complete with haughty, liveried driver, presented itself in front of the building, I had bathed myself, eaten, and drunk two carafes of spring water, and so was feeling much revived. The driver carried our belongings outside, me tripping behind in my best shirt and trousers. It was too warm to wear my favourite embroidered jacket, but I carried it over my arm, with the embroidery displayed to good effect. I nodded graciously at the driver as I climbed daintily into the carriage, supported by his gloved hand. This was wonderful. The whole of that visit was filled with such magicks.

Carmen Tricante was a magnificent villa, situated on a hill above the harbour, its steeply sloping gardens lush with flowering trees. I loved the way the house was taller at the front, although even at the rear it boasted three storeys. There was a clutch of young people resident at the Carmen, including two daughters of the house, one a few years older than I, the other, fortunately, the same age. Only two weeks parted Liviana's birthday from mine and, perhaps because of our astral conjunction, we got along very well from the first moment we set eyes on each other. There were also two female cousins, both in their late twenties, named Perdina and Voile. I think they must have been twins; they were attenuated, pallid things, who read much poetry. Finally, there was a noisy brace of brothers, Zimon and Almero, who were of the age when life suddenly becomes hysterical and interesting. Someone whom I did not see at first was the afflicted son of the household, whose name was rarely spoken. Ushas told me he was called Salyon, and that he was confined to a small pale room set high in the Carmen. I do not think that even she was introduced to the invalid until the next morning.

We took supper in the garden that first night, mother surrounded by an adoring court, relating soulscaper anecdotes; me crowded by Liviana, who never stopped asking questions. Whether it was the effect of the petal-wine we were drinking, the fragrant night, the dark-song of Sacramante carousing the spring evening, or just the strangeness of this life so far beyond Taparak, I felt as if I had fallen in love. My heart soared, my blood screamed in joy; I couldn't stop smiling. Feverishly, I extolled the wonders of this magical city to my hostess. Liviana merely wrinkled her sun-tawny nose, small and straight as a child's finger, and said, 'It's all so *busy*. I'd like to live in Taparak. It sounds so *casual*.' I wondered what absurdity of fate had cast each of our souls down in the environment that the other desired. Liviana liked air, she liked heights, and made me tell her of my life among the dreys.

There is an atmosphere in Sacramante like nowhere else on Earth. Now, I understand some of what inspires it but then, as a girl, I was intoxicated and spellbound by its hectic gaiety, its intimations of secrets. The city sprawls over a number of hills; wide avenues sweep down to the sea, and there are hundreds of little alleys, where cloistered tavernas, walled in flowering vines, sell bizarre and perfumed beverages. Walking through the maze tunnels of these alleys, you sometimes come upon a cobbled piazza, where entertainers tumble and screech for the benefit of indolent beauties seated outside the oberjas, their dark-vaned fans aflap. Every day, while my mother probed the soulscape of poor suffering Salyon, Liviana and I went out into the city. Liviana wanted to show me everything, on condition that she could visit me in Taparak later, when I might repay the favour. I was happy to comply. We were never out alone, however. Sometimes Livvy's older sister, Agnestia, would accompany us, or else we'd have to put up with the boisterous brothers as escorts. Occasionally, one or both of the languid cousins might stir themselves to take us out. Whoever came with us, it always seemed as if we were in a crowd; I had never laughed so much in my life. There was so much to see, an almost obscene plenitude of art and culture to sample. The choice of concerts, plays, and participatory art events being staged each day was over-whelming. There was something to suit every taste; even the most outlandish and grotesque.

One evening, Zimon took us secretly to a hidden taverna, deep in the city labyrinth, where two performers of exquisite slimness and beauty slowly disrobed each other to music, their eyes like polished quartz. Livvy giggled and nudged me, whispering bawdy, slightly uncomfortable, remarks, which I tried to ignore. There was a purity to the performance, a stylish reserve, which provoked only a feeling of sadness within me. Livvy appeared unmoved by such undercurrents and accepted the performance at face value, hissing in delighted embarrassment at the sight of the male's penis, the female's rouged breasts. There was nothing more to it than that. It was not erotic in any way, but art, purely that; living sculptures, their planes of vital marble catching the light, dancing with the light, using it to create new forms. I felt drunk when we went out into the evening air, although I had sipped only a citrus cordial.

One morning, Ushas dashed my hopes of yet another day's frolicking with the Tricantes. 'Today, I want you with me when I work,' she said. I felt a moment's remorse, because I had almost forgotten why we were there. We had been in the Carmen for three days; I should have offered to assist her before, or at least shown an interest in what she was doing. Liviana was disappointed she would not have my company that day – it was astounding how well we got on – but understood my responsibilities without argument. We could perhaps, she suggested, go out for the evening later.

After breakfast, Ushas led me to a steep, secluded stairway, which had banisters of intricately worked beaten iron, that curled around on itself like dried strips of fungus meat. Round windows let in a blaze of morning light, but as we mounted those stairs I began to feel nervous.

Ushas paused outside a door at the top of the stairs and said, 'I really want you to see this, Rayo.'

See what? I was unnerved. Would it be horrible to look at?

Inside, the room was very bare: just a bed, a chest of drawers, a chair for the comfort of those who sat with the invalid, and a small table. An unconscious boy lay in the bed, beneath a coverlet of white and gold tapestry. Sunlight fell on to his immobile face, and across the hands of the servant woman who sat reading a book beside him. Later, Ushas told me the Tricantes never left Salyon alone. The servant ducked a curtsy to my mother, put away her book, and left the room.

'Any change?' my mother asked her as she passed.

The woman shook her head.

Ushas sighed and walked over to the bed. I followed her. The boy looked dead: his skin was bluish white, the lips colourless, the eye sockets dark as if bruised. He was so thin. His hair looked like a discarded switch of tangled straw on the pillow. Ushas bent down and raised his body a little way off the bed and I saw that much of his hair remained on the pillow as she did so. An evil whiff of sickness filled the air. My stomach knotted; I had never seen anyone as ill as this.

Ushas examined his body and then lowered him back down. 'Is it the Fear?' I asked.

She turned and looked at me – oh, how I remember her face in that moment – and just shrugged. She cannot help him, I thought, she cannot heal him. I felt faint.

'Physically, I can find nothing amiss,' she said. 'And in the soulscape. . . .' She rubbed her face with long fingers, and then tucked her braids back behind her ears. 'If it is the Fear, then I came too late, and yet the Tricantes swear his condition wasn't that serious until just before we arrived. Otherwise, they would have dragged in a soulscaper off the street, I'm sure! I can't understand it. His father says the boy was simply listless, and prone to night terrors. Local healers suggested it was a growing sickness – it can happen – and that a good soulscaper could straighten out his mind to face adulthood. But this, this is not a growing sickness.'

'What did you find in the soulscape?' I asked, curiosity overwhelming squeamishness.

Ushas actually shuddered at the memory. 'Every day I go in there,' she said softly. 'Every day. It is a dead landscape. Utterly dead. I'm at a loss for what to do.'

'Have you told the parents?'

She shook her head. 'I can't give up yet.'

'Do you want me to accompany you today?'

She smiled wearily and shook her head. 'No, Rayo. I don't want you in there with me; you don't have the experience for this yet. I just wanted you to see, that's all. It is not very often that we come across a case like this, but it's likely you will encounter one yourself in the future, and I think it's important for you to be able to recognise the external appearance. Now, I will burn the resin, and I want you to wait outside until I'm in trance. Then, come back in, and take away the resin bowl. Observe. Will you do that?'

I nodded, and turned to the door. Pausing with my hand on the latch, I said, 'Is it possible to cure cases like this?'

Ushas was busying herself with the resin bowl and her tinder. She did not look round. 'There is always a first time,' she said.

The tutors never tell us of this condition. It is almost as if they want to deny it exists. Older soulscapers take it upon themselves to educate their juniors about it. I waited outside Salyon's door, until I was sure my mother was heavily in trance. Then, I quietly re-entered the room, holding my breath so as not to risk becoming tranced myself, and put the resin bowl out on the window ledge, dousing it with a little water I found in a flagon on a table by the bed. I left the window open and breathed the fresh air, until the pungent scaping-smoke had thinned. Ushas was sitting on the floor, straight-backed, breathing evenly. The boy was motionless as before. I leaned against the windowsill and watched. Occasionally, Ushas would curl her lips into a snarl, and twitch, but there was no other sign of distress. After an hour, she sighed deeply, and her head sank on to her breast. Then she looked up and blinked at me, with a faint smile. Her face had an unnaturally purplish tinge in the dark hollows of her cheeks.

'I am not without hope,' she said. I went over and helped her to her feet.

'What did you find?' I asked, bringing her a cup of water.

She drank it before answering. 'A small and frightened shred of consciousness,' she said. We hugged each other. Perhaps, tomorrow, she could coax that shred out of hiding.

Ushas did not ask for my company again, and the next day Liviana informed me I was to be given a treat. 'What treat is this?' I asked.

She tapped her nose. 'Aha! Wait and see. Let me lend you some clothes; you must look your best!'

I went along to her dressing room, where we spent considerable time primping and preening, accompanied by much hysterical laughter. Liviana had not asked me how her brother was, which I thought was a little strange. She was such a warm person, I could not understand why she wasn't more concerned about poor Salyon. When I began to tell her that Ushas was hopeful about his condition, she changed the subject. It was very odd.

Once we were ready to go out, Agnestia arrived. Her sophisticated calm was tempered by a flush of excitement in her cheeks. Livvy had dressed me in a simple, yet beautiful gown of dark-ruby velvet that left my shoulders bare and hugged my figure like a glove, prompting Agnestia to exclaim, 'Oh, how that suits you, Rayo dear! You look like a Deltan princess!' She leaned towards me confidentially. 'Now, my dear, we are going on a little adventure. You must promise you won't breathe a word about it to anyone – especially our parents!'

'Promise!' Livvy said, clutching my arm.

I shrugged, slightly unnerved by the feverish joy in the other girls' eyes. 'Very well,' I said.

Agnestia stood back. 'Good! Outsiders aren't generally allowed where we're going, but because you're just a girl, and some people are curious about soulscapers, I've been requested to present you.'

'Present me where?' I asked her. 'Where are we going exactly?' I wondered, with a flicker of delighted dread, whether it was the court of the Kaliph or somewhere equally grand.

Agnestia smiled broadly. 'To the atelier courts,' she replied.

I had already gathered that the creative people of Sacramante were held in an almost holy high regard. Artists and musicians were courted like royalty. Still, I could understand why they were so celebrated: talent oozed from the very walls of the city. We drove to the atelier courts in one of the family carriages. All the artisans lived in this area; it was a city within a city. Tall black gates admitted us to the hushed, reverent atmosphere, where soaring buildings blotted out the sky. The streets, in comparison to Sacramante proper, were weirdly quiet and devoid of people. Agnestia explained that the artisans needed tranquility in which to work, and that the outside world was excluded very deliberately. Around us high, balconied houses, many with glass roofs, surrounded open courts, which were occasionally ceilinged by thick, ancient rose-vines growing over trellises. There were many still pools crusted with lilies, but no fountains. Livvy told me how the richest Sacramantan families patronised the artisans of the city, be they musicians, actors, poets or sculptors, and that the Tricantes had an interest in many of these people.

The carriage came to a halt outside a huge house of matt black stone, whose front doors were at least four times the height of a man. Giant trees rustled all around us, but there was hardly any other sound. The door was opened to us by a uniformed serving-woman, whose apron was of the most exquisite lace I had ever seen. We were ushered inside the building. Here, I was silenced by the holy air of the atelier; its entrance hall possessed all the sombreness of the most ancient and brooding of cathedrals. Our shoes tapped obscenely loud upon the glossy, wooden floor. I asked whose house this was, and Livvy whispered back that the building comprised many fine apartments, and that over fifty artisans lived there. Agnestia told me we were going to visit the apartment of a famous singer named Hadith Sarim – an exotic name that had an arcane feel upon the tongue.

The serving-woman took us up two flights of stairs. Handsome statues of semi-naked elemental spirits reposed in niches and the walls were covered in tapestries and paintings. Light fell down the stairwell from far above, slightly green in colour, because vines were growing over the skylights. I was amazed at the silence. Surely there should be sounds of instruments being played, voices practising their scales or learning theatrical parts. Obviously, I knew very little about the creative process. The serving-woman, our guide, paused before a pair of double doors on the third-floor landing, and pulled on a bell-rope. I heard it ringing sonorously inside. The doors were opened, a small way, by another woman wearing domestic uniform. She conferred in whispers with our guide, and then asked us into the apartment.

The opulence within was understated, and thus more impressive. We entered a beautiful salon, whose polished wooden floor was covered only by a modest circular rug, of black and red silk, near the hearth. The white walls were hung with tapestries, worked in the style favoured by Delta Lands carpet-makers: simple designs in palest ochre, blue and gold. Huge round windows, set with stained glass that matched the hangings and rug, let in a kaleidoscope of muted light. Hadith herself came into the room as we entered, through a door opposite. I had never seen such a striking and unusual-looking woman. Her skin was utterly white, proclaiming that something other than Bochanegran blood ran in her veins. She was framed from neck to waist in long, white hair, which suggested age, yet her face was young, and she wore a bright-red robe that almost made the eyes ache: a redness echoed in her thin, pencilled lips and in the painted dots at the corner of each slanted eye. Her eyes, when I first looked, appeared dark yellow. While Agnestia made introductions, I hovered uncertainly in the background. In my own country my mother was a celebrity, but here, we were nobodies. I did not feel comfortable with that. Then, as the serving-woman was taking our cloaks, the Sarim fixed me with a cat's stare and said, 'Ah, you must be the young soulscaper! How privileged I am to offer you my hospitality!' at which I felt considerably more important, and relaxed enough to change my body posture to one of communication and interest. Hadith came and touched my elbow lightly, directing me to a seat. 'When Agnestia told me the Tricantes had soulscapers to stay, I just had to indulge my curiosity and have her bring you here! What an intriguing life you must lead!'

'Well . . . not really.' I was dazzled by her presence. 'I haven't finished my training yet.'

'You have such beautiful eyes!'

I felt my face grow hot. There was something uncomfortably intimate in Hadith's manner, an intimacy I was unfamiliar with.

We sat down on plump, rug-strewn couches, and the serving-woman brought us watered wine and biscuits. Hadith Sarim did not eat or drink anything. Everyone was speaking of the opening of a new play the following evening. It was a certainty that everyone who was anyone would be there. Naturally, the Tricantes had booked a balcony at the coliseum, and both I and my mother would be able to attend. Hadith Sarim had a cameo piece in the production. She was to play a breeze and would sing accordingly as she blew across a representation of an empty street, where the prima-donna actress would be lamenting the loss of her soul. 'The production should be of interest to you,' the Sarim told me. 'In a way, it concerns your profession.'

I was flattered by Hadith's attention. She confessed to a fasci-nation with soulscaping and asked me to tell her of it. All I could do was relate some of the experiences I had had during my training; the training methods themselves, of course, were secret. 'It must be very similar to making love with a close, close friend,' Hadith declared, interrupting one of my stories. 'To be one, in that way. It is more than sex, of course. I have an empathy with that.'

I could not comment. Virgin still, my face flamed. She noticed, of course she did, and smiled. Mercifully, she did not speak.

'At once delight and horror on us seize . . .'
From *On Paradise Lost*, Milton

Even Ushas seemed excited by the prospect of a visit to the theatre. She had told me, when I returned from the Sarim atelier, that her work with Salyon was progressing; very slowly, but it was still progress. She said she would welcome an evening's entertainment, away from the concerns of an addled soulscape. I did not tell her about my visit to the house of Sarim, not because I feared she might inform the Tricante parents, but for some other, deeper reason. Once I had departed Hadith's presence, my awe of her lessened but it left a potent residue behind. The thought of that pale, enchanting woman, with her hint of hidden menace, made me feel absurdly excited. I did not want to see her again, exactly, but I wanted to think about her all the time.

There was a great deal of feminine fussing during those blissful hours before we all trouped out to the coliseum. Breathless with anticipation, I let Livvy drape me in her clothes, giddy from the dabs of sharp scent behind my ears. In comparison to the loose, swaggery clothes of Taparak, Sacramantan attire felt very uncomfortable to me, and the evening wear was even worse, but once harnessed into silk and sashes, I felt so adult and willowy, discomfort was a minor concern. Livvy had pinned my hair into a stiff black net, studded with jet; my eye sockets had been subtly shaded with shiny, dark-green powder, my lips with scarlet clay-sugar. 'Everyone will be there! Everyone!' Liviana cried, dancing around her room, spreading out a lacy black fan and peeking over its taut vanes.

The two cousins, Perdina and Voile, emerged from their sanctuary dressed in white, their black hair loose like curtains around their pale, narrow faces. The men, comparatively dull beings in this house of female finery, were dashing nonetheless in tight clothes of viridian and iron blue, gold earrings glinting among the oiled ringlets around their shoulders. We all bundled into the Tricante carriages, which boasted torches spitting white sparks at rear and start, and polished horses caparisoned in satiny leather shifting restlessly in their harness. And then, crammed into the carriage, ear-high in crushed satin, lace and silk-net, we were off, trotting swiftly out of the Tricante court into the aromatic, torch-lit night. My heart was beating so fast, I could actually hear it echoing in my ears, and my face felt on fire with excitement. Agnestia produced a silver flask of vicious brandy, which she passed around the carriage, making her mother scold and laugh. 'Not for the children, please, Aggie!' Liviana took the flask and swigged, making a great show of coughing and groaning. I sipped more sparingly, and the fire of it gripped my throat and belly, merely fuelling the heady euphoria I felt. This was life. This: not the lazy, ritual-strung routines of Taparak. There was no occasion at home when I could ever feel like this. Tappish celebrations were laid-back affairs in comparison, loose and carefree, devoid of tension; but it was the tension that made the heart sing, that kindled the feverish need to experience, and taste and taste, until the tongue was numb. Take me, Sacramante, I thought, eyes closed. I am yours.

The coliseum was a blaze of light when we reached it, and against this radiance moved the ravishing figures of the Sacramante beau monde. Carriages jostled for position by the main doors, spilling cargoes of twittering socialites, who dripped with ropes of jewels and pearls, and were muffled in rich stoles of fur and feathers that glittered with marcasite sequins. A group of musicians played on a patio outside the foyer, and a young, female dancer stamped and spun before them in a froth of crimson skirts. Her bare toes seized bright coins off the petal-strewn paving stones, coins which the crowd had flung to her. Without pausing in the dance for a moment, she flicked these tokens into a shallow metal bowl behind her.

Artisans were present in droves. They had a curious inbred look: all very tall and attenuated, their ice-white features delicate and aristocratic. Sometimes, it was difficult to tell which were men, and which were women. Their clothes were exquisite: plain and classical. Their jewellery discreet and simple. Those who weren't artisans looked gaudy beside them. Livvy pointed out the most famous, and spoke the wonderful words of their family names: Sarim; Tartaruchi; Metatronim; Kalkydra. It seemed that artistic vocation was hereditary in Sacramante. I commented on this to Livvy. She smiled at me in a distinctly secretive way. Sacramantans were like that; *secretive*, and it seemed the secrets were of the most delicious kind.

'Surely, creativity is hereditary *everywhere*, Rayo, dear,' she said and, taking hold of my elbow, swept me into the crowd.

The play was called *The Thorn Path*, and had been written by an artisan of the Tartaruchi dynasty, a man named Avirzah'e. 'It is supposedly a controversial piece,' Liviana said to me, as we took our places in the Tricante balcony. I was craning over the rail, gawping at everyone, and Livvy had to pull me back to my seat, so that her parents could sit down. She handed me a programme of the event, printed in dead black ink on tissue-thin paper. Of the Tricante youngsters, only Agnestia and the cousins were privileged to have places on the front row of the balcony; Zimon and Almero came to sit with Livvy and myself behind.

70

Zimon squeezed down beside me and pointed to my programme. 'It is lucky you are here for this; it will be outstanding!' he said. 'The principal lady is Gimel Metatronim, and the sets are designed by her brother, Beth. Both are gifted with genius.'

Agnestia had overheard his remarks and turned around in her seat. 'I, for one, am interested in this production for the simple fact that it is a Metatronim-and-Tartaruchi connivance,' she said. 'It is no secret there has been harshness between the two families.'

'Frosh!' Zimon declared. 'You're too full of intrigue, Aggie. The artisans are not swayed by the same base passions as ourselves.'

'You talk as if they are a different race entirely!' I said, voicing a thought that had been in my head since I had met Hadith Sarim. Neither of the Tricantes deigned to follow up my observation. The house-lights dimmed, and a hush fell over the crowd. Musicians began to play the overture. The stage was a raised circular dais, far below, covered in humped, indistinct shapes. As the stage lamps were turned up, these shapes were revealed to be pieces of scenery: minimal, mere suggestions of forms. To me, it became a rocky land, devoid of moisture. As the music soared up into the theatre, a figure uncurled on the stage – it had looked just like a rock a moment before – and expanded ragged wings. The music fell in volume to a mere sobbing. On the stage, the figure dipped and swayed in birdlike fashion, accompanied only by a mournful fluted tune. I thought it would be too dark to read my programme, but the white page gleamed like phosphorescence, its black lettering as dark as if it had been burned right into it. 'The soul, set free', it said in description of this first vignette. This confused me. Surely a freed soul could only be joyful and wild; this was a being filled with anxiety and dread. Presently, the figure jumped into the air and disappeared, presumably through one of the tunnel entrances that flanked the stage. Then there was a dreadful sound: not a cry, but a lamenting sigh. A woman appeared, clambering over the rough terrain, pushing her hair from her eyes, where it hung in damp, lank tresses. Her dress was torn, her body contorted as if wracked by terrible pain. 'Gimel!' Zimon hissed in my ear. I had begun to feel unaccountably sick. There was something too realistic in this performance, a promise of horror. I didn't want to watch it any more; I was sure it was going to distress me. It was like some soulscape terror being brought into reality, with no possibility of return to normal awareness. My mother was sitting on the front row of the balcony among the older Tricantes: unreachable. Zimon was entranced, watching his heroine. The actress tottered to a stand. This was a person starving to death: emaciated and haggard. She stumbled, and the crowd drew in its breath.

'I am hungry!' she cried, and it sounded as if the words cut her throat like knives. She was bloodless; just a dry thing. I leaned towards Liviana.

71

'This is horrible!' I said, and just the act of whispering seemed to break the appalling spell somewhat.

'Ssh!' Liviana admonished. 'Don't you like it?'

I shrugged.

'She is one of the best,' Liviana hissed. 'Just watch. It's only a play.'

I was not convinced of that. Still, it was unlikely the poor woman would starve herself into such a condition just for the sake of her acting. It was obviously make-up and lighting making her appear that way. Partly comforted, I leaned back in my seat and took a few deep breaths, telling myself to be calm, and not so stupid. It was a play, and a great play; never again might I enjoy this privilege. Then the actress began to scream, and I closed my eyes.

By the interval, I felt as if I had suffered some terrible trauma. We had sat for an hour, tortured by the sight of this demented female encountering all manner of peculiar hallucinations in her lone quest for her departed soul. She was devoured alive, burned, drowned, chased by hideous demons which caught and raped her – although any graphic detail of this scene was hidden by a mêlée of cavorting actors, caparisoned in spikes and insect plates. I was not sure if I could bear to endure any more and clapped in grateful relief, more than appreciation, when the houselights flared up. 'The artisans are not receiving during the interval,' Almero said, consulting his programme. Liviana pouted in disappointment.

'Why ever not?'

Agnestia turned around. 'I told you; it's because of bad blood. I'd stake my life on it!'

'Don't be ridiculous,' Cousin Voile said, in a supercilious voice. 'Avirzah'e Tartaruchi made it known weeks ago the interval would be of short duration. The production is intense; he does not want any of us to lose the feel of it by socialising and gossiping! There'll be plenty of time for that later.'

Liviana went off with Almero to fetch us something to eat and drink from the cordial-vendors downstairs. I could only slump exhausted in my seat, smiling inanely at Zimon's chatter.

'Such talent!' he said. 'My, what I'd give to be one of Gimel Metatronim's patrons.' He pulled a face. 'Still, we have Hadith.'

'Wasn't she supposed to be in this play?' I asked, wondering how on earth the scene she had described to us could be incorporated into such horror.

Zimon nodded. 'Yes. In the second half.' He laughed. 'When it all gets damned jolly, I suppose.'

'Will it do that?' I could not dare to hope.

Zimon grimaced. 'Probably. Not even a Tartaruch could keep this up for a whole evening. We are simple folk, us Sacramantans. We need hope as well as despair for a good night out.'

'Nothing simple in that!' I replied earnestly.

Livvy came back with clay cups of citrus drink and a bag of buns in crystal honey. Once I had eaten, I began to feel better. 'You looked quite green!' Livvy said, grinning. 'I suppose we're used to this sort of thing, living here. The artisans like to make us work for our entertainment.'

I resented the implications in her comment, as if I were some untutored, uncultured rustic thing without refinement or the ability to appreciate art.

The second act was, as Zimon had anticipated, far lighter in comparison. The actress found an ally who could help her net her wayward soul and she travelled to a ruined city where Hadith, as the breeze, sang sweet melodies that wooed the soul to earth. Reunited, the actress and her soul confronted the demon prince, who lived beneath the city, and exacted a revenge for the rape by his lesser imps. This was not the gory unpleasantness I feared, but a titillating seduction scene during which the actress made the demon fall in love with her. As they embraced, the whole scene exploded into activity: shapes that had symbolised masonry and half-fallen buildings magically transformed into leaping figures whose flesh was painted with luminous pigment. The finale was a burst of firecrackers, crashing cymbals and the actress was seen with her heel upon the groin of the demon prince. When the lights swept down to blackness, the whole arena was on its feet, yelling and clapping. I had lapsed into a kind of daze, still not over the testing first half, and had to be dragged up by Liviana, who shrieked and jumped up and down at my side.

All the company appeared on stage and bowed to their hysterical audience. Liviana grabbed my arm. 'Come on!' she cried. 'We must get to the salon quickly!'

'Why?' She did not answer. Zimon was pushing me along the row of seats, urging me to move. We surged out of the balcony into a milling crowd, where I stumbled over feet and trod on people's gowns, my arm in the merciless grip of Liviana.

'*Come on*!' she cried over her shoulder. Swimming through a tide of people, I was beached by the tireless Liviana in a large chamber, reached by a curving flight of stairs. Here, many people had already gathered, causing me to wonder just how many had slipped out before the end of the performance to guarantee themselves a prominent place in this room. Servitors in costumes of stiff black feathers and wearing feathered masks sewn with jewelled sequins glided among the crowd, dispensing various refreshments. It was here that the celebrated company of artisans would gather for the edification of, and adoration by, their audience, although only patrons and their guests were allowed into this reception. Already an atmosphere of anticipation, rivalling that of before the play, was intensifying. I felt disorientated, pushed this way and that by eager people, all talking loudly and flashing their finery. My mother was nowhere to be seen and Liviana was too busy cooing and fluttering her eyelashes at any passing male to notice my discomfort. To steady my nerves and appear as if I were at ease, I sipped continually from the glass that Liviana had thrust into my hands. Someone offered me a pipe; I sucked smoke, and a giddy feeling, as of a stormy wave crashing in my head, overwhelmed any unpleasant sensations caused by my coughing fit. Within a very short space of time, I was having to lean against the wall for support, the ground beneath my feet swaying as if I were on a boat. In fact, it was more comforting to imagine that I was.

Liviana pushed back through the crowd, having left me alone for a few moments. 'The actors!' she exclaimed in triumph. 'Come on, Rayo, come and see.' She attempted to prise me away from the wall.

'I'll watch from here. . . .' My protest was unheard. Suddenly I was lurching through indignant bodies, my head aswim.

Liviana sighed, apparently oblivious to my condition. She pulled me against her side. 'Caspar Kalkydra!' she breathed. A group of people had entered the room through a curtain further back. I recognised Caspar as being the actor who had played the part of the demon prince; his face was still daubed in the gaudy make-up that, from the distance of the balcony, had seemed so subtle. He had fierce red hair, tied back in a scarf, and a face of flawless bony planes and angles. Other lesser actors, sprites and imps, came in his wake, preceding the more dramatic entrance of Hadith Sarim who was dressed casually in a belted, silk robe, bare-footed and with pale, scrubbed face. She floated to the Kalkydra's side and linked her arm through his, nodding graciously at their admirers. Then, there was another flutter of interest as the great playwright himself sauntered into the room. Avirzah'e Tartaruchi: a prince of artisans. He was fearsome to look at: I saw a murderer's soul, but perhaps that was only artifice on his part. His pale skin had a sallow tinge, causing him to stand out from his peers, and his abundant dark hair was threaded with a hint of deepest red. His mouth smiled in a lazy, sensual way, but his eyes were hooded and watchful. What is it about beautiful, effeminate men that some women find so irresistible? To me, effeminacy seemed deceitful or sly; I would never trust such loveliness. Here, I was alone in such feelings. The Sacramantans were virtually tearing the clothes from each other's backs to reach Avirzah'e. I found all the fawning adoration rather sickening. Not even the most celebrated of our scryers back in Taparak were treated to such sycophancy. This was, perhaps, the dull side of Sacramante's shiny coin; its glitter was but surface deep. With this in mind, I perched myself upon some elevated plateau of thought to look down upon these eager fools drooling over their tinsel heroes. I was above all this. Miraculously, the smoke haze was beginning to seep out from the corners of my mind, leaving a

74

sparkling clarity in its wake. I felt incredibly tall, and steady too. It was time to disengage myself from Liviana and seek my mother. She, also, must be finding this hysterical worshipping ridiculous.

'Excuse me, Livvy,' I said, 'but I have to speak to Ushas.'

'What?' Liviana turned in irritation from her spectator sport, reluctant to drag her eyes away, even for a moment. People were now queuing up to tell the leading actors, and the author of the play, just how wonderful they were: a fact I was sure they were quite confident of already. Liviana, her family being a patron of Sarim, hoped to sidle up to Hadith and thus impose on the haughty, sneering Caspar. She was welcome to this behaviour; I wanted no part of it.

Liviana did not protest as I moved away. I no longer found the crowd intimidating, but rather pathetic; they, too, were just cavorting imps and demons on a stage. Ushas stood out because of her poise. She was standing among the fronds of an ornamental tree, as if backing away from the man who was leaning towards her earnestly, his mouth moving quickly in animated speech. Sensing me approach (it really was as if we were the only two sentient beings in the room), she raised her head towards me and, with a smile, shaped a direct thought-form and tranced it in my direction. Its touch was muzzy in that riot of busy egos, and without the strengthening effect of scry-fume, but I felt it faintly. Someone else, however, had felt it too.

Even as I raised my foot to walk to my mother's side, an imminence of query surrounded me: an unmistakable intrusion in my mind. Ushas had turned back to her companion; she did not sense it. Sweat broke out on the back of my neck. What was this? I had never experienced such a positive touch outside a working situation or a scrying rite. I quickly looked around, seeking the predator, but everyone was smiling, talking, laughing, pawing each other, intent on the artisans and each other. Could there be another soulscaper here, someone who had rashly filled their pipe with a scaping mix which was now affecting me? Or were some Sacramantans making illicit use of Tappish mixes? Neither of these explanations was impossible. Many Taps came to Sacramante after all, and I was well aware of how our scaping mixes could sometimes escape Tappish control.

With a mental shrug, I composed myself, cleared my mind of transmissive thoughts and wriggled over to the ornamental tree. People peeled away in front of me, talking feverishly, merely shuffling their feet to avoid the incursion into their space.

Then I saw them.

I saw them as a dark heart within the sizzling brightness of the gibbering, yapping fools all around. From the very first instant, I knew I was looking at people very different from everyone else in the room. One was male, one female, and they stood very close together: smiling politely, nodding their heads, slowly blinking in response to whatever inanity was being directed at them. I felt a great empathy with them, perhaps because they looked as unimpressed with the proceedings as I was. Artisans, clearly, but who? I had unconsciously edged closer, until I stood at the edge of the crowd around them. A thought nagged in my head, as if I should be reminded of someone, but wasn't. I saw Zimon Tricante, just in front of me, craning over the shoulders of taller people ahead of him. I pushed up behind him and tugged at his arm.

'Zimon, who are those people?'

He gripped my arm, his hot and damp face radiant with pleasure. 'Metatronim, Rayo,' he replied. '*The* Metatronim.'

Metatronim. The name was familiar. Of course, the actress: Gimel. On stage, she had been a withered drab, but now . . . Obviously my assumptions about the make-up must have been correct. Her white skin fairly glowed as if lit by some inner fire. Her lips were the colour of red wine, purple in the shadows and her eyes, like a cat's, were oblique and dark. She wore a black robe, her obsidian hair slung over one shoulder in a thick rope of plait. By her side, taller, but only just, the man was her twin in all but the colour of his hair. He was obviously the brother, Beth, who had designed the sets for the play. I had never seen such magnificent people, and their magnificence came from inside them, I could tell; theirs was an innate beauty that eclipsed the self-conscious loveliness of Kalkydra and his kind. Although I wanted them to notice me, I had no inclination whatsoever to thrust myself forward with Zimon and try to speak to them. I did not want the Metatronim to equate me with all the others in the room. And yet, in some strange way, I felt as if the actress and her brother were well aware of my presence, even though they never once looked in my direction. The fact that I was a foreigner, and also that I was unaffected by the glamour of the occasion, must have been noticed. Perhaps they could tell I was a soulscaper. Perhaps Hadith had told these people that the Tricantes had soulscapers staying with them, and the Metatronims had seen me with Zimon or Liviana. Perhaps . . . perhaps . . . It was a fantasy. In the morning, I would doubt these feelings, would tell myself they had not noticed me at all.

The ride home was a fitting end to the evening. Everyone was intoxicated in one way or another; songs were begun, rhythms clapped, even the stately Tricante matron joining in the fun. My mood of detached aloofness faded, and I was drawn into the atmosphere of it, although my heart was curled around the delicious memory of seeing the Metatronims. There was something special about them – special only to me. From the moment I saw them, I'd felt a deep sense of recognition, some tugging within me as if I'd met them before yet forgotten when and how. I was filled with an excitement that eclipsed even the feelings I'd had after meeting Hadith Sarim. I dared to hope I could meet them again, before Ushas and I returned to Taparak.

I had a strange dream that night. What an understatement that is, and yet how accurate. In the carriage home, I had questioned Livvy about the Metatronims: she didn't have much information. I learned their especial patrons were the Di Corboran family, who had considerable influence at the court of the Kaliph and owned over a hundred massive vineyards throughout the Bochanegran Empire. The Metatronims mixed in high circles. As to where they lived, Livvy did not know. I realised that people living outside the atelier district knew very little of what went on in there. 'Who are the artisans?' I asked her, as we got out of the carriage at the back of the Carmen. 'They are foreigners, aren't they?'

'What makes you say that?' Livvy asked, quite sharply.

'It is obvious; they look different from Bochanegrans. They *are* different! Where do they come from?'

'Well, they *do* come from a far land, I suppose. I think they were driven out a long, long time ago. They have no country now. But Sacramante is their home; all artisans are under the patronage of the Kaliph and her family.'

'Why are they shut away from the rest of the city so?'

'They aren't, Rayo!' Livvy snapped. 'I don't think you should ask questions with such a tone in your voice! I suppose they have their own customs and way of life. Like you said, they *are* foreigners! We just accept what comes out of the atelier courts, and are grateful for it.'

'I'm sorry,' I said. 'I didn't mean to sound rude. Livvy?'

'Yes.'

'Can we visit the atelier of the Metatronims.'

She laughed, shook her head. 'No, Rayo, no! We are not patrons of theirs.'

I still did not understand how this patronage business worked, but how disappointing! Still wrestling with thoughts of how I might connive a meeting with the Metatronims (perhaps I could enlist the help of Zimon who undoubtedly shared my enthusiasm), I went up to my room and gratefully unbound myself from the clothes Livvy had lent me. I lay in the moonlight, still full of excitement, reliving the moment when I had first seen Gimel and her brother, and extended the memory into fantasy, imagining they had called to me, drawn me to them. In my mind, transformed into an older version of myself, I sat in a carriage beside Beth Metatronim, knowing I could look at him whenever I wanted to and therefore sweetly torturing myself by not doing so. Gimel, I talked to, but her brother was a silent presence beside me, his thigh pressed against my own. I could not really understand the powerful sensations these people had invoked within me. I did not feel like sleeping and turned restlessly in my bed, replaying my fantasies, adding detail with each repetition, which led me nearer to when I would reach their house and be taken inside. I wanted to reserve fantasies beyond this point for a later time: more exquisite torture. Half of me wanted to leap out of bed and dance and run and shout. Half of me was exhausted. I must have fallen asleep eventually, I must have, because that was when he came to me.

I opened my eyes, and my room was in darkness. The moon had slid across the sky. Everything was still. I peered into the shadows, a little unnerved. From the very first instant, I felt I was not alone. As a soulscaper, I had already been trained to deal with such feelings, knowing that the majority of them stemmed from the inner landscape exuding thought-forms into reality. It is quite a common occurrence when woken from deep sleep. We are taught to examine these things objectively. I sat up in the bed, and took a few calming breaths, willing whatever I had conjured forth to manifest itself more clearly.

He was sitting in a chair at the end of the bed, taking shape from the pale tumble of silk which was the dress I had discarded earlier. As I stared, he stood up and I could discern the wet gleam of dark jewels upon his breast. He did not speak, but somehow glided towards me, as if *through* the bed itself. I was not afraid; only fascinated, confident that he was my own creation. He curled up beside my legs, like a great cat, staring at me from dark sockets. Impulsively, I reached to touch him, even though I knew such an action would evaporate his fragile corporeality. My hand touched silky hair, felt the hardness of skull beneath. I pulled away, gasping, drawing up my knees. This was too real. He made a soft sound, perhaps a laugh, and slithered up towards me. I could not move, perhaps, deep inside, did not even want to. 'Heart's desire,' he whispered and put his mouth against my own. I felt his teeth against my lower lip, felt a sharp pain. No! Vainly, I tried to expel this vision from my consciousness, but my heart was beating too fast, I was in too much of a panic. It happened very quickly after that, and I cannot make myself remember the details. I know that he bit my face, very hard, and as he bit, a greater pain convulsed my body. I could not believe what was happening. His body was heavy upon me. Did I cry out? I don't know. All I do know is that I woke up gasping and panting, throwing myself up from the bed, my body covered in sweat. My loins tingled in a strange, half-pleasurable, half-painful way. Dream or reality? I still don't know which. But I was aware, in my heart, that illusion or not, I was no longer virgin in this body and that Beth Metatronim was responsible for it.

Next morning, I was in a daze. My mother was absent from breakfast as there had been an emergency with Salyon in the night.

Apparently he had come out of his trance and had screamed until his throat bled. Only the strongest of Ushas' potions could calm him. Still, it was progress. Wherever the soul-essence of Salyon had once fled to, it now firmly inhabited his flesh once more, albeit unhappily. Soon, we would be able to leave. I wanted to be alone with my thoughts that day, prompting Livvy to wonder whether I was sickening for something. Who are the artisans? Who *are* they? This question flapped around my brain like a trapped bird. I wanted to tell Livvy about the dream, but at the same time I savoured the secret of it. It had been so real, and yet cautious investigation of my body in daylight revealed no injury or sign of invasion.

Eventually, because I had become tearful, I sought out my mother in Salyon's room. The boy was lying with his eyes open this time, his face a mask of despair. I wondered whether consciousness was an improvement. Ushas was talking to him in a low voice; I recognised the intonation of encouragement and nurturing. She turned when I entered the room and cried, 'Rayo, what's the matter!' I just ran into her waiting arms and sobbed my heart out. When I had purged myself, I pulled away, wiping my face with my sleeve. Salyon's eyes were looking right at me, right into me, I felt.

'What's wrong,' Ushas was still asking, squeezing my arm.

Behind her, the boy raised a stick-like arm from the bed. He beckoned me to him. Puzzled, Ushas let me go and watched as I leaned towards her client. I don't know why I felt so compelled to obey his request: Salyon repulsed me. His appearance was horrific and he smelled of death. Shakily, he lifted his fingers to touch my face where I had been bitten in the dream. His fingers were dry and hot. I raised a hand defensively, paused, and then he slipped his fingers into my own. I squeezed him hard, felt the brittle bones grind in their tissue of desiccated flesh. It was instinctual: all of it. Somehow, he gave me peace. I leaned down and kissed his brow, the skin like paper beneath my lips. 'You will be well,' I said.

'Rayo?' Ushas murmured behind me.

'I had a dream, a horrible dream,' I said, and looked back at the boy on the bed. He closed his eyes slowly and managed a weak smile. If stronger, he would have nodded, I'm sure of it. 'It's all right now.' I slid my fingers out of Salyon's hold, feeling immensely calm. Somehow, he had sealed my experience within me; I would never speak of it to anyone. I was sure he knew exactly what happened to me during the night, as strongly as if he'd spoken to me aloud. In some way he had experienced it, too, and had been shocked out of his coma.

The significance of what took place in Salyon's room was not revealed to me for a long, long time.

'. . . he seemed for dignity composed and high exploit: but all was false and hollow . . . for his thoughts were low, to vice industrious . . .'
Paradise Lost, Book II

It will come as no surprise that I'd had severe reservations about working with the Tartaruch. I was almost disappointed when things turned out so well. What possessed him to invite the participation of Beth and myself, I prefer not to dwell upon. Upon discussion, neither I nor my brother could accept that Avirzah'e was merely offering us the hand of friendship; there had to be other motivations. To refuse would have caused comment among the throngs, of course; perhaps Avirzah'e wanted nothing but to humiliate us. His humour was infantile, in that case. We accepted his offer.

He had sent one of his licky-spits round, a lily-fleshed human boy with the glassy-eyed stare of the perpetually supped. The missive had been delivered on a filigree tray, sealed in the Tartaruchi wax – magenta, still warm – and penned in Avirzah'e's own arrogant hand. 'Honoured friends,' he wrote, 'may I humbly entreat your services for my recently completed work, *The Thorn Path*. A play of two acts, I can only acknowledge that its performance will be the less splendid should either of you decline to participate. Gimel, the lead part was written for you, and only your inventiveness, Beth, can bring the scenery required to life. Should you be interested in hearing more about this work, I would be delighted to call on you and discuss it.' Beth and I read the message speechlessly; the unctuous words seemed to drip with Avirzah'e's innate sarcasm. At the end of his mordant invitation was the comment, 'It would be my pleasure if you would replete yourselves upon this morsel delivering my word.' An insult! I would as soon feast upon a discarded apple core. We dismissed the messenger, and examined the parchment. No trick it seemed, and yet. . . .

'Well?' Beth asked me, as I put the parchment down upon the table. I rubbed my fingers together, conscious of the fact I had touched something Avirzah'e had held in his hands.

'I must confess to being intrigued . . .' I glanced at Beth, and as our eyes met, he said, 'At least Avirzah'e was the first to make contact.'

I nodded. 'It was just a matter of time.'

'Dangerous though. We both know the Tartaruch's stance on certain matters.'

'What has that to do with work?'

Beth shrugged. 'Nothing. I hope. This move of Avirzah'e's might have a political rather than social motivation, however. He might be interested in how we are progressing with the soulscaper, perhaps with the intention of interfering.'

I laughed and kissed Beth's cheek. 'If that is the case, he will be surprised. We are far more cunning than the Tartaruch, beloved. If he seeks to deceive us, he is sadly overrating his charms!'

We arranged to meet Avirzah'e on neutral territory, thereby signifying that although we were interested in his offer he had not wheedled his way into our lives to the point where we'd have him under our own roof. There are few public meeting-places in the atelier courts because most transactions between eloim take place in personal space, but there are one or two tavernas near the outer walls where people can pause for a flute of wine should they be out walking. We met at midday, Avirzah'e sauntering arrogantly to where Beth and I were already seated outside the taverna, beneath the awning. 'He is beautiful,' Beth said, under his breath.

'And so are we,' I reminded him. 'Don't fall for the glamour, beloved. We need our wits with us today.' We did not let Avirzah'e kiss us in greeting.

He had brought copious notes with him: ideas for set designs and costumes, an outline of the play's plot and various sections of the dialogue he presumed I might find intriguing. I read the outline and then raised my brows at the Tartaruch prince.

'I confess I don't know whether to be flattered or insulted when you say this part was written with me in mind,' I said.

Avirzah'e leaned back in his chair, balancing it precariously on its back legs. 'Gimel, rest assured I do not aim to insult you. I had your ability rather than your person in mind when I wrote the play.'

I shrugged, not totally convinced. 'Well, as you probably already know, the work is brilliant.'

'And contentious,' Beth added, 'given recent events.'

'Not that recent, Beth,' Avirzah'e replied. 'Since vigilance has been stepped up, the suicides have fallen off. Anyway, the play is not about that dilemma.' The fact that Avirzah'e did not bother to query what Beth meant signified this was a lie. 'I'm surprised you think I wrote about the sickness,' he continued. 'After all, there isn't a single suicide in this work!'

'Avirzah'e, we are not stupid!' I said.

He smiled. 'I am aware of that. Why else would I have invited your participation?'

There was a moment of tense silence, during which Avirzah'e grinned at us frankly.

'You had better send us the entire manuscript,' I said.

Avirzah'e had engaged a director, not deigning to visit the coliseum himself during rehearsals. That suited me fine, although I suspected it was not supposed to. Beth created marvellous scenery for the play, again without any contribution or even approval from the author. Even though Avirzah'e had denied it, I still suspected my rôle was designed to discomfort me. Foolish Tartaruch! I am a professional, and the part was interesting. Even having me seduce the Kalkydra puppy did not distress me. It was well known that Caspar had stolen a lover of mine some ten years back, one who had lost no time in telling Caspar all my virtues; a defection which had left neither Kalkydra nor myself happy, and which still rankled. The bitch who'd caused the upset had hived off to join a reclusive Nephelin throng in the mountains of Lansaal. I was not sorry to see her go.

There were undercurrents in the play which I knew would be criticised by the Parzupheim and which, when Metatron read the draft, caused ructions in the family stronghold. Tatriel herself came to call, slinking into my salon, wagging a talon in my face and drawling, 'Your father feels this is unfit for you, dear Gimel. I have to agree. The play is . . . contentious.'

'Convey to the Metatron that I appreciate his concern for my reputation,' I replied, 'but please impress upon him that I shall invest this part with enough of my personal mark to render it acceptable in his eyes. Also, I will not be told which work I can and cannot do.'

Tatriel nodded, saying in a wry voice, 'I thought this, and will gladly convince the Metatron you will transform the rôle. As for your latter comment, I feel it should remain within my heart.' She patted my arm. 'Allow me the privilege of being a surrogate dam to you, dear Gimel. I think I know what's best.'

I inclined my head. 'You are kind, Lady Tatriel.' My surrogate dam? She was twenty years my junior.

The rehearsals went without a hitch, other than a tantrum or two thrown for effect by the sulky Kalkydra. It was no pleasure kissing him at the end, but our dedication to our work overrode personal disgust. The director was an Elim, a flog-master, who kept us at it until past midnight some evenings. At these times I would fall into bed as soon as I got home, administered to by my sweet sibling, who brought me dainty snacks to sup upon between the sheets; lissom Amelakiveh, who would offer me his wrist and then his body. We had soon made him like us in many ways: a dear pet, this enterprising boy.

The first night, of course, had spread its own array of surprises.

The Tartaruch showed himself in my dressing room beneath the stage before the performance, bringing me a bouquet of night-blooming roses and a carafe of honeyed wine. Our make-up complete, Hadith Sarim, Floriel Elim and I – the three most prominent actresses – were sitting together, quietly conversing, to prepare ourselves for the coming performance. The room, though well-appointed, had a distinctly cave-like ambience, which I had always found uncomfortable. Avirzah'e's presence did nothing to dispel my slight feeling of claustrophobia. I had not seen him in person since he'd met Beth and myself at the taverna. He kissed my hand, nipping the skin briefly as he did so. I snatched my arm away. How dare he presume such closeness! 'Skittish before the performance, dear Gimel?' he asked me. My colleagues looked away, but they were smiling, damn them! Before he left, he addressed the wardrobe staff who had come to hover in the doorway, in order to catch a glimpse of the play's author. 'Congratulations. You have made her a hag,' he said.

He really is insufferable. Beth, having noticed Avirzah'e marching purposefully towards my dressing room, also made an appearance and pushed his way through the small bustle of wardrobe people, barely able to contain repressed cries of outrage. Avirzah'e gathered him up on the way out.

'A seat by me, of course,' he said. Because everyone had seen, Beth had no choice but to go with him.

I shook my head to regain my composure and addressed all the averted heads. 'The Tartaruchi scion has a wit about him worthy of a child!' Then, I laughed, as if in delight, and the atmosphere relaxed.

The performance was a triumph, but then there'd never been any doubt of that. I fairly floated in a daze, lines falling from my lips without conscious thought. I fed upon the concentrated attention of my audience, drawing out strands of sustenance like a web. It was annoying that the Tartaruch would claim as much tribute for the play's success as I would. The whole production sizzled with his personal observations, his discontent, his misplaced spirit of renewal. I gave life to the lines, I think, but in such a way that no one could guess his intention. That was my revenge, which I knew he would notice.

Later, we had to pay our respects to the patrons. Warmed by their adoration, I feigned disinterest; it was what they expected, of course, and in keeping with my public persona. Really I adore the humans, for all their weaknesses. They have an immediacy, a vivacity lacking in eloim-kind; their brutish enthusiasms are endearing.

I was surprised by the presence of the soulscapers. Doubtless guests of some patron family, they intruded upon this complicit gathering like harsh rays. Naturally, precautions are always taken at these functions; it is taken as fact that unsupped will be present at times, but I was still unnerved. Beth noticed them first, relaying to me a mind-line they were passing to each other. In an instant, my surprise was enriched by alarm. It was our girl, our little seed! I had been so engrossed preparing for *The Thorn Path*'s debut, I had neglected to keep abreast of her development for some months now. What was she doing there? What immeasurable convolution of fate had brought her to our city before time? For a moment I feared Avirzah'e, or one of his kin, had divined her identity and was attempting to interfere in some way, perhaps planning to damage our work in its early stages. After a quick investigation, I realised this was not so, thankfully. It surprised me that the soul-scapers could communicate in that manner without their special drugs, however, and made me wonder in what other ways I might have underestimated them. An inquiry to a nearby patron estab-lished the girl was in Sacramante with her mother, who had a commission with the Tricantes. It was because of the son, Salyon; he who was flamed. I doubted whether the soulscaper, however puissant her ability, could heal him. He had been weak since child-hood, prone to melancholy, and had withered at the first sup, or so I had heard. One of the Sarim throng had had him; perhaps someone too eager. My friend Hadith had not touched him, for which she was grateful. A tainted fruit: he should be allowed to rot in peace. However . . .

Once we returned to the courts, I was tempted to make myself known to the girl in some way, but Beth advised against this. 'There is no point, Gimel. Let her be. We must wait for the time when she's mature enough to take on the rôle we have created for her. If we intervene before that time, we could ruin everything.'

Reluctantly, I had to agree with him although I longed to visit her in her maiden's room at the Carmen Tricante. I longed to speak with her. I had not observed her for several months, and look what had happened! I vowed to be more vigilant. How fragile she had appeared in her borrowed finery and painted child's face. It seemed inconceivable she would be strong enough to mature in this world of so many perils.

Knowing what we did of soulscaper training, we hadn't thought Rayojini would leave the mountain until she was much older. Per-haps her mother liked company on the road.

Morning brought fury to my door in several forms. First, Beth presented himself in my chamber alone. I welcomed him to my bed and let him curl up against me. He smelled rather strange. 'Have you just supped?' I asked him. He shook his head.

'No, but I projected myself to the soulscaper last night.'

'What?' I pushed him away from me angrily. 'Why? You told me not to contact her!'

He smiled. 'Exactly. Told *you* not to. I felt I needed to quicken the link we have with her.'

'What did you do? Did you feed?'

'No, no. It was all subjective, as I said. I granted her an experience she will never forget.'

I was relieved, realising I would have felt absurdly jealous had Beth actually tasted the girl.

'She'll think it was a dream,' Beth said casually. 'I was careful.'

'I still think it was most rude of you to do this alone,' I said, 'especially after what you said to me about leaving her be.'

'Gimel, Gimel,' Beth soothed, stroking my hair. 'There are just some things I have to do alone; you know that. It is a complex thread we weave. Anyway, you will find it easier to influence her now. Now she has seen us, touched me, we can only be more real to her. The guardian-pursuers, such as we are, have been called from sleep.'

Although I agreed with much of what he said, I was still annoyed with him. Beth has this wayward streak, which sometimes prompts him to act independently and rather wilfully. Being, as he is, such a sensual creature, I realised he needed to establish himself with Rayojini in his own way. I hoped she had not been too unnerved by the experience but, as Beth is a gentle lover, I was sure he'd been kind to her.

After I'd dressed, and Tamaris had brought me a hot drink of bloodied milk, a servitor arrived from the family stronghold. Metatron had summoned me. Cursing, I ordered Tamaris to organise transport for me. I had wanted to spend the day refining my part; after the first performance, there were one or two details that I thought needed attention. Now, Metatron would undoubtedly keep me waiting around at the stronghold all day.

I was not incorrect in my assumptions. Upon my arrival at the family home, I was shown into one of the music rooms where an aunt played me a few tunes on her harmonium. Patient at first, my forbearance eventually wore out and I was forced to interrupt my aunt's recital in order to demand where Metatron was. At that point he sailed into the rom, trailing the usual clutch of lesser relatives, who arranged themselves on the available seating like courtesans, or a flock of carrion birds, and watched me carefully.

'Am I to be given a public audience then?' I said. An improper remark, but I was really quite exasperated.

'Forgive me, honoured daughter,' Metatron replied, with a bow, 'but I was under the impression you are far from eager to be alone with me nowadays.'

I was aghast he could speak to me like that in front of others, and could not think of a suitable response. 'I have been summoned here for a reason?'

He smiled at my lack of wit. 'Naturally. I only summon you

under the most pressing circumstances.'

'Circumstances of which I am unaware. Please, enlighten me.'

Informally, he sat down beside me and I steeled myself not to flinch. 'Gimel, I respect your strength, and your good sense,' he said, 'but I really must protest, in the most emphatic terms, about this business you have involved yourself in.'

'And which business is this?'

He was still smiling. 'The Tartaruchi abomination.'

'Abomination? I understood the news-sheet reviews were rather complimentary this morning.'

'Don't be facetious.'

'Metatron, you made your displeasure known to me before rehearsals started, and Lady Tatriel delivered my response. I cannot understand why you have left it until now to pursue the matter, if it causes you such concern.'

'It is not just the play.' His smile had faded. I had a horrible suspicion the time for games was over; he looked very serious, and not at all mocking.

'What is it then?'

He sighed. 'Gimel, it's Beth I worry for. He is still very dear to me, as you are too, but he does not have your . . . constitution.'

'I would be grateful if you'd get to the point, Metatron.'

'Avirzah'e Tartaruchi,' he said, the name laden with meaning. 'Gimel, as you know, at the direction of the Parzupheim, I maintain a watch over the deeper currents of our society. There are signs that the Tartaruch is . . . acting unwisely.'

'You refer, of course, to the content of the play. It's harmless enough. I made sure of that.'

'I'm sure you did. But his activities extend beyond play-writing. Far beyond.'

I lowered my voice. 'Are you sure we should be discussing this here?'

He glanced at our relatives, all of whom appeared to be ignoring our conversation, which must have meant they were listening intently. 'You are right,' he said. 'I will send them away, if you do not object to our being alone together.'

I made a dismissive gesture, keeping remarks about being able to look after myself unvoiced. Metatron cleared the room, the relatives looking distinctly crestfallen as they departed.

'Well?' I said.

'You remember the throng-gathering when you returned from Taparak?'

I nodded.

'Cast your mind back to Avirzah'e's little speech upon that occasion. I will be blunt, Gimel. I suspect he has taken matters into his own hands.'

I could not repress the laugh that came instinctively in response.

'Metatron, I cannot believe what you have just said! Avirzah'e is a dandy, a libertine. He is not a dark-mongerer; it would require too much effort.'

'I am saddened he deludes you so easily,' Metatron replied, without taking offence. '*Look* at him, Gimel! He will not be disciplined, and many of his kind support him. Remember his words in the Castile when you reported to the Parzupheim. I suspect that the young element of Tartaruchi are now taking matters into their own hands.'

'What evidence do you have?'

'Very little. They cover their tracks well, and I doubt whether their activities will become overt for some time to come.'

'What activities?'

'The old way, Gimel, the old way.'

I was stunned. 'You're not suggesting they . . .' The words just would not come. I could not even bear to think of the 'old way' let alone speak of it, not just because of natural distaste but because of actions of my own in the past, for which I was still ashamed.

'Yes. Someone is contravening the honourable code which forbids the taking of sustenance from unwilling victims,' Metatron said, voicing what I could not bring myself to say. A painful twinge of guilt wriggled through me, which I dreaded might be evident on my face. For a moment, I wondered whether Metatron had guessed the methods Beth and I had resorted to in Lansaal.

'I still want to know what evidence you have to support this!' I said, averting my eyes from Metatron's gaze. Was it possible he had summoned me here to confront me with what he knew about my treatment of the soulscapers? I was so frightened, I could barely breathe.

Metatron merely shrugged. 'The patrons, as you know, monitor events abroad. Something which we have foolishly thought to be a disease or hysterical condition of humans is increasing in incidence. I mean, of course, the condition they refer to as the Holy Death.'

There was no hint in his manner that he was about to accuse me. Relaxing a little, I frowned in perplexity. 'I am unfamiliar with that term.' In retrospect, I knew very little of human society beyond Sacramante.

Metatron did not expand on his remark at first. 'We are not the only ones concerned about the sickness among the eloim. Our patrons are also trying to investigate what might be causing it, and have instructed their agents to be more vigilant. The activities of these agents were confined to Bochanegra to begin with – no one imagined the cause of the sickness would be discovered outside the country. Then, a female agent travelling in Khalt picked up rumours concerning the increase in these Holy Deaths and, acting on impulse, decided to investigate the phenomenon. To her surprise, she met with great resistance from the natives who view the Holy

Deaths as sacred and resent interference from outsiders. She reported back to the Kaliph's office who conveyed the information to the Parzupheim. The victims of this particular form of death appear drained of blood; it is the only clue we have to go on, but quite a damning one.' He sighed. 'Too long we have hidden away here in the atelier courts. It seems these Holy Deaths have been occurring for many years, but we have ignored them. It is our duty to investigate all irregular events beyond Sacramante, but instead we hide behind our art and our patrons.'

For a moment, I had the ridiculous impression his thoughts were heading in a similar direction to Avirzah'e's. Surely not!

'But why do you think the Tartaruchis might be responsible?' I asked. 'There are many eloim living beyond Bochanegra. Couldn't one of those throngs have gone rogue?'

'That is a possibility; one which we shall also be examining, but I find it hard to believe that those throngs, who are so paranoid about their own safety, would risk such behaviour. And Avirzah'e did condemn himself with his own words when you returned from Lansaal. He did not take kindly to being silenced either. My instincts tell me he is planning something and it seems more than coincidence that we find unwilling sup victims lying dead in Khalt when Avirzah'e made it known how strongly he believed we should revert to such violation.'

'Have you confronted him with this suspicion?' I asked. It was difficult to imagine how Avirzah'e might react to such accusation, but a picture of his face convulsed with sneering laughter sprang to my mind.

'Not yet. Tartaruchi is a powerful throng and I am loath to offend Tartarus outright. If I manage to gather enough incontrovertible evidence the Tartaruchi Lord will be unable to voice official complaint, so I will have to be patient.'

I sighed deeply. The knowledge my father had passed to me had crushed any euphoria I had felt at the success of my performance the previous evening. Until then, I had believed the selection and continued observation of Rayojini would be more than an adequate contribution on my part towards the solving of the eloim's dilemmas. Now, it was clear that the sickness was not our only problem, and that my father would not allow me to remain ignorant of it. Was this the penance fate had placed upon me for the murders I had committed in Lansaal?

'I am sorry to have distressed you,' Metatron said, obviously noticing how my spirits had fallen, 'but it is important that you know all these things. Forget what I have said, on a conscious level, but *be aware* of it within. Be vigilant. Take care of your brother. I fear that in years to come Avirzah'e will attempt to intrude upon your plans with the soulscaper. Be alert for an approach. You, I

89

have no fear, will be able to repel it, but Beth. . . It pains me to admit this, but he has . . . weaknesses. Thus, he will be your weakness. Remember this, Gimel. Remember it well.'

'What are you going to do?' My voice sounded very small. At that moment, I wanted to curl into his arms, feel his strength around me. He knew that, and kept his distance, knowing also that I would regret such behaviour later.

'Do? Nothing, for now, but observe and collect information. The time may yet come for the Harkasites to be awoken and released.'

'No!' I put my hands over my ears.

'Yes,' Metatron replied softly. 'Many things from the past are buried or kept hidden, the Harkasites among them; I know their power can be ungovernable, but the way events are developing I may have no choice but to use them.'

'Please, I pray you, do not make me hear this!' I cried.

The Harkasites hailed from an earlier age when we had needed warriors to protect us. They were dark creatures, unpredictable, almost like beasts. Lord Sammael, who had long been absent from our society, had initiated their creation in a time of great need when humanity had turned on us and driven us into hiding. The eloim had been grateful when they'd felt secure enough in their environment to retire the Harkasites to retreat-slumber, but perhaps there'd always been a fear that, one day, the warriors would have to be recalled from sleep. I did not know where they reposed – only Metatron and the Parzupheim knew that – but it made my skin crawl to think they might be nearby, hidden somewhere in the atelier courts. Whispered legends suggested the Harkasites, when pursuing a particular directive, were unconcerned whether the victims of their investigations were eloim or human. And those whom they interrogated *were* victims: I had little doubt of that. These were not things I thought about normally. I was upset, almost angry, that Metatron felt he had to share this information with me, making me face such uncomfortable images.

'Gimel, I trust you,' he said, apparently divining my thoughts. 'As you know, if I had my way, you would administer this House at my side.'

I lowered my hands. 'You flatter me, Metatron, but I am unsure whether I am worthy of your regard. What you have told me frightens me very much.'

'I would be uneasy if it didn't,' he said, and briefly touched my hands, where they were knotted in my lap. 'Now, I have told you. Later, we might need to speak of this again, but meanwhile do me the honour of sharing a light sup with me.' He grinned at me, quite boyishly. 'I have the best. It will be a treat.'

I gulped; never had I felt less like supping. 'I have . . . work . . . at home,' I said.

'It can wait. You work hard enough. Do I have to command my

daughter to spend the day with me?'

I looked at him helplessly. 'No, my lord, you do not.'

He stood and offered me his arm. 'You were really very good last night, my dear.'

'Oh, thank you. I must admit I did not see you there.'

'I did not stay for the reception. Yes, very good. However, there are one or two points I feel need criticism. . .' Together, we walked into the hall.

CANTO TWO

'. . . who shall tempt with wandering feet the dark
unbottomed infinite Abyss?'
Paradise Lost, Book II

A summer of drought was followed by an autumn of unceasing
deluge; those that were late with the harvest watched their grain
rotting in the fields. And I, Rayojini, daughter of Ushas, daughter
of a skilled line, found myself in the waterlogged land of Khalt
wishing myself anywhere, *anywhere* else in the world. What an
unfortunate time for wanderlust to strike!

Walking north through the ceaseless downpour, I had need of a
new pair of boots. The rough tracks that, in drier days, served as
roads for caravans heading north-west had been reduced, through
the attention of the elements, to little more than muddy streams
that sucked at my soggy trouser-legs causing irritating sores, and
they had destroyed the leather right off my feet. I was convinced
one of my toes was suffering from a fungus blister. My long, heavy
coat – one of my favourite garments – was thick with mud up to
my knees and my wide-brimmed hat had become distinctly droopy;
I'd had to remove the face-guard netting completely. As for my
carryback, it had been getting heavier and heavier as I trudged
along. Next town, I told myself, next settlement, the next cottage
by the way . . . I had been travelling without having seen another
human creature for three days now. Naturally the rain kept people
inside, but I had expected to see some form of life. A ghostly herd
of deer had crossed my path the previous evening – heads down,
pelts matted and furrowed – but other than that, I hadn't even
glimpsed a bird. My bivouac was still wearing well, thank spirit and
will, and I was tempted to turn my back on the uncomfortable
outside world and bed down under canvas until the weather cleared.
Only the promise of greater comforts kept me travelling. How I
would welcome a roof over my head, a hot potage, and someone
to rub my feet! I struggled on, resting as little as possible.

I knew it had been more than a little unwise to venture into this
territory, because it had a reputation for foul weather at this time
of year. I was bitterly regretting my decision now, but summer's
end had promised balmy, fruity days, and the scent of the ripening
plains had led me out of Truskania by the nose. I had veered away
from the well-trodden track, inspired by a sense of adventure, and
had intrepidly decided to explore lands unknown to me. I had a

95

map, because no soulscaper worth their life travels without one and if it was correct, I should come across a settlement any time now. I was worried, though, that the scale of the map was deceptive.

In spite of the discomfort, I was still glad to be away from familiar ground. I felt as if I'd accomplished some kind of escape, as indeed I had. I had not felt haunted since my feet had left the western road. For a while, at least, I was free of my inner demons. Demons? a foreigner might ask. A soulscaper haunted? Yes; it shouldn't be mocked. We are all haunted, every one of us, marked from the day of our ascension into the craft. Hag-ridden, in fact. I am talking of guardian-pursuers, those ever active voices from our inner selves who, once invoked, never shut up. During my childhood they had been a source of comfort and reassurance, but once I reached puberty they turned into an invasion from which I could never escape. Even in my most secluded moments, I was never truly alone. In my youth, as a self-righteous teenager, I had privately accused the scryers of handicapping every soulscaper that left the mountain. After all, it was they who invoked the demons that snagged at our ankles in the form of our guardian-pursuers. I could not understand why the ceremony was perpetuated; in my early twenties, dreams of these legendary overseers had often left me exhausted. As I matured, a weary philosophy had planed the edges of my anger, leading me to think that soulscapers, because of the potential strength of their skills, had to be curbed in some way and the threat of a judgemental spectre hanging over your head was as good a way to curb a person as any other. A long time ago I had come to the conclusion that something very unfortunate must have occurred in the past, which had inspired the Scaping Guild to invent this particular torment. And it is a very private torment, too. We soulscapers do not speak of it even to each other. When we meet, we celebrate and joke, make love and talk together. Sometimes we might discuss scaping cases of mutual interest and compare notes, but our haunt is never alluded to. As a child I had thought the guardian-pursuers to be very real, but as I grew older I concluded they were simply products of our own imaginations, shaped into being by the trauma of the scrying rite we all undergo at eight years of age. It's not impossible that the scryers conjure them forth from the murk of the soulscape itself, anchoring the vigilant images to our conscious minds by an insidiously instilled sense of guilt. This theory seemed to be reinforced by the fact that since the age of sixteen I had given my guardian-pursuers faces that belonged to people who were very much alive, or at least had been at one time. No matter how often I had tried to change the image in my head, whenever I thought of my guardian-pursuers I masked them with the faces of the Metatronims I had seen in Sacramante.

It had begun as soon as Ushas and I had returned home from the city. Even now as I plodded down the road of life towards the end of my thirty-fifth year, I could still remember vividly, as if it had occurred only weeks before, how deeply I'd been affected by the Metatronim artisans; the experience had left clawmarks on my soul. As I grew older, I recognised that the erotic dream I'd had in the Carmen Tricante, which at the time I had invested with all kinds of significance, must have been nothing more than the flexings of a developing sexuality. On my return to Taparak I'd quickly found myself a lover – to exorcise any residual anxiety my fantasies of Beth Metatronim had caused. I had felt that I needed an emotional protector. In my heart, I'd worried that the presence of the Metatronim would follow me back to Taparak and haunt my dreams for ever. It did not happen that way, exactly.

Despite the intensity of our brief friendship in Sacramante, Liviana Tricante never came to visit me. Not long after I'd left the city we did exchange one letter each, six months apart, but neither of us pursued the relationship beyond that point. I think I realised that, despite Livvy's enthusiasm to visit my home, Taparak would bore her. Sometimes I wondered what had happened to her and whether her brother, Salyon, recovered fully from his mind-sickness. Occasionally, out on the road, I'd think about heading towards Sacramante and finding out for myself but, for some reason, I kept away from Bochanegra. Inside, I harboured a deep aversion to returning there. It was strange because as a girl I'd enjoyed myself there so much, but perhaps memories of poor Salyon's hideous illness, and my bizarre reaction to meeting the Metatronims, put me off. Even now, the Metatronims haunted my soul, in the form of my guardian-pursuers. It is difficult to articulate what function these images actually have. I suppose that in simple terms they are a symbol of the striving for excellence in our work and a reminder that, because of the delicate nature of soulscaping, we should never become complacent or careless. If we foul a job, the guardian-pursuers will notice and fill our souls with dark despair. If we succeed, they nurture us with feelings of love and protection. I still believed it all to be a self-inflicted judgement. As for my personal guardian-pursuers, they never manifested themselves more tangibly than as a pressure in my head and a constriction around my heart. It felt as if they watched me from afar. They were invisible beings, but I still found their scrutiny oppressive. Occasionally, I'd become especially impatient with this sense of close attention, whether it was the product of my own imagination or not, and needed respite from it. I had discovered that the concentration required for crossing new territory seemed to quell the phantoms, dim their shapes, and silence their whispers, which was probably the real reason why I had not headed back to Taparak when the weather turned. With relief I'd waved goodbye to my guardian-pursuers on the coast of Lansaal and headed north, visualising them as diminishing specks on the shore, impotently ranting at my defection. See, it is a joke. I am not afraid of them.

I had come on to the mainland in southern Atruriey, the beginning of a long meandering, which I envisaged would take me up through the mountain state of Truskania and from there into what are known as the unmapped lands – although they have been thoroughly mapped now for over sixty years. I had become restless at home in Taparak, even though I had only recently returned from a long ranging in Lansaal. Without analysing my feelings or arguing with myself, I had packed my bivouac, crossed the sea to Cozca, hurried down to Toinis and taken a ship north.

The Atruscans are an astonishingly healthy race, devoid of most ailments – soulscape ones included – so it was more like a holiday for me to travel that way, rather than business. I was hired to tell stories of my experiences more often than for my soulscaping skills, because Atruscans love stories of any kind, and pester all travellers to tell a few. The Atruscans are as hospitable as they are hale; it is a shame we soulscapers so rarely have an excuse to tread their lands. After shambling slowly north through Truskania, I led the autumn up into the death of Khaltish summer. The Khaltic lands are peopled mostly by nomads, although there are also a number of settlements ranging in size from small hamlets to walled towns. The nomad tribes are notoriously superstitious people, prey to fears, haunts and other mind-sicknesses, and therefore rich pickings for the enterprising soulscaper. It is not a circumstance without dangers, however, as very often nomad superstition extends to a general mistrust and fear of soulscapers themselves – lynchings are not unrecorded – but if a person has taken the trouble to learn the three most common tongues of the North, they can generally get by without making gross offence. Another problem is that nomad shamans tend to regard soulscapers as professional rivals, so careful treading is required when meeting new groups. I always prostrate myself to the shaman's goat, or show whatever form of humility is asked for, before attempting to offer my services around. If the ground seems too hot, I just make it a social visit, wave farewell and move on. It is best to be prudent in these matters.

So, there I was, trudging miserably through the mud of Khalt, hoping the land had not mysteriously become deserted around me, hoping desperately that any people I did come across would be friendly to soulscapers and anxious to make me feel at home. I was making for a settlement called Yf, where stone-cutters harvested the earth, sending their produce east, west and south, to build the palaces of shahs, kaliphs and lesser nobles. Khaltish stone was also widely used in the construction of temples, as it was generally believed to be of the very best quality. There are so many temples throughout the civilised lands, I sometimes wondered where all the deities came from. Gods were instrumental in my work, so I always paid close attention to their temples and felt confident I was familiar with most religions. All deities are present in the soulscape: they are as mutable as ocean, flowing and ebbing, coming into prominence, declining into obscurity, but always present. From careful observation as I travelled, I had noticed that new gods tended to arrive in the community in waves; and almost like some bizarre soulscape emigration, they always came from the West. New cults sprang up like spring growth, claiming followers in droves. At first, a fresh religion would be passed by word of mouth; new names would be used in oaths, new prayers would appear on the tongues of the afflicted. Later, shrines would sprout up along the road and, later still, temples that clung to the hills from Sacramante to Atruriey and beyond. I had sometimes wondered if there was a common fount to all this spirituality, whether some priestly wits, perhaps closeted in a high room in Bochanegra, spent their time inventing new gods and dispersing the invention through a team of professional travellers. The eastern races have a fondness for antiquity, never throwing anything away, whether it be an idea or an object; they tend to tack new god-forms on to their existing pantheons so that most religious cults in the East boast a bristling forest of idols in their temples, each more specialised than the last. There are scryers in Taparak who have no occupation other than to catalogue this rich, ever-expanding divine population.

Sundown was barely recognisable as such, although the rain had thinned to an all-pervading mist, drenching my clothes to the skin. I had vowed to keep walking until Yf came into view and my persistence was rewarded. Through the grey, murky twilight, lights appeared beside the road up ahead, and I could smell wood-smoke and food cooking.

The town was flanked on either side by dark stone cliffs, most of which had been burrowed into and excavated. Yf patronised the mason god Mofi, and I passed a roadside shrine where a statue sat with chisel upraised, humourless face staring out into the rain. Mofi was a stocky god, renowned for his skill rather than his beauty, which was unusual. It is fair to say he was rather oafish in appearance.

The buildings of Yf are sturdy block constructions, all of stone, with slate roofs. I could see none more than single-storeyed. Too exhausted to be circumspect, I waded up to the nearest door and knocked loudly. After a few moments, a fair-skinned woman answered, carrying a heavy kitchen utensil which I guessed would double as a weapon should her unexpected visitor prove hostile in some way.

'Glad eve to you, madam,' I said in Middle Khalt, of which most people could at least speak a few words. 'I am a traveller from

99

Atruriey. Do you know of anywhere I could lodge for the night?' I thought the Yflings would be familiar with travellers, given their wide-spreading trade.

The woman put her hands on her hips, which were generously proportioned to say the least, and cocked her head on one side. She wore a thick woollen shawl with dangling fringes, which I would have given anything to wrap myself up in at that moment. 'Buying, are you?' she asked. It was neither welcoming nor antagonistic, just a question. I wondered whether it would be easier to lie. Sometimes, stating my profession meant a few long minutes of explanation would be required.

'In a way. I took a detour in my travels to purchase a gift for my mother here in Yf.'

The woman laughed, tucking a few straggly fronds of pale hair back into the untidy knot behind her head. 'You purchasing a house for her, then?'

'No, a sepulchral plaque. Alas, she is recently dead. The work of Yf is renowned. I want nothing less than the best for her.'

The woman had assumed a pitying expression. 'Sympathies, madam. Excuse me. Well, there'll be no obsequy-smiths trading at this hour. You'll have to wait until morning.'

What an astute conclusion! I nodded. 'As I mentioned, I seek accommodation for the night.'

'You can pay, of course.'

'Truscan zehs. Will that pass for currency here?'

She nodded. 'We take all here, long as it's money somewhere. I have a couch you can use, if you like.' She stood aside. 'Come inside, out of that rain.'

The cottage was spacious; long and low, with a large central room that doubled as kitchen and daily living space. My hostess had an extensive family of brats, sticky-mouthed and staring, who were huddled around a delightfully huge fire. 'Such a sudden end to the sun,' my hostess observed as she bent to stir her cooking-pot over the fire. I agreed, unstrapping my carryback with chilled fingers and gratefully relieving myself of its weight. 'No weather for travelling on foot,' the woman added, looking me up and down. Perhaps she was wondering how I could afford to pay for a plaque if I had no animal transport.

'I couldn't agree more,' I said, pulling off my hat and scratching my damp head, 'but I always travel this way. Keeps me fit.'

'Oh. Yes,' she replied vaguely and barked a few shrill orders at her brood, who moved aside to let me sit down on a stool and steam among them.

After asking my name, she told me her own was Annec and that her husband was a master cutter, presently working away from home at a quarry, north of Yf. 'He supervises,' she said importantly. 'No cutting now for him! He marks the stone, of course, and tells

100

the youngsters where to ply. If you knock in the right place, a block comes out of the mother-cliff the size of this room!'

'Really!'

'Oh yes. Princes of the Delta Lands come here to buy their stone, you know.' She peered at me. 'Forgive my importunity, but I was wondering, from your skin, do you claim Deltan blood?'

I smiled. 'I have more than a few drops of it, as it happens.'

She nodded. 'Thought so. The mountains are very fertile here-abouts, you know. We can supply any need, no matter how great or how particular. We have a temple made all of quartz.'

'Indeed? I must visit it while I'm here.' Thinking me Deltan, poor Annec thought she smelled money, and was attempting to ply the local trade with me.

'Yes, you must take a look at it,' she said. 'Now, take yourself a seat at the table, Mistress Rayojini, and I'll dollop you a potful of this boilings.' I had peeled off my soaking top coat and, as I sat, Annec draped a welcome shawl around my body. She pinched the bones of my shoulders and made a fussing comment about how I could use more than just one of her meals. Eyeing the trough she had set down before me, I doubted whether my naturally spare frame could bear that. Annec set about mixing us both a hot rye drink, and then sat down beside me to gossip. 'I'm expecting again. It'll be my seventh. Father says, when they're grown, we'll have our own cutting team! Won't that be grand!'

'Mmm.' I smiled round my food. 'You don't know how grateful I am for this.'

She beamed back at me, pleased, in a motherly fashion. I thanked all the spirits that such creatures as Annec existed, whose apparent sole function was the nurturing of others, and that it gave them such pleasure. All you had to do was be weakly grateful for their ministrations, and they puffed up with maternal urges like a sail full of wind. I anticipated a comfortable stop-over in Yf.

'So Rayojini, where do you hark from? Living in Atruriey, are you?' She must have been trying to translate my clothes, which I kept eclectic to confuse such analyses. I saw no reason to hedge now.

'I was born on Taparak,' I said, watching her carefully. Her face lit up.

'You are a soulscaper! Of course!' She slapped her thighs in self-congratulation. 'I should have realised from the first! Walking in all weathers, and such a long way! A soulscaper! Do you plan to work here?'

'I am here to purchase a plaque, remember?' I smiled, feeling my face fold into a now perfect copy of my late mother's wry expression.

Annec made a gesture to indicate her stupidity. 'Of course! Still . . .' She paused. 'There may be work if you're willing.'

'Oh?'

'Yes. Our town steward, Mouraf, has sent to Taparak for help, as it happens. And now you turn up! If it wasn't too soon to be a response to his petition, I'd say you were fooling me now, and had come to see Mouraf after all.'

'I'm not here to see Mouraf but, naturally, if I can be of help, I shall assist in any way . . .'

'Tomorrow, I will introduce you,' she said. 'Mouraf will be pleased!' By that, I deduced he would be pleased with *her*; I could see Annec enjoyed people being pleased with her. Still, for all her simplicity, she was a well-meaning soul. She exclaimed over my feet when I eased them out of the remains of my boots and not only treated me to an aromatic-salve rub but also, after we'd ascertained that, happily, our feet were of a similiar size, gave me a pair of her own boots – telling me her husband had recently equipped her with two new pairs. I was not sure whether to believe that but, despite my protestations, she would accept no payment for her gift. I slept like a babe, as I'm sure she desired, upon her plump, enveloping couch where I lay smothered in thick blankets, with a cat stretched over my toes for extra warmth, and woke feeling much refreshed. As an echo of my tranquil, contented mood, outside the skies had cleared somewhat. There was no sunlight, but neither was there any rain. I hoped these were conditions that would keep up after I left the town.

Annec stuffed me with breakfast, which I consumed amid a babble of fractious child-noise. Later, accompanied by two of her younger children muffled up in thick winter coats, she escorted me to the residence of Mouraf. The mud-streets of Yf were full of people hauling stone up and down in carts. I imagined the air must be very dusty in summer; even the fruit on the shop-stalls we passed was spattered with thick droplets of mud. The Yflings were an affable community, perhaps because so many foreigners passed through, and were totally devoid of the usual suspicious wariness found in Khalt. Recognising me for a stranger, even the cart-boys would pause from their hauling and paw my sleeve, so that they could show me what they were transporting to the workshops. All the blocks were carefully wrapped in waterproof cloth, and would be reverently unveiled for my appraisal, as if they were the most precious of jewels. I was so charmed by this behaviour, I nearly bought a cut of rose marble, thinking how much a Lannish friend of mine would have liked its colour. She was the wife of a fairly successful merchant, and liked to commission sculptures. Her sitting-room had rose-quartz walls, and I knew she would love to have an ornament cut from this exquisite stone to match them. Luckily, common sense interrupted my benevolent thoughts, and reminded me it would be rather a problem lugging a block of marble around with me until the next time I was in Lansaal.

Mouraf's abode had the distinction of being called a hall, although its size was modest in comparison to what was generally considered hall-like. Mouraf himself was a dwarf, uncannily similar in appearance to the local god-form, but with a handsome face framed in thick black beard and well-groomed hair. After Annec had pulled a bell-rope and announced herself to a servant of some kind, Mouraf had come to the door to meet us. He stood pugnaciously on the threshold, thumbs in belt, while Annec explained who and what I was. Then, he cocked back his head and treated me to a blistering inspection from brow to toe.

'Perhaps you could tell me how I may help you,' I said, inclining my head.

Mouraf did not smile. He glanced sternly at Annec, before turning and marching smartly back into his hall, calling over his shoulder, 'Well, follow then.'

We did so, brats trailing, one beginning to grizzle.

Mouraf had a winsome wife named Tarelyn. She was only a young girl, of comely and homely appearance; clearly a second marriage. Mouraf's son, Harof, was very sick. I guessed there was not that much of an age difference between the wife and son. Annec, her brood, and I were taken to a bedchamber where the wife sat feeding the ailing son. I immediately warmed to the tableau, sensing the strong family bonding, the loyalty and affection, which were soaked into the walls themselves. Mouraf was tetchy because he was worried. It was also obvious that his son would not have lasted until help could come from Taparak. What lay on the bed was a person very near the end of existence in this lifescape. I walked to the bed, smiled warmly at the girl, and bent to inspect the boy's eyes. He gazed back unblinking; a handsome youth, despite his damp pallidness, who had inherited his father's features, if not his small stature. I could see the Fear very strong inside him, looking out through his eyes like a sly beast. But it was more than that, I felt.

'Tell me the history of this illness,' I said.

'He cannot speak,' Tarelyn said quickly. 'He cannot walk, and sometimes he is sick after food. You see, he is wasting.' She indicated the bed earnestly. I turned to Mouraf.

'Fever? Or injuries?'

The steward shook his head. 'Strangely – neither. Not that we know of. He simply came in from the yard one eve, after littering the chickens, wandered in here and lay down. He has not risen since.'

'I see. And your healers – what is their opinion?' I took it for granted they would have had a healer to the house.

Mouraf shrugged helplessly. 'Foxed, she is. Herbs aplenty, needles to the pulse-points, assuaging fumes; all are useless. Which led me to believe it was a soulscape malady.'

I nodded. 'Perhaps. Perhaps.' I sat down upon the bed and lifted the boy's hand. It was heavy and lifeless; damp and cold to the touch. I shuddered, my flesh acrawl with memory. If anything, the appearance of poor Harof reminded me strongly of Salyon Tricante, when my mother had tried to heal him all those years ago. As she had predicted, I had come across the odd similar case during my travels, and I had also picked up whispers from my colleagues about cases of their own that shared the same symptoms. It was more than the Fear, it was a condition I had coined 'the non-death'. However, I knew appearances could be deceptive; I would not know for sure what ailed the boy until I had inspected his soulscape. Requesting a lighted coal, I unpacked some fume-grains from my bag. 'I need to work alone,' I said. 'Would you mind leaving the room?' Tarelyn began to protest, but the steward waved her objection aside.

'Whatever you wish. How long will this take?' I noticed a sand-timer beside the bed, turned it over to begin the flow and handed it to Mouraf.

'Precisely this measure,' I replied.

They left me.

For a few moments I paused to collect myself, sprinkling a pinch of the grains on the lighted coal, and inhaling deeply of the smoke. The boy was still staring at me, but I knew he could not see me; I was not looking forward to discovering what it was he *could* see. The reddish-grey smoke of the fume-grains began to fill the room. I removed the pillow from beneath the boy's head and arranged his limbs straight in the bed. As a matter of routine, I quickly checked the body for signs of injury. There was no sign of great trauma, only the usual array of scratches and minor knocks a boy of that age would collect from day to day. I smiled when I discovered the bruise of a love-flower on his neck – quite a large one, in fact. It was one of those poignantly sad moments; whoever had given him that vigorous caress would never do so again. The inspection completed, I composed myself on the floor, legs crossed, palms upward, and breathed deeply of the scaping-fume.

I heard a small moan escape the lips of the boy on the bed; it suggested the fume was beginning to take effect and that, in his dazed state, he was encountering the boundaries of my own mind-scape. His own appeared to me as a murk of poisonous smoke; a barrier. I could feel his consciousness trying, so desperately hard, to break through into my mindscape. He was in a state of flight. Quite harshly, I pushed him back and followed his wailing essence into the murk. It was terrible. All that was left of him was a thread, a dim spark. Usually the scape of an individual is a panorama of colour: thoughts blooming like flowers into what are seen as concrete forms; great spreading vistas, bizarre constructions like cities, which when approached may only be a honeycomb or a cloud. All of a person's thoughts, memories of the past, ideas for the future, emotions and intuitions, exist in the soulscape. It is also the home of those symbols and ideas generated by the racial soulscape: the home of gods and demons. As a contrast, the shallower mindscape is conscious thought: a geometric territory, functioning like a machine. Sometimes I have to work in that territory but, with Harof, it was only the soulscape I sought. I found it to be a depressingly barren place. There was little light, although there was manifestation of a rudimentary landscape. The horizon was an image of crumpled stone while, above it, luminous-edged clouds fled in streaks across a sky of dark grey. Even as I watched, the panorama was dimming and decomposing. There was no life in that place; if anything it resembled the soulscape of someone recently deceased – a place which may be entered though I would not recommend it. As bodily functions wind down, it is possible to glimpse how the inner landscapes decompose – a necessary part of departing the flesh – for they are only of use to the incarnate being. As to what comes after incarnation, no soulscaper has been able to report back to the living about it. We did not believe in ghosts, except those that could be explained away as projected thought-forms from living minds. It seemed clear to me that Harof should be dead and yet, even in this wilderness, I could discern a pathetic shred of being rattling around, lamenting and confused. This spiritual essence, though small and insubstantial, was not degrading as one would expect, but neither was it redeveloping. Unless extinguished and released, thus permitting it to rejoin the rest of its substance (an irresistible attraction wherever it roamed), the soul-shred would eventually inhabit a void and be powerless to escape it. The body would live on, if fed and cared for, but the vestigial soul-essence would be trapped in the flesh, waiting only for the release of death. An unspeakably horrible situation. Mulling all this over, I had already decided upon what course of action to take, and had prepared myself to retreat from the soulscape, when a tremendous roaring started up around me.

It was like being pelted by flying boulders. Powerful sensations gripped my consciousness, preventing any action, and I was momentarily paralysed. To a soulscaper, helplessness of this kind is the most terrifying thing; it is imperative, for the well-being of both scaper and client, that the scaper remains constantly in control. Now, something huge, formless and extremely forceful had invaded my being, preventing my departure from Harof's soulscape. I did not recognise this presence at all; it fitted no known manifestation. My first instinct was to wriggle and struggle desperately, break free; the sense of repulsion and fear was so strong. What was it? There was an overwhelming desire to give in to panic, and it was only my training that pulled me through. Be calm, spoke my inner resol-

105

ution. Relax into this. Finding an inner rhythm, I let go, ceased struggling, and managed to extrude myself by slipping under the power of the aggressive form. I could tell then that the thing, whatever it was, wasn't really that powerful; it was all bluster, but formidable, nonetheless. It did not belong in the soulscape of this boy, for it was not part of him. Just exactly what it was doing there, I could not guess, but the reason would not be pleasant, I was sure.

My flesh shuddering with cold, I opened my eyes in the smoke-filled chamber, gasping for breath. I was freezing, yet I knew the room was warm. Or had been. I stood up, steadied myself against the bed, and went to open the window. I breathed deeply of the clean air outside, listening to the comforting everyday bustle of Yf: the clang of hammers, the trundle of carts, people calling out to each other. Then, I turned and gazed for several long minutes at the boy on the bed. His eyes were still open in a rictus of uncomprehending confusion. I cursed aloud, and thumped my fist against the window-sill, because I knew what I had to do. There was no alternative, no matter how much I detested the procedure. It made no difference how many times it needed to be done – and I'd had to do it three times before – it never got any easier. I took a jar of paste from my bag. It was wrapped in several layers of cloth and etched with warnings. I loosed the cap, took a small spatula from the bag and scraped off a tiny amount of the paste inside. Then I poked the spatula into Harof's mouth and left it there for a few moments. During this time I sat and held his hand, even though he did not know I was there. Still, some rituals have to be observed. I felt the shreds of his soul tug free of the flesh and fly out of the window, pulled inexorably to wherever in the universe the rest of his essence lingered. I removed the spatula from his mouth, closed his eyes, and tidied away my things. For a few hours the empty body would continue to exhibit minor signs of life, until the motor mechanisms in the mindscape wound down. It was important this effect was maintained, otherwise it would be too obvious what I had done, and no soulscaper wants to be branded a murderer.

I didn't wait for the family to re-enter the room, but opened the door and went out to find them. Mouraf was comforting his weeping girl-wife in the main hall. From that, I understood her instincts had already informed her the boy was dead, although she was probably not yet aware of it on a conscious level. Other women of the household hovered nearby, ready to swoop in with accommodating bosoms, should they be needed. Annec, apparently, had left.

I put my bag on the long centre table and said, 'Do you trust me, Master Steward?' Mouraf stood up. No matter what his size, he was tall in that moment. He came towards me, touched my arm, and led me some distance away from the crying woman. He searched my eyes intently. This was not a man to be fooled. 'It was too late,' I said plainly. 'I suspect it was always too late. I'm sorry.'

'What do you mean? Is he . . .' He balked from saying the words.

I shook my head. 'Not yet, but it will be soon.'

His face had hardened, but he betrayed no emotion. He would only give in to that later, alone with the woman. 'Can you tell me what caused this?' he asked gruffly. 'Is it a sickness, or was he attacked?'

I hesitated. 'I do not think it was a sickness exactly. A precaution, Master Steward: sometimes there are things in the air that none of us can understand. Have your people take care at sunfall for a while.'

'Take care? In what way?'

I sighed. 'I wish I knew. It is difficult to give advice in this area, but there have been other cases like this. Widespread. Victims have always seemed to be alone when the "sickness" attacks them. Always at day's end. It is a strange time, when the domain of the moon and sun cross paths. Sometimes, I feel, soulscape denizens can break through into our world at this time. It is just a hunch. Rarely is there more than one casualty in each community, but I advise caution at least.'

Mouraf was all for more than caution. 'Tonight we will search the area. If there is a scape-beast around here, we will find and burn it!'

I nodded. 'As you feel best.' I did not want to say that there are no such things as scape-beasts, not as he might understand them. There are no fearsome creatures of flesh and blood that can be fought and vanquished, but I knew the hunt would provide release for his grief, so did not argue with his decision. Perhaps he and his hunters would come across some stray wild dog and kill it, believing themselves avenged. I hoped so.

'Thank you for your time,' Mouraf said to me. 'I would like you to stay until . . . this is over. Stay for the hunt. I will reward you.'

I appreciated this gesture. Quite often in these situations, relatives of the afflicted, driven furious by grief, tend to shun, or blame, the soulscaper concerned, and can't get rid of them quickly enough. 'Please,' I said gently, 'no payment is required.' I shook my head firmly as Mouraf opened his mouth to protest. 'I mean it. I do not feel comfortable being paid for failed healings. But I will gladly stay beneath your roof until morning, if you wish.'

He nodded. 'I do. Now, I will muster a search group for later. If I may entreat your services again, have you anything for Linni, my wife? A potion of some sorts . . .' He waved a hand. 'Something to let her rest.'

'Of course.'

Mouraf voiced a difficult question. 'How much life has Harof got left to him? I want us to be there at the end, if that's possible.'

'A few hours. Enough time for Tarelyn to rest and for you to

107

accomplish your business. I will sit with him, and call you when I feel it's time.'

He gripped my arm. 'Thank you, Mistress Rayojini.'

The house of Mouraf fell to stillness. I went to sit in the sickroom, sipped at the hot drink one of the house-women brought me and nibbled on a delicious filled-bread snack, while writing up a page of notes on the case. Afterwards I leafed through my leather note-binder, reading over the notes of previous cases of this kind. If I had hoped to find succour in my faded words, the hope was short-lived; they brought me only uncomfortable reminders. The last time it had happened, which had been over three years ago, in Atruriey, I had been prey to a disturbing idea, concerning the origin of the sickness. It was an idea which I had banished once easier, more straightforward assignments had blurred the memory. I had written feverish notes back then, garbled thoughts tumbling out upon the page, of how I feared there were other people travelling the land, adept as soulscapers in the sifting of souls but perhaps not as benevolent. Sometimes I had suffered the sensation that another had passed before me, and that I merely patched together the remnants of this other's deeds. The thought had been so strong, I'd almost been able to visualise this unseen predator; it was a creature wrapped in shadows. Others had developed their own theories concerning the non-deaths.

A friend of mine, Sard, a man with whom I had been infatuated as a girl, had once voiced a highly controversial opinion. He suggested that victims of the soul-shredding were actually people who should have died the Holy Death but, for whatever reason, *hadn't*.

'Think on it', he'd said. 'All Holy Deaths take place at sunfall – as do the soul-shreddings. Like them, there is no evidence of sickness or injury. I believe the shreddings are the same thing, but somehow failed.'

As their name suggests, the Holy Deaths are sacred. To suggest that the process might sometimes fail, leaving an individual mindless and virtually soulless, on earth, was a heresy. People believed the gods chose the honoured victims of the Holy Deaths themselves. It was said that divine messengers plucked the most god-favoured individuals from earthly life, in order to transport them to everlasting bliss in the shining realms beyond all knowledge. And gods, to humankind, are infallible. The majority of people were possessive of their theologies, and strongly resented disbelief or criticism from others. Personally, I was convinced that deities were nothing more than inventions of the human soulscape, which meant that if people died Holy Deaths, they had unconsciously chosen to do so themselves. However, I'd scolded Sard for his outlandish ideas, and advised him to take more care where he repeated them. The idea had been related to me across a pillow. I hoped Sard was not so open with all his lovers.

Mouraf and the people of Yf killed a black-bristled boar that night. They brought it home amid a blaze of torchlight and triumphant chanting. One man voiced my thoughts: 'How can you tell that's a scape-beast? It looks like a simple hog to me!'

Mouraf had scowled. 'Fool! It disappeared before our eyes a dozen times, before appearing behind us again in an instant! Simple hogs are not capable of that! See its eyes? They are red, and the tusks are crueller than the norm. You tempt the spirits by mocking. Had we not killed this beast, members of your own household might have been at risk!'

The criticised man turned to me. 'Mouraf's son was not gored by a hog,' he said. 'You saw this. Are scape-beasts so wise as to kill without their beast weapons?'

The man was canny, but then he had not lost a son. I shrugged. 'The killing of this animal was a release,' I answered. 'Above all, that is most important.'

They burned the carcass of the hog as an offering for the deceased boy, the whole town filled with a sense of celebration, as well as one of loss. Annec sought me out in the crowd. 'Mouraf has many sons,' she said. 'The cut will mend soon enough.' I smiled. The people of Yf all had massive families. It bred, perhaps, a certain fatalism concerning the loss of children.

Later, I walked out into Mouraf's yard, gazing out across the modest paddocks and orchards behind. Mountains loomed above the town, silent and still beneath the wind, filled with their own prescience and wisdom. They, and the trees, the grass beneath my feet, the very air, had witnessed the fate of Mouraf's son, but they could not speak to me. I was discomfited. Not only did failure oppress me, but I could no longer deny the pattern revealing itself before me. There was a message to be translated, symbolism to be aligned and understood. I could not ignore it. Information nagged in the air around me, incomprehensible for now, but existent all the same. If only I could pluck it forth, and give it form. I had a feeling, should I be at a soulscapers' gathering this moment, everyone would have tales to tell of the increase of this soul-shredding phenomenon. A sense of urgency filled my mind. The wind blew over the mountains, whipping the tree branches around me, bringing in the clouds from above the eastern seas. It was filled with unheard voices and spiralling spirit forms. Soon the people of Yf would forget this tragedy and their lives would resume a contented rhythm. Mouraf's wife would bear him more children, the memory would fade. If they were lucky, this would not happen to them again. But I, come morning, would leave the town, my mind full

109

of this moment, repeated endlessly. Come morning, I would follow the way of the wind.

'. . . we are decreed, reserved and destined to eternal woe; whatever doing, what can we suffer more, what can we suffer worse?'
Paradise Lost, Book II

Everything reached crisis point far sooner than we had anticipated. Time is no enemy to the eloim; we supposed we had many years in which to investigate the phenomenon of the suicides. We felt as if we were controlling the sickness.

For several years we had suffered no more fatalities, as all cases had been recognised in their early stages, and the throngs had sent any potential self-destructees hastily into retreat. This gave us a respite. I wanted Rayojini to be in her forties by the time I summoned her to Sacramante; then, she would be approaching the peak of her powers. The innovation and impulsiveness of youth might be dulled, but she would have accumulated vast experience: a far more potent tool. However, events began to accelerate beyond our control well before that time.

Metatron's dark suppositions, which he did not broach with me again for many years, seemed to have been correct. Over the years my differences with my father had seemed to fade and although we had never resumed any intimate physical relationship, we now spent more time in each other's company. I was aware that as well as enjoying my conversation Metatron was subtly grooming me for a rôle he expected me to undertake later in life. It was never actually said, but I sensed he had chosen me to be his successor in the family stronghold. The day when he would step down as leader of our throng seemed so distant to me, I did not worry about it particularly, but occasionally, in private moments, the spectre of what I'd done in Lansaal would insist on coming to haunt me and I wondered whether Metatron would still view me as his direct heir, should he ever find out about it. Sometimes, though rarely, I'd dream of being the beast again, and those dreams were erotic and pleasurable, a feast of blood and sex. Perhaps Beth suffered the same dreams, although we never discussed it. I could only hope that time would eventually dull the sting of those memories.

One evening Metatron came to call on me. From the moment he stepped into my salon, I sensed an agitation in his manner. My mood changed immediately from lively anticipation of an agreeable evening's discussion to joyless apprehension.

111

'I regret we must discuss subjects of a serious nature tonight,' Metatron said. He held out his coat to Tamaris, who was waiting to see whether I would order a light refreshment. I waved her away quickly.

Metatron sat down opposite my couch, resplendent as usual in tight yet flexible garments of black crushed velvet, his jewellery exquisite but understated: a single ring, simple hoops of thick gold in his ears, shining through his dark hair.

'Not bad news. . .' I said, hopeless of reassurance.

My father frowned. 'Gimel, I spoke to you some time ago concerning potential, illicit eloim activity in Khalt. Well, patron agents have reported further phenomena.'

'More deaths?' To dispel my unease, I stood up and went to my liquor cabinet to pour us both a measure of brandy.

'The deaths appear to have continued,' he said, 'but it is more than that.'

I handed him a glass. 'I cannot imagine anything more serious.' I sat down, sipped some brandy, grateful for its warming piquancy.

'There are reports of . . . *unusual* events in Khalt,' he said. 'Events that to ignorant minds might appear – well – *supernatural* in origin.'

'Such as?'

'Would you believe corpses that walk, monstrous ghosts, quantities of blood appearing spontaneously on ground where there are no victims, human or beast?'

'I would find it hard to believe such things,' I said carefully.

'Much of it might be exaggeration, of course,' Metatron added hastily, 'but these are the reports we are receiving from patron agents.'

'Surely all cultures have such legends,' I said. 'The agents are obviously looking for evidence and are perhaps taking more notice of folklore that the Khalts have believed in for centuries.'

'There is merit in that assumption,' Metatron said grudgingly. 'But the agents claim to have seen certain things themselves – the blood, for example, and peculiar figures in the night. These people are highly trained; it is doubtful they would be prey to idle fancies like uneducated peasants! I'm afraid I am inclined to pay attention to their reports.'

'And do I take it you also believe the Tartaruchis are responsible?'

Metatron glanced at me sharply, clearly aware I still doubted that possibility. 'I cannot help but believe that. But if they are, I admit they cover their tracks well. With the sanction of the Parzupheim, I have been discreetly monitoring their behaviour, but so far have been unable to produce proof that any members of the Tartaruchi throng have even left Sacramante over the past few years.'

112

'From which you might draw the conclusion none of them actually has,' I suggested.

Metatron sighed. 'I am disturbed by your tendency to defend Avirzah'e's throng,' he said.

'I am not defending them,' I replied, 'but merely voicing the remarks Tarturus himself would no doubt present should this investigation become public. I am only trying to help you formulate a suitable reply to any objection he might raise.'

Metatron narrowed his eyes at me. I was unsure myself whether the explanation of my remarks was true or not. I was intrigued by Avirzah'e, but had had no direct contact with him for years, and certainly harboured no especial regard for him or his people. Some instinct within me, however, could not accept the Tartaruchis were responsible for the events Metatron had described. The Tartaruchis were known as a flamboyant and outspoken throng, and their behaviour had often irritated the more sedate members of our community, but I did not believe them to be corrupt.

'I suppose you are right,' Metatron conceded reluctantly, 'and my answer in that case is this: at any one time, the majority of throng members are concealed in retreat-slumber within the atelier courts. Therefore, it is not impossible that the Tartaruchis harbour progeny of which the rest of us are unaware, and who could therefore depart the city to re-enter it undetected. There might be hidden thoroughfares beneath the Tartaruchi stronghold.'

I thought Metatron's theory a little outrageous and desperate, but did not say so. 'Well, it is *possible*, I suppose, but I am sure that if the Tartaruchis are involved in these phenomena, it is because certain younger, hot-blooded individuals are petulant, arrogant and short-sighted. I am sure that, whatever they are doing, it can't be that effective. Do you seriously think Tartarus would condone such behaviour? Surely by simply confronting him with your suppositions, his insubordinate progeny could easily be curbed.'

'I can't do that, Gimel. I have no proof.'

'Mmm,' I murmured, and risked a smile.

Metatron appeared offended by my expression. 'Do not forget, beloved daughter, I still have a greater verse to quote: the Harkasites!'

I shuddered. The mere fact that my father hadn't yet initiated that particular course of action encouraged me to think he was actually reluctant to do so, despite his threats.

'The verse is long and complicated,' I said, 'its content menacing to well-being, its conclusion as yet unwritten. It might also be received unfavourably by your audience. . . .'

'Unless I recite it to myself alone,' Metatron concluded darkly.

I shrugged. 'I can only caution you to delay the performance.' My heart was filled with foreboding.

* * *

Metatron's fears proved to be the least of our problems. As the sickness had been eclipsed in my father's mind by events beyond Bochanegra, so a more immediate threat in Sacramante itself dispelled the spectre of renegade eloim for a while. Only two days after Metatron's visit to my salon, a terrible incident occurred.

Because of our longevity, which of all our racial characteristics is the hardest to conceal, we cannot blend easily into human society. We are constantly shadowed by the threat of suspicions being aroused, which could lead to the revival of old hatreds and prejudices. Therefore, at a crucial time in our history we instituted our own ethnic community within the atelier courts, the streets of which are never frequented by humans, other than patrons or our own trusted retainers. If we were not the creatures we are, and if we were prepared to abandon the very point of our existence, this seclusion might have been enough to protect us. Unfortunately, we cannot forsake our duty; we are impelled to transmit our artistic spirit throughout the world. This is not a selfish gesture because, should they be deprived of our creativity, humanity would be spiritually impoverished and, more profoundly, would find themselves in a very vulnerable position. Even the patrons are unaware of this. Our vocation demands that we perform in public, exhibit our art and publish our philosophies, which forces us into closer contact with humanity than is either safe or desired. Should we neglect to take adequate precautions, the least astute human would soon notice that his or her favourite performer never seemed to age. To offset this possibility, all eloim are required to take regular retreats – normally, once every sixty or seventy years. Retreat is essentially a sleep-time of refreshment and meditation and, at its conclusion, reawakened eloim are reintroduced into society as younger members of their families, newly fledged in the arts. The eloim throngs all possess a strong family resemblance, so there is little likelihood that non-patrons will suspect anything. Obviously, we take extra precautions, and rely heavily upon make-up and masks when performing in the streets, just in case some aged member of the audience has a good memory. Also, at any one time, only a select group of eloim practise beyond the atelier walls; the majority of throng-members cluster like bats in the high towers, away from public sight. No one, not even the patrons, are aware of how many of us there are. Eloim living beyond Sacramante have developed their own methods of concealment but, all in all, this delicate balance has been maintained for centuries. We were aware, however, of the vulnerability of our position. Our most potent tool of security operates on the soulscape level of humanity, because humans tend to believe everything they are told by spiritual or political leaders. The patrons of Bochanegra, a powerful country, have effective influence on world politics. But we control the spiritual life of humanity ourselves. There are a select group of eloim whose sole creative function is simply to invent gods. These religious ideas are disseminated throughout the world via the patrons' agents, and it is therefore relatively easy for us to sow particular seeds into human culture, which have effectively preserved our secret. Since the phenomenon of the Holy Death was brought to Metatron's attention, he'd seen to it that this religious creativity had increased. Without explaining why exactly, he had encouraged the artisans concerned to throw out all manner of exotic ideas in the hope of creating a smokescreen around incidents which might, or might not, have been instigated by rebel eloim.

However, despite our considerable influence, our careful disguises and precautions, both the patrons and ourselves were perpetually vigilant for individuals who might have seen through our defences, whose curiosity and suspicions had been aroused. It was as if we knew in our hearts that one day the difficulty we all dreaded most would arise, that it was inevitable.

One afternoon, Hadith Sarim came to my salon. She was a regular visitor and I was very pleased to see her, but that day she was restless and remote. I questioned her, naturally, and found her strangely reluctant to speak. Eventually, she confessed that she feared she had transgressed eloim code in some way. The remark shocked me, bringing, once again, uncomfortable memories to mind, but I took her hands in my own, assuring her I could not believe such a thing and urged her to confide in me. At first she was practically unable to articulate her anxieties.

'Gimel, you are wise. I cannot speak easily of my feelings to anyone – not even members of my own throng, but I must confess I would value your counsel.'

'Speak freely,' I soothed. 'Rest assured that what you tell me will be kept in confidence.'

Slowly, after further gentle nudging, I extracted the information that she had noticed a human male paying particular attention to her at a recent set of concerts. On a couple of occasions, he had even followed her home to the gates of the atelier courts. I laughed at her disquiet, patted her hand, and told her that her duty was simply to satisfy his curiosity! If he was the son of a family with whom she did not enjoy formal patronage, then of course the liaison must be discreet, but it was a problem quickly vanquished. Hadith only frowned.

'You don't understand, Gimel,' she said. 'He is not a patron at all!'

Not a patron? I was astounded. Non-patron society in Sacramante had been thoroughly permeated with a subtle antipathy towards eloimkind in a carnal sense, so that we did not appear that attractive to them. There would be an even greater risk of discovery if non-patrons started desiring us as lovers, because we knew that love

115

inspired far greater curiosity than any other human condition. The flimsy boundary between admiration for our work and physical desire was delicately balanced. I was horrified by what Hadith had confessed.

'You must tell your patrons at once!' I said. 'At once!'

She shrank from doing so, knowing the consequences would unavoidably involve extinction for the besotted non-patron.

'Hadith, our need for security transcends the welfare of the individual,' I said firmly. 'You must not even think about the man concerned, never mind feel sympathy for him.'

'He presented me with a poem at the final concert,' Hadith said, glumly.

'You have it with you?'

She nodded and took it from her purse. I silently scanned the maudlin lines. He more than desired her, poor fool; he loved her! However, the work did not contain enough literary potential to consider elevating its creator to the ranks of the patrons. 'You must go home and summon the Tricante elders immediately!' I said, handing her back the scrap of paper.

Hadith swallowed painfully. 'Gimel, he is . . . he is *most beautiful*.'

'Hadith!'

She covered her eyes with her hands. 'I'm sorry. I know. I know.'

By this time, I was very concerned for her. 'You must take a measure of brandy, my dear. Compose yourself. Under the circumstances, I think it would be best if I sent Tamaris to the Carmen Tricante straightaway with a message. Meanwhile, I will escort you home and speak to the Sarim on your behalf.'

'Thank you, Gimel. I will never be able to repay this favour.' Hadith wearily put her head in her hands and let me take control.

That should have been an end to the matter. The Tricantes should have discreetly exterminated the nuisance. Plans went horribly awry, however. Two days later, after careful investigations had been made, Hadith's doting admirer – a man revealed to be Oro Mervantes – was annihilated by Perdina, a young woman of the Tricante family. Unfortunately, Mervantes' mistress, a woman named Rosalia, had become aware of her lover's interest in Hadith. She had been making jealous investigations of her own, observing her lover's apartment and hoping to catch him in flagrante. On the night in question, while surveying Oro's rooms from a neighbouring building, she witnessed Perdina entering Mervantes' apartment by a rear entrance. Supposing this cloaked and furtive female to be her dreaded rival, Rosalia silently followed Perdina at a distance. Thus, the Tricante was caught red-handed with a knife in her hand and Mervantes, throat slit, at her feet. Regrettably, Rosalia had had the presence of mind to crack Perdina over the head with a bed-warmer before running out into the street, where she fell to her knees screaming for someone to fetch the judiciary. A semi-conscious Perdina was subsequently taken into custody, whereupon the Judificator of Sacramante discovered he had an embarrassing situation on his hands.

The judicial system of the city is, of course, run by the patrons, so it should have been a simple matter to compensate the murder victim's family discreetly with no further questions asked. However, the grieving mistress would not let the case rest, and recruited Mervantes' brother Zalero to her cause. Between them, they kicked up a tremendous fuss, and demanded the execution of Perdina Tricante. All the patrons' efforts to subdue the situation were to no avail. Encouraged by Rosalia, Zalero Mervantes embarked upon investigations of his own, and consequently published a pamphlet on the affair, which he distributed in the streets. He raised excruciatingly uncomfortable questions. What was the motive for Perdina's crime? Using Rosalia's evidence, he did not believe it had been the action of a lunatic; it had been too premeditated. Inspection of Oro's journal did not disclose any romantic attachment to Perdina, but it was rather revealing concerning his infatuation with Hadith Sarim. Winsome poems asked the beloved why she shut herself away in the atelier courts. Why were her people so distant and aloof, as if they had a thousand secrets to keep? Zalero considered these questions himself – although unlike his unfortunate brother, he was starkly devoid of any sentimentality. He concluded it was more than a coincidence that Oro had been murdered after falling in love with an artisan. It was as if his eyes had suddenly been unsealed, after a lifetime of blindness. He realised no one ever had any relationship with the artisans, no one saw the interior of the atelier courts. What secrets were hidden there? Who exactly *were* the artisans? What race were they? From where had they come? And why did the ruling families of Sacramante do so much to protect them? Had Perdina Tricante been involved with Hadith Sarim herself, thus murdering Oro out of jealousy, or were her motives darker, and less obvious, than that? His inquiring pamphlet was widely read by Sacramantans and according to reports we received from the patrons' agents, the question upon every non-patron's lips was simply: why have I not stopped to think about these enigmas before?

An emergency meeting of the Parzupheim was called, attended by elders of many of the patron families and the Kaliph Izobella herself. The most significant point addressed was the practicality of ridding ourselves of Rosalia and Zalero's unwanted attentions, by exterminating them. Or had they made themselves too visible to the public eye for that to be a safe option? If they died, or disappeared, would others take up the flag of their activities? It was a desperate moment. One eloim even advocated that we should take Zalero and Rosalia into our confidence and elevate them to the

117

ranks of the patrons, in the hope they would understand the greater implications and let the matter drop. Few of the eloim, and none of the patrons, thought this was a good idea. Rosalia and Zalero were too incensed and excited for the subtly addictive properties of being supped to affect them. Our familiar reality had changed; humanity had begun to question our existence. Sadly, Izobella resolved that in her opinion there was only one way to safeguard eloim secrecy; Perdina Tricante must be sacrificed to the executioner's blade. Even then, there was no guarantee such drastic measures would be enough to satisfy the Mervantes. Understandably, the Tricantes objected strongly to the Kaliph's suggestion. They could not countenance Perdina being executed for something her family had ordered her to carry out. They pleaded for reconsideration. Yet, there seemed no alternative. Some patron families supported the Tricantes, others pressed for a passionless resolution of the problem. The meeting fell into disarray, forcing the Parzupheim and the Kaliph to call for an adjournment.

Later the same day, Perdina herself resolved the situation by taking her own life. She left a note claiming she had murdered Oro out of jealousy which, given that she must have been in an unhinged frame of mind when she wrote it, sounded convincingly hysterical. The Mervantes were quickly heaped with palliative compensations: money, privileges, goods. Perhaps that would be enough. Of course, it was not.

Zalero had indeed woken up. He had transcended all the subtle restrictions placed upon his people, and set about incubating a racial hatred for the artisans throughout his society. He insisted that his brother's death must not be in vain; something sinister was going on in the atelier courts and he intended to discover what it was.

The eloim prudently abandoned all street performances and withdrew into the atelier courts, appearing in public only in establishments frequented exclusively by patrons. Perhaps unwisely under the circumstances, the patron families insisted that Zalero and Rosalia were public nuisances and demanded their incarceration in the judicial stronghold. Naturally, this caused a furore, although many Sacramantans took the opposite stance, speaking out for the artisans, and urging us to return to public performance. The fact that we were wary of doing so only provoked further suspicion. Mervantes' followers – a minority, but loud-voiced – complained about the artisans' privileges and riches. They declared we were nothing more than maggots in the heart of Sacramantan society, barring anyone who was not of our race – people who could undoubtedly be just as successful, given a chance – from attaining prominence in the creative fields. Could it not also be said that the artisans' selfish dominance of the Arts possessed distinctly political overtones? Who, in fact, inquired Mervantes' followers, really reigned in Sacramante while the Bochanegran dynasty clearly danced exclusively to artisan tunes? Money poured into artisan coffers from the vaults of the old Sacramantan families, they said. These same families would not sponsor common people and, as their old money controlled all the galleries and theatres, they would not contemplate the exhibition of unsponsored work – never mind the purchase of it. Mervantes' people declared that this situation effectively prevented anyone who was not favoured by the old families making a living as an artist or performer. This was, of course, true to a degree and the way both patrons and eloim wanted things to be, but we could hardly admit that. However, we did not actively suppress natural flair in the un-supped and would, should an individual case merit it, elevate a talented person in rank, absorbing them into the patron community.

Zalero and Rosalia, with their rebellious demands, undermined the delicate status quo. Even after they had been imprisoned, demonstrations were staged beyond the atelier walls with non-patrons marching up and down demanding that the gates be opened, and that poets and artists of their own be allowed to take up residence.

Everyone was thrown into profound anxiety, and I paid a visit to the family stronghold, hoping to be reassured by my father.

Clear morning light fell into the small, comfortable room Metatron used as his private study. Beyond the windows, the Metatronim garden bloomed in profusion beneath a serene summer sky. The whole scene was one of tranquil contentment and it was hard to believe there was anything amiss in the world.

Metatron embraced me warmly, offering me brandy and a seat beside the window. His voice sounded blithe although his face betrayed his anxiety.

'Are the un-supped right?' I asked him. 'Has the time come when they no longer need us? Is our star on the descendent?'

Metatron sat down beside me and gripped my arms firmly. 'Gimel, beloved daughter, do not lose your faith! Do not let despair into your heart, for it is certain I shall need your help in the near future. I believe all this upheaval is merely another result of the subject we discussed before. Someone, somehow, has upset the equilibrium. It is this that has allowed Mervantes to wake up and view things with an objective eye.'

I wriggled in his hold. 'But where is all this leading us, Metatron, *where?*'

My father relaxed his grip. 'Sadly, I am concerned it might lead us once again to war.'

I could not bear the thought of that, and stood up quickly, needing to make some physical movement. I pressed my hands against the window glass, wondering if I dared break it, and whether the pain of cutting my flesh would lessen the pain of terror in my

119

heart. 'And if it doesn't?' I asked. 'What then? Do we have a chance? In comparison to humanity, the eloim are few on this world. They would overwhelm us, no matter what dark verses you might dare to quote!'

Metatron pulled my stiff fingers away from the window, and gently pushed me back into my seat. 'Gimel, you know as well as I do that we fought for our lives once and could, if necessary, do so again. We might have become indolent over the years, but we are not powerless, although I sincerely hope it will not come to war.'

'I don't see how you can prevent it!' I said. 'For years you have talked of taking action and yet have done nothing but use the patron agents as spies. You have succeeded only in gathering a collection of folklore tales! Forgive me, but I fail to perceive how this can help us now!'

'That information has been more useful than you think,' Metatron said stiffly. 'I am sure that if we remove the disruptive influence at work in the world, the situation will calm down, and we will be able to resume our activities unmolested.'

His words did not reassure me. 'I am not so sure,' I said. 'We are interlopers in this world; it is not ours. Therefore, the question has to be asked: do we even have the right to fight to remain in it?'

Metatron looked at me in disbelief, almost anger. Then his expression changed to one of great weariness. 'Gimel, forgive me, I sometimes forget how young you are. Let me explain. We have given so much to these people, *so much*. It was through Lord Sammael's love for humankind that we, his followers, lost our power in the old world. We did not have to follow him here. We could have stayed in our natural realm, but Sammael convinced us humanity was in peril, so what could we do but give him our support? The traitor Mikha'il sent all his legions against us, we suffered great losses, yet we adhered to our beliefs – for the sake of humanity, not just for ourselves. Essentially, we relinquished everything we had to live here among the people.'

If his explanation was designed to appease me, it failed. 'Do you know, in some ways, I'm beginning to think Avirzah'e is right!' I said. 'Your words have only served to remind me how little gratitude we've received for our sacrifice. Humanity thanks us with war! With hatred!'

Metatron's voice was gentle. 'Remember we gave in love, Gimel. And the Tartaruch is *not* right. You must never think that. There is nothing to be gained by going backwards.'

My conversation with Metatron threw me into greater turmoil. I could not speak to Beth about it; his reaction to the Mervantes affair had been to shut himself away in his brush court and apply himself mindlessly to his work. If I attempted to confide in him, he only grunted in reply and then changed the subject. I was tempted to shout at him, shock him into facing reality. Hiding behind a canvas would not save him if the non-patron Sacramantans ransacked the atelier courts. Feverishly, I considered fleeing Sacramante. Perhaps I might reveal myself to Rayojini and live on the road with her for a while, until the situation in the city was resolved one way or the other. During those days of anxiety and fear I know I was hard on Rayojini, nipping her heels from a distance, somehow transferring my helplessness on to her through persistent assaults on her mind. Other times, weighed down with guilt, I would attempt to soothe her and bring her pleasure, but she had become so adept at coping with me, it was easy for her to repel my gentler approaches.

Then, another inevitability manifested itself upon my threshold; one which Metatron himself had predicted years earlier. Avirzah'e Tartaruchi made his approach.

I had risen late that day. The skies were overcast, which miserably reflected my less than carefree mood. Sitting in my salon, I was reading through a manuscript for a new play; although when we would be able to perform it, I could not imagine. Tamaris came hurtling through the door, her face flushed, her hands aflutter. 'What is it?' I asked in dread. We had come to expect the worst when our servants were agitated.

'You have a visitor,' she replied, her eyes round with excitement. '*Tartaruchi*!'

'Avirzah'e?'

'*Yes*!'

I arranged my gown more artistically around my legs. 'Then show him in, Tamaris, and bring out the brandy.'

It did not occur to me Avirzah'e was about to fulfil Metatron's prophecy. I expected some kind of immature silliness, but nothing sinister. Avirzah'e and I had not been in the same company for several months, and I hadn't spoken to him properly since *The Thorn Path* had ended its season fifteen years before. If he'd hoped to achieve any kind of intimacy with either Beth or myself through involving us in his production, he'd been sadly misled. I supposed he'd since given up trying to command our attention.

I was uncomfortably stunned by Avirzah'e's appearance when he swept into the salon. His presence filled my tasteful little room like a ball of flame. He was dressed in garments of the deepest, bloodiest crimson with muted gold embellishments. Ropes of dark, polished crystal beads adorned his neck and glinted in his carefully coiled hair. He bowed, and the heavy beads rubbed together with a gentle clinking sound. 'Gimel, thank you for receiving me.'

I inclined my head. 'The pleasure is mine. Please, make yourself

121

comfortable. Tamaris, relieve the Tartaruch prince of his travelling cloak.'

He sat down opposite me – in the place, coincidentally, where Metatron always chose to sit when he visited me – flicking back his black, red-ticked hair. I instinctively curled up my limbs.

It was all very formal to begin with. Tamaris poured out the brandy, while Avirzah'e and I swapped chilly pleasantries. I began to wonder what he had come for. He'd asked me how Beth was. Splendid, I replied. He is splendid. Avirzah'e smiled, thinned his lips and sipped his drink – very pointedly, I thought.

We'd begun to discuss a new ballet that the Eshim were working on, when Avirzah'e suddenly changed the subject. 'There have been no suicides among the artisans for three years now,' he said, not looking at me.

I was rather taken aback by his comment. 'No,' I replied carefully, with a faint note of interrogation.

'Has the sickness passed us, do you think?'

'We can only hope so.' I wondered whether he was aware of how many eloim had been forced into retreat for exhibiting overt signs of depression and self-destructiveness. I knew, because Metatron kept me informed.

Avirzah'e laughed. 'You are transparent, dear Gimel! You know as well as I do what is going on. Still, there has been a marked decrease in casualties, I understand.'

I made no comment on this, but reminded myself firmly of Metatron's suspicions and, however much my instinct was to discredit them, vowed not to let the Tartaruch deceive me. 'I have a feeling you are leading this conversation to a predestined point, Avirzah'e.'

He leaned forward earnestly in his chair. 'Never think I underestimate your intelligence. We, as a race, are balanced upon the point of a needle; a needle which stands in corrupting fire. Soon, there is every likelihood we will fall – again.'

I shivered. 'You touch upon a delicate issue – one which I am not prepared to discuss.'

'Every cell proclaims you Metatron's spawn! It is time you woke up, Gimel!'

'Speak plainly, then, but do not be surprised if you offend me.'

'Do you want to die?' he asked. The silence which followed these words was almost vertiginous. I stood up.

'I would like you to leave my house, Avirzah'e Tartaruchi.'

He remained sitting. 'No, you wouldn't and, if you will permit me to answer my own question, neither do you want to die. At least hear me out, Gimel.'

I sat down again, and sighed. It struck me how much I was enjoying the Tartaruch's company. He was right; I did not want him to leave, no matter what obscenity he was about to blurt out.

122

'Very well, I will listen. But, please remember at all times exactly who I am.'

'Assure yourself I am incapable of forgetting that! I know the consensual Metatronim opinion of my throng. But I have to say this, Gimel. You *will* die – we all will – unless preventive measures are undertaken. The Watchers have. . . .'

'No!' I interrupted. 'You'll not speak that name here!'

The Watchers were Mikha'il's creatures. Wary of their power, which might traverse the boundary between the worlds, we were forbidden to name them. The spoken name alone might be enough to invoke them.

'Avirzah'e, I implore you, guard your words!'

Now, the Tartaruch stood up, and began to pace my room. 'Guard my words? What are you afraid of? You are as conditioned as the human rubbish who populate this world!'

'Perhaps so, but for good reason!'

'Words cannot summon *them*, Gimel,' Avirzah'e said scornfully. 'They are here already! They have always been here. Now, are you the unique creature I think you are, or are you a craven, spineless wraith like the majority of our pathetic race?'

I bit my lip until the ichor ran, sucking my own juice in a moment of total indecision. I swallowed. My voice was hoarse. 'Spit your venom, then!'

Avirzah'e made a genuflection of respect and sat down again. 'My gratitude, Lady Gimel. Now, in plain words, we are on the brink of many calamities. Our minds are attacked by an unknown malady, for which there is no apparent cure. Human puppies are snapping at our ankles, puppies which may well grow into fierce, aggressive hounds with powerful jaws. Years ago, I suggested to the Parzupheim that we take hold of our own destiny and propel humanity into a position where they could no longer be a threat. My suggestion was ignored. Look what has happened! Can you sit there and, in all honesty, deny that the sickness and humanity's sudden aggressive interrogation might be connected? I don't think so. It is too coincidental. We have existed for centuries in this world, without one incidence of disease, or one human ever having the wit to question our origins or existence. Now, the question is, what event instigated these two dilemmas?'

I had to interrupt his speech. 'Avirzah'e, didn't the impulsive and irresponsible behaviour of certain crusading eloim, who for courtesy's sake I will not name, predate the incident with Oro Mervantes?'

Avirzah'e was silent for a moment. I raised an admonishing eyebrow. 'Well?'

'It is hardly relevant! Think of this, Gimel. The Watchers will have been monitoring our activities since we fled the other world. If they are not directly responsible for what is happening now, I suspect they have, at least, been waiting aeons for this moment. You can be sure they certainly intend to take advantage of the situation! Ask yourself this: who has kept the world free of their oppressive machinations, if not ourselves? If the eloim fall, the Watchers will swamp this world with their own philosophy, something which our people fought to prevent in the past. You think I am self-motivated in wanting to take drastic action, but this is not so. It is true we might have to kill in order to maintain the balance, but it is a vital unpleasantness. Your father feels my methods will bring about a dark age, but the Watchers would bring far worse I assure you. Without us, the world will fall into stagnation, and its people will succumb to the worst form of oppression. The Parzupheim know this, so I cannot understand why they are being so squeamish! Much as it pains me, I am forced to conclude they have become complacent and indolent over the centuries. In short, they are no longer fit to guide us.' He ended his speech quite breathlessly.

I wasn't sure whether to rage at Avirzah'e, humour him, or fly to Metatron immediately and betray him. 'I am puzzled as to why you have chosen me as a confidante for your heresy,' I said.

'Because the flame of life burns strong in you, that's why, and you are not a fool.'

'And you trust me?'

He nodded, smiling.

'Then it is you who is a fool, Avirzah'e!'

He shook his head. 'No. For all my weaknesses, I am never that. Soon, I will leave. For a while you will consider informing the Metatron of our conversation. Then, you will actually think about what I have said and you will realise I am right. Our people are threatened, Gimel. This situation involves more than just humanity and ourselves. We are caught between two blades, but I do not think the situation is irredeemable.'

'Why come to me now?' I asked. 'What do you need of me?'

He stroked his lips with a casual forefinger, pausing before answering. 'Your soulscaper, Gimel. At first I must admit I considered your plan to be without merit. I questioned whether a human soulscaper would be strong enough to confront the perils I am now convinced face our people. But I have reconsidered. In my opinion, this woman's ignorance of the Watchers would be her power, because she is not conditioned to fear them as we are. You are right in thinking the soulscape is the arena in which this battle might be fought and won. If the Watchers have penetrated this world, that is the portal they have used. You have groomed the soulscaper since her childhood, and I trust that your influence will have honed her abilities to perfection. Now, she is ripe for her task.'

'How do you know that?' I asked abruptly. I was aghast, not just at the ideas he was coming out with, but at the fact that he seemed to be familiar with Rayojini.

He shrugged. 'That is irrelevant.'

'I disagree!'

'Very well. Although I lack the benefit of a psychic link with Madam Rayojini, I have made prudent use of certain patron agents who roam Lansaal. I instructed them to make discreet inquiries about any soulscaper carrying the name Rayojini – perhaps it was a mistake on your part to divulge her name at the meeting at the Castile that day – and discovered that only one individual was of the appropriate age. I have followed her career with great interest. She is highly respected apparently, but of course you must be aware of this. I can't understand why you haven't summoned her here earlier.'

I felt as if he'd dug the ground out from beneath my feet. I was scrabbling helplessly for purchase in a world he had turned inside out. I was appalled he knew so much. 'Your remarks are indeed interesting,' I said, 'and deserve careful consideration. I must admit I had not envisaged bringing Rayojini into play until she was a little older, but perhaps events have accelerated to the point where we no longer have the time for that. However, I have to think about what you've said, Avirzah'e. Perhaps you would leave me now and allow me to contact you later.'

He frowned and then nodded, reluctantly. 'Very well, but please do nothing rash, such as running to Metatron about this. I am not concerned for my own safety, which is unassailable, I assure you, but for the security of far greater issues. If you try to impede me, the results could be fatal. I cannot urge you too strongly to remember this.'

I nodded. 'As you wish, Avirzah'e.'

After he'd gone, I sought solitude in my bedchamber, lying down among the draperies whispering in the afternoon breeze. I descended into trance and sought out my soulscaper. She was so bright! I knew she was drawing conclusions of her own about the strange events she was witnessing. Were these things the results of machinations of Avirzah'e's, or of a greater plan? I was unsure. He had seemed genuine enough but perhaps I underestimated his acting skill. Metatron had counselled patience; now, I wondered whether we should act. Not as Avirzah'e insisted, but in our own way. I could not believe Metatron and the Parzupheim were ignorant of the implications Avirzah'e had mentioned. No matter how forbidden it was even to think of the past, it must have occurred to them that the Watchers might be involved.

I walked with Rayojini in the land of Atruriey, even though she had effectively shut me out of her mind. I trailed her like a sad ghost. The Tartaruch was right about one thing; I would have to make contact soon.

125

That very night, I took my carriage to the family stronghold. I told Metatron everything Avirzah'e had said to me. He did not react as strongly as I had anticipated, but thanked me formally for giving him the information. I had a feeling I'd told him nothing he hadn't known already.

'Soon, I shall leave here,' he said. 'Already the preliminary waking calls are being sung to the Harkasites. Soon, I will lead them into the world.'

I made a sacred sign. 'Have you no other choice?'

He shook his head. 'No. Avirzah'e Tartaruchi is no fool, Gimel. His diagnoses are largely correct, but his treatment of the malady is misguided. He is aggravating the situation.'

'You are still convinced he is responsible for the phenomena in Khalt, then?'

'I would be stupid to dismiss it as a possibility.'

'So, you will deal with him?'

Metatron looked at me sharply. 'He is a mote, nothing more.'

'Maybe so, but a mote of disease infects the whole organism, eventually.' I resented Avirzah'e's meddling with Rayojini. I wanted Metatron to prevent him getting more involved.

Metatron rubbed his face wearily. 'I will do all that is necessary. If I find Avirzah'e or any of his kin in Khalt, they shall be dealt with summarily, believe me!'

I shuddered, trying not to think about what being 'dealt with' by the Harkasites might be like.

'Bring your soulscaper to Sacramante, Gimel,' Metatron said. 'As soon as you can.'

I hurried home and began to make preparations. The plan had long been perfected in theory. It was time for my beloved brother to face reality; he could no longer hide within his brush court. Much to my annoyance, Beth was out when I returned to the house. I immediately summoned Amelakiveh, Ramiz and Tamaris and asked them if they were aware of Beth's whereabouts. Ramiz said he thought my brother had gone to the opening night of an art exhibition in the outer courts of the Kaliph's palace. He was not expected home until late. I could do nothing until he returned, so I would have to issue a mind-chime to recall him. After a few minutes of concentration on the summons, which I knew had reached its target, I resentfully went to my bedchamber, taking Amelakiveh with me.

'Are you ready, lovely boy, for the work I have for you?' I asked him, stroking his face. His flesh bloomed with the vigour of life. I knew Beth and I had transgressed eloim code by what we had done to Amelakiveh. We had introduced him to the sup, made him like Tamaris and Ramiz through giving him thimbles of our blood, without asking permission of the Parzupheim. Any humans who were candidates for becoming special retainers had to be examined

126

thoroughly for taints and weaknesses. We excused our evasion of this procedure because we knew the boy would be instrumental in our plans concerning Rayojini, but I was unconvinced that would stand up as a defence should our action be exposed.

'I am ready,' Amelakiveh said, and flexed his fingers. 'I am tired of your house. I am looking forward to freedom.'

There was a darkness about him, a faint aroma of bitterness. I realised he was more potent a force, in his own way, than any smouldering Harkasite. 'You are my heresy,' I told him. 'You!'

Beth did not respond to my summons. Even though I had strengthened the call with my desperate need for his presence, he did not come home at all that night, but returned early in the morning. Tamaris informed me of this when she came to wake me. After a spare breakfast of bloodied milk, I requested Beth to join me in my salon, a request which he ignored. After he had kept me waiting for over an hour, I flew down to his room in person, intent on scolding him. I was met by a stranger.

Beth was in his sitting room. Ramiz was in attendance, half-dressed, which indicated Beth had recently supped. I directed a meaningful glance at Ramiz which prompted his swift departure. Beth, for some reason, would not look at me. 'You seem agitated,' he said, adjusting his clothes in a mirror. In the glass, his eyes were evasive and dark.

'If I am agitated, you are distinctly strange. What has happened?' I asked stiffly. He shrugged. 'Beth, I *needed* you last night. Why did you ignore me? The time has come! We have to pool our strengths now.' I had to admit he really didn't look fit enough to accomplish what we had to do. His hands were shaking, his face ashen. 'Tell me!' I demanded, in desperation.

'I have nothing to tell you.' The chill in his voice was terrifying. I realised that for the first time in our lives, we were not in accord. I ran up behind him and gripped his bony shoulders with my fingers, digging my nails into his flesh. He did not feel like he was mine any more.

'Beth, there is nothing you cannot tell me, nothing. I love you. Please, *speak to me!*'

'I can't Gimel,' he said, bowing his head. 'I really can't. But I can show you, if you like.'

'Then please do so.' I stepped backwards.

Wordlessly, he turned around to face me and began to unlace his shirt. There was a challenge in his eyes, as if he expected me to scream or lunge at him. The white skin of his chest was marked above the heart. I saw a large bruise there, the flower of the sup and, in its centre, there was a tiny wound. Someone had fed there. I closed my eyes and turned away. Not even I had ever supped upon my brother's ichor; it was an act so rare among eloim, and so potent, I had never imagined I would encounter it. It signified subjection, total surrender; it signified possession. In darker times, the Harkasites had fed upon each other to hone their powers; we had been told it had made them beasts. It was barbaric to feed upon each other; unclean. It encouraged morbid humours and hysteria. It prompted obsession. I could not believe Beth had let such a thing happen to him.

'Who?' I demanded. He did not answer. 'Did you taste them too?'

He nodded.

'Why?' I asked. It was such a small sound. There was no answer that he could give that would relieve my shock.

There was a short silence, and then Beth said, 'You went to Metatron yesterday, didn't you? You told him everything Avirzah'e said.'

The sound of that name cut me like a whip. I felt as if Beth had punched the breath out of my body. His words told me all I needed to know. I turned slowly to face him, and he was smiling at me. It was not my brother's smile.

'I have answered your question,' he said, 'satisfied your curiosity. Come, sister, embrace me now. Give me your love.' He held out his arms and simply because I knew I was not supposed to, I threw myself against him and hugged him fiercely. He was as unyielding as iron, and kept his arms outstretched.

'You must tell me, Beth,' I said. 'I have to know what happened.'

He gently pushed me away from him. 'I suppose you do,' he said. 'But your knowing will change nothing.'

'This is a spiteful act of revenge. You do realise that, don't you?'

'It will comfort you to think that, no doubt.' He sat down casually and crossed his legs, leaving his shirt unlaced so that the wound glared at me like a baleful eye. His tawny hair hung about his shoulders like combed silk. 'I went to the opening last night. An astounding display! You really must see it. Raphael has incredible talent, and will certainly go far.'

'Beth, I don't care a spilled drop about the paintings,' I said, in a low voice.

He shrugged. 'Avirzah'e was there . . .'

I nodded. 'That much is obvious.'

'He invited me back to his apartment. He wanted to talk to me. I must confess, the things he said were unbelievably controversial. Still, he speaks from the heart, and you have to respect that. He also talks sense.'

'You are wrong. It is your heart speaking now, not your mind!'

Beth shook his head. 'Oh no. Don't deceive yourself, sister. The heart did not become involved until later. We sat upon the floor, in candlelight, and talked deep into the night; we ventured into the darkest territories of conversation. We untombed the past. It was

128

fascinating. Then, it was the strangest thing, we both went quiet, as if everything that had to be said had been said.' Beth frowned. 'I looked at the Tartaruch. He seemed . . . somehow vulnerable, but also, he seemed to be a . . . potent warrior. A doomed and tragic figure. I did the only thing possible. I pledged him my allegiance. I gave him my strength. I opened up my shirt and said nothing.'

'What did he do?' I asked, more for interruption of the ghastly narrative than because the question was required.

'Why, he opened his own shirt too, of course. What did you think? It was a very . . . holy . . . time. We just stared at each other; we were staring at the potential more than anything, I think. Maybe, in another reality, we would have done no more than that. But it must have been preordained. I can't remember how, but suddenly we were lying next to each other and . . .' He paused and put his head on one side with a quizzical smile. 'Are you sure you want me to continue?'

I shook my head. 'No, I've heard enough.'

'I thought so.'

'You realise I can no longer allow you to have contact with the soulscaper, don't you?'

Beth laughed. 'And how do you propose to do that?'

His laughter enraged me. In an instant, I had leapt the distance between us and hit him hard on the face. His mouth dropped open in shock. 'Don't presume to try and compete with me, Beth!' I said. 'I am ready for you; both of you! If you try to interfere with Rayojini, I will take whatever action is necessary, however drastic. You can tell Avirzah'e I have accepted his challenge, and also that he has made a great mistake.'

My determination, and the reality of what he had done, became clear in Beth's mind; I could see it in his eyes. His mouth opened and closed, but issued no sound.

I turned to leave the room, but delivered a final remark, which I knew would hit him sorely. 'I do not blame you, Beth,' I said. 'I blame myself. Metatron warned me long ago of your weakness, and I never really believed him. Obviously, I was a fool.' Then, I closed the door behind me.

For once I worked alone, leaving Beth behind me, far behind me. The Tartaruch would pay for what he'd done, I would make sure of that. Before I initiated the procedure that would bring Rayojini to us, I saw, in Beth's eyes, a seed of sickness that filled me with fear. Of course, he came to my rooms begging for forgiveness and understanding. Of course, he pleaded for me to help him undo what he had done. But it was irreversible. I had to harden my heart and concentrate on the future. For the time being, Beth was lost to me, at least until Avirzah'e was dead. I felt so tired as I climbed the spiralling stairs to the highest tower of our house, so tired. I entered the small room where the windows are open to the winds, and lay down upon the black-veiled couch. Amid the lamentations of the elements, no more pitiful than those of my own heart, I willed myself to trance. I projected my personality into another body, one which even now mounted a swift Bochanegran steed in the yard below, and it took me travelling.

'. . . and winds with ease through the pure marble air his oblique way . . .'
Paradise Lost, Book III

The plains are lovely in the autumn; a sea of grass, moving like quicksilver. I rode the horse many leagues into the Kahra Flats, tassels of seeds around my thighs. It was like cleaving an ocean. For a while I could enjoy the physical sensations of the journey: sun on my hair; the smell of ripe grass; the chewing of the horse; the scream of wheeling birds. My body felt fit and supple; I enjoyed the sensation of wearing it.

The nomad trails are very easy to see from a height. Sometimes I would leave the flesh and let my soul soar into the body of a bird. Then I would look down, sick with vertigo, afraid, yet knowing I could not fall. The bird did not even feel me there, gliding on the waves of air, dipping and curling. I could not decide which tribe to concentrate upon, and realised that fate would have to take me in her hands.

It was a relief to be away from Sacramante. Metatron had left the city before me, leading the stuff of legends out into the world. I recognised the spoor of their passing. Now, for a time, my father had become Harkasite himself; I might not even know him if I saw him. The Harkasites had slept for centuries, perhaps dreaming of the time when Lord Sammael had led them against Mikha'il's legions, and the humans that had sought to oppress our race. Sammael himself slept on. As I rode in the sunlight, my hair warm around my shoulders, I thought of him, our estranged Lord. Was he aware of what was happening to us? Did he care? Was it heresy to wonder if someone should have tried to attract his attention, wake him up, make him help us? I could not believe he was dead, but if he still lived wouldn't the Parzupheim have approached him in his sanctuary? Perhaps they had, and had found him to be unwakeable, or perhaps he had refused to get involved. Now, his warriors, the Harkasites, followed a new general, whom I hoped was capable of controlling them. Metatron wanted them to gather information and, if necessary, deal with any situations they came across in the most expedient manner. It didn't sound beyond his powers — he was the strongest person I knew — and yet I still felt uneasy about it. The Harkasites were not like us; they were driven by a fanatical urge to protect eloimkind, but they lacked com-

131

passion, and respect for all human life. Their eyes missed nothing; they could not be lied to.

I released the horse to freedom and walked on, without food or belongings until my path crossed that of a roaming tribe. The spoor was recent. I followed it.

For a day or two I merely observed their routines, a shadow in the grass, and as luck would have it a night came when the men and women separated to conduct their personal mysteries. I observed the women at their rites.

It must be true that they are half-breeds, these people, because I recognised many corrupted eloim gestures in their ceremony. They were groping towards a light they would never uncover, but the passage of it was pretty. The women swayed and moaned, graceful as deer. I watched entranced for a while, although it was not with them that my objective lay.

The men had taken over a shallow cave for their rituals. At its threshold, a still pool, which was swarming with frogs and cuffed with scum, reflected the impassive countenance of the lady moon. When I came upon them, they were stamping in a circle outside the cave, a fire having been built in their midst. Their shaman was sitting on a rock beyond the circle, painted in ritual finery and naked but for a skirt of crow feathers. His face was fearsome, black and white, a skull. The outline of female breasts had been drawn upon his chest, to signify he was a receptacle for the spirit of Helat, their androgynous deity. To me, he looked like a sacrifice. The men would hurt him, I could tell. He was expecting that and was drugged with torpine essence to still the pain. Presently, certain of the stamping men assumed the personae of warrior knights, Harkasites, and picked up beautiful long knives, whose hilts were inscribed with symbols that were simple approximations of more powerful glyphs used among the eloim. One by one they danced by the shaman and lightly cut his flesh. The wounds were minor, but enough to make the blood flow. He began to chant, his voice shaking to the rhythm of the flashing knives. After a few minutes, he raised his hands. The men placed their knives on the ground and, between them, carried their shaman into the cave. I followed, unseen among them. I watched them cover him with a diaphanous shroud; they bowed and moaned before his body. Then, they left him alone to commune with the host of Helat. They hoped to invoke these immortal beings with the gift of blood; so wet and fresh upon the skin of their holy man. What could I do but approach him? Had I not been invoked?

For a while, I sat upon the rock by his side, listening to the concluding calls of the rite outside. Soon there was silence, for the men had melted out of the glade and gone to hunt among the grasses, sure in their hearts they were the supernatural scions of a god.

A single candle shivered in the cave, illuminating the still contours of the holy man lying on the rock. Blood had soaked into the shroud like water into a sponge. The stains looked like a map of the world – not this world, but some other, unknown place. As I watched, the countries grew, rising up from an ocean of dark warmth.

I lifted the shroud away from his face. He did not feel it. He was deep inside what the Tappish call the soulscape. I had him to myself, I could do whatever I liked with this man. Sweet pleasures. The body I inhabited quivered with interest. I, as a black silhouette against the feeble light, leaned over the shaman. I could see myself from all angles at once: attenuated, sleek, powerful. I kissed his lips, just once, and he exhaled abruptly through his nose, like someone coming awake from a deep sleep. Then I cast back the shroud from his chest and began to lick the skin.

The sweet ichor tasted of paint – an earthy, chalky tang. Gently, once the skin was clean, I sucked each wound the knives had made and the pure essence filled my mouth. My body awoke with a concentrated, keening tingle, while he, unable to resist the delicious thrill of my touch, filled up with desire. My head was aching, but in that moment I was as fully alive as a person can be, bursting with energy and sheer joy. I let him wake as our bodies joined, knowing all he could see was a dark shape above him; he would think me some avatar of the night, some incubus bringing him the forbidden thrill of unholy union. I told him, so quietly, that our communion was holier than all others, and he believed me utterly. Who would not? The evidence of sensation proved my words.

I rode him into the vales of ecstasy, urging him onwards with my thighs as if he were a horse between my legs. Stretch for the fastest gallop. Stretch! Gallop faster than time, my beloved victim. He ran till his heart would burst with the effort, and then I jumped him through the flame, releasing the reins of constraint.

His cry of repletion was a woman's scream, a woman in childbirth, a woman dying. He asked me: 'Who are you?' and I bent once more to lick the drying wounds.

'A traveller,' I said, 'who begs forgiveness for intruding upon your rite.'

'Why ask forgiveness when you were such an essential part of it?' he said. I saw he was an intelligent man, and pious. I did not answer, but smiled in the dying candlelight. He began to speak, as I had anticipated, of the bizarre things he had seen the past few days, and how my appearance seemed just another inexplicable strangeness. Would I vanish away with morning? I shook my head. No, I would not.

'And yet, I feel you are some part of the strangeness in the world,' he said, wondering.

I would not commit myself entirely. 'Maybe, I have seen things too,' I said, 'and maybe I can interpret some of them.'

'Tell me,' he said, but I kept quiet on that subject.

'The tribes look towards the Taps now for help,' I remarked.

'Some do, but not I,' he replied sternly. 'It may be that the activities of the soulscapers are the cause of the disruptions.'

I shook my head. 'Oh, no, they are not.'

'Are you a soulscaper?' he asked, suspicious.

'Not at all. Would that I were, for you need one.'

'Do I? By what authority do you say these words?'

'My own, but it is true.'

'Well, there are dozens of them roaming about. Shall I kidnap the next one I see?'

I laughed. 'Not the next one, sweet shaman. I will tell you which one.'

'How do you know?'

'Easy. You see, in essence, there is only one and already her feet are leading her towards you.'

'You know her?'

'Yes, though she doesn't know me. I will tell you about her.' In fact I told him very little, but it was enough for my purposes, nevertheless.

'With even step and musing gait, and looks
commercing with the skies, thy rapt soul sitting in
thine eyes . . .'
From *Il Penseroso*, Milton

Once I left the town of Yf, the Khaltish plains were warmed by a
ghost of summer; magically, the clouds moved southwards, leaving
the sky as blue and scintillant as polished sapphire. It was as if,
once Harof's soul had been freed, a foul and predatory breath that
had been souring the air passed on.

Mouraf had insisted on loading me up with goods: food, items
for barter and, suggested by Annec, a stone plaque which had been
elaborately etched with my mother's name the night before. Heavily
laden, I bade farewell to the Yflings and, to silence their entreaties,
I agreed to return in the spring, and join in with the celebrations
of their vernal religious festival. It was a lie, for in my heart I knew
I would not return, no matter how much I would like to. Since
I had stood in Mouraf's yard and faced the wind, since I had
acknowledged that something, *something*, was stirring in the world,
if not in the soulscape as well, I knew I had taken hold of the tail
of a dark and slippery serpent, one which might well turn and give
a fatal bite before I could analyse its venom.

The night before, I had lain awake into the chill hours before
dawn, thinking, yes, yes, it will become clear to me, it is getting
clearer *now*. Secure in my soulscaping philosophies, I was convinced
that simply by *deciding* to look for an answer to the soul-shreddings,
the non-deaths, I was sure to find it. The hunt itself was an irresistible compulsion because, as someone who stripped bare the most
secret imaginings of the human mind, I disliked mysteries. However, the very nature of the predatory force I had encountered in
Harof's withered soulscape, meant there had to be dangers – the
biggest being my lack of information. I could only hope there was
a simple explanation, but I was not without unease as I made my
goodbyes in Yf.

Very soon, however, the bright warmth of the day banished my
nocturnal misgivings and once out on the road, striding west into
the narrow mountain range that girdled the lower plains, my spirits
were soaring along with the wide-winged birds that rode the thermal
breezes, high above. Maybe there were new gods up there, too,
winging their way forward on the wind.

135

By noon the following day, I was already leaving the mountains behind. There had been little climbing, as the trails were well-defined and often trod. An old woman living in a cabin on a shelf of rock, where I paused for the night, had few tales to tell other than the usual gossip of weddings and funerals, none of which were remotely interesting. She did have a little icon, however, which she claimed had been left as payment by a traveller, some days before, for a night's lodging. 'And who is this?' I asked her, picking up the crude carving.

She made a sacred sign – a new one – and said, 'One of the lost children, madam, one of the lost.' I replaced the carving in its niche.

'And the child's name?'

'She has no name. Not yet.'

It was not really an uncommon thing to find.

I resumed my journey and made quick progress to the other side of the mountains. Nothing untoward occurred, and neither did I uncover any mysteries. In fact, I was beginning to wonder whether my dire premonitions in Yf had been nothing more than an emotional reaction to the unpleasant procedure I'd had to initiate with Harof.

Before me, the seemingly interminable plains of western Khalt, known as the Kahra Flats, rolled out to the horizon; the place where nomads roamed, and soulscapers trod carefully. Vast herds of beasts sailed the sea of waving grasses that hissed in the balmy breeze and whose feathery autumn tassels shook to fill the air with downy seeds. As I descended the foothills, I could see the plain was laced with the darker ribbons of flattened roads, where the great caravans from the Delta Lands carried their exotic produce to Bochanegra and the North-west. It was the first time I had travelled this way, having confined my activities to Lansaal and Atruriey for most of my career. This was a wild and beautiful place which, although flat, was blanketed in places by thick forest. Occasionally, there would be areas where eastern Khalts had come to farm the land, defending their territory from any nomads who objected to the Flats being enclosed. Settlers tended to be wary of travellers, because it was not unknown for nomad scouts to disguise themselves as southerners in order to penetrate the farmsteads and sow poison in the grain or water. Having been alerted of this by other soulscapers, I kept to the roads, ignoring any narrower tracks which would lead to settlements. Nomads, on the other hand, were gregarious and generally welcoming to strangers, as long as their rather unpredictable and superstitious instincts weren't aroused, and they didn't feel threatened. I was amply stocked with currency and victuals, so had no immediate necessity to ply my trade. Therefore, I intended to mingle with the nomads as much as possible, posing as a simple tinker with goods to barter in the West. This

136

was not because I yearned for company but because I sought clues to the non-deaths. If anything of that nature had occurred among the nomads, they would be bound to have exaggerated it and invested it with all kinds of ominous significance.

Chewing on a sweet plucked stem of honey-grass, I was sauntering dreamily along one of the wide roadways when I came across my first group of nomads. It was a glorious morning, the sun beating down from a cloudless sky on to the drying grasses that were shoulder-high beyond the road. Lizards and small rodents skittered across the path in front of me, diving from one stand of grasses to the next. I felt full of optimism; the world was a beautiful place and I, that morning, was its centre. I had been happily visualising myself returning to Taparak with the reason for the non-deaths, and its solution, written concisely in my notebook. It would presage a new age for soulscaping; all scapers would be summoned from around the world to discuss my findings, and new techniques would have to be developed and implemented. The daughter of Ushas would leave her mark upon history; she would change the course of soulscaping itself. I was quite content to be alone with these cosy thoughts, so much so that the noise of approaching people was a source of indignant irritation at first. The chaotic sounds of the nomad troupe, moving down a side track to join the main path, assaulted my peace long before I could actually see them.

It was customary for the head shaman to lead a tribe line, chanting rhythmically to dispel any demons blocking the road ahead. I identified the tall and feral-looking creature who first appeared before me as being of this category. He stepped out from the minor track, stooping in a hunter's crouch and warily scanning the road. Although I had stopped walking, and was standing only feet away from where he had emerged with an expression on my face which must have registered displeasure, the shaman made no sign that he had seen me. He warily stamped his left foot, which summoned the rest of his troupe. His immediate acolytes, trainees, wise women and smoke-readers, filed out behind him, shaking rattles and ringing handbells. Next, came the ritual dancers, swaying slowly to the rhythm of the chant, stamping and turning, with expressions of intense concentration on their faces. They milled in an unorganised crowd, absorbing me into their midst, yet there was still no recognisable communication between us. Finally, the remainder of the tribe appeared through the tassels of grass, children racing up and down beside the more intent adults. Goats, mules and long-eared sheep wandered haphazardly among the group, bleating and chewing, and there were skinny, furtive hounds with cautiously wagging tails. Only the dogs took any notice of me, warily sniffing my clothes before backing away. I began to smile; never had I encountered such a chaotic social entity as this. Then the shaman raised a

137

pointing finger in my direction, and for a moment or two the performance of his followers intensified, with much shrieking and shaking of rattles; women lamented at the sky, lifting their hair with clawed fingers. I folded my arms and watched, tempted to applaud, but wise enough not to risk offending them. Eventually, the shaman must have realised enough was enough and he raised his hand above his head. Everyone stopped leaping, groaning and wriggling, in order to stare at me. To a person more nervous than myself, it would have been a terrifying sight. I stepped forward and touched my brow and my lips with steepled fingers, addressing them in the ubiquitous Middle Khalt. 'Glad day, sir, to you and your people.'

He replied in a brutish tongue, pig-Khalt or somesuch, which I could barely understand. Gestures accompanied the speech, which sounded low and angry, much like the language used by the Abomina Priests of Lansaal, a minority cult, among whom the acts of self-denial and self-mutilation were much-loved. The shaman was an impressive sight. Like all Khaltish seers, he wore the tangled garb of a priestess and may even have been a eunuch. The Khalts, like the Taps, often feel moved to emasculate themselves when ascending to a higher plane of communication with the soulscape. His skinny, well-muscled body showed through rents in his robes. Grasses and flower stems had been woven through other threadbare areas, along with shells of many sizes (from the shores of the Bitter Lakes, no doubt), long shiny feathers from the tails of birds and hanks of hair, whose origin I preferred not to think too deeply about. After waving his arms and grumbling incomprehensibly for a few moments, he made a dismissive gesture with his hands and then spoke a few gruff words to one of his acolytes, a young girl carrying a tabor thick with rattle plates. She nodded and then addressed me directly in halting, yet perfectly enunciated Tappish.

'You are a soulscaper,' she said.

I wriggled my shoulders, noncommittally, but a gesture which perhaps would be taken as an answer. So much for being a tinker!

'Q'orveh speaks of the stealing of souls, not just the scaping,' the girl continued, oblivious.

Q'orveh, presumably, was the shaman. I was watching him covertly as the girl spoke. I realised this man, whether through his scent or soulscape emanations, had already kindled a spark of interest within me. It is always this way with soulscapers; we know immediately when we have met someone with whom we can resonate on a physical level. I had an itch in me to touch him; it had been a long time since I had given in love, and the shaman was a beautiful creature, all hair and quivering mania. I inclined my head in the noblest manner I could muster. 'Please relate to your master, he has no reason to fear or doubt my presence. I am not seeking work, but merely travelling across the plains of Khalt to the western lands. I would linger with your people, true, but only to share a bone or two.' I smiled. The shaman was peering at me suspiciously, flicking back his hair with his hands, shifting restlessly. I hoped he had not mutilated himself too badly.

He leaned down to listen to his acolyte's whispered message and then grunted a few words back. The girl addressed me once more. 'Q'orveh says you may walk with us,' she said, and then turned away, skipping back to her position in the troupe. With a resigned shrug, I shifted my carryback into a more comfortable position and joined a group of women who all looked at me with great suspicion. Rattles hailed into life, feet stamped, voices found their pitch, and the tribe moved off again towards the West, me in their midst, barely tolerated.

All day they walked, eating and drinking on the march, never pausing except to relieve themselves and even then, the men barely bothered to slow their pace, pissing confidently into the grass beside the road. The nomads are bizarre people. Had I not known better, I would have thought they'd somehow crossed from the soulscape into reality; they were so faery-like, so unpredictable and swift. There are folk tales to be found among most cultures of the known world about people who, while travelling on the plains of Khalt, have been tempted away from the road by nomad lovers – quick, lovely beings who tantalise and lure, who offer unimaginable pleasures and strange elixirs. These stories always end with the seduced individual, by this time a lovelorn wretch, being left alone in an unknown wilderness – generally with a destroyed mind, and with no way of finding their path home. I had always regarded these tales as being the result of severe culture clash, but marching along with these ragged, black-eyed tatter-sprites, I wondered, with a smile, if there were not more truth in them than I had credited. The nomads wore clothes the colour of Earth itself, but far from dull: leaf-green, rich red-browns, sandy yellows and duns. They were festooned with protective talismans, some of which gave off strong and disagreeable odours. Their goats, sheep and mules roamed uncontrolled among them, as if human themselves. The whole tribe just poured forward, a randomly moving mass, somehow managing to find order in its chaos and progress further up the road. Most of the men walked behind the holy people and their dancers, clad in trousers of deer-hide pelts that were roughly sewn together, their long, tangled hair hanging over bare bronzed backs to show off their tribal marks. These included tattoos from rites of passage, or even metal rings that pierced the skin in the most unlikely places. None of the men, not even the older ones, wore beards. Perhaps it was in their bodyscape, bequeathed through the generations, for them to be clean-skinned. The children were often naked.

By late afternoon I had fallen into the rhythm of the chanting up ahead, and was walking in a dream, happily investigating old memories and thinking up new ones. The sun sank into the hissing grasses around us, and we came to a place where a finger of forest reached out from some distant higher ground, invisible from the road. Here the tribe turned off the track and snouted around for somewhere to make camp. It was clearly a site used regularly by nomads, because the grass had all been nibbled short, and the trees bore signs of having been cut for their wood. No one had paused here for a while, however, because the black ashes of cooking fires were obviously months old. I was just wondering where I should erect my bivouac which, I must confess, I did not intend to sleep in if at all possible, when one of the nomad women finally deigned to speak with me. She was young and imp-faced, with tangled red hair, dressed in a motley of russet rags – layers of skirts, leggings and shirts – and had marched by my side all day; in nomad terms our proximity on the march probably meant she could now consider herself an old friend of mine, although her first words, in Middle Khalt, did little to inspire closeness.

'I'm Sah'ray. Soulscaper killed a kidling of ours once.'

'Oh.' I didn't know quite how to respond. Her tone was not accusatory. 'I'm Rayojini. Where are you people travelling to?' She accepted this change of subject smoothly.

'Bochanegra garter lands, the Strangeling. Have business there, does Q'orveh. Has a price to pay, they say.' She fixed me with a steely eye. 'So do you, I'm thinking. Told it to him loud on the road, you did.'

I was again unsure how to react, rather flustered that my carnal interest in the shaman had been so obvious. Then Sah'ray grinned and pawed my arm. 'You can share my space, if you like. Help me make it stand?'

I nodded. 'Thank you.' I considered it would be useful to become closer to this woman, although I still had plans of my own about where I would be spending the night.

Sah'ray chose a spot between two trees, where the branches hung low, thick with ripening berries. She told me they were not good to eat, which was slightly erroneous, as I recognised them as being an ingredient for a particularly efficacious remedy against lung-thickness. Perhaps I should impart this knowledge to one of the healers at a later time. I helped Sah'ray erect her tepee, which seemed barely large enough for one person to occupy, never mind the pair of us. I dearly hoped I would not have to share it with her. Nearby, the cooking pit had been lit, and the resinous fragrance of burning wood filled the air. Some of the tents being pitched around us were large enough to contain several families, others were tiny, like Sah'ray's. It seemed there were no social guidelines concerning whether people should sleep communally, or alone. I would have to question the girl about this.

140

Once Sah'ray's tepee was firm and solid among the trees, I asked her, 'Where do I find him?'

As I had anticipated, she needed no more detail than that to understand my question. She pointed through the smoke at a large, skin-coloured tepee of bleached hide, whose flanks were painted with the tribe's personal glyphs and seals.

'Thank you,' I said. 'Do you think that now would be a good time for me to request an audience?'

Sah'ray smiled at my choice of words; she was obviously not as ill-informed and ignorant as she appeared. 'Oh, he'll speak with you. Always looking for soulscapers now.'

'Really? Why is that?'

She screwed up her nose, clearly reluctant to tell me. 'The dead have come down from the trees,' she said, her expression betraying she did not think I'd believe it.

I briefly touched one of her hands. 'Then of course I must speak to him.' Her words intrigued me. Like many nomad tribes throughout the world, the Khalts left their dead on wooden platforms high in sacred trees, so that the birds of the air could pick at the flesh, thus releasing the spirit into whatever heaven the tribe believed in. (There were many heavens available to the people at that time.) Bearing in mind that the nomad shamans had never, to my knowledge, actively sought consultation with a soulscaper, I wondered whether I had already uncovered one of the clues I sought. I did not believe for one instant that the dead were actually climbing down from their perches, but perhaps one or two cases of the non-death had occurred, blurring the lines between what was death and what was not. It seemed the obvious explanation, and fortuitous I should come across it so soon.

The night had moved in quickly around us. I tongued the wind and it tasted of Mouraf's orchard, a cold vein coming down from the mountains, hiding fatal secrets. 'Go now,' Sah'ray said, pushing me away. 'Before we eat. You may share your food with me.'

'Take what you need from that pack,' I said, gesturing at my belongings. She would investigate whatever else I was carrying, of course, but I did not think the nomads were thieves, so I was happy to let her satisfy her curiosity. Waving to her cheerfully, I moved off through the trees towards the shaman's tent.

A circle of men and women, whom I took to be the elders of the tribe, sat around the entrance. As I approached, they looked at me through tangled hair with fierce eyes, and stopped speaking amongst themselves, but two old women shuffled aside to allow me to squat down among them. I thanked them with a murmur and bowed my head, lacing my fingers over my knees. Conversation was not resumed, but a smoking mix rolled in dry leaves was passed around, of which I inhaled too deeply. It seemed my harsh coughing awoke something within the tent. Abruptly, the flap parted and a youth came out, prompting my companions to look away. This told me quite a lot about the boy; he was not a favourite with the elders. In fact his position within the tribe was immediately obvious to me through something associated with the arrogant stance, and the down-sweeping gaze with which he raked the gathering. I was sure that if he was an acolyte, it was to sciences other than the religion of the tribe. Although he was dressed in similar garments to those seated around me – feather-and-bead decorated rags and tatters – his appearance was somehow tidier, as if he usually dressed himself in a very different manner. His long dark hair was sleeker, too, his skin finer than that of the nomads. He looked at me and I went cold. Never had I had to drop my eyes from someone else's stare before. I felt absurdly young and awkward. I felt like a dog.

'You,' he said, in strangely-accented Middle Khalt. 'Q'orveh commands your presence.'

I knew, even though I was staring at the crushed grass at my feet and not at him, that he was speaking to me.

The interior of the tepee was thick with the smoke of burning perfume oil, and some other, mind-stimulating substance. Q'orveh reclined on a mound of cushions and brightly coloured rugs, where he was being rubbed with aromatics by a female acolyte. Treasures were heaped at random around the floor: delicate metal jugs and censers; piles of fringed silk; and many articles of carved dark wood. The youth who had summoned me sank down behind me and I could feel his attention riveted on my back like needles; the skin between my shoulder blades prickled and crawled.

'A woman of the tribe told me you might wish to speak with me,' I said, because it did not appear Q'orveh was going to initiate verbal communication between us. I wondered whether he understood Middle Khalt, but if his acolytes could speak Tappish, it was unlikely any dialect of Khalt would be strange to them. I began thinking of the legendary seducers, who stole people away with desire, and wondered whether the girl who had first spoken to me on the road, in Tappish, could have been a product of such a liaison. I spoke again, in Tappish.

'What tongue would you prefer me to speak in?'

The shaman laughed. 'Whatever you choose,' he replied in faultless Bochanegran.

'You travel widely,' I said.

'We are nomads.' He nodded at the girl, who was kneading one of his thighs. She stood up, wiping her hands, and went outside.

'So how may I help you?' I asked.

'You can't,' he replied. 'But I speak to people whenever I can; to gather news, to listen to their opinions. But I do not believe anyone can help, as such. We are living a shaping-time, soulscaper. Our lives are moving, all of our lives. Gods march down the road

142

from Bochanegra, they pour like wine down the road, and strange things happen along the way.' He paused as his girl came back into the tepee carrying a pitcher and cups. 'You drink?'

I didn't know what he was offering, and I had heard that some of the stuff they brewed could be positively evil, but nodded all the same to be polite. '*Strange things*,' I said, as the girl poured the dark beverage into cups. 'Such as?'

He did not look at me as he spoke. 'The air is full of beings we cannot see. More than usual. Others think this way too. The shamans of many tribes have gathered to discuss the phenomenon. Also, we find blood upon the grass in unusual places, and mourning things trail us, lamenting, but there is never anything to see. A virgin became pregnant and she gave birth to a creature that was half-deer.'

'In your tribe?' I was quite shocked. He spoke so seriously.

'No, not this tribe.' He shook his head. 'Now, you disbelieve my words.'

True enough, although I did not think he was deliberately trying to deceive me. However, now was not the time for debate or education. 'Far from it,' I said. 'I too believe there is movement in the world, strange things *are* happening, and not just to your people. I am anxious to discover the cause.'

'You think it is something to do with soulscape phantoms, no doubt.'

'It is possible, but I am not convinced. I do think whatever *is* happening has been brewing for a long time, for years, maybe.' I took a drink from the cup and it was not bad; sweet and fiery.

Q'orveh drank also. 'I have found many strange things in my path,' he said, and he was looking beyond me at the youth sitting against the tepee flap. I shivered.

'Perhaps such things should be left upon the path and not picked up,' I replied lightly, and buried my nose in the cup. Perhaps I had been too forward. I could feel the boy's attention quicken; the needles had become daggers. Think what you like, I thought. You cannot harm me, boy. I visualised a light of protection around my body and the effects of his personal power dwindled instantly; I no longer ached from unseen darts.

'Sometimes we have no choice in the matter,' Q'orveh said. 'Sometimes it is destiny.'

'I prefer to shape my own destiny,' I said, hoping he wouldn't be offended.

He shrugged. 'Each to their own beliefs. So, tell me what you have seen and heard concerning strange events.'

I was reluctant to tell him. It had been remiss of me not to realise he would believe himself to be the interrogator, rather than be content to answer my questions. The non-deaths were soulscaper business. I groped around for something to say. 'Well . . . as you

143

have said, people talk of spirits in the air, evil spirits perhaps. . . .'

Q'orveh laughed. 'I am not a fool, woman! Soulscapers don't believe in spirits! What have you heard? Tell me!'

'Strange deaths,' I said dryly.

'And what is strange about them?'

I had been staring at the rug beneath me, now I looked up and fixed him with what was intended to be a commanding stare. He was smiling back at me. I had been stupid to underestimate him. 'Q'orveh, there are some things I cannot speak of that are connected with my craft. Please respect this.'

He frowned and nodded, waved a hand at me. 'Of course. Tell me what you can.'

'Deaths that are not deaths.'

'The dead walk.'

'Not exactly.'

'But they do!'

I closed my eyes and made an assuaging gesture. 'As you wish. I have a feeling, Q'orveh, that there are predators about.'

We looked at each other keenly; it was a long, long moment. He would have nodded at me, but obviously couldn't, and merely blinked twice.

'Soulscape predators?' he asked lightly, as if I were the one with the ridiculously superstitious belief-system.

'Acting through people, maybe. I can't explain. But something.' Even as I talked to him, ideas were tumbling through my head; he was just a sounding board. Yes! I thought, soulscape predators, a consensual enemy, a mind-sickness of vast proportions, passed from person to person like a disease. Maybe?

'So, in your wisdom, soulscaper, what do you suggest we do?'

His question took me off-guard. 'I will have to observe,' I said.

'Mmm, we don't know what to do either,' he answered, with a kindly smile.

Q'orveh was handsome. I wanted him, and even once he'd made it clear our business was over for the time being, I hung around making light conversation in the hope that he would reciprocate. My own voice sounded ludicrous in my ears as I asked him pointless questions about sheep and mules. He must have been aware of my intentions, but I could not work out what he was thinking. He took time to consider his answers, no matter how banal the inquiry. Perhaps he was mocking me. I know the limits and strengths of my own power, and how to exert it to kindle desire, but all my attempts to use it on Q'orveh just seemed to fizzle out. Maybe there was *another*, somewhere; someone whose claim could not be breached. I doubted strongly whether it was the female acolyte who'd fawned over his body, or even the silent, deadly youth at my back whom I had surmised Q'orveh feared in some way. Disappointed with myself and him, I eventually abandoned my efforts and took my leave. Q'orveh said we would have to talk again at some other time. We would indeed. I had hoped that I'd be spending the night in Q'orveh's tent, but now I'd have to take advantage of Sah'ray's offer, after all. A pity. It left a sour taste in my mouth as I ducked out of the shaman's tent and into the clear night. I inhaled deeply. Was I losing my touch? Two failures in such quick succession did not rest easy with me. Admittedly, there was nothing I could have done about Harof, but I had never been unsuccessful in a seduction attempt before.

I paused outside the tent before making my way back to Sah'ray. I needed time to indulge in a little analysis of my conversation with Q'orveh. Then, a voice came up out of nowhere and hissed intimately in my ear, cruel as truth. 'He cannot please women. You were wasting your time.' I jumped and looked round swiftly. The silent youth had crept out of the tent behind me. He must have stood and watched me for several moments before hissing at me. I shuddered involuntarily.

'How assiduously you defend your territory,' I said, quite sharply. A strong smell of ambergris emanated from his body; surely not a perfume the nomads could have access to? I doubted whether they had much of value to barter.

He shrugged. 'Not *mine* – just a park to wander through, that I enjoy from time to time.'

I had no answer for that. The youth snickered in the darkness. 'You want a man? Find one in your soulscape, sister.' Then, he was gone. I shivered; suddenly time condensed, convulsed, and I was sixteen years old again, my body skewered by a dream. A man from my soulscape . . . Even though I had developed my own explanations for the imaginary ravishment I had suffered at the hands of the Metatronim, some primitive part of me which I could not control and which burst forth into my mindscape at unexpected moments still believed I had lost my virginity in that dream. Was it coincidence that Q'orveh's boy had invoked a memory of that time, or had his remark been deliberate? I found myself wondering more keenly about him. Q'orveh had intimated he had found the boy upon the road, and there had been undercurrents of fear and coercion in the few words he had spoken about it. I reviewed what I had learned. The nomads had encountered peculiar things; most of which they had, as I had already anticipated, exaggerated and expanded. However, I was intrigued by the way Q'orveh had associated the migration of gods with the phenomenon. The boy had been found upon the road; I would have to discover in what way he had managed to become annexed to the tribe, given that Q'orveh clearly had mixed feelings about him. The boy seemed to have considerable power or influence and, in some way, resented my arrival. There could be many reasons for that, of course, some

145

of them depressingly mundane, but there was no doubt he had intimidated me, a fact I was far from comfortable with. It would be easy to give in to the romantic fancy that he was some kind of dark vapour, who had cleverly penetrated the defences of the nomads, and resided in their midst as an unsavoury infection. I felt a compulsion to remove it – him – permanently. Although I knew there were dangers in following this path of thought, my instincts insisted the boy was somehow instrumental in whatever was happening. Also, how dare he laugh at me!

I slept very badly on the first night; Sah'ray had kicked my legs continually, whimpering in her sleep. Fortunately, her tent was larger inside than it appeared, although she was clearly used to having it all to herself. If she had guessed my intentions concerning the shaman, she was sensitive enough not to comment upon them and had made me most welcome when I'd crept in from the night after leaving his tent. The food she had prepared for me was rather congealed, however.

The tribe emerged from their tents at dawn, some of them seeing to the first meal of the day, others packing up the camp, preparing for another day's travel. Young men and women danced in the damp ashes of the previous night's fire to release any lingering flame spirits, and there was a great feeling of imminent departure all around us; in the air as well as in the camp itself. I crawled out of Sah'ray's tepee, stretching and yawning, stiff as wood, and yearning for a draught of water because Q'orveh's liquor had shrivelled my mouth as I'd slept. There was a spring some distance off, where twittering people had gathered to draw water, flushing themselves down with it as they stood in the springy grass along the banks. I sauntered up slowly, admiring the wet, naked bodies shivering in the cool morning; all laughter was shaky because the air was chilly enough to set everyone's teeth chattering.

Q'orveh's boy was squatting by the stream. He was fully clothed, although his trousers were wet to the knees. His hair was tied back neatly at the nape of his neck. I recognised him instantly because he glowed with dark. From yards away, I could tell he was aware of my approach, prompting me to think, 'Well, I have made an enemy here.' Indignantly, I walked right up to him and said, 'My sleep was peculiarly free of dreams.' He was rinsing his face in the stream and did not turn for a moment or two, leaving me unacknowledged for long enough to feel insulted. Then he sprang to his feet, causing me to jump back, uncontrollably, in alarm.

He grinned. 'Come and see this,' he said, and leapt over the stream. I made a sound of irritation, because my heart was still hammering with shock. I'd thought he was going to attack me. Squatting down, I took a few handfuls of the pure water, which revitalised my palate and my spirit. The boy watched me silently from the other side of the stream, hands on hips. Then, when I had drunk, he said. 'Well, follow then. The others will be moving off soon and I suppose you'll want to eat before.' He sauntered off into the knee-high scrub, confident that I would follow him. I did so, without qualm. No way could I allow this creature to see I was wary of him. Q'orveh had made that mistake; I had no intention of doing so.

The sounds of the tribe members by the stream faded very quickly, swallowed up by the thick, green murk of the forest. Birds were calling through the morning, drawing up the sun from rest. Animals rustled away from our path. I kept a fair distance between us. The boy had the self-assured grace of a person whose body is often fondled and admired. It was as if he'd been trained to be an actor or a dancer, or had at least been well-schooled in the arts of the flesh by one.

We ducked into deeper growth, scrabbled, almost bent double, through a tangle of thorny shrubs, finally emerging into a rough clearing. I had been able to smell something distasteful for a few minutes; now I understood why. This was a nomad burial circle. Platforms about ten feet off the ground ran like a balcony around the trees, littered with indistinct and colourless shapes. I have no fear of the dead, but I do respect them and kept my eyes averted after a quick glance.

'Why have you brought me here?' I asked. I had a feeling he intended to frighten me.

'Do you believe the dead can walk again?' he replied.

'Do you really want an answer from me? Is that why I'm here?'

He smiled. 'Look, one of us is going to have to answer a question. I've brought you here so you can see. Soulscapers see much more than the normal person, they say. Tell me what you see.'

'You are not a normal person,' I said. 'You are playing with me. I do know this, boy. You are a shadow.'

He laughed. 'A shadow am I? What kind?'

'A dark one, naturally. '

'In that case, aren't you afraid I might have brought you here to hurt you?'

'No, because I am more powerful than you. I actually still believe you are jealous because I wanted your master last night. You are playing and you are a snake.'

'Please answer my question. I want to know what you think.'

We are not communicating at all, I thought. I don't know what we're doing. Still, I wandered to the nearest tree, put my hand upon the bark and gazed upwards to the platform. It creaked slightly and there was a sudden rattling, whirring sound as a bird flapped out of the foliage. I did not receive any bad feelings particularly; this place was truly dead. 'If corpses really are climbing down from the trees, this is not a place where it has happened,' I said.

147

'But then, I expect you know that already.'

'You will be needed soulscaper,' he answered. I looked at him sharply, and realised that he was not of Khaltish stock; he was too pale, his eyes were too wide, lacking the catty, slanty look of the nomad. His hair was matt black, an absorber of light.

'Do *you* need me, Shadow?' I asked, teasing. 'Is that the reason for this performance?'

He shook his head, a grin splitting the serious expression on his face.

'I don't need anyone, soulscaper. I'm just telling you, so you'll be prepared.'

I nodded, warming to the game. 'So tell me, what *is* happening in the world. Your master doesn't know. Do you?'

He twitched – no other word for it. 'No, I don't know. I only watch. Whatever is happening won't be solved in this reality, I do know that.'

The pertinence of his remark astounded me. He was probably right. I folded my arms and gazed around the clearing. The dead do not walk, I was sure of that. 'So you have shown me. What *exactly* you expected me to learn from this, I am unsure, but I will remember the place. Now, I am hungry.' I turned around and headed back into the trees. I expect he followed me, though I did not look.

'Of forests and enchantments drear, where more is meant than meets the ear . . .'
From *Il Penseroso*, Milton

Q'orveh had said I could not help him, and yet his people came to me steadily, relentlessly, from the moment we trod the same path, asking about my art, and often begging me to exercise it. Because they were travelling westwards and I was intrigued, both by the rumours flying in the air and the people themselves, I elected to join them for a while – perhaps even until we reached the Strangeling. There was much to record in my notebook, and even as I wrote I visualised myself reading the words aloud to the scryers back in Taparak when I returned. Sah'ray was glad to share her company and her tepee, although she was a restless person who disturbed my nights. Very soon, however, I became adept at avoiding her flailing limbs, even while half-asleep.

I would not have said the nomad Khalts were a people often prey to the Fear. They had their own rituals and customs for dealing with it, which seemed effective. Their shamans were powerful. Strangely, I learned that none of these holy people were female – wise-women were another caste entirely. And yet all nomadic shamans were expected to take on a female rôle, even going so far, as I had suspected, as emasculating themselves. Perhaps because of this, they possessed a unique mystery, a finely tuned polarity of gender. Khaltish shamans were, on a spiritual level, both sexes. One thing I learned later was that the dark-shadowed boy had lied; Q'orveh did know how to please a woman.

The tribe is an extended family in Khalt. I had joined the Halmanes. They claimed their blood was mixed with ground-sylph stock, because sometimes children would vanish, drink blood or turn into animals. I saw no immediate proof of this, but being in their company made me feel as if I had stepped into another world – the soulscape itself perhaps. The nomads had the unpredictable, surreal ambience of soulscape creatures. The Halmanes were destined for a meeting with another tribe – the Toors – in order for their shamans to commune over a marriage or two to be arranged, and religious celebrations to be shared. Sah'ray told me that everyone would wear knives in their hair during this meeting. Relations were delicate among the tribes and could often dissolve into conflict. The nomad Khalts are a deeply religious breed, although their

149

beliefs do have a flavour of defiance. Often, I felt they mocked their god. Rituals generally involved some kind of pantomime, usually of divine beings making fools of themselves. Grinning, moronic masks, pendulous false breasts and phalluses abounded in such rites. The men and women had their own mysteries, which were exclusive to gender, but any woman walking the path with them was automatically admitted to the women's rites. It was taken for granted I would participate.

After my encounter with the Shadow, which had amused and stimulated me rather than caused the discomfort I'd expected, I ate with Sah'ray, and then joined the tribal line for the day's travelling. Sah'ray kept me by her side, linking her hard, skinny arm through mine. She was eager to talk about herself and was anticipating finding a man at the coming celebration.

'I have no desire to marry outside the tribe,' she told me, 'but it is time for a kidling, and Q'orveh rewards those of us who bring new blood to the family.'

'Rewards in what way?' I couldn't help asking.

'He elected my friend, Madlin, to his inner circle for a moon or two. She took a prominent part in the women's rites because of that. It is said he gives red liquor to the favoured.'

'Red liquor?'

She tapped her wrist. 'The life fluid. Blood.'

I tried not to grimace. 'Blood-drinking seems to play a prominent part in both your rites and your legends.'

She nodded. 'It is the sylph in us. We are an old race. If you know the magicks, you can be immortal. Some of us achieve that, but most of us have forgotten how. It's said we are under a curse which makes us forget this important thing.'

'Have you seen an immortal nomad, Sah'ray?'

She gave me a sneaky look. 'How would I know if I had? They would disguise themselves, wouldn't they?'

I shrugged. She had a point, I suppose.

What interested me more than the old legends were the new rumours and stories that were springing up: blood places, mutant births, angry spirits. As I got to know the Khalts, I began to wonder whether it was simply part of their racial behaviour to surround themselves with these stories. Perhaps it was not a new phenomenon after all. Sah'ray, naturally, was not loath to talk to me about it.

'The shamans say things have been building up for years, like an energy. Now, it cannot be contained. We have seen many strange things.'

'Such as?' I prompted, probably needlessly.

Sah'ray wrinkled her nose to think. 'There have been deaths that are not deaths among us for several seasons.'

150

'Non-deaths?' I asked excitedly.

Sah'ray nodded. 'You could call them that. They are like the Sacred Paling, but not so. It is like a Holy Death that begins but does not end. Do you understand?'

It astounded me that these primitive people had been drawing virtually the same conclusions about the non-deaths as myself. Q'orveh had deceived me; he knew more than he had suggested. 'Yes, I think I understand,' I said, grimly. 'How many have there been among your people?'

'Maybe five since the last Farless – that's what you call winter. Three of them were children, which is unusual.'

'Indeed. What else have you encountered?'

'Blood places. The grass is flattened and there are the marks of great carnage, but no flesh. The blood is always wet, as if whatever happened only *just* happened. A couple of times we've heard other tribes approaching us at night. We hear the road-singing. Nobody sings the road at night. Nobody travels after dark unless in fear and then they wouldn't sing, they'd be silent. When you go out of your tepee to take a look, there is nothing at all to see. Then the sounds just stop. We crossed the path of Sho'wl tribe, two moons back, and they were jumpy as deer. Maybe too much like deer. Their shaman told Q'orveh one of their girls had got pregnant and her child had four legs and hooves.'

'Ah, the mutant virgin birth.'

'He told you that, then.'

'Yes. He told me that. Now, tell me something else. Tell me about the black-haired boy in Q'orveh's tent.'

'Keea?'

'I don't know his name. He is not one of you.'

'It is Keea; there is only one boy in Q'orveh's tent now. He came to us a short while back. It is to do with the men's mysteries. I don't know about that and couldn't tell you if I did.'

'He spoke of the dead coming down from the trees.'

Sah'ray visibly shivered. 'Q'orveh tells us it is part of the non-death. Perhaps people have sent their dead to the trees when they haven't really been dead, and they come down again. Keea knows something about this, which is why Q'orveh keeps him close.'

'What does he know?'

Sah'ray gave me a keen glance. The urgency in my voice must have alarmed her. 'You ask a lot of questions, Rayo. Why do you want to know so much about us?'

I could see no point in lying. 'Let us just say I too have encountered those who have suffered the non-death. In eastern Khalt. It is horrible and I want to know why it's happening.'

'You must speak some more with Q'orveh, then.'

I nodded. Paused. 'Another question, Sah'ray. Is it possible to speak with Q'orveh when Keea isn't there?'

151

An unspoken knowledge passed between us. She pulled a rueful face. 'Not easy, but I have friends in the inner circle. No promises, but I'll see what I can do.'

That evening, we paused again in a habitual nomad resting-place. After we'd erected the tepee and Sah'ray was preparing us something to eat, I sat down, with my notebook on my knees, and reviewed what I had learnt. It seemed my instincts about Keea were right, or was I deceiving myself about him? I would have to observe him more closely. It was possible he wasn't human at all, but if that was so, *what* was he? I certainly didn't believe he was a soulscape emanation who'd taken on flesh. Still, it was not unheard of for great concentrations of thought to produce manifestations in the physical world, and the widespread panic caused by the strange events occurring all over the place would certainly be capable of producing the required power. Greater implications seemed to loom within my head; approaching swiftly, but under a cloud.

Sah'ray brought me a broadleaf full of minced goat. She sat down beside me, licking her greasy fingers. I ate carefully. Khaltish cuisine tended to be rather gritty, they were not too fussy about what they threw into their cooking pots. 'You must go to Q'orveh's tepee again tonight,' Sah'ray told me.

I was surprised. 'You have gained me private access so quickly?'

She shook her head. 'No, but I have talked to someone. You must become part of Q'orveh's talking-wheel. Keea will be there. Keea is always there, but you must become so regular a visitor to the talking that you will be invisible to him.'

'I see. What do your people think of Keea?'

She shrugged. 'Nothing. He just is. It's you that wants him out of the way, not us.'

There were questions I wanted to ask the shaman and they referred back to a subject I was already keenly interested in. I already knew that the majority of religious people, whatever their particular creed, reacted violently against the bodies of their Holy dead being inspected. It was very unfortunate that the only people objective and rational enough to study the condition – the guild leaders in Taparak – never had local corpses at their disposal. Recently I had been mulling over the idea that the Holy Deaths and the non-deaths were connected. Now it seemed Q'orveh might have reached the same conclusion. I felt it was time to establish exactly what the Holy Death was, in order to understand what the non-death might be. Perhaps Q'orveh would be receptive to my ideas, and would even let me examine one of the corpses should the opportunity arise, but instinct cautioned me to keep my thoughts to myself and him alone. I needed privacy in which to speak with him about it.

As Sah'ray instructed, I presented myself at the shaman's canopy

152

that night and was again admitted. The tent was full of people, tribe elders, both men and women; acolytes of the shaman clustered together, heeding the wisdom being spoken. Keea was a vibrant, dark presence by the tent curtain. The discussions involved only tribal gossip: speculations about what other tribes were doing, arrangements for the coming celebration. I was not called upon to speak, although Q'orveh did acknowledge my presence as I entered the tent. I would have to be patient.

The meeting with the Toors nomads was destined to take place at an especially sacred nomad site, known as Helat's Sink. Helat was a deity worshipped by all the nomad tribes. It took us only three days to reach the location, during which time I was frequently approached by members of the tribe requesting my services. Sah'ray was delighted by this and decided to manage my appointments. Each evening a few people would queue outside her tent, and she would usher them inside, one at a time, where I sat burning a minor fume. Generally these people wanted no more than simple mind-purifying rituals from me; they were unnerved and jumpy. I was happy to comply and, while burning assuaging fumes that calmed the mind, would murmur some gentle, reassuring words and mass-age the face and scalp of my clients. I was rather concerned that, by my undertaking this work, Q'orveh and his healers might think I was undermining their rôle within the tribe. I remained alert for signs that I was causing upset within the shamanic circle, but picked up no whisper of reproach.

One night, as I attended the talking-wheel, after having worked on a couple of people, Q'orveh commented that the fume-smell I carried into his tent on my clothes helped him relax. I took that, warily, as guarded approval of what I was doing.

Helat's Sink was an enormous crater in the plains as if, in ages past, some heavenly body had crashed to earth there. Its creased sides descended steeply to a wide, flat expanse which, but for a cleared area where nomads can pitch their camps, was mostly cov-ered by forest and scrub. A large lake dominated the centre of the crater, which Sah'ray claimed was bottomless. Many shrines had been built around the sides of the Sink next to the lake, and even within the forest itself, some of which were now falling into decay. All bore the signs of recent offerings on their altars.

A road had been hacked into the side of the Sink and spiralled down at a gentle curve; it took considerable time for us to reach the bottom. I noticed a palpable change in the atmosphere as we descended; the chanting of my companions took on a lower note.

There was plenty of space for several tribes to make camp in the Sink without feeling too close to each other. The Toors had already arrived and erected their tents. The usual riot of children and animals milled beside the lake, and I noticed that the Toors used wheeled transport, for there were about a dozen hide-covered wagons standing around. To me, the Toors were indistinguishable in appearance from the Halmanes. This surprised me, seeing as Sah'ray made such a fuss about tribal identity. Both tribes made a great show of ignoring each other as the Halmanes made their way around the lake to an unoccupied spot. I wondered whether this presaged some kind of conflict, but Sah'ray reassured me by explaining mutual lack of recognition was polite behaviour until the point at which the shamans had greeted each other. Among the Toors I noticed several people who were clearly foreign travellers like myself, although they were too far away for me to ascertain what race they were. I wondered whether any of them were soul-scapers.

We erected our tents and fetched water from the lake before any approach was made to the Toors. An atmosphere of excitement was building up. Eventually Q'orveh emerged from his tepee with a straggle of keening entourage, and stalked magnificently over to the sprawling, decorated tent of the Toorish shaman beside the lake. Sah'ray and I linked arms and, with the rest of the Halmanes, edged forward to watch. Likewise the Toors stopped what they were doing and gathered nearby. Q'orveh was admitted to the shaman's tent and at this signal everyone sat down to wait. Naturally the two shamans spent considerable time catching up on gossip, which meant we had to sit around for over an hour.

Sah'ray, noting my impatience, began to tell me what I could expect to experience over the next three days. 'Tonight, the women will gather together and perform a group ritual, as will the men,' she said. 'Tomorrow, marriages will be solemnised, matings arranged, and I will find a man. You could, too, if you'd like.'

She grinned at me. I smiled thinly in reply. Since setting my attention at Q'orveh and failing, I'd had little desire to seek carnal company elsewhere. Perhaps I should.

'Tomorrow night, we will have the festival with dancing and wildness and special magicks. I can't wait!' Sah'ray could barely contain her lusty enthusiasm.

Q'orveh eventually emerged from the Toorish tent and made a sweeping signal with his arm. Gratefully the Halmanes stood up and began to disperse. Members of the Toors approached them, some people embracing as they met old friends again, or relatives who had married out-tribe. I was relieved everything had become so friendly. Sah'ray introduced me to a group of Toors that she knew – I think a sister of hers was involved somewhere – and I was invited to their tent for refreshment. Then the Shadow slithered up to my side and said, 'I have to drag you away. Make your excuses.'

'Why?' I demanded, far from pleased.

'Work for you, scaper,' he said, with a sarcastic curve of his lips.

'Q'orveh, in his wisdom, wants you to represent the tribe.'

His annoyance gratified me. 'Then, of course, I shall. But in what respect?'

'There is trouble among the Toors, I think.'

'What kind of trouble?' I didn't want to get involved in any inter-tribal dispute.

'It's scaping work, that's all. You'll find out. Just stop asking questions and follow me!' He marched off towards the Toorish shaman's tent and I was forced to run after him. I was intrigued. Soulscaping work, here, and why me? It must mean that the foreigners I had seen did not include any Taps.

The Toorish shaman, Toortaki, was little more than a boy and would not speak to me directly. In some tribes the shaman will speak only with his acolytes. Q'orveh was sitting beside this sha-manic stripling, magnificent as a god-form in comparison with the boy who was skinny and rather pinched of face. Q'orveh gestured for me to sit, which I did. Prudently I held my tongue, waiting for Q'orveh to speak.

'There is work for you here, soulscaper,' he said.

I nodded. 'I was told that, yes.'

'The Fear is in one of the Toors. No scaper has yet been able to remove it.'

I didn't like the sound of that. 'I'm not sure I can work miracles where others have tried and failed,' I replied. 'There is no such thing as a good or bad soulscaper. We are all equal.' That wasn't exactly true – some of us were more skilled than others – but we never admitted that to outsiders.

Q'orveh's expression did not change, yet I think I had embar-rassed him. 'Nevertheless,' he said smoothly. 'I have assured the Toors our soulscaper is the best. You must try, Rayojini.'

'Of course I will try,' I answered, wondering since when had I become 'their' soulscaper.

The afflicted girl was lying in a covered wagon, attended by a woman I supposed was her mother, or at least a close relative. A whole party of individuals set out from the shaman's tent, all of whom insisted on being present during my initial examination. Inside, the wagon was pungent and dark, the space cramped. They were not the best conditions in which to conduct a physical inspec-tion. I addressed the girl's relative. 'Other soulscapers have exam-ined this girl?'

She nodded, her mouth pursed tightly as if she had been forbid-den to speak.

'Are any of them still with the tribe?'

Again, a nod.

Q'orveh was squatting beside me, his bare knees poking out of his robes and touching my thigh. Not one to resist an impulse, I

155

put my hand on his shoulder. He did not move away or tense himself, so I applied a gentle pressure. 'I would like to speak with these other scapers,' I said in a low voice.

'Of course,' he murmured back, his face so close to me I could smell the herbs on his breath. 'Perhaps you should examine this girl yourself first, though.'

'Very well.'

She was in her early teens, a pretty little thing, whose eyes were wide and staring. I opened her mouth, looked inside, sniffed her breath. It was rank, a sure sign. I rolled back her eyelids, noted the colour of her eyes, the marks upon this colour, the size of the blackness at its core. I felt her skin, and scrutinised the palms of her hands for signs of mental illness. It seemed she was a straight-forward case. I couldn't imagine why other scapers hadn't been successful in healing her. Obviously they wouldn't have revealed their difficulties to the Toors; I would have to speak with them myself. On an impulse, I made a quick examination of the girl's torso and belly. A thought came to me. 'Your tribe healers have examined her?' The woman nodded again. 'You must understand there will be a degree of risk involved in scaping; the girl is preg-nant.'

'No!' the woman said indignantly. 'That is not possible.'

'The signs seem clear,' I replied gently. 'Perhaps a healer should be summoned to make sure.' There were discrepancies between the physical symptoms and those of the eyes, but I was positive I was not mistaken. Very shortly, an elderly woman came into the wagon and all the men, but for the two shamans, were dismissed. Both the healer and myself made a careful examination of the girl. She was, as I had suspected, with child. She was also, and again I'd had my suspicions, virgin. Q'orveh and I exchanged a glance. I whispered in his ear. 'This pregnancy should be terminated.' He nodded and turned to Toortaki. The boy was looking rather stunned and green about the face; I suspected it might have been the first time he'd encountered the genitals of a female. Q'orveh briefly told Toortaki what he had heard on the road concerning virgin births. He gave rather a lurid description of the deformed deer-child. Although the implications in his words were clear to me, I could tell they weren't really suggesting the same thing to Toortaki. Q'orveh could not be as blunt as was obviously necessary, because some tribes had very strict religious codes about pregnancy, and he would be wary of giving offence. I ended up becoming impatient and, offensive or not, stated my recommendation in plain terms. The whole situation was repellent.

'I feel this pregnancy should be terminated immediately,' I said. 'At least before any further attempts at soulscaping are made. It may be a fluke this has happened. Shared bathing water, I have heard, can lead to the quickening of a child, but even so, I do not

156

think any risks should be taken. A girl's life is at stake, if not her sanity.'

Support came unexpectedly from the girl's relative. 'You are right. I will boil some water,' she said, and squeezed her way past the shamans to leave the wagon. I was not sure how the Toors felt about such procedures, or even if their healer knew how to accomplish them. All soulscapers have a fair amount of medical training, and resolving unwanted pregnancies was a common feature of our work. I was perfectly capable of dealing with it and said so. The Toorish shaman gave his permission for me to proceed, almost without thinking about it. The healer readily agreed to assist me. A shadow of the Fear was over all of us in that wagon, I am sure.

There is little need to dwell upon the details of what we did to rid that poor girl of whatever had come to inhabit her body. The foetus was indeed bizarre, yet it was difficult to discern whether its expulsion from the womb had deformed it, or whether it had grown that way. I knew we were most likely to see peculiarities in everything at that point and tried to remain objective.

'We need to talk,' Q'orveh said to a white-faced Toortaki. 'Both tribes.'

The boy nodded. He looked so ill, I thought I'd better mix him a quelling potion as soon as we left the wagon. 'We will meet before the celebrations,' he said, in a thick, constricted voice. 'I will summon the elders.'

'And the soulscapers,' Q'orveh added.

Toortaki shrugged. I sensed reluctance, but he said, 'If you wish. I think we should talk privately first, however.'

'I would like to confer with these scapers myself,' I said. 'Perhaps we could talk together while the tribe elders are meeting.'

'That seems sensible,' Q'orveh said.

I smiled at him gratefully; he was being an ally.

As we came out of the wagon, eager to escape its stink of blood, I said, 'Q'orveh, I would like to speak with you, too. Alone, if that's possible.' It was too good an opportunity to miss.

'It is difficult to be alone,' he said, but seemed amenable to the idea. 'Among the tribes, aloneness is a thing to be avoided. We thrive in each other's company.'

'I have things I want to discuss and, being a loner, I thrive in intimate situations,' I replied, with a careful smile. Already, I could see members of the Halmanes preparing to converge on the focus of their tribe. I wanted to say, 'Get rid of them,' but realised that might be going too far. 'Where shall we go?' I asked hurriedly.

'My canopy. You can have your privacy there.'

'I thank you. However, I feel certain of your intimates will attempt to prevent our being alone.'

He gave me a strange look. 'There is no one there,' he said. 'I am sure of that.'

'Q'orveh, what is the Holy Death?'

We were sitting in his tent. It was dark, with the door curtain shut fast. Incense smouldered sullenly in a dish; we were wrapped in smoky perfume. Q'orveh reclined upon his cushions, long-limbed and lithe, like an archetypal soulscape vision of male beauty. His tangles of matted hair were like an animal's mane, trailing the length of his spine, dusty and lighter in colour at the ends where the sun and rain had bleached it. He smelled like an animal; clean, but muskily aromatic. We were so close, yet I was aware that his body language did not incline towards me. I kept my voice low, expecting the shadow of Keea to manifest at any moment in a corner, his dark eyes watching keenly.

Q'orveh appeared puzzled by my question. 'I cannot believe the soulscapers don't know,' he said.

I shook my head. 'No, you misunderstand. I just want to know what it means to *you*, your tribe, your own explanation for it.'

Q'orveh narrowed his eyes. 'You are soon going to say something connected with this subject that I will not enjoy hearing.'

I raised my hands. 'Maybe so, but until I have spoken with the other soulscapers here, there is no one, other than yourself, whom I can trust. Also, you said you wanted to discover the cause of the strange phenomena on the road, how and why. Please answer my question. I will explain its relevance shortly.'

'Very well. To us it is the Sacred Paling, which is when a person takes on the colour of the moon, glowing from within to symbolise its holy connotations.'

'What do you mean by *holy*?' I interrupted. I knew little of nomad mythology, not having had much opportunity to meet its glyphs in the soulscape. Soon, I felt, that would change.

'The god takes them. They are sacrifices to the Gardling, Helat.'

'Your god?'

He nodded. 'We have only one. Helat. An androgyne who regenerates and has a host of offspring, all of whom hide in the world and influence the ways of men. Helat has three breasts. One squirts nectar, one blood and the other poison. You can imagine how this symbology is incorporated into the most secret of our rites.'

'I think so. So, those who die the Holy Death are taken by Helat.'

'Well, we say that the members of the host take them.'

'The children of Helat?'

'Yes. Some believe we are the product of these children mating with men and women, which is why we are part unman. The children of Helat are very beautiful. It is said they can appear to a person out alone on the plains, and lure them into an endless embrace. People have died that way.'

'It is *said* . . .'

Q'orveh shrugged. 'We have only imagination. No one survives the embrace of the host to tell of it.'

'Until now . . . maybe.'

Q'orveh raised an interested eyebrow. Perhaps my heresy wasn't as fearsome as he'd thought it would be. 'What are you suggesting?'

I shrugged. 'It is only a guess . . . May I present my theory? It is this. Suppose the non-deaths are "failed" Sacred Palings.'

'Intellectually, I might suppose it. But what do you mean by that? The host are losing their power?'

I doubted whether it was a good idea to tell this man I did not believe in his god, or its children. I did not believe in any god outside the confines of the soulscape. I had stupidly thought Q'orveh to be as rational as a Tap. He wasn't. He still gave his inner symbols external life, as his people did.

'What I mean, Q'orveh, is that I feel we have to establish exactly what the Holy Death is, to understand why it has changed. If it has.'

'There are some things we must not question too closely,' he replied. 'We are only human and must not presume upon divine territory.'

I smiled. 'Q'orveh, I do that all the time. It's my job.'

Unfortunately, he took offence at that. His face hardened. 'I think I can understand why so many of the shamans will not tolerate a soulscaper in their path. They say you rival the host, or presume to. Rayo, you are only a woman of flesh and blood.'

'So what do we do? Sit back and let things happen?'

'I don't think there is anything we can do. It is beyond our powers. We can only appease the Helat in whatever way we can. Rites, prayers. . .'

I had to interrupt him. 'You called me to speak with you first, Q'orveh. Now I *am* speaking! Why are you backing away?'

'I feel it is becoming too dangerous. Anyway, your flimsy theory hardly explains the other things we've discovered; the blood places, the . . . births.'

I had no answer for that. He was right. 'I just don't have enough information, that's all.' I stared at him steadily. 'Q'orveh, don't try to deceive me; you yourself suspect the Sacred Palings and the non-deaths are connected. I know you do.'

'I do not deny it,' he answered smoothly. 'But I still question whether we have any right to interfere.'

'Even when your dead walk?'

His face had become stone. 'I'm sorry, but I don't want to discuss this any further until the tribe elders have met. Perhaps you should go and find your compatriots now.'

I was stung; he had dismissed me.

* * *

159

The two soulscapers travelling with the Toors were unknown to me. They were brother and sister, natives of the eastern eyries of Taparak, and a good deal younger than myself. Aniti was a strong-boned handsome girl with wide, thick eyebrows, while her brother Juro was more slender, his eyes unusually pale. Perhaps their youth and inexperience explained why they had not been able to heal the Toorish girl.

It was late afternoon by the time we were able to speak and I, feeling superior in the face of their lack of years, doubted strongly whether I would benefit from our consultation. They, on the other hand, might learn much from me. They had a tent to themselves – clearly demonstrating just how valuable soulscapers were becoming to the nomads of Khalt, who at one time used to interact with stray Taps by plucking out their eyes, or skewering them through if they dared to practise their art among the tribes.

Aniti and Juro were shy in my presence; I felt my voice was too loud and hearty. I wasn't sure where to begin and asked them who their mentor was. It was someone I was only vaguely familiar with, a woman of no particular note. I wondered whether these two were actually being coerced to stay with the Toors in some way. 'You have been travelling on the plains long?' I inquired.

The girl, Aniti, shrugged. 'A while. Suddenly there is much to be learned from the Khalts, but we have found it tiring.'

'Really?'

The boy nodded. 'It is as if the Fear itself flits from person to person among the Toors. We drive it from some poor soul, only for it to manifest itself moments later in the being of another. The shaman is impressed with our ability; whereas we are unsure of our level of success.'

I had been tutored in how, among close communities, people could develop sympathetic soulscape discrepancies. What the children should have done was to have travelled deep into the collective soul of the tribe and rooted out the rot from there. All individual soulscapes are connected; it is merely a matter of perception, and the use of a more potent fume, to enter a consensual scape. I told them this. The girl took exception to my tone. Her face flamed a little.

'We have tried that!' she said indignantly. 'It hides.'

I couldn't repress a laugh. 'Hides? Really, child. Those are not words I'd hope to hear a soulscaper say.'

'You have not experienced it,' she replied. 'Perhaps you should – before you upbraid us.'

Her brother muttered a warning, but I did not take offence. Both of them looked bone-tired, muddy of face, and drawn.

'The nomads seem to be experiencing a number of delusions,' I said. 'Soulscape hallucinations, maybe.'

'If you are referring to the blood places and the un-beasts, they

160

are not delusions,' Juro said. 'We have seen them, or perhaps you think we are suffering the same delusions?'

'It is sometimes dangerous to believe the evidence of our eyes,' I replied. 'We are fallible, after all. Use your art.'

'Use our art? Are you blind, Mistress Rayojini?' snapped the girl. 'I am frightened. There is something happening, and it is beyond us. The nomad shamans consider themselves superior to soulscapers, yet now they turn to us in desperation. We cannot help them.'

'There is an answer to everything,' I said. My patience was beginning to fray. 'We have only to gather up the clues. Now, the elders of both tribes are meeting and soon they will expect us to speak to them. I feel it is important we present some plan of action. I, for one, have no wish to invoke any negative assumptions the nomads might still have about us. Even if we are confused, we must not let them know it.'

'You admit to confusion, then?' Juro asked me, tartly.

I shrugged. 'I feel in the dark, yes, but panicking won't solve anything. We must be vigilant. If I were you, I'd return to Taparak as soon as possible. The scryers must be informed of what is occurring here.'

'You mean we should leave these people to their fate?' Aniti asked. She was clearly an idealist.

'Or leave them to you?' added Juro, who was a cynic.

I declined to answer their impertinent questions. 'Listen, we three will journey into the soulscape of Toor. Maybe you are right and we will find nothing, but we can plant assurances, seeds of strength. This is what we shall tell the conclave of elders.'

'And when the sun begins to fling his flaring beams, me goddess bring to arched walks of twilight groves and shadows brown . . .'
From *Il Penseroso*, Milton

Q'orveh hosted the meeting of elders and, later, I and the young scapers were summoned to his tent. There was hardly any room to sit down, and I sensed that our presence was not welcomed by everybody. Ignoring any hostile resonance, I spoke confidently to the elders of both tribes, impressing upon them how strongly I believed that there was a simple explanation for all they had experienced recently.

'The answer lies in the soulscape, I am sure,' I told them. 'The strange things you have seen and experienced might well seem very real, but they could just be the products of your imaginations.'

This caused a cacophony of angry denial. I raised my hands.

'Please, let me explain. It is possible to create physical matter, or at least a convincing illusion of such, by the power of thought alone. For example, the virgin births; perhaps the girls concerned imagined they were impregnated and because the illusion of coupling had been so real they *created* something that resembled a child.' Juro and Aniti were sitting just behind me, and I could sense they thought I was speaking utter folly. I had no doubt this opinion was shared by everyone else sitting in the tent. Perhaps I should have kept my mouth shut. Nobody actually contradicted me; they simply ignored my words. I had hoped for intelligent debate. I should have known better. These were nomads, not a select gathering of Tappish adepts.

One of the old Toorish women followed my remarks with an impassioned and ignorant sentiment of her own. 'You could be making the problem worse with your meddling!' She was an ancient, stick-like creature, whose lips had receded and tightened so much, her face strongly resembled a grinning skull.

I remained calm. 'We do not meddle, madam, I assure you. We bring light to the places that are overrun with shadows.' At that point I could not resist flicking a glance at Keea. He was staring right back at me and smiled slightly when our eyes met. Incredibly, my face grew hot.

'Some places are meant to be shadowed,' the woman continued relentlessly, casting narrowed eyes around the tent, seeking allies.

163

'Of course they are. Notice I said "overrun". Please don't warp my words.'

Q'orveh raised his hands, clearly having little desire for individuals annexed to his tribe to argue in public. 'Perhaps you have formed an opinion while speaking with your fellow Taps,' he said, hopefully.

I shrugged. 'Seems to me we should enter the *tribal* soulscape, and root out the problem from there.' That the tribe possessed a soulscape of its own was clearly a new concept to the Toorish elders. My original opponent slapped her gums together juicily and took up the sword again.

'Blasphemy!' she screamed. 'The soulscapers intend to violate the gardens of Helat!'

I turned around and rolled my eyes at Juro and Aniti, who grimaced back. At that moment, I was glad to have fellow rational beings with me, whatever their youth and inexperience.

'I think if any soulscape is to be entered,' Toortaki said, 'it should be that of the girl we attended this afternoon. Can more than one soulscaper work together?'

'Of course,' I said. 'Once within the girl's soulscape, we could perhaps extend our consciousness to encompass that of the whole tribe.'

'Well, then, everything is clear,' Q'orveh said. He turned to me. 'Mistress Rayojini, you and the other soulscapers will enter the soulscape of the Toorish girl, and report back to us. Then we shall have the answers we need.' His faith in me, even if it was only for appearances' sake in front of these others, was endearing.

It was decided that we would begin our work as soon as possible, so that it would be concluded long before the women's rite was due to commence. I understood the mystery ceremonies were destined to take place just before midnight.

I asked the Toors to take the sick girl out of the wagon; it had a miasma of despair about it, in which I had no desire at all to work. Juro and Aniti helped me choose an alternative working-place among the trees nearby, where we would be screened from noise and the eyes of others. Q'orveh thoughtfully provided a company of young men – who would stand apart, but keep the curious away.

We erected a canopy around the working area to contain the scaping fume, and then built a fire on to which we would cast the strongest of our scaping mixes. The sick girl lay comatose at our feet, oblivious of our preparations.

'This is a waste of time,' Aniti grumbled. 'Believe me, her soulscape will be filled with happy spirits and sweet memories of childhood. There will be no fear to find, no shadows hiding.'

'I leave no stone unturned,' I said to her quite sharply. 'In the

164

soulscape or outside of it. The Fear *is* there. It just hasn't been recognised as such.'

Aniti stomped off to gather twigs for our fire. I appealed to her brother. 'Whatever it sounds like, I don't mean to be harsh. But having *that* attitude won't solve anything.'

'What if Aniti's right?' Juro asked me, carefully neutral in tone.

'Then I'll admit I was wrong, naturally, but I think the chance of that is very slim.'

When the fire was ready, Aniti cast a generous amount of my scaping-mix into the flames. The three of us arranged ourselves in sitting positions around the prone body of the Toorish girl, and linked hands. Breathing deeply, we began to suck the sweet smoke of the fume into our lungs. Aniti's fingers gripped me tightly; I had a feeling she was not without fear herself at that time.

As Aniti had predicted, when we passed into the soulscape we emerged into a landscape of exuberant radiance, where everything was gilded with light. 'Yes,' I thought, 'this is indeed the summer land of childhood.' Our presence was the only dark thing there.

Normally when a scaper enters the soulscape, the Fear will come to flap around their head. Its guises vary; sometimes it is just a black wing of darkness, sometimes an ugly and malevolent apparition but, whatever its shape, the Fear is a senseless force. It has no consciousness and therefore lacks the instinct for self-preservation. To defeat it, a soulscaper has only to visualise weapons of a suitable nature. The material of the soulscape is malleable. It is possible to form anything you need there, simply by the power of thought, whether that is fire, or steel or ice. Sometimes confrontation alone will expel a weak fragment of the Fear; you can chase it away or simply visualise its evaporation, order it to depart. Conflicts vary. There is rarely any need for a scaper to roam a great distance into the soulscape, because the Fear will come hurtling towards them like a stupid, savage dog. However, in this case, it seemed Aniti might have been right in her assumptions. The Fear, if here at all, was in hiding or at least disguised in some way. I felt uneasy with the implications in that. Could the Fear develop intelligence, a kind of survival instinct? Was that the new demon we were facing, Fear with consciousness? Would that explain all the strange phenomena? I hoped not. If the Fear had evolved significantly, then soulscapers would have to develop a more puissant form of combat to defeat it.

I perceived Aniti and Juro as bright globes of white light beside me. It took them a while to assume a definite shape – which was a manifestation of their inexperience. I, too, had found it difficult to manipulate my own form in the soulscape during my first scaping range. Sending them a reassuring pulse of sympathetic thought, I concentrated on our surroundings. For a moment or two I extended my consciousness outwards, hoping it would brush up against some-

165

thing suspicious, some core of condensed matter. I found nothing. There were spots of heat which suggested event-plays of some kind, but they held no taint of Fear. If anything, they were concentrations of pleasure. On an impulse, I changed tack, and advised the others to focus on these areas of ecstasy instead of trying to locate pockets of Fear. It was a gamble, and I disliked gambles in the soulscape, but we had nothing else to go on.

There, we caught it; a fizzling radiance. Homing in on it was no difficulty. And this is what we found.

The soul-spark of the ailing girl was being embraced by a god-form, which clearly did not come from nomad mythology. They were copulating in a white shrine, surrounded by ivy trees, the sky a pale-lemon colour above them. The girl was manifested, quite typically, as a veil-clad female – although the draperies suggested an image I would expect to find in the land of Atruriey rather than from a Khaltish nomad girl. She appeared to lack awareness, to be drowsy in a sensual heat. It was obvious to me that she had lost touch with reality, perhaps even the very concept of it. There was not the slightest vibration of distress emanating from her. Perhaps there was no Fear to remove . . . and yet.

The god-form raised a heavy head, crowned with antlers, to peer at us with curious yellow eyes. Fortunately, these archetypal manifestations never possess intelligence. He had a large, red phallus, which was unashamedly erect and dripping with fluid. His nether parts were those of a deer or goat. I realised that my theory concerning the virgin births might well be correct. Still, this was not a threatening image and I knew I could remove it easily, by performing a thought excision designed to expunge any unwelcome phantoms. After I had directed this simple command, the god-form vaporised instantly, without a struggle, leaving the girl mewing and squealing with the horror of loss. Presently her image faded and I guessed she had been sucked back to reality.

It was time for us to leave. I did not, at that juncture, wish to continue our journey into the tribal soulscape. Aniti had not been wrong, it seemed, but then neither had I.

When we came back to our senses, the girl was curled into a foetal shape on the ground, sobbing piteously. I sent Juro to fetch the women of her family to attend to her, leaving me alone for a few moments with Aniti. There are some things that men must not be privy to – even soulscapers. Without discussion of what we had done, Aniti and I gently murmured a few relaxation mantras, straightened the girl's limbs and held her in our arms, crooning softly. Presently her sobs abated to gulps, but there was no more we could do for her. The familiarity of her people would be more healing.

As we walked back towards where the wagons and tents were clustered round the lake-side, Aniti cleared her throat gruffly and said, 'I have to stand admonished, Mistress Rayojini. You were right and I was wrong. I apologise for my arrogance.'

I put a hand on her shoulder, feeling altogether more sympathetic with relief. 'No, you were not wrong. Neither of us was. What we discovered in that poor girl's soulscape is not a completely unknown phenomenon, but it is very rare.' I squeezed her fondly. 'We have all been panicked recently, what with all these strange goings-on. I don't think any of us was sure of success when we entered the soulscape.'

Aniti shook her head emphatically. 'No, you don't have to absolve me. It was you who thought to look for the opposite signs, not me. I would never have thought of that.'

I shrugged. 'Perhaps so, but don't worry about it. You have learned something and, if it was a mistake, it won't be one you'll make again.'

'Soulscapers shouldn't ever make mistakes though!' she said hotly, angry with herself. 'We can't afford to. Too much is at stake.'

'Well, I can't dispute that, but what's done is done. Don't be too hard on yourself.' Her capitulation made me feel protective towards her. I was, in truth, feeling particularly high at that moment.

'You were right in all you said,' Aniti blurted presently. 'I shall return to Taparak, with or without my brother. Clearly this is not a time for me to be practising my art afield. I need more guidance . . . more. . .' She shook her head. 'Where are our guardian-pursuers when we need them most? Where? Sometimes, I wonder whether they are real at all, and not just a dream put into our heads by the scryers!'

Her words cast a chill over my mood. 'My guardian-pursuers are very real to me,' I said softly. We had stopped walking, standing together in a shadow of the trees.

'How do you invoke them?' Aniti asked in a hoarse whisper. 'How do you commune with them? I can never feel them, never!'

'I can't answer your questions,' I replied. 'It's too personal.'

Aniti chastised herself again. 'I must be the only soulscaper who has never met her guardian-pursuers, never felt them near her, never communed with them!'

I did not answer. The truth was, I felt that her experience was the same as all other soulscapers, and that it was my ambivalent familiarity with my guardian-pursuers that was distinctly unusual.

We ate beside the fires; the tribes mingling, children splashing through the shallows of the lake. Dogs roamed from group to group, seeking titbits, musicians tuned their instruments for the approaching rites. At the appointed hour, everyone began standing up. There was no particular signal given; people just knew when the time was right. The remains of the meal were quickly cleared away, and the fires were amply stoked so that they would still be smouldering when we all returned to camp. Older children not yet of an age to participate in the ceremonies had been instructed to guard the younger ones, and had stationed themselves importantly around the tents, brandishing knives.

I had been sitting with Aniti and Juro among a crowd of Toors. Now, Sah'ray materialised at my side from out of the dark and urged me to accompany her. I grabbed hold of Aniti, because I wanted her to be with me. She was still so furious with herself, I feared that, alone at this potent occasion, she would be vulnerable to soulscape intrusions.

The women had begun to creep through the trees. Sah'ray told us there was a special ritual place hidden in the forest, used by all the tribes and rich in power. The elder women of the tribes had assumed a kind of leadership over the rest of us. They glided ahead with the authority of priestesses; their tiered skirts swirling round their ankles, heads held high, long braids loosed down their backs.

The excitement of the nomad women was infectious. We all acknowledged our own feminine power as we hurried through the dark; we had our own mysteries that no male would ever penetrate. Anything could have watched us from the thick undergrowth; I would not have been surprised to see manifestations of imps or sylphs. Gradually, the happy excitement of the women mutated to controlled hysteria; soon, I sensed, it would erupt.

Eventually we came to a wide clearing where there was short, springy grass underfoot. Above us, queen of the rite, the pregnant moon shone down fiercely through the gap in the trees. I wondered if the men were conducting their own rite nearby, but could hear no sounds other than the natural music of animals and birds going about their nocturnal business. Nobody seemed to want to venture out into the naked arena beyond the trees, where the grass had been bleached to a bone whiteness beneath the moon's colourless radiance. Sah'ray tapped my arm and gestured. She had begun to unlace her bodice. I understood. The women must be unclothed to endure the painful, white light. Clothes might shrivel and burn to blackness beneath its touch, but flesh would only absorb it and glow. In the world of the night all is black and white, and we were there to celebrate its colours. I disrobed myself, telling Aniti to do likewise and we folded our clothes and placed them in a neat pile beneath one of the trees. Then we felt brave enough to bathe in the shower of light.

Cautiously, the women stepped out on to the grass, feeling with their hands for the cold rays, slowly turning their bodies, stretching their spines, reaching up to the sky. Aniti and I hovered on the edge, unsure of the movements. I noticed she flicked a glance at my body; I felt absurdly tall and masculine beside her. Aniti was a voluptuous creature, whereas I am mainly skin-covered bone.

I'd noticed that some of the women had carried large objects

168

wrapped in cloth, which I'd thought might be poles to support a canopy. Now, I could see that these objects were actually enormous wooden horns. Four of the elder women stationed themselves at equal distances around the roughly circular glade, each in possession of a horn which they supported on the grass. At some unseen signal, they placed their lips against the mouthpieces of these horns and began to blow. Aniti and I moved into the gathering of women; we could no longer observe from outside.

At first, the sound felt like a wind passing over the flesh, below the threshold of human bearing. Then the ground began to vibrate with the sound and a deep belling could be heard. This was the voice of the earth herself, calling out to her white sister of the skies. We, in the centre of the glade, were filled with the vibration of this sound. Our hair crackled with the power of lightning, our ears popped with the pressure of it. Every pore of our being, and we *were* one being, was filled with the sound. I felt as if I had lost my identity to it; all I could do was move to its monotonous note. Then the drums began, and we found we were free to dance.

I have never heard music so eerie or compelling as that of the nomad women's rituals. In any other circumstances I am sure it would have sounded hideous. But at that time, in that space, it was the only permissible sound: *our* sound, that of the blood flowing in our veins; the throb of womb-power; the invisible potency of the female spirit.

Then, as the moon travelled across her kingdom, a new secret was revealed. At the edge of the clearing an immense statue appeared. I had not noticed it before and for a superstitious moment or two I actually considered whether it was a living, breathing thing that had slipped out of the soulscape and into reality. Common sense rebuked me. It had been in shadow and had only been revealed by the gradual movement of the moon; more time must have passed than I thought.

The statue represented Helat. Its serene face beamed mysteriously down at the dancing women, sensual lips curved into a perfect smile. Its body was slim, lacking voluptuous female shape around the hips, but possessed of three large breasts that looked as if they were bursting with nourishment. The statue was seated, hands upon its thighs, its knees apart. An erect phallus pointed to the belly, straining up from a dark crevice where the stone was stained by a thin trickle of what I took to be water. Maybe it was a natural spring incorporated into the carving. I could not imagine the nomads ever having been able to carve this monstrous idol themselves, but as far as I knew no other races worshipped Helat the androgyne Gardling. Perhaps, they had adopted this god-form from an earlier race of the plains. It looked incredibly ancient, as if it possessed the innate wisdom of an idol who has been worshipped for centuries. Whoever had built it, Helat knew who its people were now and

169

smiled down benevolently on the dancing women, impassive and pregnant with potential. On its brow, the symbol of the moon; on the back of its hands, that of the sun.

I became dizzy with the dancing, and was almost in trance watching Aniti's swift dark shape flitting among those of the paler nomads. Then I noticed that one of the women was approaching the idol. She climbed up the few shallow steps between its legs to reach the pool that had formed in its lap. She dipped a cup into the liquid, only a small cup, which she brought back to the dancing women. There must have been nearly a hundred of us, swaying there in the glade, but there was a sip for us all from that cup. I expected it to taste of something rank and stagnant but, although there was an earthy flavour to it, the water was pure and indeed earth-born. I knew I had tasted the life fluid of Helat.

After this, the drumbeat faded away and all the women began to sit down on the grass, everyone panting a little and wiping sweat from their eyes. Aniti sat down beside me. 'What now?' she mouthed. I shrugged. We soon found out. It was time for rites of passage to be conducted, young virgins being brought, for the first time, into the mysteries. The nomad women did not trust men to deflower their children. Following the symbolism of Helat, each girl must deflower herself. To the unsuspecting these rites might seem alarmingly primitive and barbaric, yet I who had been privy to the ceremonies of many religions and cults upon my travels, simply prepared myself, with interest, to spectate.

Perhaps, though, I was too complacent and underestimated the potent emotion being invoked. Aniti and I observed – Aniti, with a rising sense of unease, for she took hold of my arm – as the first girl was led to the lap of the god by two old women. She placed a garland of small, woodland flowers over Helat's stone phallus. 'They can't!' Aniti hissed into my ear. 'Surely. . .' I put my finger to my lips, trying to signal that we were only guests and must not show discontent. The girl bowed to the idol and then sat in the cold water of its lap, facing outwards, raising her knees so that her feet were planted firmly on each thigh. I felt rather relieved at that point, having been convinced she had been about to spear herself on the statue; I was unsure whether Aniti would have been able to contain her disgust at that. Chanting softly but insistently, the old women blessed the girl. Then they summoned a woman younger than themselves, who walked up the shallow steps carrying some object wrapped in a dark cloth. The old women unwrapped this object and handed it to the girl. I could see it was a carved phallus, perhaps of wood or bone. One of the old women nodded at the girl and led the others back down the steps. The significance of this object was obvious. Aniti made a muffled sound at my side.

At first, the girl seemed reluctant to pierce herself and my heart went out to her. She must have been horribly conscious of how

170

intently everyone was watching her. Did she feel humiliation, shame, or fear? And yet she must also have been aware of how she had no choice but to complete the ritual; there was no other way she could become a fully-fledged member of the tribe. I saw her close her eyes, screw up her face with the fear of pain, and press the tip of the phallus against herself. To me, a man of flesh and blood would have been less of a trial. All the women began to sing, swaying slowly, building up a rhythm of power. I realised they were actually invoking Helat, calling down the spirit of their god into the flesh of the girl before them. The rite was symbolic of the androgyne; Helat impregnating itself. The girl had also adopted the traditional position of giving birth among these people. I was quite moved, despite the barbaric aspects of the rite. The girl's face was changing, becoming enraptured. The support of her people entered into her and she took the plunge, abandoning nervous pokings, and thrust the phallus inside her. It must have hurt her horribly, but I could see she was beyond pain. She slithered upwards into a standing position, barely shaking, and I could almost feel the thunder of her heart. So mystical a thing is sexuality; it made me realise that we Taps, with our scientific cool, sometimes missed the intention of its power. Before me, stood a trembling girl who had been deflowered by a god, and the god was herself. Maybe I would be able to use this symbolism during my work sometime. Not all of my commissions involved expunging Fear or mental sickness. Sometimes, I am called upon for lesser maladies – anxiety about sexuality can be one of them.

The following rites – eight girls in all – did not seem as powerful to me. The initial image was the one that stayed with me. I was looking forward to discussing it all with Aniti later; I was glad that another of my kind was present.

The rite was ended by a circle dance; all the newly initiated girls skipping around in the centre, joyous because the trial was passed. Their blood had mingled in the sacred waters of Helat. The over-spilling pool would eventually instil their essence into the earth beneath by flowing over the damp steps. All the women had become excited, laughing shrilly. When the circle broke, I noticed most of them only gathered up their clothes in their arms before running off between the trees. Aniti and I, left alone because Sah'ray had scampered away somewhere, solemnly began to dress ourselves.

'It was very powerful,' Aniti said lamely.

I nodded. 'Yes, very.' I realised I had become quite aroused by the rituals and, thinking Aniti must feel the same, asked her if she would like to slip off somewhere and make love with me. 'I do not feel this is a time for men,' I said.

She smiled. 'No, it is not. Why don't we stay here? Everyone else seems to have gone.'

We sat down beneath one of the trees and I began to undo her

171

fastenings once more. She giggled, complaining of being tickled. I was thinking of the impassive idol at the other end of the glade; at that moment I envied Helat's androgynous form. I would like to have had a phallus myself, to plunge into this young and willing body and, in turn, would have appreciated Aniti being similarly blessed. The strength of the rite was insidious. I was quite surprised at how it had affected us. We didn't even bother to undress fully; we simply groped for each other. I squeezed Aniti's breast with my free hand. 'Not so fast, lovely. Let's take our time.'

'I feel so strange,' she said wistfully. 'So hungry.'

'I'm glad we witnessed their mysteries,' I said. 'It will be useful.'

Aniti laughed. 'Rayojini, you seem so cold, so analytical all the time. Can't you just feel what has happened and accept it?' She made a scoffing sound. '*Useful*! Really!'

Her skin looked like dark, polished wood in the dappled moonlight; I stroked the smooth planes of her generous hips. Her pubic hair was a shadowed, impudent bush. Perhaps she was right about me; perhaps I was too cynical.

'Do you still want us to enter the tribal soulscape?' Aniti asked. I really didn't feel like discussing it.

'To be honest, I wonder whether there is any point,' I said.

'You have changed your mind, then.'

'I don't know. At the moment, I don't care!' I lowered my lips to her breast. This was not a time to worry about work. Aniti moaned sweetly and ran her nails lightly over my back. It felt exquisite.

Then, she tensed. 'What was that?' she hissed.

'What?'

'Listen!'

There was a sound among the trees behind us; just a slight sound, but enough to alert us that it wasn't an animal. I sat up and tried to peer into the darkness. 'Is someone there?' Aniti asked nervously.

'I don't. . .' Before I could finish speaking, a man stumbled out of the shadows. He looked like a hunted animal; his naked flesh was scratched and bleeding, and his eyes were wild and round. Matted hair fell on to his chest, tangled with twigs and leaves. It was Q'orveh.

I guessed his condition must be the aftermath of the men's ritual and that he had not intended to come across any women. I had a feeling someone was chasing him, but perhaps I was wrong. He leaned down, panting, his hands braced on his knees. Then, he looked up and seemed to see us for the first time.

'Soulscapers,' he said. I could not interpret the emotionless tone of that single word.

I became aware of my dishevelled condition, my shirt hanging open, my trousers unlaced. 'What do you want?' I demanded, expecting him to flee.

He did not speak, however, but limped over and squatted down beside us. Aniti was still lying down, her breasts exposed, her trousers round her knees, lips all full with passion. She was looking at Q'orveh with hooded eyes. Aniti, little wild thing; so easy for her to let go, become one of these people.

'We are busy, shaman,' I said. 'I thought men respected the women's rites.'

'The women's, and the men's, rites are over,' he replied. 'Don't you know that?'

'Well . . .'

He flopped down and lay on his side, supporting his head on his hand. I felt a familiar longing flash through my mind. Q'orveh: beauty, the words were really inseparable. Had he been looking for me?

'Rayo, he's ours,' Aniti said. 'Lay him down.'

I was amused, more than shocked, by her words. Perhaps, at that moment, I wished she wasn't there. 'Do we need this?' I asked, rather sharply.

'Need it? No. But he needs us, I'm sure. This is still part of it, Rayo. He's lying; the rites haven't ended.'

She sat up and Q'orveh rolled on to his back. Aniti looked splendid: a satiny black spirit, her braids lovingly accentuating the curve of her full breasts. What a little goddess she was! Her eyes were those of the primeval huntress as she slithered towards the shaman like an oiled serpent, kicking off her trousers, intent on seizing what she considered to be her prey. I was older than Aniti; sometimes it is necessary to claim the privilege of age. The older huntress would have to take prevalence.

I playfully pushed her away. 'Mine first,' I said.

Aniti grunted and then laughed a little. Q'orveh had closed his eyes; his arms were spread out in the wiry grass. He knew what to expect. As he was both priest and priestess, he knew all about submission. I kissed his body, tasting salt and clay, and ran my hands over the ripple of his ribs. Just to let him know I understood more about him than he thought, I used my hands in a way he probably didn't expect. An androgynous deity has many ways of manifesting itself. He arched his back in pleasure, and my ministrations made him ready for us.

So much for Keea's words, I thought as I took Q'orveh inside me. Little creeping liar. Jealous snake.

Tomorrow, I might be wryly appalled at my behaviour but for now . . . It felt too glorious for words. Q'orveh was a sacrificed king beneath me; I couldn't stop looking at his face. I realise now we really should have had those moments to ourselves.

Then, Aniti became impatient, and threw herself on my back,

173

her nails digging into my shoulders. We fought over the slippery phallus, passing it between us, a tangle of fingers and moist folds. Once, I looked down, almost oblivious of the man but for his sex, and it seemed the face of Keea was looking back at me, smiling triumphantly. Why had my mind projected him in this way? Who, or what, was this boy? Perhaps my own soulscape was trying to give me a message, but the illusion made me uncomfortable, and I closed my eyes to banish it. For a while, at least, Keea did not exist.

'Roaming to seek their prey on earth . . . And when night darkens the streets, then wander forth the sons of Belial . . .'
Paradise Lost, Book I

We awoke, lying in the dew, with mellow autumn sunlight coming down through the trees. By daylight, it was possible to see how the leaves were turning, all nourishment seeping back into the branches, so that energy would be conserved until the spring. There was little chill, however, although we shivered because our clothes were damp.

Q'orveh had left us during the night, a fact which surprised neither Aniti or myself. 'I thought he was a eunuch,' she said to me, and then laughed. 'Perhaps he is – normally!'

Although we were hungry and wanted to bathe, we sat for a few moments in the privacy of the trees, feeling meditative and weary. 'I feel better today,' Aniti said. 'Not so apprehensive. What an experience! It feels like a dream.'

'Most primitive cultures involve sexuality in their rites,' I said.

Aniti scoffed. 'There you go again! Rayo, these people aren't primitive. In a sense, I feel we are underdeveloped in comparison.'

I shrugged. In truth, I was feeling edgy because the power of the previous night's rituals had affected me so deeply. I hate to lose control of myself, and the abandonment of our communion with Q'orveh had been nothing if not uncontrolled. I believed the act of love should be a measured and gentle practice.

Eventually, we wandered back to the camp site. Surprisingly, there was little activity; only children hurried between the tents, carrying water or preparing food. I supposed the adults to be wrapped in blankets, recovering from their excesses. It was also possible most of them were still asleep in the forest. Aniti wanted to stay with me and suggested we should go and bathe together, but I needed time alone and also wanted to discourage any attachment on her part. Last night was last night. Rayojini was a loner; she did not thirst for a satellite. Rather crestfallen, Aniti went away to find her brother, and I strolled back to where Sah'ray had erected her tent. As I had expected, it was empty. Inside, I sat on the rolled bed-mats and took a drink from the pitcher of water Sah'ray had drawn the night before.

Some time, perhaps on the way back from the sacred glade, a

175

decision had set within me which now surfaced in my mind. It was time to part company with the nomads. Perhaps, all along, I had only wanted to have sex with Q'orveh. Now this had been achieved, I felt restless. Clues to the mysteries I had encountered must litter the grass-lanes of the Kahra Flats, crowd the minds of its natives; I was eager to discover them, and knew I could travel faster alone. There was little more to be learned among the Halmanes. I had catalogued all the information I'd acquired in their company, clearly marking in my notes all the accounts which I considered had been exaggerated by hysteria – such as the idea of the walking dead. As for the virgin births, this was bizarre and biologically inexplicable, but it seemed unequivocal to me that the girls concerned had somehow impregnated themselves through the power of unconscious thought. At least, they had *mimicked* the formation of life. I strongly doubted whether these self-generated offspring could survive beyond their mothers' bodies. It was Helat's privilege to create life by itself; perhaps a symbol that the nomads, panicked by fear of what they thought they'd seen and heard, had interpreted too literally.

I also considered the possibility that recent events presaged only the imminence of yet another new faith, one characterised by miracles and bizarre occurrences. New religions, Host of Helat, Holy Deaths, non-deaths, walking dead: what was the connection? It was a puzzle which I was frantic to solve. The nomads, while being peripatetic in their lifestyles, were static in their beliefs; the religion of Helat had been theirs for centuries. There was evidence too that Helat was a deity that predated the nomads themselves. It had great power and had carved for itself an exclusive territory, where other god-forms held no sway. This was rare. I was juggling these ideas in my mind, scribbling as I thought. There had to be a connection, surely? All questions. No answers.

I decided I would stay with the nomads for the festivities that night and then move on in the morning. If the Halmanes felt they had a claim over me, they could think again, but for convenience's sake, I would slip away without advertising my departure.

Just as I was tidying away my notes, Sah'ray came rampaging through the tent flap, destroying my contemplations. 'Oh, Rayo!' she cried, 'I'm so glad you're here! I have to talk to someone!'

She smelled strongly of earth and sex; her flesh muddied, her clothes in disarray. I fastidiously drew away. 'It seems you've been enjoying yourself,' I said diplomatically.

She patted her belly. 'I hope so! I found three men who were handsome enough to father a child with me, so I had them all! Do you think I'm pregnant? Rayo, you're a soulscaper – won't you be able to tell?'

'Not so soon,' I replied.

'Where did you go after the rite?' she asked me, favouring me with a particularly lecherous grin. 'What did you get up to?'

I certainly did not want to discuss my experiences with her. I shrugged. 'Nothing as adventurous as you, I'm sure.'

'Oh, come on, tell me! It's not secret. Today, we will find the most interesting gossip around the fires.'

I could believe that, but had no desire whatsoever for the exploits of Rayojini the soulscaper to be part of that gossip. 'So who were these three men?' I asked her. 'Were they Toors?'

She was happy to talk about that. 'Yes. Toors. It's always more exciting with strangers, don't you think. You can do or say anything, *be* anything!'

I suppressed a shudder. 'And what were you?'

She sighed languorously and brushed her fingers through her hair, head flung back. 'Oh, I was beautiful, beautiful!' she exclaimed. 'It was a perfect night, no strangeness anywhere! I think it was the power of our rites that drove it away. What do you think?'

I shrugged again, noncommittally, although I had reached for my notebook. Sah'ray's observation might be worth recording.

In the afternoon, after Sah'ray had fed me, I went alone to bathe, alert for the presence of Aniti because I still did not want her company. Feeling refreshed and invigorated by the cold water, I wandered into the woods. It was a truly magical spot. I fantasised about having a little shack there, somewhere I could retreat to when the wideness of the world outside became oppressive. Perhaps one day I could return when the Sink was empty of nomads. What bliss to have all this to myself!

As if my feet were led by unseen agencies, I found myself emerging into the sacred glade. Even by day it was an arcane place, and the face of Helat, shadowed by trees, smiled down with ambivalent mystery. Spreading out my arms, I turned a few circles in the centre of the clearing. The sun was hot on my hair. I lifted it up in handfuls, recapturing, for a moment, the spirit of the rite. And then a voice intruded on my solitude.

'So, the warrior-priest can dance!'

I staggered a little, disorientated, dazzled by the bright sunlight. For a few moments I could see nothing in the shadows of the trees and my heart contracted. Was there a body attached to the voice? Was it familiar to me? Shadows pulsed on the edge of my vision; I experienced a great feeling of imminence. It was like wings over my head, wings I knew too well.

Then someone laughed; it was a spiteful sound. 'Relax, Rayojini, your cavortings have not been discovered by the barbarians!'

The voice came from the edge of the clearing, the place where Helat sat. And, when I looked, I could see there was a shadowy figure crouched in the statue's lap. As I stared, it became more focused, somehow, more real. The concentration of my senses

177

conjured me the image of Keea: a shadow condensing into reality. Keea, damp in the lap of Helat, perhaps spawned by the god itself. I blinked: no, there was nothing unreal about him, I would not let myself think that. He jumped down the steps and I could see that his clothes were wet through. He really had been sitting in the water, bizarre creature.

'What do you want?' I asked sharply.

He walked towards me, shaking his limbs like a wet animal, as light on his feet as an athlete. 'Well, what I wanted was a little peace to commune with the spirit of the god, and I find my meditations violated by a prancing soulscaper!'

'Forgive *me*!' I answered, sweeping a sarcastic bow. I realised it would be wise to leave immediately, before he tried to humiliate and confuse me further.

'Oh, it's quite all right,' he said, disarming me with a frank smile. 'This place is for everyone, isn't it? I'm sorry I disturbed your dance.'

'It wasn't a dance. I was just. . .'

He halted a few feet away from me, flicking out the damp ends of his hair. 'Don't make excuses. How did you like Q'orveh last night?'

I was almost speechless. 'You unspeakable little . . . !'

'All right, all right,' he interrupted. 'I shall not speak. It is strange though. Taps are eager enough to share in the rites, but loath to be honest about it after the event! Perhaps you look upon it as research. Anyway whatever your reasons, you still made a pretty tableau last night, you and that lovely girl.'

It occurred to me, with terrific shame, that Keea might have spied on us after the rite, an idea which I banished swiftly. Instinct told me that if Keea had been near us, he would have been unable to resist making his own contribution to our private ceremony in one way or another. I dismissed the illusion I'd seen of Keea's face, convinced I'd conjured that myself. Q'orveh had obviously told him about what had happened; Keea was only trying to discomfit me now. I did not want to imbue this impudent youth with any power.

'Well, at least I've proved you a liar!' I said.

He shrugged. 'And you have proved yourself to be a woman of passion. So we have both experienced revelations!' He glanced round into the trees. 'Now, are you ready for further surprises, or do you want to scamper back to camp away from me? I have wonders greater than burial platforms to show you here!' He had immense impertinence for one so young.

'I doubt you can surprise me,' I said stiffly, intrigued in spite of myself.

'We'll see.' He turned around and began to walk away from me, raising a summoning arm above his head. 'The adventure begins! Follow me, soulscaper, follow me!'

* * *

178

Keea led me to the great stone toes of the statue and then squeezed into the undergrowth on Helat's right side. I followed him, rather nervously. It seemed somehow irreverent to be thrusting ourselves into Helat's territory; I wouldn't have been surprised if the idol had suddenly groaned and moved a limb at our effrontery. My rational self scoffed at such primitive fantasies, but I still felt uncomfortable at having to lean against the ancient stone for support. If there was a path, it hadn't been used for a long time. Most of the time, we had to claw our way forward through leaves and branches that scattered a powder of insects, twigs and autumn spores. I shuddered to think what might be making its way down the back of my neck. Soulscape monsters I can handle; anything small and with more than four legs reduces me to gibbering panic. I was gratified when Keea screeched ahead of me and starting beating frantically at his shirt. For a few moments we paused to discuss the monster spider he'd encountered in the nauseated yet morbidly fascinated manner of habitual arachnophobes. After that, Keea used a stick to make a path and there was a certain sense of companionship between us.

As we struggled onwards, I saw evidence that at one time this path must have been used regularly. If I peered carefully into the foliage, I could see that it concealed lichened, stone pillars, bound in vines and some of them half-crumbled. I did not ask Keea where we were going. In fact after the spider episode we did not speak at all, but I felt strangely at ease in his company almost as if I'd known him for a long time. Only a short while ago, I'd felt strongly that he was an enemy. I could not believe this new intimacy had been prompted simply by our discovery of a shared phobia. I cautioned myself to be on guard. Keea was a complex creature; I must not let him beguile me.

Suddenly, he stopped moving forward; I had been lost in my own thoughts and stumbled against him. 'What is it?' I asked.

He tapped his chin with his fingers and squinted around himself. 'Yes, this is the place.'

'What place?' Shrubs and low growth pressed in from all sides. We were thigh-deep in greenery, our trousers thick with spurred seeds and down.

'Help me, will you.' He started clawing at a bank of vines ahead of us, throwing out webby debris behind him. I advanced cautiously. Reluctantly, I grabbed hold of a gnarly old ivy stem and tugged. Something ripped among the leaves. I pulled hard and an immense length of greenery peeled away. Beneath it I was amazed to see stone. My interest kindled, I forgot my nervousness about what might live in the vines and started tearing the leaves away. The foliage concealed an ancient building. Keea squatted down and started scrabbling round the base of the wall. 'There must be an entrance round here. . .'

'What is this place?' I asked him.

He paused and wiped his damp forehead with a grimy hand. 'This is the temple of Helat.'

'Oh, of course it is!' I said, rather sarcastically. 'How do you know that?'

He resumed his excavations. 'I've done my research more thoroughly than you. Just listen. At one time the whole of this crater was a religious community. Nearly all of the ruins have disappeared now, of course. Caravans of stone merchants crossing the Flats stole most of the masonry but, fortunately, this inner temple remains virtually untouched.'

'How do you know these things? Who built this place?'

'There is no mystery, soulscaper. All this information is recorded if you know where to look for it. Also I passed my time productively last night, while you were gratifying your baser instincts with Q'orveh and the girl.'

I refused to respond to his latter remark, determined not to let him provoke me again. 'And just where are these records you speak of?'

He paused again to conduct a swift inner debate, finally saying, 'Oh, I suppose there's no harm in telling you. There are libraries in Sacramante that detail the history of the older races of the plains.'

'Are the nomads descended from them?'

'In a way, I believe.'

'Then what changed their society? Natural catastrophe, plague, conquest?'

'I don't know.'

I had a feeling he was lying, which meant perhaps that there *would* be harm in telling me too much. I wondered why. Just who was this shadow-boy, and why was he with the Halmanes? He was clearly educated and appeared to be Bochanegran. He seemed to be more interested in my investigations than Q'orveh was. Was it possible he could be following a similar line of inquiry? If so, for whom, and what had prompted him suddenly to include me in his plans? His manner towards me up until now could, without exaggeration, be termed hostile.

'Keea, just what is your interest in Helat and the nomads?' I asked, but a timely discovery allowed him to sidetrack my question.

'Here! Here! Here!' he said, excitedly. He had found the doorway. I couldn't tell whether vines from outside were growing into the building or whether its interior was filled with the stuff, which was bursting outwards. I hoped it was the former, having little desire to spend the rest of the day defoliating the inside. When we had made enough of an opening to get within, Keea wriggled through it. I paused for a moment before following him into the temple, sucking my scratched fingers and taking the time to examine

180

the carvings on the outer wall. They were so worn, it was difficult to decipher them, but what I could make out reminded me strongly of the hieroglyphs which were used in the sacred texts of the Delta Lands. I wondered whether they were, in fact, the same. It was possible that the Kahra Flats, whose name itself suggested Deltan heritage, had once been colonised by the Deltans. Most places in the known world bore evidence of their influence. In the past the empires of the black-skinned Delta kings had risen and fallen along with the centuries. Sometimes they had owned nearly all the known world while, at other times, they had retreated to their own country, driven back by indignant races who objected to the Deltan fondness for conquest. Now, the Deltans were fascinated more by spirituality than war, and empire-building had lost its attraction for them. Still, the Temple of Helat might be a remnant of the times when their armies had covered half the world.

'Rayo! Come here!' Keea called from deeper inside, his voice muffled.

I ducked down and stepped cautiously into the gloom beyond. All the inner walls were shrouded in dead vines; the floor was a riot of ground shrubs. Birds had nested among the higher growth and were squawking madly at our impertinent intrusion. Bats hung like clusters of furry fruits from thick branches overhead, sleepily uttering inquiring squeaks. There was not much to see, everything was hidden beneath a blanket of bird and bat guano, rotten vege-table matter, and new, paler growths. Slim rays of sunlight fell like spears from holes in the roof high above our heads. Keea was standing ankle-deep in rubbish, his hands on his hips, staring upwards. I joined him and we stood in silence absorbing the atmos-phere. There was, without doubt, a hint of holiness about it. The air smelt of rich loam and I thought I could detect just the faintest whiff of old incense: surely my imagination? Then Keea sighed and rubbed his hands together, breaking the stillness.

'Is this it, then?' I asked.

He smiled at me thinly. 'You are indeed hard to impress.' He began to wade purposefully through the ground debris towards the right-hand wall, as if striding through water. I watched as he started to scrape at the rustling garlands of dead vines that lined the temple.

I struggled to Keea's side. 'I'm not putting my hands in that!'

'Did I ask you to help?' He threw a handful of leaves at me and smiled.

Sighing, I began to pull at the dead vines. 'What do you want to show me?'

'Wait and see.'

The tough woody stems inflicted further damage on my fingers and tore my nails. 'This had better be worth the effort!' I said.

'You will really have to learn to trust me,' Keea replied.

I pulled a particularly stubborn vine-rope from the wall and threw it over his shoulders. 'You are a real showman, Keea. I commend your performance.'

'This is not for your entertainment, Mistress Rayojini, but your enlightenment.'

'Then why not just tell me what this is all about?'

Predictably, he did not answer.

'There,' he said at last, standing back and folding his arms, which were scratched to the elbows. I glanced at him, wordlessly, and then went to examine the wall. We had uncovered a series of pictorial carvings, a picture story, which related some mythological or historical event. At one time they would have been brightly painted because, in places where the vine-roots had not been too destructive, flecks of colour remained. I leaned forward to peer at the pictures, but Keea, standing behind me, put his hands on my arms and pushed me to the left. 'No, they start here. Read it.'

I let him guide me.

The first picture represented the androgyne Helat. It was crouched in a huge hole in the ground, perhaps the Sink itself, with its legs spread wide, delivering an obscene amount of infants into the world who poured from between its legs in a torrent. Above it, figures that might have been angry spirits thronged the sky, shaking their fists and throwing down bolts of lightning. In the next few pictures, Helat's spawn – clearly the creatures now known as the Host of Helat – were shown dispersing into the societies of mankind. They were much taller than the humans, and were depicted in a stylised way that again reminded me of Deltan art. Whereas humanity was shown as an active bundle of chaos, the Host were towering and rather sinister creatures, and even though they were only carvings, I detected a great sense of stillness about them and a focused intention. The humans paid them no attention. Perhaps the Host were invisible to humankind. But no, further panels revealed members of the Host apparently teaching people the science of medicine, of the stars, the arts. In most of these panels the sky was represented as being full of boiling clouds and thunderbolts. Then the pictures became rather more fascinating.

The first of this sequence presented a member of the Host leaning over a recumbent man in a manner suggesting the act of love. The Host creature was female, her breasts bare, the nipples clearly erect. Her hands clawed into the shoulders of the man, whose head was flung back, his face, even after centuries of weathering, wearing an expression of ecstasy. The next panel showed the Host-female and the man engaged in copulation, although now the female seemed to have been overcome by lust because she was biting her lover on the throat! The man, apparently helpless but enraptured beneath her, seemed to be a willing victim to her ravages. His face was still ecstatic. I was smiling to myself, wondering about Keea's motive in wanting me to see this. I was just about to make a facetious remark when the next picture I examined made me gasp. It depicted the unfortunate lover of the female-Host lying dead in his house. His family were shown grieving around his bed, although the corpse was smiling radiantly. This was followed by a representation of the man's funeral procession – the obsequy cart, the line of dancing mourners – but that was not all: every symbol, those on the cart itself, on the head-gear of the mourners, on the shroud of the deceased, were those of the Holy Death. *This* was the Holy Death! Copulation with a member of the Host while being preyed upon. Sex as death. The symbol of the succubus was an ancient one and quite common in the soulscape, but this was different. Succubi and incubi did not mingle with humanity; they attacked under cover of night. Here, the spawn of a god imparted great wisdom, all the sciences and arts, and then preyed upon the people to whom they had bestowed this knowledge. What allegory was this? I had never encountered it in the soulscape, which was not just unusual but impossible. All human mythology could be accessed through the soulscape, however ancient, so why not this? I knew that old religious symbolism was often a metaphor for historical facts. How could I interpret all this? Was there a shred of truth here? Had some ancient race preyed upon humanity in some way, so that certain conditions of death now echoed those old legends?

'Well, are you impressed or not?' Keea asked. I turned to look at him accusingly.

'You know what this is?'

He merely smiled.

'Keea, how did you know this was here?' I demanded. 'How could you have known? It hasn't been touched for centuries?'

'I didn't know for sure. I just read it somewhere and had to come and see.'

'*Just read it somewhere!*' I could have hit him. Did he think I was so stupid? 'Is this why you're travelling with the nomads?' I asked, gesturing at the walls. 'Were you hoping they'd lead you to this place?'

'Partly.'

I folded my arms. 'So, the time has come for illumination! Come on, tell me what interest you have in all this. You know that I'm researching the cause of the non-death, and that I suspect it may be linked to the Holy Death, otherwise you wouldn't have shown me this. You stroked it out of the shaman, I suppose. Well, it's no secret. What I want to know is, why are you researching the same thing? How are you involved?'

'Personally? Not at all,' he said. 'I'm in the service of someone else.'

'Who?' I was desperate to know.

183

'Maybe you'll find out,' he replied. 'Maybe you'll meet them. One day.'

'Your love of mystery is really quite tiresome, you know!'

He shrugged.

'Do I have to guess? Is it someone in Bochanegra? Have the weird phenomena spread that far? Is that it?'

'They are interested in the same subject as you, yes. There are questions to be asked.'

'Do they know the history behind these carvings?'

'The history is obvious, isn't it?'

'Is it? Keea, I really think we should be working on this together. We could help each other, exchange information. You must tell me all you know. It might save lives.'

He laughed. 'What I know is more likely to end them!'

'Keea!'

'Work it out, Rayojini. The truth is here. Work it out.'

I had a thousand more questions to ask him, but he was already heading back for the doorway. 'Wait!' I called. 'You can't just leave! There's so much more to see! What about the other walls?'

He did not pause. 'No, there's nothing more,' he said. 'You've seen it all.'

I stood there helplessly. Damn him then! I would investigate the rest of the place by myself. He paused in the doorway. 'Your time has expired, soulscaper. The permit has been revoked. If you are wise, you will follow me out of here.' I opened my mouth to protest, but could not utter a sound. Maybe Keea invoked something through the tone of his voice, or maybe a breath of the wind coming down through the cracks in the roof made it happen, or even the thundering of my own heart. Maybe all of these, but suddenly the temple became a violently hostile place. For no apparent reason all the birds swooped down from their nests and subjected me to a vicious attack. Even as they were flapping and screeching round my head, veils of bats lifted from the high foliage and poured down around me in a great squeaking maelstrom. The air became chaos; leaves and twigs swirled up from the floor. Hitting out blindly with my hands, I felt claws and feathers snag in my hair. Panicking, and shielding my face, I could only crouch down and scurry out of the building as quickly as my legs would carry me.

Keea had waited for me a little way along the path, but he did not turn around as I emerged. I called his name, stumbling forward, and he began to trot ahead of me, slapping branches from his path. The air was full of the angry screams of birds, the whirr of their wings. I ran after Keea with my hands over my head, the birds seemingly in pursuit.

After a while everything went silent; all I could hear was my own ragged breath and the rustle of foliage as I pushed it aside. My chest ached so much I had to pause and catch my breath, or risk

184

collapse. Keea did not wait for me. Perhaps he was more frightened than I was, or perhaps now that he had shown me the temple, he no longer cared what happened to me. I did not call him back. Later, I would corner him and he would answer my questions willingly or have the information beaten out of him! What had taken place back there? Had Keea made it happen? Gasping, I turned around.

Behind me, there was no evidence of anyone having disturbed the foliage, not for a hundred centuries.

By the time I emerged, groping along the flanks of the statue of Helat, the glade was mostly in shadow, the sun having fallen into the embrace of the highest trees. There was no sign of Keea at all. Helat's presence was very strong; I felt as if the nerves in my spine were being tweaked by unseen claws. Quickly, I crossed the open space without looking up at the statue, and plunged into the trees beyond. I wanted to find the camp as soon as possible; even Sah'ray in her most abrasive mood would be a relief after this! Luckily, the tribes were preparing for their evening festivities with a good deal of noise. My ears led me back.

Sah'ray was indignant that I'd disappeared, having arranged several consultations for me with some of her Toorish friends that afternoon. As she had mentioned none of this to me, I failed to be apologetic. I suspected she must have planned to make a clandestine profit from these appointments. 'You said you were just going to bathe, Rayo! Where have you been! You're so . . . so *secretive!*' she complained.

'I went back to the sacred glade actually,' I said. 'I wanted to see it by daylight.'

A frown furrowed her brow. 'Oh,' she said. 'That's supposed to be unlucky, you know. Helat only allows people into the glade at sacred times. I hope you didn't cause offence.'

'I was most polite,' I said. 'I'm sure the god will forgive the blunderings of an uninformed foreigner.'

'Hmmph!' Sah'ray grumbled, unsure whether I was mocking her or not. 'Why are you such a mess? What did you do there?'

'I went for a walk in the woods and got a bit lost.'

'Helat's Eye, your hands!'

'Had to burrow my way out at one point.' I knew I sounded sheepish, but mercifully Sah'ray abandoned the interrogation.

'That soulscaper girl was here looking for you,' she said.

I was not surprised.

I quickly wrote up an account of everything I had experienced in the Temple of Helat. Sah'ray insisted on looking over my shoulder the entire time, but fortunately she couldn't read Tappish. Well, at least I knew where I was heading now: Sacramante. I would have to interrogate Keea to find out where the libraries he had spoken of could be found. If only I could ascertain who his masters were. He was being most obstructive. It was obvious they'd want to know my findings as much as I wanted to know theirs. I considered what I'd learned: could the Host be a metaphor for a disease? Perhaps the Holy Death had been more common at one time and people had tried to explain it by anthropomorphising it. Yes, that made sense. Still, it was strange how Holy victims were always taken at night. What could that mean? Something to do with the temperature of the air changing at dusk? Holy victims smiled in death, as if they had welcomed it. Why? Hadn't they known they were going to die? Pleasurable nocturnal deaths would, in primitive minds, give rise to the idea of incubi and succubi perhaps. And how could all this possibly relate to the advent of miracles and inexplicable events? I tidied away my notes. More information was needed. The fright I had suffered seemed nothing more than the product of a feverish imagination now. Keea had scared the birds and bats somehow. He was not just a showman but an accomplished magician!

I was now in the mood for celebration. A night of drinking, eating and general wildness would be quite a fitting end to my partnership with the Halmanes. Soon, I would be alone again with my thoughts and the sound of my own footsteps. I knew I should make the most of human company before this time. Perhaps even a final dalliance with Aniti! I supposed I owed her an explanation, at least. Sexual partners who dropped you without a word caused the most horrible of self-doubts. I was also anticipating getting my hands on Keea; he would not evade my questions so easily again. In a way, I was excited and pleased that others were making investigations in the same direction as myself. Realistically it was inevitable that someone would be doing so; my intellect wasn't unique.

I changed my clothes, and allowed Sah'ray to line my eyes with black kohl and tidy up a few of my braids, which had come loose in the scrabble through the wood that afternoon. She had forgotten her annoyance with me and, as we preened ourselves in the murky confines of her tent, happily babbled to me about whom she intended to snare as a sexual partner before the night was over. We shared a few cups of thick, sweet wine, but before the festivities one of Q'orveh's female acolytes appeared outside, and I was summoned to the shaman's tent.

I anticipated our meeting might be rather embarrassing, but Q'orveh greeted me with casual friendliness, as if nothing had transpired between us the previous night. Keea was nowhere to be seen; irritating that he should be invisible at the only time when I wanted him. I asked Q'orveh why he'd summoned me.

'I want to discuss our approach to the Strangeling,' he said.

I knew the Strangeling to be a wide area of ruins, inhabited by every kind of rogue imaginable. It hugged the border of the

186

Bochanegran Empire; perhaps the ruins were those of ancient cities that had been abandoned by the Bochanegrans centuries before. The Strangeling was not a place regularly frequented by soul-scapers, and it was certainly not somewhere I intended to linger on my way to Sacramante. 'Oh?' I replied, carefully.

'Things will get more . . . bizarre, I feel. The Toors have come from the West and they say the incidence of strange occurrences is much more frequent back there. Also, Toortaki has told me of evil riders on the road who have no faces. They inspire terror in the heart of anyone who sees them.'

More tribal fairy-stories! 'What has this to do with me?'

He seemed puzzled by my coolness. 'I thought you were interested in these things. I had hoped to help you. Also, I feel very strongly we will need a soulscaper among us in the western lands.'

'I see. Do all the tribal shamans feel this way, Q'orveh? Since when has the soulscaper's rôle changed from rival to saviour?'

'Your bitterness surprises me,' he said. 'I think the strangenesses are things that we should face together, Taps and tribes alike. I supposed you felt the same.'

'Yesterday, you spoke of prayers to appease your god, and no interference in divine activity. In fact, you reprimanded me. Now, I am essential. Your turns of mind confuse me, Q'orveh.'

'Are you with us or not, Rayojini?' he asked sternly.

I sighed. 'Q'orveh, I am a healer. My vocation is to help people wherever I find them. In that respect, you have my commitment.'

My words seemed to satisfy him. 'Go out and enjoy the festival,' he said.

'Nor uglier the night-hag, when called in secret, riding through the air she comes . . .'
Paradise Lost, Book II

After leaving Q'orveh's tent, I sought out Aniti and Juro as I had intended. We sat together, with a group of Halmanes, and the evening passed in a pleasant haze of intoxication. We all drank the nomads' vicious brews far too liberally and, at Juro's insistence, he, Aniti and I had shared a pipe of our secondary scrying mix. Dreamy illusions crowded the corners of my vision. I rambled on incoherently, to an equally incoherent Aniti, about the sacrifices I had made for my lone life's path, which precluded all intimate relationships of a long-term nature. She accepted this without apparent upset, but asked me to look for her when I next returned to Taparak. This I agreed to do without question, although I had a feeling it would be a very long time before I saw my home again.

I had kept alert for signs of Keea but he made no appearance throughout the night. Before my mind fuzzed up completely with smoke and alcohol, I had made a cursory search for him among the groups of celebrating nomads gathered around the camp fires. I was not permitted access to Q'orveh's tent, because youths stationed outside informed me that a private rite was being conducted within. They did not think Keea was involved.

I did not disclose to the other soulscapers that I planned to resume my travels alone the following day. They themselves talked about returning to Taparak very shortly, and clearly assumed I would remain with the Halmanes until we reached the Strangeling. I did feel a little nervous about my proposed escape. Would Q'orveh come after me when he realised I'd abandoned his tribe? Did some part of me hope that he would? Was having a soulscaper around that important to him or, more worrying, would he see my flight as a sign of culpability in some way? I could only find out once the camp was behind me.

As the fires sank low, and people began to drift off into the trees, I saw Q'orveh come out of his tent. Perhaps it was no coincidence Aniti and I had chosen to sit quite nearby. The shaman appeared shaken, perhaps drunk; he was naked to the waist. I watched him stretch up his arms to the sky, saw him extend the magnificent muscles of his lean body and let his tangled mane fall back in a ragged flag to below his waist. A brief pang crossed my heart.

189

Should I go to him? Would I be rebuffed if I did? Aniti touched my arm. I looked at her sharply, expecting some provocative remark. But she was not looking at me. 'Rayo, can you see that?' she asked. 'Look at his throat, just above his chest. What has he done to himself?'

'A ritual cut,' I said, glancing at the mark she indicated. 'The nomads are like that.'

'He looks . . . ill.'

'Drugged. He has his acolytes in there with him.'

Aniti shrugged. 'Are you going to speak to him?'

Q'orveh stood motionless, staring up at the moon. For some reason, at that moment I could not bear the thought of touching him again. 'No,' I said. 'Some delicacies can only be sampled once.'

'Am I one of those?' she asked archly.

I patted her hand. 'You are a Tap,' I said, 'a woman – not a delicacy.'

'I admire you greatly,' Aniti blurted.

I squeezed her hand. 'I don't deserve it!'

She sighed. 'You are no longer touched by the magick of this place, are you?' The disappointment in her voice tugged briefly at my heart, but I hardened it swiftly. Seeing Q'orveh had somehow choked the urge for intimacy with anyone from my body.

I shook my head, not entirely without regret, and Aniti gently pulled her hand from beneath my fingers.

At dawn, after a few hours sleep alone, I removed myself as quietly as possible from Sah'ray's tent. A fog had come down, lying thickly in the basin of the Sink, so that the rock walls were invisible. Only the peaks of other tents showed as smudges in the immediate vicinity and I could hear the muffled tocking of the bells worn around the necks of the mules and goats hobbled nearby.

It was chilly enough to warrant wearing my long, heavy coat; I bundled my hair up into my hat, so it wouldn't get too damp. Carryback firmly in place, I carefully picked my way through the camp, treading deliberately so I wouldn't make a noise by accidentally thrusting a foot into a pile of pans or something similar. The Sink looked utterly enchanted, as if everyone were under the spell of a magick sleep. The air smelt of damp ashes and spilled wine, and many people were asleep where they'd fallen – drunk – the previous night. I nearly stumbled over a slumbering youth, who lay motionless on the ground outside one of the tents. Thankfully, he did not wake. All the rubbish from the festivities remained: dead fires, tumbled pitchers, half-eaten bones. Sound was deadened; not even the murmur of a child broke the stillness. I passed the tent of Q'orveh, and had to resist a powerful impulse to glance inside. The strength of this urge made me realise that, for a few days at least, I was going to miss being able to look at Q'orveh. It also made me

190

realise that I wasn't leaving any too soon.

The thickness of the fog meant that it took me some time to find the curving road that led up to the plains. Once I had found my bearings, and had begun the long climb, a lone black bird cawed desolately from a ragged tree sticking out of the crater wall. It seemed a bleak omen. I increased my pace, grateful to be leaving the Sink and all its secrets behind. It was a nuisance I hadn't been able to speak with Keea again, but at least he'd given me enough information to know what to look for in Sacramante. What would he think when he found out I'd slipped away? I had a feeling he'd be quite annoyed at losing the person he enjoyed tormenting.

If I thought to escape the fog on the Flats I was mistaken, but under the circumstances it was probably fortuitous. If Q'orveh did discover my departure shortly, at least I wouldn't be visible on the road. My footsteps seemed to make hardly any sound; I was surrounded by a wall of soundless whiteness. At first, I enjoyed the sense of isolation and then the noises crept in upon me and I became aware that I was armed only with a knife.

A thud of hoofbeats came through the mist, sounding as if some-one were riding alongside of me, just out of sight. I could hear the jangle of harness, the grunts of a labouring horse. For a moment, I paused. There was suddenly silence and I could see nothing moving, other than the thick banks of cloud roiling across my path. I was glad I had wrapped myself up well; my coat had become soaked within an hour of leaving the camp. I shivered and held my breath. No, there was definitely nothing to be heard. Obviously, I had caused the sounds myself: buckles rattling on my carryback perhaps, and the muffled thump of my own tread upon the packed dirt of the road. I starting moving again, humming a simple tune under my breath to create an aura of security around myself. Then I heard it again: jangle, clop, thump.

I halted immediately, hastily flexing my senses in an effort to pick up some sign that I was not alone. But, again, all the noises ceased when I stopped walking, leaving an eerie, waiting silence as if reality itself were holding its breath. I was not altogether free of the fear of pursuit.

I had picked up some talk the previous evening concerning the mysterious strangers who had been seen riding across the plains. The Toors spoke of cloaked men who rode heavy, white horses and whose behaviour was somehow threatening. One woman said that the riders wore armour that looked like skin. How I wished these people could be more objective! It was like trying to work out a puzzle, translating their superstitious prattle into hard infor-mation. If there really were sinister riders flitting about the Flats, there had to be a sensible explanation. I did wonder whether, after having played unwilling host to one or two strange events, a local landowner had sent some of his people out on horseback to scout

191

around. It was possible. Perhaps I was being followed by one of these riders now. I tried to peer into the long grasses beside the road, but if anyone lurked there it was impossible to discern. I am rarely frightened when travelling. Human beings, I can usually deal with in one way or another. I can run fast; I can fight with an unfaltering arm and without squeamishness; I can talk the spirit from the craziest of madmen until I have them eating out of my hand. Things I cannot see, that are not human, I deal with in the way I deal with anything in the soulscape: with my will. Thought-forms manifesting themselves in reality are the easiest of creatures to cope with. With all this in mind, I slowed my pace, breathed deeply to regulate my heart and summoned my inner strength. It was senseless to feel afraid or threatened. And yet a premonition of dread was creeping all over me like a swarm of insects; my skin actually *crawled*. The blood drained from my face and I found it hard to breathe. Was this how it felt when the Fear took someone? Was it? I knew that was the most dangerous thought to dwell on, because terror of the Fear builds it the widest of portals into the mind. You are a soulscaper, Rayojini, I told myself firmly. What you are thinking is nonsense and worthy only of nomads! I reminded myself objectively that although there *were* recorded cases of soul-scapers becoming victims of the condition they attempted to eradi-cate, the instances were few, and those who did succumb were always weak individuals who had neglected their training. *Never*, in the history of soulscaping, had a seasoned professional like myself been taken, or at least, if they had, no one had ever heard about it. Then, I definitely heard an equine snort in the grass on my left and the sound of hoofbeats accelerated to overtake me.

I stopped walking and pulled out the knife from my belt for comfort. It was a useful and well-loved instrument that had spitted my food and provided me with protection for many years. I straight-ened my spine, closed my eyes and extended my senses out into the fog. If anything was there, soulscape effluvia or not, I willed myself to become aware of it. Nothing. It was like trying to see through thick cloth. Then I opened my eyes and, for a moment, believed I had manifested some thought-form of my own into reality.

Just ahead of me, on the road, stood the motionless form of a gigantic white horse. It was caparisoned in a tasselled mantle of purple cloth, over which ran a complicated harness of embossed leather. On its back sat a stooped, cloaked figure wearing a lemniscate hat. Two hawks were tethered to the saddle in front of it. The horse's head was turned a little to the side, as if to examine me more closely, and I could see its eyes were pink like an albino's, with long, white lashes. Its rider's face was indiscernible beneath the brim of the hat; whether male or female I could not tell, but the ambience of authority was unmistakable. I had no doubt come across one of the mysterious riders the Toors had talked about. I exhaled gustily in relief. *This* I could cope with. This was not a problem; both horse and rider were real, larger than life itself. My step buoyant with relief, I confidently walked forwards, saying, 'A less than bright day to be abroad, my friend. Are you lost?'

I had rarely encountered a creature with less of an air of lostness, but I had to say something. There was no answer. I was close to the animal now and, as animals do, it swung its nose around to sniff my coat. I was reassured and cupped my palm around its muzzle, tucking my knife back into my belt. I could see the grain in the leather of the rider's boots. I could see the stretch of the thin, black kid gloves across the knuckles where they gripped the reins. I could even see, I fancied, the glimmer of eyes beneath the brim of the hat, and the suggestion of an unsmiling line of a mouth. The rider's demeanour was not exactly welcoming, but I detected no immediate threat. Perhaps we could conduct a trade in information. I realised how silly it had been to let myself get frightened before; *that* was a failing of the superstitious and the ignorant. Being so intimate with the nomads must have infected me with their thought patterns.

'There is talk of you, I think, among the nomad tribes . . .' I said as a bait, using the Khaltish tongue. The figure stiffened a little, I was sure. 'My name is Rayojini. I am a soulscaper of Taparak.' Giving my identity so freely was deliberate and designed to inspire trust.

'I know who you are,' the rider replied. It was a young man's voice, without particular inflection in the tone but possessed of a silky, Bochanegran accent.

'Really? Well, perhaps you could return the privilege?' I did not believe his claim; it was a ploy to discomfit me, as was the fact that he refused to answer my question. He was as bad as Keea! I affected a laugh. 'Well, if you will not converse with me, that is your own choice,' I said. 'Ride east, and you will find a pair of nomad tribes, camping in a vast depression in the plains. Maybe you want to speak with them. There is much they can tell you, I should think.' Then I raised my hand in a wave and began to walk past the horse.

'Rayojini!' The sound of my name stopped me dead. I looked around. Although I had heard no movement, the horse had turned to face me and we were in exactly the same positions as when I had first approached the animal. They must be silent and quick movers these Bochanegran steeds, I thought, feeling slightly disorientated. *Had* I walked past it?

'You did not see enough of Helat's shrine,' the rider said. 'Or rather you saw, but did not understand. The nomads have more intelligence than you, Tappish clown!'

'Now, wait a minute!' I marched towards him, frowning as grimly as possible. How dare this dandy insult me! Who was he, and how he had known about my visit to the temple? Could it be that he was one of Keea's mysterious employers? I reached out to grab the horse's reins by the bit-ring but at that moment its rider squeezed the animal sharply with his legs and uttered a sibilant command. Obediently the horse rose into a splendid kicking rear, plunged forward into a canter – virtually from a standstill – and thundered straight towards me. It all happened so quickly, my first instinct was to throw myself aside, which I did – landing in the tall grass beside the road. I had a glimpse of dangling hooves. The guttural sound of a low and terrible neigh was in my ears. Summoning every shred of strength, and despite the heavy carryback on my shoulders, I rolled madly further into the grass, waiting for the sickening and agonising assault of iron-shod hooves on my body. I was convinced I was going to be trampled no matter how quickly I moved, and I curled tight into a ball, my arms over my head, awaiting the impact . . . which never came.

After a few moments, I relaxed enough to uncurl my arms and look up. The horse had vanished. All was silent in the fog, but for the hiss of the grass rubbing against itself, high above my head. I wriggled out of my carryback harness and stood shakily, brushing myself down and peering towards where I thought the road should be. Through the mist I could see nothing: no rider, no horse, and – most importantly of all – no road. Well, that was easily remedied. I unbuckled one of the flaps of my carryback and searched the pocket where I kept my compass and maps. Empty! 'By all the gods!' I sat down again, heavily, pulling a shroud of grass about my body. Had Sah'ray stolen some of my possessions? Surely not. It was more likely that I hadn't packed up properly and had left some of my things behind in her tent. Still, whatever the reason, in losing my compass I had effectively lost the road. What should I do now; blindly look for it or stay put until the fog lifted? Surely it would lift by midday? Hadn't the weather been warm recently. It certainly wasn't now. I hadn't really been aware of how cold the air had become until my journey had been interrupted; suddenly despite my heavy coat, I felt chilled to the core. I wondered whether the mysterious rider's intention had been to harm me or merely frighten me. Was he still stalking me now, silent in the mist, perhaps only a few feet away? Surely the road was near; the mist was warping my perception. If I walked a few feet to the left, I was bound to find it again. I had only rolled a short way into the grass, after all. My back was in agony where the carryback had dug into me as I rolled and I noticed that one of the straps which connected it to its frame had torn loose. It would be twice as difficult to shoulder now. Sighing at this unexpected misfortune, I stood up, strapped myself in the harness as best I could and began to push my way through the tall grass, trusting my sense of direction to lead me. I was also alert for signs which might indicate that the white horse and its rider were still in the vicinity.

Minutes passed and I was no closer to finding the road. Angrily, I began to slash out at the grass around me. 'Helat's tits and cock!' I cursed, an evocative little phrase I'd picked up from Sah'ray. I was lost, and to go blundering about like this only increased my chances of not being able to find my way once the fog lifted. I was beginning to curse my decision to leave the Halmanes. I knew, deep inside, that the reasons for my flight were more abstruse than a simple desire to travel alone. In truth, I was running from an aspect of myself. Now, I was trying to control a rising sense of panic and I made a quick, impassioned plea to Helat. If I was allowed to find my way back to the road, I would return instantly to the Sink. Once there, I would stay by Q'orveh's side whatever the consequences for my equilibrium, and would do all that I could to comfort his people until we reached the Strangeling. Someone must have heard me, but I don't believe it was Helat.

I was standing there, helpless, wondering quite what to do, when I thought I saw a movement ahead of me. It was just a dark blotch, but in no way suggested a horse and rider. My attacker could have dismounted, of course, yet I did not feel that it was him I'd seen. I began to push through the grass, hoping I wasn't just following some animal that would lead me further into obscurity. Then – oh bliss, thank Helat – I stumbled out on to a hard, flat surface: the road! Before I'd finished congratulating myself, I realised I was not alone. Someone else stood upon the packed dirt, but this time it was not a horse and rider.

This figure was alone, and I knew instinctively that it was female. She was standing quite some distance away: a slim body clad in a dark, hooded cloak. A nomad woman? I began to run towards her, my broken carryback banging painfully against my body. Then I heard a voice.

'Don't be too hasty, Rayo!' It was my mother's voice.

I stumbled and glanced quickly over my shoulder. The words had sounded so close, but behind me I could see nothing except the closing fog. It wasn't easy to run with the damaged carryback but at that moment I needed human company more than anything. Such was the state of my panic, I did not for one moment consider that what stood upon the road was anything but human. As I drew close, I could see that the woman was quite tall; one white hand was holding her cloak together at the neck. I must have called out, some nonsense or another, but she made no sign of having heard me. She, like the rider when I'd first seen him, was neither welcoming nor threatening; she simply *was*. Then I realised that in a strange way which did not relate directly to physical appearance, I recognised her. At that precise moment, she opened her arms wide. Her great cloak became feathers, became wings. They flapped slowly, arching with living muscle, framing a naked body as white as death. I fell to my knees on the road; my silently gaping mouth open so wide, it hurt. I filled it with my fingers and bit down to conjure pain, to conjure feeling. Slowly, like a flickering picture cast by the shadow of flames, the monstrous shape of the bird-woman came to hover over me. I could see her face, her slitted yellow eyes. She opened her mouth to reveal pointed, dog-like teeth and out came a raw croak.

'Don't you know me, sweet Rayo?' she asked, and laughed. It was the sound of a dozen ravens screaming.

And then I knew her, oh yes! Led me from the grass she had: guardian. Now hanging over me like a nightmare: pursuer. As real to me as my own pain. 'Help me!' I said.

'How can I? Am I real to you, real enough to count?' She laughed again and then, bunching her wings up behind her, she swooped down towards me, her pale face the colour of bleached decay, her red mouth wide like a cavern of the firepit. She knocked me backwards, and something grazed my face, something with hot breath that stank of old meat: a sweet and infinitely corrupt perfume. My head hit the road, my back arched painfully over the carryback, so that my heels dangled in mid-air. Wet, stinking, black feathers flapped in my face and I was surrounded by laughter, an evil stench and the feeling of imminent destruction. Helplessly, I held up my arms, calling out for my mother: my only true goddess. Hard claws dug into my flesh, dragging my hands away from my face. I struck out again and again, one hand groping for my knife, which I could not find. I screamed, eyes screwed up tight, and flailed my arms. I hit something soft and there was a sound of surprise. Yet above this sound was the cacophony of scraping feathers and distant shrieking. Behind my closed eyelids the world was red and black, shot with flames and blood. Then something sinuous curled around my wrists, and I could not move. I flexed my fingers helplessly, sobbing like a child. I kept my eyes closed tight; for all my bravado in the soulscape I dared not look upon what held me.

'Rayojini!'

The voice seemed to come from very far away, and then swooped up close as it spoke my name again. 'Rayojini!' I was being shaken. Gulping, I opened my eyes.

Keea's face was hanging over me, his hair touching my face. He was smiling, but the smile was not convincing. I saw fear there, too. 'Had a fright, soulscaper?' he asked shakily. 'What is this scrabbling with the fingernails like a girl?' His hands were firmly holding on to my wrists, as if he was afraid I might attack him. 'You have scratched yourself,' he said. 'What is the matter with you?'

And I am ashamed to admit that despite my pride, my principles and any resolution of spirit I had made, I threw myself against him and wept like a frightened kidling.

Q'orveh had sent him after me of course, although he denied this vigorously. I had resigned myself to returning to the Halmanes, yet once I had recovered my wits enough to regain composure, Keea made no suggestion we should do so. He sat me down in a nest of grass, next to a neatly furled pile of luggage, bound about the dismantled twig-plait frame of a tepee. Keea, it seemed, was travelling too. Had he anticipated a long journey before he caught up with me? He gave me water to drink – warm, but minted – and the herb brought a little coolness to my brain. I was in a state of shock and answered Keea's questions honestly, as to what I thought I'd seen. 'The rider knew about our visit to the temple,' I said. 'Is he a friend of yours?'

Keea shook his head.

'Then he is associated with your employers?'

He was reluctant to answer. 'That is always a possibility. How can I say? I did not see him.'

'Surely you would know!' I said angrily. 'Keea, the man was insane. He attacked me! He appeared to know my movements! If you know who he was, tell me!'

'I don't know, really I don't. And how can I answer whether the people I work for have other agents in Khalt or not?'

'So, you are an agent,' I said. 'That sounds sinister.'

'Why? It simply means I am an information-gatherer, that's all.'

'For whom?'

'It is confidential.'

I made an angry noise and rubbed my face vigorously with my hands. Stupid boy! Did he want to play games at a time like this? As if sensing how much he was infuriating me, Keea tentatively touched my arm.

'Rayo, don't get angry. Tell me what you saw.' His voice was gentle; his concern even sounded genuine.

'I think I saw a ghost,' I said.

He smiled, but did not laugh outright. 'A ghost? Do soulscapers believe in ghosts?'

'This soulscaper might believe anything, at the moment,' I answered.

Keea listened to my description of the guardian-pursuer and, instead of asking what I meant by that, as most people do, said only, 'If it *was* one of your guardian-pursuers, why were you afraid? Aren't they supposed to be looking after you all the time?' The question appeared innocent. I was dazed but not enough to be easily fooled.

'You seem to know a lot about Tappish custom, boy. . .' Perhaps I had told him too much. 'Nobody but soulscapers know about the guardian-pursuers. How did you find out about them?'

197

He shrugged, remarkably casually seeing as I'd just cornered him. '*You* just spoke about them,' he said. 'Perhaps other Taps have as well.'

I wondered whether he was implying that Aniti or Juro had confided in him. It was hard to believe; Taps just didn't tell outsiders their secrets, and yet Keea did have a point – *I* had babbled out my story to him. Now, calming down, I wished I hadn't.

'You are an intelligent boy, Keea,' I said. 'So you must realise that soulscapers work with symbols. The guardian-pursuers are merely metaphors for our own consciences, self-discipline and self-control.'

He laughed. 'Really! Then your conscience just attacked you in the road, did it?'

'I'm not sure *what* just attacked me,' I replied, trying to speak with some authority, 'but I cannot dismiss the possibility that it was self-generated.'

'The rider, too?'

It was obvious to me that he was looking upon our conversation as some kind of game. 'The rider was real enough,' I said, 'and the bird-woman seemed so, but I shall retain an open mind as to their origin.'

Keea smiled at me slyly. 'Perhaps with the advent of these new times your personal authority will continue to hound you in the flesh, soulscaper!'

'What new times?'

Keea narrowed his eyes through the grass. 'You have to admit strange things are happening in the world.'

'Perhaps.' I sipped for a few moments from the drink he had given me, eyeing him obliquely. For one so young, he sometimes spoke with the confidence of a far older person. Perhaps appearances were deceptive. He looked about eighteen years old. 'You mystify me a little,' I said.

He smirked at me. 'How flattering!'

'Not necessarily. I just wonder why you've made sure I'm aware you have information I need, and yet you refuse to share it. I wonder why you're trying to play with me. Are you foolish enough to believe the things that are happening are part of a game? You are interested in me, Keea. I know you are. Perhaps you too realise that if there is danger in Khalt, only people like myself can cope with it.'

He laughed. 'From the state I just found you in, I wouldn't count on that!'

I made an angry sound and he took hold of my hands. 'Let me see to those cuts. I don't mean to insult you, Rayojini. I quite like you.'

'How fortunate I am!'

Keea produced some balm and lint from his luggage and wiped

my face and hands. 'I didn't do this to myself,' I said.

'Perhaps not, but do you still think the creature that attacked you was your guardian-pursuer?'

The horror of it was fading. It would be easy to doubt what my eyes had seen. Why would one of my own guardian-pursuers attack me? It didn't make sense. 'Somehow I made her real,' I said. 'Somehow. I *saw* her!'

For a few moments, Keea studied me carefully. I could almost see him sifting through several things he wanted to say. For a moment, I was tempted to offer, 'You need my help, don't you?', for his expression held ghostly shreds of confusion and anxiety.

'They are important to you,' he said, staring me steadily in the eye. 'Those *creatures* . . .'

The last word held a tone of pure disgust. 'Why are you so interested in my guardian-pursuers, Keea?' I asked.

He glanced at me sharply, almost guiltily. 'I don't want you to lose your mind, that's all, and there is a danger of that around here.'

'Thank you for your consideration . . .' I finished the minted water and handed him back the cup. 'It was very fortunate you found me, I suppose. So, are you going to escort me back to the Halmanes, now? They, at least, have confidence in my sanity!'

He seemed puzzled. 'You want to go back?'

'That *is* why you're here, isn't it?'

'I don't run errands for Halmanes, Rayojini.'

'Yet you were following me . . .'

He grinned and gestured at the road. 'See this? There is a choice of two directions. There was a fifty-per-cent chance I'd run into you.'

'I don't really feel you have answered me but if you want to believe you're travelling independently, so be it. Where are you heading?'

'We're going to the Strangeling, aren't we?'

At his words, something contracted around my heart. For a moment or two I was afraid that some invisible net was closing in, tightening around me and yet, on another level, I was relieved not to be alone. 'Why do you want my company?'

'To tantalise you with what I do and do not know.'

'And what if *I* don't want company, hmm? I usually travel alone.'

'Why should we separate when we have the same goal?'

'Which is?'

'Enlightenment, naturally.'

I nodded, pulling a sour face. 'If you can promise you will not try to frustrate my investigations . . .' I glanced at him quickly. 'And what of Q'orveh? You are prepared to leave him?'

'Q'orveh will survive!' Keea stood up, obviously not wishing to discuss that subject with me. 'Do you feel well enough to travel?'

I snorted disparagingly and clambered to my feet beside him. 'Keea, I am always well enough to travel. I can travel in my sleep, if needs be.' All around us the fog was thinning, becoming transparent. Already the sun was a pale disc in the sky. Keea helped me re-strap my carryback and we started to walk towards the West. There was no conversation, but Keea whistled between his teeth: a low, marching refrain. I squinted at him beneath the brim of my hat. Now was I getting way too jumpy or was it possible, however unlikely, that Keea had somehow engineered all that I had just experienced? All that had happened in the temple of Helat indicated he might be an illusionist of some kind. My instincts did not trust him. Were his motivations benevolent? Yet, despite these reservations he intrigued me, not least because of his intimacy with Q'orveh. It would be as if I carried a tangible memory of the shaman with me if I travelled with his boy. Q'orveh would be aware by now that both Keea and I had left the camp. In a way that gave me satisfaction. I wanted him to think we had left together. This was most unlike me. Could such emotional flotsam cloud my judgement of Keea? As I thought this, he glanced at me and smiled. I would have to remain alert.

CANTO THREE

'So soft and uncompounded is their essence pure,
not tied or manacled with joint or limb, nor founded
on the brittle strength of bone like cumbrous
flesh . . .'
Paradise Lost, Book II

A few weeks after I had projected my spirit out into the world, and
had initiated certain vital processes, I returned to my body in
Sacramante. It felt stiff from disuse, even though I'd only been
away from it for a short time. Now the ingredients had been thrown
into the cauldron and I could only wait until the slow fusion was
complete to discover what fascinating result they would produce.

Awaking to an autumnal chill, I felt as if I had been away for a
hundred years. A questioning wind fluted around the high tower;
above me the black veils of the bed flinched restlessly to its tunc.
As I returned languorously to full consciousness within my body,
the hayfield aroma of the plains slipped away from my memory,
overcast by the echo of the last angry words I had exchanged with
my brother – Beth. I was afraid of what might have happened in
my absence.

Tamaris came to help me when she heard me stumbling down
the stairs of the high tower. She took me to my rooms, bathed my
body and let me feed from her wrist as I floated in the perfumed
water. The curtains were drawn against a glum afternoon, and
lamps, made fragrant with essential oils, were burning low. 'Has
anything . . . happened?' I asked.

Tamaris' dark eyes were cloudy with concern. She looked tired.
Soon, we would have to perform the ritual for her rejuvenation. I
didn't want my faithful servants dying from neglect! 'Lord Beth has
been working hard,' she replied. I closed my eyes and relaxed into
the water, grateful he was still in the house, at least. 'Madam . . .
?' The tone of Tamaris' voice suggested she was about to address
a difficult subject.

'Yes, Tamaris?'

'We – Ramiz and I – are aware all is not right between you and
Lord Beth.'

'It could hardly have escaped you, dear Tamaris. We made
enough noise about it!'

'Well . . . we want you to know that Lord Beth has not . . .' She
screwed up her face in vexation.

'Speak, for the sake of Light! I won't bite you!' We both smiled at the joke. She stroked a sliver of amber-scented soap down my arm.

'Avirzah'e Tartaruchi has not been near the house, and neither has Lord Beth been near his. We thought you should know that.'

'Thank you. It is gratifying news.' I stood up in the bath and Tamaris wrapped me in a voluminous towel. I would dress and then visit my brother.

I was relieved by the helpless welcome in Beth's eyes when I approached him in his brush court, although the ambience of the room itself was not that which I had expected to find. Gentle afternoon light came in through the north windows, and the room was full of tranquillity. Beth was dressed in a loose, paint-smeared shirt, the sleeves rolled back to his elbows. His hair was unbound, hanging round his shoulders; usually he tied it back severely when he was working. Smiling, I walked past him without attempting an embrace and went to examine his latest work. Some of my relief condensed into a harder substance.

'A good likeness,' I said.

The painting was of Avirzah'e. He was represented naked, but his loins were modestly shrouded by the tips of long feathers of purple hue. These feathers were the curling pinions of the enormous wings which Beth had painted sprouting from Avirzah'e's shoulders. The wings rose to bony joints high behind the subject's head and swept around to fill the edges of the canvas. His hair poured like red and black flames to the upper corners of the picture, his head thrown backwards, reflecting a divine light that shone from above. His hands were raised in helpless supplication. Somehow the attitude did not seem typical of the Avirzah'e I knew, but perhaps I did not know him as well as I thought I did. Poor Beth: keeping his distance from the Tartaruch must have felt like slow and agonising death. This work of art was but a poor substitute.

'Gimel . . .' he sighed. 'I don't know what to say to you.'

I turned to inspect his condition more thoroughly. If I had hoped to see signs of physical decay which would have given me a reason to reprimand him, I was disappointed. He appeared to be in the peak of condition; the Tartaruch's juices must be potent indeed! Still, his face was creased in anguish. 'I commend your continence,' I said.

He made a bitter sound and threw the brush he was holding into a pile of rags. 'I am torn two ways,' he said. 'Don't make light of my predicament.'

'You committed an impulsive act, Beth. I cannot lessen the burden of that.'

He shook his head. 'No, the act was not impulsive, and neither do I regret it. I have been thinking hard while you were lying alone

204

on the black-veiled bed, beloved.'

I should think he had! 'And yet you have not gone to the Tartaruch . . . Has he attempted to summon you?'

'Of course!'

'Then there is a puzzle. If you truly have no regrets concerning your action, I cannot understand why you did not obey the summons . . .' It was as it I were forcing him to say hurtful things. It was as if I wanted him to surprise me and dissipate my fears. I was also aware of how my harsh words violated the peaceful atmosphere of the room. My presence was insensitive and destructive, as if it were I, not Beth, who was in the wrong.

Beth's shoulders slumped. He picked up a rag and began to clean his hands. 'I share Avirzah'e's philosophy to a degree, but I cannot involve myself in his activities. He has my support – on a spiritual level.'

'Such lofty talk, Beth! It is rubbish!'

'I am very confused, Gimel. You cannot guess how much . . .' He smiled at me sadly. 'Look at you; you are so self-assured, so confident in your beliefs. There are more than two sides to every issue, you know. Blinding yourself to all but one is not the answer.'

I was alarmed by the calm reason in his voice; he made it sound so plausible. 'Beth, we committed ourselves to a course of action. You have betrayed me by abandoning it!'

'I did not abandon it! You didn't want Avirzah'e near your soulscaper, so you forbade me to assist you. It is your doing!'

'I saw you drunk on Tartaruchi blood, that is all. Your involvement would have contaminated the whole procedure!'

He raised his hands and threw down the cloth. 'If you wish to believe that, do so! How is Amelakiveh?'

'Competent. As I expected. He will soon establish contact with the soulscaper.'

'And what does he think of you working alone?'

'It is not his concern!'

'Don't be so arrogant, Gimel. He is faithful to me as well as to you.'

I sighed and rubbed my face with weary hands. I didn't want us to be arguing like this but the hard, painful core in my heart, caused by Beth's betrayal, made me reluctant to assuage the situation. Still, it was clear to me that Beth would not make any concessions; the rôle of peacemaker would have to be mine, whatever my feelings. 'We mustn't fight,' I said. 'It's what the Tartaruch wants.'

Beth did not deny it, but was chivalrous enough to acknowledge my attempt at reconciliation. 'Tonight, there is a private distraction for the eloim at the Castile,' he said. 'May we go together?'

I nodded. We put our arms around each other briefly and Beth kissed my face. 'Will you ever again smile at me with love?' he asked.

* * *

The gathering at the Castile was remarkably well attended, but many of the faces I had expected to see were absent. While I had been away from the city, two Metatronim had taken forced retreat. It was said that the trouble with Mervantes had sparked a host of terrors in eloim hearts, and some were not sturdy enough to withstand the conflagration. Since supping, I myself felt greatly invigorated, but still wished my father was present to advise me over more recent and personal concerns.

Lady Tatriel was in evidence, surrounded by the usual group of Metatronims. Beth and I spent a few minutes in their company, in the outer hall of the Castile. Tatriel had adopted a certain authoritative air during Metatron's absence, which I found rather irritating; she clearly fancied herself as a Metatronim matriarch. It was certainly time our mother came home from her wanderings; much more delay and she might find her belongings out on the street! Scanning the faces of eloim entering the hall, I was alert for an excuse to abandon Tatriel's abrasive company. Fortunately, Yara Sarim arrived and I was able to free myself from Tatriel's circle under the cover of inquiring after Hadith. A sizeable portion of the Sarim throng had turned out for the evening and were being escorted by their patriarch, Sandalphon. I could not see Hadith among them. I was worried she might have succumbed in some way, but Yara reassured me instantly; Hadith was one of the evening's performers and was preparing herself elsewhere in the building. She had, apparently, recovered her composure entirely after the unfortunate incident with Mervantes. Still, it was no secret that Hadith could not for the time being perform for the public; feelings concerning her continued to run high among some of the unsupped. Events had progressed while I'd been away. Yara said that, to a degree, things had calmed down, but it was an uneasy calmness.

'The Judificator might be forced to release Zalero Mervantes and the woman,' Yara told me. The Sarim naturally kept a close eye on what transpired in that direction.

'That is only to be expected, I suppose,' I replied in a commiserating tone. 'They were only being held in confinement on the flimsiest of pretexts. I hope they won't be moved to further indelicacies upon their release.'

Yara pulled a face. 'Seeing the effect their crude mouthings had upon my dear sister, I must admit I am tempted to take matters into my own hands! The insufferable arrogance of that man!'

I laid a restraining hand on her arm. 'His ichor, undoubtedly, would be sour. You must trust that Izobella will deal with the situation.'

Yara nodded, sighing.

'So,' I said, brightening and linking my arm through hers. 'Tell me what is in store for us tonight! We will be going to the Aurelium

206

Chamber? The Castile looks so beautiful! The torches are like jewels!'

As I walked with my friend into the Aurelium, she told me of the entertainment which had been arranged for our pleasure. I had left Beth in the company of Metatronims, but now he had disappeared. Horribly anxious, I felt for him with my nerve-ends; it had been senseless of me to let him drift away. Members of the Tartaruchi throng, if not Avirzah'e himself, would be present at this gathering.

As an almost hysterical reaction to adversity, the eloim had outdone themselves in their finery. Walking into the Aurelium was like immersing myself in a coruscating hoard of remarkable treasures. Shimmering, sultry velvets hugged bodies that were encrusted with jewels and precious metals; feathers and beads were wound into fabulous coiffures and stitched across bodices. I felt somehow warmed by this brave effort. Some eloim had been paired for centuries, and had always sought retreat at the same time as their lovers; I noticed that at least two of these people were there without their partners; their grief-ridden attempt at conviviality showed plainly.

Yara, smaller and slighter than her sister Hadith, had sheathed her impossibly slim body in a soft gown of darkest blue. Her silvery white hair was dressed with ropes of pearls, and she looked utterly enchanting. In black and gold, I felt rather morbid and looming beside her. She tapped my arm with her fan and whispered, 'Oh look, Gimel, the Tartaruchis are here.'

I had not expected otherwise, but my flesh still condensed in chill. I scanned the group and saw Avirzah'e's arrogant beauty flaunting itself beneath a lamp of ruby glass, but mercifully, there was no sign of Beth among them.

'Avirzah'e is in love. Did you know?' Yara said, with a small laugh, which indicated she didn't really believe such an impossible thing.

Her words cast a stone into the pool of my soul; the ripples they caused were fierce and shallow, but the knowledge itself sank deep into my spirit and lodged there in the dark, deep currents; immutable. 'No,' I said, lightly. 'I must admit this is news to me. And who is the lucky recipient of the Tartaruch emotion?'

'Well, nobody knows.' Yara said, with relish. 'Two nights ago, Avirzah'e attended a soirée at the Sarim court. He was being *most* theatrical, and read out a remarkably sentimental poem. Between you and I, dear Gimel, the effort the Mervantes morsel wrote to my sister was more profound! Anyway, my cousin Haniel later remarked to Avirzah'e that he looked distracted. She was flirting, of course! Avirzah'e merely smirked and told her, if he *was* distracted, it was because he was in love. Personally I think he was just bored! Haniel questioned him immediately, but the Tartaruch was vague. "Some loves," he said, "are for experiencing not gossiping about." He made it sound so sinister, but then, of course *he* would! The rumour got around after that. There is naturally great interest in this unprecedented phenomenon!'

I felt as it Avirzah'e had spoken those words solely to me. I could see his face, his laughing eyes! My instinctual reaction was to go and cause a scene among the Tartaruchis immediately; a course of action which would be both unproductive and regretted keenly at a later, calmer hour. I tried to tell myself I was being too subjective; there was every possibility the Tartaruch had been referring to some other dalliance (in truth, he was supposed to indulge in many at a time!), but I dreaded he had been speaking of Beth. Yara's innocent remark concerning the sinister tone of Avirzah'e's declaration conjured other, darker ideas.

These ideas were to do with the concept of love itself. To humanity this simple, familiar word kindles images of sexual desire, family security, harmony among friends. These are all images shared by eloimkind, expressions of emotion which we have adopted from humanity, and which provide a satisfying yet ultimately trivial reward. There is also another expression of love, peculiar to our kind. It is a remnant of ancient times and, because in the distant past eloim attempted to minimise the differences between humanity and themselves, has been discouraged by eloim elders. The concept has been bound up in chains of taboo and fear. According to our legends – and it must be remembered that some legends still resided as fact in the memories of our oldest kin – it was this love that caused our fall, our desolation, while at the same time being the very thing that elevated us. A paradox. An unwritten law forbids us to speak of it, and even the thought conjures dark names, dark times. But I must say this: the expression of love among eloim can transcend sexuality and flesh; it can transcend reality itself. When impelled by intensity of feeling, eloim can combine their separate corporeal forms into one entity which inspires exceptional sensations, both physical and emotional, unimagined by any human creature. Not having experienced it myself, I was ignorant of how this might actually feel, but I was assured that on this world at least, it was an uncontrollable and dangerous practice. Physical conjunction of this nature was one of the things my people had surrendered because they wanted to live on Earth. Eloim never indulged in it now. *Never.* For this reason, I had a feeling it would be a highly attractive concept to Avirzah'e Tartaruchi. I was sure, as if he'd told me himself, it was this forbidden thing he had referred to in the House of Sarim.

Comfortable chairs had been arranged in the Aurelium in front of a small stage. I sat down among Yara's relatives, mouthing pleasantries, while nervously scanning the crowd for Beth. Eventually I spotted his bright head nearby, and stood up rather abruptly to call him. Sarim looked at me quizzically as I struggled with my skirts. I was unconcerned for my dignity; not for one minute did I intend to let Beth leave my side again. He waved and smiled when he saw me and sauntered over, bringing me a crystal tumbler of fortified fruit cordial which was both salt and sweet to the taste.

'Sit down,' I told him. He did so meekly. My heart was fluttering madly as if I were in the presence of a new lover of whom I was uncertain. Later, Beth and I would have to reforge our intimacy; we had been strangers for too long in that respect. Perhaps my neglect had been the cause of his transgression with the Tartaruch. Had I been too wrapped up in my own thoughts and the problems of others recently? Had I unwittingly estranged my brother through lack of attention? I put my hand over his own. 'Do you feel all right?' I asked him, in a low voice.

I could tell he considered making a cutting remark and then thought better of it. 'You mustn't worry,' he said.

Usually when eloim perform for their own kind, they stage pieces of a complex or ambitious nature. But tonight, the entertainment was whimsical and unchallenging; a balm to frayed nerves. Hadith sang amusing little songs, and acted out a small play with a few friends. It was a silly romance, full of double meanings and misunderstandings. Though it was supposed to be humorous, I could not help but notice parallels with events in my own life. Perhaps I was over-dramatising the situation. Avirzah'e and Beth had got drunk one night and in high spirits had engaged in a little amusement of their own. Their act of mutual supping had been stupid and perhaps impetuous, but if everyone concerned remained objective it could be forgotten. The symbolism of what they had done meant nothing in this world, this life, unless we ourselves empowered it with meaning. Later, I would tell Beth that we should both pretend it had never happened. I knew I had the power to draw him back to me and, in view of Avirzah'e's careless words to Haniel Sarim, it was perhaps vital that I did so.

After the entertainment drew to a close, and the performers had taken their bows, everyone left their seats and began to mingle once more for conversation. The Sangariah and his staff moved among the crowds, speaking briefly with everyone. I wondered whether this was the true reason for the gathering: a discreet inspection of eloim morale.

Hadith swept gloriously through the crowd to embrace me and thank me again for my compassion during the Mervantes crisis. I was gratified to see how well she looked. Sandalphon, her father, noticed us together and came to talk to us. He kissed Hadith's brow and smiled at me, murmuring further grateful words. I felt rather embarrassed; there was no need to thank me. I had only done what anyone would have done in my position. Sandalphon is such a gentle soul; I had often envied Hadith having him as a father. Though his power is as formidable as Metatron's, he has a tempering streak of tender serenity. He and my father had connections that went back a long way, and he was instrumental in much of Metatron's business even now; a quiet yet vigilant presence. Before leaving Sacramante, my father had urged me that if I needed help in any way while he was absent, I should approach Sandalphon.

While I talked socially with the Sarim, Beth hovered restlessly at my shoulder and I could sense he was not completely at ease. As soon as propriety allowed, I intended to suggest we take our leave of the gathering and return home. I was anxious to talk with Beth, to drive the phantoms from our relationship. Then we could talk about all I had seen and done in Khalt. We would lie in bed together and make further plans. Sandalphon, however, showed no sign of wanting to end our conversation and, because of his rank, I could not excuse myself until he was ready. People were talking excitedly all around us; it was difficult to imagine the eloim were suffering any difficulties at all. Sandalphon was enthusing about a new opera he was working on. He said he needed Metatron's advice and looked at me keenly. I took it to mean that in the absence of my father, I would do equally well as an adviser.

'Perhaps I could call on you soon,' I said, far from eager to enmesh myself in operatic details at that moment.

Sandalphon nodded thoughtfully, sucking his lower lip. It is difficult to imagine his true age; sometimes he appears to be no more than a boy. 'I would appreciate that – as soon as you can,' he said.

'I will look forward to seeing your manuscript.' I smiled at Hadith who had been listening to our conversation, adding the occasional affectionate observation of her own. But she did not smile back. Her eyes focused somewhere behind my shoulder, her expression strangely bleak; it was enough to make me turn round.

My eyes slid straight into the attentive gaze of Avirzah'e Tartaruchi. He had obviously sidled up while my back had been turned. His proximity made me flinch; it was as if a flame had passed too close to my skin. I took a quick internal reading of the situation. Beth was calm, but somehow bemused, while my own mind fizzed in anticipation and anguished excitement. Why did the Tartaruch have this effect on me? I reached for Beth's right hand and said in my coolest voice, 'Good evening, Avirzah'e. I hope you are well.'

He blinked slowly and smiled, inclining his head the merest fraction. 'I am in the best of health, Lady Gimel.'

I could not stop looking at his mouth: the finely sculpted lips, the hint of his perfect teeth. I kept imagining that mouth against my brother's skin; more than that, I could feel it on my own, above the heart. 'Good,' I said. 'I am immeasurably glad . . . Beth, perhaps we should leave now. I feel a little tired.'

'Leaving so soon?' Avirzah'e said, his voice full of mockery. 'I

210

won't hear of it! Let me summon an attendant to refresh your glasses!'

'No, thank you, Avirzah'e,' I said.

He smiled at me in an intimate fashion. 'Aah! You have been travelling, Lady Gimel, haven't you! Hence the feeling of enervation! I had not thought it would be so soon, but then events have taken a turn for the dramatic haven't they!'

I was aghast he could talk so plainly in company. Hadith had half veiled her eyes; she looked interested in our conversation and deeply aware of my discomfort. Sandalphon's boyish face was curiously blank, as if he were waiting for someone, or something, to imprint an expression on it. Beth was utterly still and silent beside me. I did not look, but I knew his eyes were fixed on the Tartaruch. I felt as if we were enacting a scene from a tragic play – deaths, deceptions and pierced hearts were sure to follow.

Avirzah'e shrugged abruptly. 'Well, you are clearly too exhausted to string a sentence together, so don't let me detain you!' His eyes, damn them, looked right into my heart, my mind, my soul. We hadn't spoken since the day he had called on me; since then I had betrayed him to Metatron, and he had tried to steal Beth away from me. It was absurd that we were standing here talking politely, however superficial that politeness. I inclined my head to him and addressed the Sarim.

'Your performance was excellent tonight, Hadith, a welcome relief.' I smiled at her father. 'I will call on you soon, Sandalphon, over the next day or two.' Everyone made noises of farewell, and I linked my arm through Beth's and made to leave the Chamber. My heart had begun to beat erratically; I should have realised the confrontation was not over. As I passed him, Avirzah'e caught hold of my arm.

'Everyone is friends tonight, Gimel' he said. 'We need to close ranks, don't we? Whatever ill feeling has passed between us, forgive me now, as I have forgiven you. Kiss me farewell.'

I could not believe his audacity. His voice had been loud enough for the Sarim to hear, but I did not care if they thought me ill-mannered.

'I would as soon kiss a heap of ordure!' I said.

Silence fell in our immediate vicinity.

'Gimel!' Beth hissed. Up until then, he had not spoken a word.

Avirzah'e had narrowed his eyes. I realised, too late, that I had played into his hands. 'You are a wilful creature, Gimel,' he said. 'I admire your spirit, if not your social graces. So, there is to be no reconciliation between us? I am disappointed. However, if you won't make amends, at least allow me to kiss your brother in proxy.'

'That is a ridiculous request!' I said, although the words were difficult. My mouth had gone utterly numb. 'I cannot speak for my brother; he has his own mind.'

'Do you?' Avirzah'e asked Beth.

'I resent the implications of this conversation,' Beth said weakly. My heart contracted at his predicament.

'She is a strong creature!' Avirzah'e said with a laugh and then, with serpent speed, he grabbed hold of Beth's left hand. Beth tried to pull away, but the resistance was feeble. Avirzah'e raised both their arms to shoulder height, his eyes full of fear and challenge. A nauseous presentiment bleached the whole room to mist in my eyes. I could see Beth's knuckles straining through the flesh; yet his face had gone curiously impassive.

'Let me go,' he said.

Beside us, Sandalphon made a small, anguished noise, as if he were about to intervene.

'You let *me* go,' Avirzah'e said, and then Beth's face went completely ashen. I squeezed his other hand hard; his whole body was shaking. The Aurelium dipped and swayed; conversation receded like a twittering tide. I could no longer see Beth's knuckles stretching his skin, for the simple reason they were no longer visible. His hand, and Avirzah'e's, had become light, become another substance, become *one*. I felt the thrill of it course up my own arm; I was part of it. Through the medium of Beth, Avirzah'e plunged straight into my soul. It happened so quickly, nobody but ourselves and the Sarim was aware of it. The conjunction seemed to last an eternity, but then I became aware of noise around me again. Avirzah'e laughed, released Beth's hand and kissed him briefly on the cheek.

'Good night, Metatronim. Hurry home and sleep well!' He bowed to Sandalphon without looking once at me, turned smartly on his heel and swept off into the crowd. I could not believe my ominous presentiments had been so accurate.

Sandalphon's face was stern, to say the least. 'I think we should talk in private,' he said. 'Now!' Hadith looked simply stunned, her mouth hanging open.

'I . . . It was . . .' I groped for words. I felt soiled, responsible, defeated.

'Gimel,' Sandalphon said, 'I think it would be best if you and your brother accompanied me to one of the private chambers annexing this room. This should not be discussed in public.'

'Yes . . . yes.' I nodded helplessly. Hadith extended her arms to embrace me, but Sandalphon, in an uncharacteristic moment of aggressiveness, slapped her hands away.

Beth began walking swiftly towards the door. Making further confused gestures at the Sarim, I hurried after him. He had no intention of seeking a private room, I could tell. At the gilded doorway to the Chamber, I took hold of my brother's arm. By the

212

time we came to the outer hall, he had shaken me off. Around us jewelled lamps burned dimly, throwing out long, gloomy shadows. Beth was unsteady on his feet, and his eyes were full of rage. He stood for a moment and pressed his fingers against his eyes. I wanted to soothe him, but my mouth was dry of words. It was as if I had forgotten what language was; I was simply a maelstrom of feeling.

My brother lowered his hands and sighed. He blinked rapidly as if to dispel an illusion. He turned his head and stared into the darkness, beyond the dim colours of the lamps. Then he began to walk towards it.

At the end of the hall, in a place where there are no doors, is a dark statue. It is of an eloim in armour, twice life-size, and carved from unpolished black marble. One hand of the statue wields a sword, the other hand claws at its beautiful face which is contorted by pain. The reason this carving stands in the Hall of the Castile is very complex: it is both a reminder and a regret. It symbolises desolation, loss, betrayal, unavoidable sacrifice, the conflict of beloved brothers. The name of that statue is rarely uttered. Its name is Mikha'il.

Beth stood there, staring up through the darkness into the anguished stone face. There were no lamps around it; Mikha'il is ever in shadow in this world. I padded to my brother's side and took his hand; this time he did not pull away from me. Together, we stared into the face of Mikha'il.

We could not speak. I felt tears gather in my eyes. Did Beth really see a parallel between himself and Mikha'il? Standing there, I had to admit there were similarities. Beth broke the silence.

'Is he grieving still, do you suppose?' he asked.

I did not bother to answer the question; it was impossible to conjecture. 'I think we should speak to Sandalphon.' I said. 'He is wise, and kind. We must speak to somebody!'

Beth did not look at me. He dropped my hand. 'I will speak to the only person who can advise me,' he said. 'Sandalphon cannot possibly understand this situation.'

He put his hand upon the leg of the statue, in the place where the thigh was bared. He stroked the stone. Mikha'il's ferocity is contained, and therefore more devastating. He has a sword in his hand and, above the heart, his armour is pierced. He is wounded there, above the heart.

Light as a cat, Beth leapt up on to the statue's plinth. 'What are you doing!' I hissed, looking round to see if anyone else was in the hall. 'Get down!'

Beth ignored me. He climbed the statue and balanced on the stone armour. He put his arms around Mikha'il, and lifted his head to the unsmiling lips. 'Don't Beth, don't!' I tugged at his clothes, but it was no use. He kissed the statue on the mouth. I was

213

transfixed, unsure of whether what I was witnessing was heresy, invocation, madness or blessing. Beth rested his head on Mikha'il's shoulder. I think he was weeping.

We were torn apart. I was at one end of the world, he at the other. So distant. He did not look upon this as our problem, but his alone. He did not want me to be part of it.

There was a movement behind me. I knew who it was without having to turn around and confirm my suspicions with my eyes. I knew now that I would recognise his presence on a spiritual level, for ever. 'Avirzah'e you are evil,' I said. 'Evil and stupid!'

'Cruel words,' he said affably. I turned around, then. He was looking at the statue, smiling gently. There was no malice in his face, but his eyes were bright and feverish.

'You cannot understand,' he said. 'If you were sensible, you would join with us, but you are not. You are Metatron's creature and simply that. It is a shame, but . . .'

Overcome by rage, and other more complex feelings, I spat in his face. Avirzah'e merely flinched. 'You have no idea of the strength of my regard for you,' he said. 'It has always been there. Beth is a beauty, a watery spirit; while you are earth and fire and air combined. I have always been drawn to you both, always, knowing that the following of that call was dangerous and that its consummation would invoke unprecedented wonders. I think you have known this too, but Metatron has disciplined you too well,' He looked at me. 'I cannot help you, Gimel, and for that, I am sorry.'

His words were like strong hands around my throat; I could not speak and could hardly breathe. I could only stand there, stripped of my powers, as he walked past me to the foot of the statue and said, 'Beth, come down, I will take you home.'

Beth looked at him. 'I can get home by myself,' he said.

Avirzah'e shook his head. 'No, you misunderstand me. I am taking you to my home.' He held out his hand and after a moment's consideration Beth jumped down, although he avoided Avirzah'e's waiting arms.

'Beth, don't go with him!' I said.

'We have things to do.' Avirzah'e said reasonably. 'Eloim power must be rekindled. If no one else is strong enough to take responsibility, I will do so myself.' He looked at Beth whose face, in those moments, was uncannily similar in expression and appearance to the statue's. Beth closed his eyes painfully and nodded.

I felt completely bloodless. Avirzah'e had beaten me, or had I defeated myself? 'Beth, why did you kiss Mikha'il?' I asked. 'You clearly do not intend to follow his path.'

Beth sighed. 'Some would say that a long time ago Mikha'il himself took the wrong turning.' He took my hands in his own. 'Do not judge me, sister. I have to account for my actions, impulsive or not. I have to do what is ordained. There is no choice.' He kissed me on the lips, very briefly. 'Do you love me?'

I looked at him steadily. 'You know I do – in all but one way which, as an eloim and a creature of good sense, I have forsaken. You are contemplating folly, Beth, you are risking ruin.'

He nodded. 'I understand how you feel about this,' he said. 'But I cannot agree with you. Do not worry for me.'

'You are welcome to join us,' Avirzah'e said. I dared not look at him.

'No,' I said, and turned to face the statue until I was sure they had left the Hall. I stared at the wound on Mikha'il's breast, which some say will never heal. On Earth, eloim had individuated. We lived in isolation, but it was a condition we had become familiar with. Once, it had not been so. Beth was right. Sandalphon was not the person to talk to. I knew, in my heart, who was.

'. . . but his face deep scars of thunder had
entrenched, and care sat on his faded cheek, but
under brows of dauntless courage . . .'
Paradise Lost, Book I

Sandalphon came to our house just after dawn the next morning,
but I was ready for him. In fact, I hadn't slept. After returning
home, I had conducted Tamaris' rejuvenation and checked Ramiz
over for signs of degeneration. Satisfied that my household was in
order, I'd bathed myself and projected my consciousness out into
Khalt to check on proceedings. All seemed to be progressing steadily, although I was slightly disturbed by the fact that Rayojini
seemed more difficult to make contact with than usual. Perhaps
Amelakiveh's proximity to her was affecting our link. Beth, of
course, did not come home. I shut him out of my mind.

When Sandalphon presented himself, I was sitting composed in
my salon and Tamaris was in the process of blending a light breakfast. I had never seen the Sarim so stern, but I was sure there was
a galloping frailty beneath his exterior. Sandalphon was not a
person to deal happily with issues of conflict. Sometimes, I questioned why Metatron had chosen him to be his deputy.

'I am disappointed you did not want to talk to me last night,' he said.

I smiled. 'Do I take it, then, you are not here to discuss your
opera?'

Sandalphon made an exasperated noise and sat down without
asking my permission. 'You do realise what we witnessed last night,
don't you?' he said. 'The Tartaruch and Beth . . . Gimel, they were
beginning to *conjoin*. Such is the way that monsters were conceived,
at one time.'

He was, of course, referring to the Harkasites who were all, but
for Metatron, composite beings – creatures composed of multiple
eloim souls. They had been that way so long, it was doubtful they
could separate now. The fact that Sandalphon referred only to the
creation of monsters was also evidence of the unnatural aversion
to conjunction that had been imprinted into eloim society. He
seemed to have forgotten that its essential purpose was the purest,
most ethereal expression of love.

'Avirzah'e has developed quite an insistent longing for my
brother,' I said. 'He means no harm. He is just unsure of how to
satisfy himself.'

217

'The longing, if it can be called that, is not just for Beth,' Sandalphon said, eyeing me grimly. 'What is going on between you three? I am sure Metatron would disapprove strongly, whatever it is!'

I signalled discreetly to Tamaris, who had been hiding behind a curtain covering the entrance to an adjoining room. She brought in the breakfast immediately, forcing Sandalphon to collect himself.

'Have you mentioned this matter to anyone?' I asked.

He shook his head emphatically. 'Of course not! I would not speak of this to anyone until after I'd seen you, but naturally the Parzupheim will have to be informed very soon.'

'Mmm.' I tapped my lips and then leaned forward. 'Might I speak to you in utter confidence, Sandalphon?'

'I would be grateful if you would speak at all, Gimel!'

'Let's just say that what you witnessed last night was simply a development of a process that has been evolving for quite some time. Metatron is quite aware of what is happening.' I kept my voice low and steady, anticipating his outburst.

'Metatron has made no mention of it to me!'

I nodded slowly, letting my eyes glaze as if I were deep in thought. 'Mmm. Perhaps I should elucidate further. Beth and I conceived a strategy with Metatron; Avirzah'e is a component of it. More than that, I am not at liberty to disclose without Metatron's express permission, because the proposal is bold and audacious. However, if it is allowed to proceed as we have designed, it might be the answer to all our problems . . . Last night the Tartaruch prince became a little too . . . presumptive, I suppose. It was an accident. Avirzah'e's enthusiasms do tend to run away with him in their jaws, you must admit!' I smiled wryly, but Sandalphon would have none of it.

'Metatron would devise no stratagems that involve the Tartaruchis!' he declared darkly.

I nodded in agreement. 'I know it seems hard to believe! However, think about this: if Metatron *was* involving the Tartaruch in his plans, he would be very reluctant to tell you of them. He knows the Sarim view of Tartaruchi.' I reclined against my sofa, and delivered the final thrust of the needle to his heart. 'Wouldn't you agree?'

Sandalphon considered my words. 'Is this true?' He shook his head. 'Metratron has never kept information from me before.'

'I assure you it is quite true.' As I spoke, I wondered myself why I was taking this deception so far, why I was hurting this lovely, gentle soul whom Metatron trusted above all others. I was poisoning their relationship with my words. Why? Was it simply to protect Beth and Avirzah'e? I could no longer be sure of my motives.

Sandalphon sighed. 'Perhaps you'd better tell me more – if you can.'

I shook my head. 'No, I regret that I can't – for now.' I leaned towards him and spoke in a low, urgent voice. 'But it is absolutely imperative that the Parzupheim are not told of what occurred last night. Nobody must know. Can you make sure of this? Would you prevent Hadith from spreading the news?'

Sandalphon hesitated.

'My father will be able to explain everything when he returns to Sacramante,' I said. 'I promise you. Please, give me your word. Give me the silence of Sarim!'

He sighed again. 'Gimel, I don't know if I can. The implications are awesome. You know that the Tartaruchi throng is suspected of certain other transgressions. This is vital evidence. Forgive me, but if Avirzah'e has infiltrated the Metatronim throng, it is a matter which should not under any circumstances be kept secret.'

'Don't you believe what I've told you?' I asked sharply.

'Yes, I believe you, because of who you are, but you said yourself that Avirzah'e acted . . . *presumptively*. You know Metatron would not approve of that.'

So, I would have to cast my sharpest hook, along with the smaller. There was little chance Sandalphon would wriggle free of this. 'Very well, I understand your dilemma. However, there is something else I have to tell you. After hearing it, you might give me your assurances more readily.'

He glanced at me sharply. 'Then speak,' he said.

I drew myself up straight in my chair. 'Sandalphon, I need to gain access to the Bale Tower.'

For a moment, he looked at me blankly, clearly believing he had misheard. 'Access where?' he said.

'I think you heard me, Sandalphon. The Bale Tower.'

A certain incredulity dawned in his sad, tawny eyes. 'You mean . . . you want to try and communicate with *Sammael*?' he said. 'But . . .'

'No buts! It is essential! Metatron left me with instructions to be followed only if certain conditions arose. They have! The future of our race is at stake, Sandalphon. You are, if I am not mistaken, the Keeper of the Key in Metatron's absence. For the love of my father, please help me.'

'You know Sammael has forbidden us to approach him, Gimel. No one has seen him for centuries. I don't think . . .'

'Forgive me, but I am not asking you to think, Sandalphon. I have to carry out Metatron's instructions and – if I may be rather direct – so do you.'

He asked no further questions.

The Bale Tower stands alone in a neglected corner of the atelier courts. It is the most ancient building in our enclave, the first that was built for us by the patrons. Its summit kisses the lower clouds, for ever sheathed in tears of mist. As far as anyone knows no one

219

ever goes there, for its occupant has shut himself away from the world. Twice a year, on the solstice nights, a newly matured human of comely aspect is taken to the foot of Bale and the dark doors open to allow admittance. In the summer a maiden is taken; in winter, a youth. They never come out again.

Long ago, the occupant of the tower had been a great prince of eloim; the most beautiful, the most powerful. They had called him the Lord of Light. What he was now exactly no one knew, for he never showed himself. He, like his brother the sad Mikha'il, had a wound above the heart that never healed. Once, they had fought terribly; it had been a war that neither side could win. We eloim upon the Earth were Sammael's minions, although he ignored us now. It was said that on windy nights he stood upon the pinnacle of Bale and called his brother out through the clouds, from the old world that had cast us out. It was said Mikha'il obeyed this summons and that they scratched each other through the storm. It was, of course, utter fantasy. There was no contact with the other world. However, it was believed that Sammael knew everything – every thought in the world, every deed, every question and answer.

He knew all about the conjunction of eloim; he would have banished nothing from his heart and mind, no matter how many millennia had moved across the sky above him. He remembered. And if anyone knew the cause of all that was happening to us now, it was him.

Metatron, if he'd been in the city, would have prevented my action. He observed the law whereby Sammael had excommunicated himself from our reality. We could not go to Sammael for advice, even if he was the only creature who could counsel us, simply because he did not wish us to. The law had been created centuries before, and was respected with a stringency that was almost fearful. I had no regard for this law. The previous night I had experienced a profound revelation at the feet of Mikha'il's statue. Sammael's solitude must be invaded; he must be forced to speak to me. I had no idea what I would find within the Tower, whether my mind could withstand it, or even how I would be received by this powerful being, but I was prepared to risk annihilation to attract Sammael's attention. My little Rayojini was no longer enough; I needed to secure unimaginable support for her. It might be that, should I be able to interest Lord Sammael in our problems, we would no longer even need a soulscaper. I could still draw Rayojini to me, but perhaps without having to put her in peril. That idea alone was attractive. Beth had bitten through the rein of love that bound him to me; he flirted with potentially catastrophic desires. Avirzah'e was stronger than I had thought. I no longer knew what the real problem was. Whom else could I turn to, but Sammael?

* * *

220

My father, under the jurisdiction of the Parzupheim, controlled the only key to the Tower of Bale. In his absence Sandalphon was responsible for it. I knew I was abusing the power Metatron had invested in me, and I was also abusing the trust of Sandalphon, but the previous night I had stood before the statue of Mikha'il, floundering in a sea of dark and turbulent emotion, and I had made up my mind. No one could change that conviction; I felt as if the direction had come from Mikha'il himself.

Sandalphon walked with me to the Tower. I could see that he was even at that last moment struggling within himself. His instincts told him he was doing something very wrong but because I was Metatron's daughter and had learned how to speak with my father's voice and command with his eyes, Sandalphon felt he had to trust me. I had dressed myself in simple black and had unbound my hair. I'd removed all my rings, including the family seal that Metatron had entrusted into my care, and the locket around my throat that bore my father's likeness. I became an eloim essence, little more. As I walked I let all but my sense of purpose drift away from me into the Tower; there was no other way to face Sammael.

As we mounted the final stretch of hill through an avenue of thick, dark cypress trees, a bell began to toll down in the atelier courts. I turned back and studied the tall buildings, the narrow streets, the high walls. The brighter sprawl of Sacramante beyond them was perhaps four times as large as our crowded enclave, where we clustered like a vast colony of nervous bats. An image flashed through my mind: blood-suckers with bright eyes hanging from crumbling towers, pressed close together, trembling, stinking of blood. I swallowed thickly. Beside me, Sandalphon shivered and pulled his cloak more closely around his body. The wind whipped his pale, fine hair around his face. 'Gimel, we can still go back . . .'

I shook my head and turned into the wind, climbing, climbing, up through the avenue of restless trees. Above me at the end of this tunnel of foliage, the Tower itself loomed solid and dark and silent. Soon we stood upon its lichened steps.

Still shaking his head and sighing, Sandalphon put the great black key in its lock, where it turned as smoothly as if it were used every day. At the push of his hand, the door swung open without a sound. A slight thread of panic wove a line across my heart. I put my hand on Sandalphon's arm and said, 'Wait for me'. Then the thread unravelled and was blown away down the hill.

Sandalphon nodded. 'If it takes a century, I will wait for you.'

I smiled, although it was hard to do so. 'I might not come out again.'

'I will wait,' Sandalphon said, and sat down upon the steps, from where he looked up at me like a sweet, trusting boy. I wanted to kiss him, but knew I should not. I went inside the Tower.

It was very plain; there were no carvings on the grey stone. It

221

was also bigger inside than I had imagined. Flights of steps ran everywhere, garlanded with dusty webs, scattered with faded straw. At random I chose one and began to climb it. Many landings punctuated my ascent, where I saw numerous closed doors, but I did not pause because I knew that Sammael, if he was still there at all, would be at the top of the Tower. It was utterly silent. Thick glass in the narrow windows shut out the moan of the elements. The air smelled of old books and musty incense and there was a definite mousiness to it, too. As I climbed in this atmosphere, all trepidation fell away from me; this was the sanctuary of a scholar-hermit. It did not feel in the least sad or frightening.

I had not estimated how long the climb would take, and I had to allow for several rests to ease the muscles of my legs. When I looked up, the tower still seemed to rear upwards for ever. I wished I'd brought a flask of water with me, for my throat was dry. At one point I emerged into a dark passageway, along which I would have to walk if I wanted to climb further. I could not see any more steps in the immediate vicinity. The floor appeared recently swept and there was a faint smell of soap. Still no sign of life though. There were doors set into the wall, some of which I felt brave enough to try and open. All were locked, the handles rust beneath my fingers. I quickly dismissed the idea of trying to open them. Centuries of neglect had warped the wood and rotted the locks, so that they were sealed by disuse rather than the turn of a key. After a while I came across a drinking fountain set into the wall, where a simple metal cup was chained to the stone bowl. The water looked cool and clear: irresistible. Would it poison me if I drank? I looked around myself: the dark corridor extended to either side, lit gloomily by narrow windows paned with green glass. Nothing moved in the shadows, not even a mouse. I filled the cup and lowered my head to drink.

'Who are you!'

I had heard no one approach and wheeled round frantically at the sound of the voice. Behind me stood a young human girl of maybe eighteen summers. Her hair was pale and confined messily behind her head; her clothes were simple but spun of fine, expensive-looking wool. She was carrying a bale of linen and was looking at me with angry accusation. 'What are you doing in here?' she demanded.

I straightened up. 'I might ask the same of you,' I replied, 'given that the occupant of this tower is reputed to live alone!'

The girl narrowed her eyes. 'You're one of *them*,' she said. 'How did you get in?'

'Where is he?' I asked. 'Where is the Lord Sammael? Is he . . . is he still here?'

'I'm not telling you that!' the girl cried. 'Get out!' She came towards me quite menacingly. 'Get out!' She dropped the linen on the floor and picked up a broom standing beside a doorway, which she brandished in my direction. I was so surprised by this aggressive behaviour from a human, I was temporarily confused, and knew not how to respond to her hostility. The girl poked me with the broom. She was not of patron stock, that was clear; she was far too brutish and common in attitude. That meant she could not be one of the solstice offerings. For a moment I was afraid that Sammael no longer existed and the Tower had become overrun by unsupped vagabonds! After all, no eloim really knew what went on in this place any more.

'Is Sammael here?' I asked again, holding up my hands to fend off the broom.

'Get out leech! Get out hag!' screeched the girl, savagely thrusting her weapon at my body.

Then, a voice bellowed out of an adjoining room. 'Lilian, Lilian, what *is* the fuss? I can hear nothing but your rude farmyard cacophony!'

'A she-rat has bellied her way into the Tower!' the girl replied.

'A what?'

'A she-rat! A big one!'

There was a sound of a chair being scraped across the floor. I stood there, utterly confused, as a tall, painfully thin man with shaggy red hair came out of the room. He saw me, allowed himself a few seconds of mute shock, and then sighed and folded his arms, leaning on the doorframe. He was not a man; he was eloim. I could see that now, but undeniably there was a certain human casualness about him. He reminded me, in a way, of Avirzah'e.

'What *have* we here?' he said.

'Shall I push her down the stairs?' asked the girl.

He shook his head. 'No. Who are you, how did you get in, and what do you want?' he asked me.

'Are you Lord Sammael?' I asked, trying to sound dignified. Only hours before I had been poignantly balancing on the rim of a terrible abyss, my heart and head full of profundity; now, I was living in a nightmare of farce. Where was I?

'Who wants to know?' he replied.

'Gimel Metatronim does,' I said.

He laughed. 'The fruit of the Metatron's loins? Ah yes, I see the family resemblance now. What are you doing in the Tower?'

'Looking for Sammael.'

He extended his arms. 'Well, you've found him. There's little point in further procrastination. What do you want from me?'

I glared at the girl, and asked him, 'May I talk to you in private?'

'Hm? Oh yes, I see. Run along, Lilian, all is under control. The she-rat is unfanged and affectionate, you see.' He gestured for me to enter his room.

'Well, Gimel Metatronim, you had better sit down. May I offer you refreshment? We have a choice selection here.'

I had no doubt of that, but shook my head. 'No, talking with you will be refreshment enough.'

'I do hope that wasn't simple flattery . . .' He bade me be seated, and I looked around the room. It was comfortably furnished and a fire burned fiercely beneath a huge mantel. All around were books and papers: on the floor; on shelves that lined the walls; flowing over a large, heavy desk under the window. Beneath my feet the rug was threadbare, and a few animal skins had been scattered around to cover the worst spots. I attempted to regain my composure.

'I have not come here to flatter you,' I said. 'I need your advice.'

'I do not give advice,' he said, leaning against his desk and folding his arms. 'It is generally ignored, anyway. Before you decided upon this visit, didn't you think about why I'd shut myself away from worldly concerns? What makes you think I will make an exception in your case?'

'Nothing whatsoever. I took a risk.' I gave him a frank glance. He was nothing like I'd expected. The Parzupheim were more ethereal, my father more regal. Was this really the one they had called the Prince of Light? I found it hard to believe. He was sinewy, his face lined more strongly than was usual in an eloim, but they were the lines of expression, not age. He was handsome in the way that human men are handsome, not eloim. What did he do here in this place all alone? Why hadn't he gone insane? Perhaps he had.

'Did the Metatron let you in?' he asked me.

I shook my head. 'No, I used deceit to gain entrance.'

'Well that's commendable at least, I suppose!' He peered at me. 'So, do the atelier courts still stand and surround my sanctuary . . . ?' Then he shook his head before I could respond. 'No, I'm not curious. I'm not going to ask questions. After all, if I'd wanted the answers I'd have come outside, wouldn't I?'

'I don't know,' I answered carefully. 'If *I'd* locked myself away for so long, I might be a little afraid of open spaces and many people . . . But still, I think I'd yearn for company now and again.'

Sammael smiled widely; my answer had pleased him. 'Strangely enough, I find I'm glad you came,' he said.

I told him all about what had been happening. He listened eagerly as if I were a new book that had magically acquired the ability to speak its text aloud. He did ask questions, some of them probing inquiries about my narrative, others apparently unconnected; brief demands about various individuals, a thirst for gossip. His mind flitted from thought to thought like a frantic bird, but he kept his conclusions to himself, only listening and then stabbing a finger at the air, saying, 'Yes, yes!' I was patient, but hoped he would enlighten me when I'd finished the story. I ended it by describing

224

my ascent of the hill, and the state of the weather outside, the tolling of the bell. Here, Sammael stopped me.

'Sandalphon is here?' he asked abruptly.

'Waiting outside,' I replied. Sammael turned away from me, to look out of the window. There was a moment's silence, the meaning of which I divined easily. I had breached the defences he had constructed between himself and the world. For a while, at least, the Tower door was well and truly open.

'Would you . . . would you like me to fetch him?' I asked quietly.

He pondered the question. 'I don't think so.'

An uncomfortable atmosphere had settled in the room. Sammael was lonely for his kind, I could see that now. And I, in most respects a child of the Earth, was not in his eyes one of his kind. What had impelled him to prolong this insufferable torment of loneliness?

'I have everything I need here,' he said.

'Are you still glad I came?'

He turned around and smiled at me. 'Tell me what you think your problem is.'

I respected his reticence. 'Well, Avirzah'e thinks the Watchers are instrumental in what is occurring. He thinks that nothing is coincidental.'

'Does Metatron share this view?'

'It is hard to say. He believes my idea about the soulscaper is a good one, but quite honestly in view of everything else that has happened, it seems such a small solution – too small.' I shrugged. 'I don't know. That's why I came to you. It wasn't a decision lightly made.'

'The smallest solutions are generally the best ones,' he replied. 'Grand plans, grand ambitions are easily reduced to ashes, whereas a small plan can sneak through to devastating effect. At least, I have come to think that.'

'Maybe, but I have been wondering recently whether we should be here in this world at all, whether my attempts at restoring our position are against natural law. We have tried to assimilate with humans haven't we? But we cannot fulfil that desire completely. We have been living on borrowed time.'

Sammael laughed. 'You poor creature! There is no natural law; anything is possible in this universe, *anything*. If eloim want to remain here, they probably can, but change is an inevitability. They might not remain as they are.' He sat down on the floor in front of me, leaning back against a chair, and clasped his arms around his knees. 'You are wrong in saying that eloim have tried to assimilate with humanity; they haven't. They have made what they see to be massive compromises, but they hang on to the past, to approximate memories of their past forms. They cling to immortality in a mortal world and yet, at the same time, they relinquish

225

certain powers which would be useful. Oh, Gimel Metatronim, I gave up trying to philosophise about this millennia ago! The eloim have reached the horizon of a great decision: they can reclaim their heritage, or they can sacrifice it and be absorbed into the world. It is that simple. Your soulscaper will be able to tell you this, if she can withstand a journey into the eloim soulscape.'

'Is it really that simple? Is it nothing to do with the Watchers and . . .' I had to say it, ' . . . Mikha'il?'

Sammael blinked at me slowly. 'We are observed, of course we are. We lost our battle with them, and yet we won. We were cast out of our world, true, but we came to inhabit the one coveted by our enemies.'

'But even this world turned against us,' I said, 'otherwise we wouldn't be confined here in Sacramante, hiding our true selves away from humanity.'

'That, too, was inevitable,' Sammael said. 'You should not feel indignant about it. We gave humanity knowledge and, in return, they gave us sustenance. It seemed a necessary thing at the time. Eloim could no longer feed from one another, not if they wanted to pass for human. Only human blood can maintain the fleshy shape that we had chosen for ourselves, and which has been held by eloim to this day. It was the first mistake we made in this world – perhaps the worst. I foresaw the results, much to the displeasure of my brethren. We should have mingled utterly with humanity, interbred with them. If we had discarded our psychic abilities, and much of our creative spirit, we could have held on to flesh without needing human ichor to sustain it. We should have rid ourselves of eloim traits.'

'Yet you have not done so!' I interjected.

He smiled sadly. 'No, but I am ancient and eccentric, and I have hopes that one day an unlikely and enraptured reunion will occur, for which I will need *all* of my eloim characteristics . . . Anyway, allow me to continue. Humanity eventually came to resent the tithe of blood demanded from them; they found it unsavoury, despite the advantages. At the time, many eloim insisted on supping to the point of death for the donor; they drank spirit as well as blood. This is what caused the war between the two races, which was no doubt observed by our estranged kin from the old world with much grinning and gleeful hand-rubbing! A minority of humans, namely those referred to as the 'Old Blood', realised that the relationship was symbiotic, and all that was required to achieve the correct balance was a control of our sustenance-taking. Not all humanity agreed, of course, which resulted in our furtive seclusion in Sacramante. All this happened a long time ago. We had to connive and plot to secure our position. For a long time we were in hiding, until enough years had elapsed for us to creep forth and call ourselves artisans. I wanted no part of it. Give me enough to eat and let me

226

rot in peace is what I told them.'

'Do you feast until death then?' I asked. 'Every time?'

'It is the nearest I can get to . . . the things that I miss,' he replied, unflinching. Then he stood up abruptly. 'The things that I miss! They basked in pleasure as I suffered, damn them!'

I jumped in alarm; the outburst had been so unexpected. 'Who is the girl?' I asked him quickly. 'The one you called Lilian?'

He calmed down instantly, and ran a hand through his brilliant hair. 'Just that; a girl. I have them with me, just a few. I can't bear to be totally alone. They keep me company.'

'They? How many?'

He made an irritated gesture as if the question were trivial. 'Oh, I don't know. A few. They come from the Strangeling. They come here to find me. I let them live and die here, if they want to.'

From the Strangeling? I thought. How was that possible? 'But how do they get here?'

'Gimel, humans occupying the Strangeling lands are not quite like other humans. I think they consider themselves to be another race entirely, living there among our ruins as they do. They have been affected by the memories of our history, they have absorbed all the feelings that haunt the place.' He grinned. 'They are pantomime eloim!'

'So you brought them from the Strangeling yourself then?' I wished he'd answer my questions.

Sammael shook his head. 'No. In the old days when this tower was built an underground route was dug from here to the Strangeling. Naturally I wanted a back door, in case of emergency. Also, in the beginning I was drawn back to the Strangeling often. I liked to walk among the ruins.'

'And you made contact with humans who'd come to inhabit the ruins?' I was visualising the story in my head. It seemed so vivid.

'Not exactly,' Sammael aid. 'After a short while I stopped my secret excursions and went into retreat-slumber here, perhaps imagining I would never awake. Life was painful. I could no longer bear to think, to remember. Then as time eroded the stones and locks around the tunnel's entrance in the Strangeling, humans living there found my hidden road and came creeping along it. They came into the tower and woke me up. It didn't happen that long ago, perhaps only a few decades.' He shook his head smiling. 'I think they thought I was an ancient corpse – I was covered in dust and rubbish, my bed long-rotted – but I still wore my jewels and they sought to rob me. One of them started tugging at my rings, which brought me back to reality. It was quite amusing to see their hysterical reaction when I sat up and roared, showering them with my mantle of dust.'

I found the image quite chilling. 'You are lucky they didn't kill you.'

'Oh, they wouldn't have done that. They sense something in me that links me to the Strangeling and its past I suppose. I am their secret, but then the humans in the Strangeling have many secrets.'

'Do you sup from them?' I asked.

Sammael smiled. 'They would like me to. Sometimes I do, just a little. It pleases them, although I have been off my food for a thousand years; supping does not give me great pleasure.'

'You are a strange creature,' I said.

He grinned. 'What did you expect? And then he said, 'Would you like to see some of my work?'

I accepted the change of subject without argument. 'I would be honoured.'

He brought me a leather-bound book with beautiful, creamy parchment pages, all covered in delicate curling text written by hand.

'It is all about love,' he said.

I tried to read it. 'Is it?'

'Yes. You know why I dislike the sup?'

I paused from my examination, looked at him and shook my head.

'It is because of . . . I drank, as your brother did, eloim ichor. Anything else is like muddy water after that. I think we should sustain each other, don't you?'

'When did you do that? After you came to Earth?' It was a loaded question. I knew whom he was referring to but in eloim lore there had been no contact between Mikha'il and Sammael since that time.

'Yes, afterwards. In our old territory mutual supping was a way of life. It is different here; a different world. And yet I had to experience the taste of eloim fluid on Earth; I was always too curious.'

'I thought your brother . . . I mean, *people believe* your brother never came through to Earth after the conflict.'

Sammael pulled a rueful face. 'Well, our meetings were not exactly advertised with banners and trumpets! We met a few times before the thoroughfare between the worlds was closed for eternity, but nobody knows that. As we were building Ykhey, he came to me there, and we loved one another in flesh.'

'But you had fought! He was responsible for our eviction! I don't understand why . . .'

'Oh, these things happen you know,' Sammael interrupted. 'People fall out, and fall in; then they can't make up their minds and just claw at each other. It was like that, but not like that. We had divided loyalties.'

I realised that more than anything, he wanted to talk about himself. But even now, with me an eager audience, I could tell he was reluctant to speak plainly. I was a little nervous of what I might hear. Even so, only someone open-minded like me could take his confession. Metatron would say things like, 'You mustn't think that way, ever!' and that would be an end to it. Mikha'il and his kind could only be statues, icons, in this world. We could not admit they were actually *real*. Sammael seemed to pick up my thoughts. He smiled wistfully and shook his head.

'Do not judge *your* brother,' he said. 'His way might be the right way. It is certainly *one* way. Why not let him proceed and see what happens?

'You mean I should tell him to stop taking sustenance from humans and feed solely off Avirzah'e?' His advice, as I should have known it would be, was useless. 'And I suppose, also, that you think they should be allowed to conjoin?'

'If that is what they want. You cannot criticise them, Gimel Metatronim, because you have not tried it.'

'I very nearly did – and against my will!'

'The eloim are foolish if they think they can be happy living as humans, with only humanity's shallow grubbing in the flesh to fulfil them!'

'All right,' I said, to appease him, 'but if we chose the eloim way, how could we coax humanity to accept us?'

'That's your problem. That's your soulscaper's problem. Don't you see, that is the way she can really help you?' Eloim are invisible in the human soulscape. She might be able to manipulate the soulscape, much as you have manipulated humans in Sacramante, but in this case to forge a positive image of eloim, not an invisible one!'

'You are saying we could live among humanity as ourselves?'

He shrugged. 'Just a suggestion. It needs discussion, of course. Anyway, I doubt whether you *will* choose that way.'

'You are not being very helpful, Sammael.'

'Don't be so ungrateful. I could have let Lilian sweep you downstairs!'

'I'm sorry. Just tell me one thing; where do I go from here?'

'The Strangeling, I think. You could use the underground route, if you like, but parts of it are difficult to negotiate now, so other tunnels have been dug, not much wider than a fox run. They might be difficult for a lady such as yourself to negotiate in places.'

I shrugged. If that was a criticism, I could hardly deny it. 'Why should I go to the Strangeling?'

'There is a dead city there called Ykhey that is the seat of the eloim kings: the last ruin on this world of our once magnificent communities. If your soulscaper is to investigate our malady, there would be no better location than Ykhey for her to attempt it. The emanations of our past are so strong there; Rayojini will be able to pick up memories and feelings that should help her in her work. Ykehy is drenched in ancient blood. Once war was done, and we

229

had come to Earth, we began to build in that place. Mikha'il came to me there to say "I told you so", and gloat. He never believed I wanted anything but power. Our father had control of his mind, while I had only his heart. I needed both.' He sighed. 'Mikha'il came to me in Ykhey. It was the last time . . .' His voice faltered and his face became introspective.

'Do you really have a wound that doesn't heal?' I asked him.

He glanced up at me. 'Hmm? Oh, *that*. I was wounded once, above the heart. Mikha'il struck me as I and my people fled Elenoen. It healed quite naturally, but later, when Mikha'il and I fed upon each other, I made him open up the scar with his teeth. Perhaps I was trying to make a point . . . Anyway, if you feed from the same place regularly with earthly flesh around your soul, it gets a bit messy, that's all. It's healed again now, on the surface.'

'Mikha'il too is wounded above the heart,' I said. 'There is a statue in the Castile . . .'

'We are brothers,' Sammael said quietly, 'and more than that. Where I bleed, he bleeds. As he wounded me, he wounded himself. I have never seen that statue though.' He smiled to himself, and his hand hovered to touch his chest. Then, he rubbed at his face vigorously.

Impulsively I reached out and touched his wrist. 'Come with me,' I said. 'If you cannot help us yourself, at least guide our soulscaper!'

He looked down at me, so full of sad hope it was pathetic. 'Well, I don't think . . . No, it wouldn't be a good idea. I might just blow away out there.'

'You can't stay here for ever!' I said.

He laughed shakily. 'I thought I already had!'

'Sammael, don't *you* want to know what is really causing this sickness? You are so powerful.'

'Was,' he corrected, but I shook my head.

'*Are*! All we have is a human woman to help us. Do you really think she can succeed?'

'Yes. Well, I think she has more chance than I. Do not underestimate the Taps, Gimel. Even before we were driven into hiding, they were a force to respect. I am not a soulscaper. In our old world, she would have been no match for me, but not here on Earth. My power – our power – has atrophied. Whatever abilities I still have, there are none that are equal to the skills of a Tap.'

'I don't believe that!' I cried. 'And if you do lack a certain knowledge, then Rayojini could teach you!'

'In that case, she could teach you!' he said quickly.

I shook my head. 'No eloim has your experience, Sammael, nor your strength.'

'What strength? Look at me!' There was a note of despair in his voice, but in his face I thought I could see a yearning to leave the tower. In his pain, so long ago, he had wanted to hide away from

230

others and indulge his grief and his sense of failure. Now the grief and shame were dulled. My visit had plainly stimulated him, awoken his curiosity. I knew I would have to persuade him quickly, while the thought of escape was in him, before he remembered too much of the past and changed his mind. 'Sammael, we need you!' I said desperately. 'You brought us to this world. You *are* eloim. Cast off your fear of the outside! I do believe that's the only thing keeping you in here now – fear.'

He considered my words, took a few breaths as if he was about to speak, before frowning and shaking his head. Finally, he said, 'Suppose I was ready to leave this place. Imagine my situation. It would be very embarrassing. How would I be received among my people now?'

'No one need know.'

'You said Sandalphon sits on folded paws at the Tower's door.'

'I could send him away. Oh, Sammael . . . please!'

He sighed. 'Damn, damn, damn, you're like all the others, aren't you! I tried to age a little, I tried to become something else, but I'm still me, ultimately. It's a curse, sometimes.'

'You can't escape what you are.'

He held out a hand to me; a glowing, fiery hand. He really was the Lord of Light, the most beautiful. I took it in my own, let his energy pulse into me. He would come down out of the Tower now; I knew he would.

'. . . but pain is perfect misery, the worst of evils, and excessive, overturns all patience.'
Paradise Lost, Book VI

On the walk down from the Eastern mountains, the plains of Khalt had seemed an open, innocent place: a seed-ground of primal thoughts and with the ambience of the Supernal Child. Whether it was travelling in the company of Keea that changed my perception I am unsure, but from the moment I left Helat's Sink the Kahra Flats became a secretive, threatening place. Its whispering grasses concealed unimaginable terrors; their constant hissing sounded like malevolent voices muttering in a language I could not translate. Something dark had hooked itself into my heart.

Many times, the dreadful suspicion that the Fear itself was slinking at my heels recurred, and I had to fight to push it out of my mind. Sometimes, when the mists came down, I thought I could hear it panting close behind me, that I could feel its hot, steamy breath through my clothes. Each time, the banishing was harder. If Keea suspected the way I was feeling, he gave no sign. We conversed quite easily as we walked, although neither of us broached the subject that had thrown us together. Perhaps he had his own Fear to dread. Talking aloud kept my horrors at bay; night-times, for this reason, were the times I hated most.

Keea and I did not share sleeping space, although sometimes I would have welcomed the presence of another living soul nearby. My dreams were chaotic, full of potent symbols; time and again I relived the original dream I'd had in Sacramante, years before. I held Beth Metatronim in my arms. In these dreams I was no passive victim lacking knowledge. In these dreams, I embraced him with hunger. Sometimes he had the face of Q'orveh, but the struggle always took place in Liviana Tricante's house. I awoke with longing after these dreams; with a thirsting for beauty, and intimacy beyond flesh, that could not be easily quenched in this world. I knew I could mix my fumes and enter the soulscape to obtain satisfaction, but I was afraid of doing so; I was afraid of what I might find there. Obsessions crowded my mind, pulsing in my blood to the rhythm of my footsteps. I was falling. Falling.

In honest moments I admitted I was helpless and terribly afraid, and walked swiftly on the road. I kept hoping that in the next settlement we came across there might be a soulscaper whom I could turn to for comfort. I needed to be among my own kind, not just to arrange my thoughts into perspective, but to experience the reality of their healing touch. Even in the darkest moments, I still said nothing to Keea. As a travelling companion, he was surprisingly easy to get along with, and more than easy on the eye. He was certainly a lot older than he looked; how much so, it was impossible to tell. He seemed completely different from the person I had met among the Halmanes and I had begun to like him, to appreciate his quick mind. He was a sensitive creature and from day to day did many small things to increase the comfort of travelling for me.

'Let me rub your feet for you,' he might say when we rested for the night, if I pulled a face and groaned as I sat down.

'Look, Rayo, your favourite,' he would say, having found some fruit or nut of which he'd learned I was particularly fond.

And yet, despite this thoughtful behaviour, I could not and would not trust him. I wanted to, desperately. I wanted to tell someone about the whispers I heard that seemed to say my name, the shadows on the edge of my vision suggestive of cloaked figures with pale, attentive faces. I could not speak, only walk faster, and he, without questioning, adjusted his pace to my own, talking carelessly of life in Sacramante. It helped, if only through the rhythm of the sound of speech, yet I realise now that he actually told me very little.

Inevitably, because he was intelligent, Keea became aware that my self-confidence was deteriorating, and that something more than the long hours of travelling was responsible for my obvious exhaustion. His attempts to overcome this manifested itself as lively sarcasm, with which he flogged my limping spirits. He mocked my occupation, and what he saw as my arrogance, even my clothes. I responded with similar cutting remarks, calling him a whore, a parasite, a precocious upstart. All of this sparring seemed good-natured at heart. I was unsure whether Keea was the cause of my condition, or not. If he was, I was a fool, and subjecting myself to needless danger by remaining close to him. If he was not, I was fortunate to have him with me. I was so confused, I could not decide; my powers of perception were weak and prone to inaccuracy. Nevertheless, saviour or tormentor, Keea's presence helped me maintain my sanity throughout some quite absurd experiences in the land of Khalt and beyond.

Each evening we would pause in our journey and erect our sleeping tents – in the shelter of trees, if they were available. We'd build a small fire and take it in turns to cook a meal. Game was plentiful and Keea seemed to know where to find succulent roots, which we cleaned and baked among the embers of our fire.

One night, we had just settled down to eat – and we ate well

234

during those weeks – when Keea suddenly put down his plate and sat up straight, his nostrils quivering like an animal's. 'What is it?' I asked. I'd had a bad day. It had been warm again, after a few days of cooler weather, and the heat haze had been full of moving shapes just beyond my sight. Keea never seemed to notice these things, although I kept hoping he would, just to confirm I was not losing my mind.

He shook his head at my question and took a cautious mouthful of food, still staring above the grass. 'The night is quiet. Have you noticed?'

When he mentioned it, I could sense the stillness. There were no animal sounds and even the grass itself was silent. Not so long ago I would have noticed these conditions at the precise moment when sound had died away. It made me realise, yet again, how vulnerable I'd have been had I travelled alone at that time, preoccupied as I was.

'Predators about? Maybe we should take it in turns to stand guard tonight.'

He nodded thoughtfully. 'Yes, I think we should.'

We finished our meal with little enjoyment.

In the morning, we discovered a dew-soaked figure sitting beside the ashes of our fire. We had taken it in turns to remain awake throughout the dark hours, and neither of us had heard or seen anyone approach. Keea had been on last watch and we'd decided he should sleep for a couple of hours before we began travelling again. I almost stumbled across the stranger as I went to replenish our water carriers from a nearby spring.

The figure was hunched low to the ground and dressed in dusty garments, the colour of the grass itself, and did not move a muscle at my approach. I called for Keea and we both stood looking at this person from a few feet away, for several moments.

'A nomad?' I asked. There was something unspecifically repellent about our uninvited visitor, even though we could only see the back view.

'Nomads don't usually travel alone,' Keea replied.

'Looks sick,' I said, and stepped forward. Just a few minutes' appraisal at close quarters revealed that the creature was more than simply sick. I offered water, and the stranger did not respond. I squatted down in front of him or it or she, to see the face. I could not tell what sex this person was. The stench coming off the body was disgusting; it spoke of deep-seated disease. The face itself was distorted and discoloured. The eyes appeared blind; just a mass of milky discolouration in sticky sockets. Instinctively I drew back.

'Plague!' I hissed at Keea.

Instead of retreating swiftly as any sensible person would, he came to squat beside me. Our visitor still had not moved.

235

'No, not plague,' Keea said quietly. 'I have seen this before, Rayo.'

'You have?'

'Yes, look around you.' He gestured upwards. We had camped in a copse of tall trees. Among the leaves, high above, dark wooden platforms could be seen. We had camped in the midst of a nomad funeral site.

'Are you suggesting . . . ?' I could not speak the words and opted for, after a pause, 'Is this thing alive or not?'

'Not in any sense we understand,' Keea replied.

'How can you be sure?'

'Easily. If you examine this unfortunate semblance of humanity, you will discover there is no heartbeat, no physiological activity whatsoever. It is animated to a degree, yes, but I can't tell you by what. It has no function, it is not part of the life-chain. It just *is*, decaying about itself.'

'Then I must deal with it immediately!' I said, wanting more information about this poor creature's condition than Keea's words, which sounded more than a little ignorant and superstitious to me.

'No! We must just burn it!' Keea said emphatically.

I could not believe what I was seeing. There had to be some kind of explanation. I did not think that this creature was literally a dead thing brought back to some semblance of life. That was the kind of primitive conjecture I would only expect from nomads! Surely, Keea did not believe such a thing; he seemed so intelligent. Nothing in this world could persuade me to burn someone alive, and I was astounded Keea had suggested it. Yet perhaps our discovery of this creature was what I'd been waiting for: an ideal opportunity for investigation. Some of the answers I was looking for might exist within this wretched creature's mind, or brain-cells: answers that Keea claimed he was seeking, too.

I stood up and began to walk quickly to my tent. 'What are you doing?' Keea asked, irritably.

I pulled out my bag of scry mixtures and equipment. 'I'm going to explore this person's soulscape,' I replied.

Keea stomped over angrily and knocked the bag from my hands. 'Don't be insane! You're not capable!'

Indignation flared within me. I felt stronger than I had for days. 'How dare you!' I cried, snatching up my bag once more. 'You have neither the right nor experience to question my ability! Also, this might be the only opportunity we get. I'm not going to let it pass by.'

'Rayo, be sensible. There is no soulscape in that thing! If you breathe the scry-mix and enter *nothingness*, it may be impossible for you to return. It could suck away your life-force.'

'Superstitious, old women's fire prattle!' I replied. 'I may have been affected by strange influences recently, but I'm not afraid of doing my job. This is familiar territory to me, Keea. I understand it. There's no danger.'

'Yes there is! You're so blinkered. You think that thing's still alive, don't you.'

'Keea, it has to be, in one sense or another. Now, let me get on with what I have to do.' I was sure we had another case of the non-death on our hands, a person whose spirit was barely in this world, but still recognisably alive. I'd not come across one who could walk around before, but evidence was scanty; it could be a fairly common phenomenon.

As I prepared my mixes, I told Keea about Mouraf's son in Yf. 'You see, this may be the same. *Think*, Keea: do you really believe a dead body can walk around among the living? It's preposterous!'

My exclamation seemed to mollify him a little. I was pleased about the way the balance of power had changed. Since I had met him on the road, Keea had seemed much stronger than I. I'd not been happy about that and welcomed this chance to reassert myself – and not just in his eyes.

He watched me moodily, hands thrust deep into his trouser pockets. 'How do you know the scry-mix will affect them? They look too far gone for that.'

'It affects anyone; therefore, you should move away from the smoke.' I paused. 'I may need you.'

'You are not wholly confident then, *are* you?' he said, with a certain tone of triumph in his voice.

'Only a fool would not take some precaution,' I replied. 'But the risk will be worth it. Think what we could learn.'

'What did you learn from the boy in Yf?'

'I've seen and heard a lot since then. Now, move back.'

I positioned my charcoal-holder in front of the motionless figure and sprinkled it with a generous pinch of scaping-mix. Keea backed off reluctantly and went into his tent.

The pungent fume odour swelled around me, bringing a thousand comforting memories of Taparak, and soon eclipsed the foul stink of the stranger before me. I arranged myself into the habitual cross-legged position and took long, deep breaths. Before the fume took effect, I made an objective study of the face in front of me. The muscles were slack, the skin mottled. One cheek seemed pushed inwards, as if the person had been lying on a hard surface and the flesh had not sprung back to its usual shape. Bodily functions were clearly running down, and I was amazed it could actually still move about. As the thick, grey smoke surrounded us, the figure's left hand twitched a little and, through the fug, I saw its mouth tremble. These signs were reassuring. I crooned a few comforting words – they may have been of some help – and concentrated on leaving one reality for another.

* * *

237

A regular pinch of scry-mix produces a fume of perhaps ten minutes duration, which is enough to affect both a soulscaper and their client sufficiently for scape-sharing to occur. A trained soulscaper can 'step back' into normal reality at any time, an aspect of my training that I was soon destined to feel particularly grateful for.

As usual, I became aware of the consensual soulsape taking shape around me and prepared to enter the individual scape of our peculiar guest. The soulscape scenario around me was shimmering oddly, as if in a heat haze. I could not see very well, and there was no immediate sign of the stranger's presence. This was most unusual, but I had expected something out of the ordinary, so was not too concerned at first. I instructed my body to reach out, in reality, and touch the sick person in front of me. This might facilitate soulscape contact. I was totally unprepared for what occurred. The minute my flesh touched the cold meat, I was engulfed, within the soulscape, by a great, icy cloud of thick, grey fog that was tinged with a sickly, putrid yellow and which stank of corrupted flesh. It was a far stronger stench than that of the sick stranger's physical body. I sensed my own body gagging, although my soulscape form was unaffected in that way. Then I noticed movement in the fog. Collecting myself, visualising a core of sustaining light within me, I summoned whatever lurked there towards me.

It was the eyes I saw first. Pitiful, yet empty, they were the only aspect of the shambling figure approaching me that retained any semblance of normality. The thing was a stray thought-form trapped into a disintegrating shape, which was decomposing even as I looked at it. Tatters of flesh ran, semi-liquid, from spongy bones. One thigh-bone had departed company from the hip, attached only by stretched rags of flesh. The face was an indescribable horror, features melting from the skull. And I had summoned this thing towards me! I backed away, my soulscape form now also experiencing the stench – which was spiritual more than anything – and beginning to lose its cohesion. It seemed as if this dreadful creature were contaminating the soulscape as it struggled forward. It was like a disease eating at the substance of the inner world; it should not, under any circumstances, be allowed to remain there.

I had to claw my strength back to me, strain to regenerate my flame of protection but, thank Helat, again my training did not let me down. Visualising an enormous wave of pure, cleansing water rising up around me, I projected it as forcefully as I could at the yellow-grey fog and the foulness it surrounded. Testing my belief to the extreme, I convinced myself the water was destroying the fog and the stumbling monster. Again and again I fashioned this elemental weapon and hurled it forth, becoming almost hysterical, so that I was creating tidal waves and throwing them out for several minutes after I needed to. Eventually I realised the soulscape was clean – steaming, but clean – and I directed the water to sink into the ground. My work was over.

The procedure had not been as dangerous as Keea had feared, but neither had it been as informative as I had desired. Utterly drained of strength, I forced myself back to conscious awareness. My nose was full of a disgusting stink, and I vomited copiously into the grass. I could not bear to look at the thing in front of me, and got shakily to my feet, averting my eyes. Keea had come out of his tent, and was waiting anxiously just beyond the perfume of the smoke. I had only been in the soulscape for a few minutes, because the smoke was still potent. I looked at Keea steadily for a couple of seconds, and then wiped my mouth. He did not speak, but watched me as I scattered the fume-mix and damped the smoke with handfuls of grass, holding my breath the entire time. I did not want to be aware of the soulscape just then, even though the contamination had been successfully dispelled. I kicked the ashes and made a gesture with my hand, signifying to Keea that it was safe for him to approach. He came and took my forearms in his hands, peering into my face, his eyes full of concern. At that moment we were utterly in accord.

My mouth felt thick. It was hard to speak, but somehow I got the words out. 'Burn it!' I said.

He did not ask me what I had seen, nor could I have spoken of the foulness I had encountered in that poor creature's soulscape. In fact it had not really been a soulscape at all, but only the reflection of a memory, haunted by a confused fragment of deteriorating consciousness.

Keea carried out the grisly deed while I packed away our things. Afterwards, we fled from that place and, from that moment on, every movement in the grass beside the road had both of us jumping in alarm. At any moment we expected to come across another ragged remnant of humanity that the nomads had, quite rightly as it turned out, dubbed the walking dead. Yet I was relieved to find that I felt a lot better, my mind did not seem so strained and fearful. This, I think, was simply because I now *knew* the strange, conflicting feelings I'd been having, the presentiments of weirdness, were *real* and external. Before, I had not been sure.

After the encounter with the dead thing, I noticed that Keea began to meditate for up to an hour at a time, once every few days, at sunfall. He shut himself away in his tent, tying its entrance flaps together firmly, so I could not glimpse what went on inside. Afterwards, he would seem tired and irritable, and refused to answer my questions.

Several times, we caught sight of the mysterious riders in the distance. On one occasion we were trailed for nearly an hour, but we were never accosted. Keea tried, unsuccessfully, to hide how much these figures worried him; I noticed his jumpy unease when-

239

ever we saw one. I asked him if he knew who the riders were, but all he would say is that he believed they came from the Strangeling.

'And the person who employs you, do they come from the Strangeling too?' I asked.

'I can't tell you about that,' he answered.

'You are anxious to reach the Strangeling. Is that the place where we will learn the truth? Does everything come from there?'

'Wait and see.'

He was so impenetrable. At times it drove me to distraction and once I physically had to restrain myself from striking him. 'Tell me what you know, Keea.'

'In time you'll know it too.'

He would never tell me.

'So strange thy outcry, and thy words so
strange . . .'
Paradise Lost, Book II

Before a traveller passes on to Bochanegran soil, the fertile plains
of Khalt diminish into the bizarre landscape known as the Strangeling. I had never visited it before, although I had heard much about
it from other soulscapers. Legends told us that the Strangeling had
once been a collection of thriving and affluent small kingdoms
which at some distant point had become involved in an unusually
extensive conflict with another country; a war which the Strangeling
kingdoms had lost dramatically. The victors of this war had obviously attempted to erase all evidence of the race they had vanquished, for no information remained in any library I had visited,
or even within the oral tradition of other races, concerning the
civilisation that had existed there. The old kingdoms of the Strangeling, however, were not the only ones to suffer such expunction
from human history. In primitive times it had not been unusual for
war-mongerers to put all surviving conquestees, including civilians,
to the sword. Some of the ancient Delta kings had been fanatical
about how certain races, whose philosophies and religions were
widely different from their own, were so abhorrent to them that it
was nothing more than a Deltan duty to obliterate their genetic
lines. There had been special phalanxes within the Deltan army
whose sole purpose had been to march in after a war was over and
clean up, by methodically scouring the land and butchering any
natives they came across. At first I had believed this to be an
exaggeration, but the records were so cold-bloodedly descriptive of
these acts, and full of such detail, I had eventually (and reluctantly,
because the ancient Deltans were my ancestors) acknowledged it
as fact. Nowadays, the Deltans were embarrassed about this aspect
of their history, and treated such records with a kind of whimsical
unease. As part of my initial training, I had spent time studying
the Deltan archives in Ahmana, and was therefore familiar with
much of their history. Deltan records, however, did not mention
the Strangeling specifically, although the extent of its devastation
would suggest Deltan interference, but the country would undoubtedly have been known by a different name in the past.

Whereas other countries had recovered from earlier ravagements,
the Strangeling had never resumed its former glory. Perhaps that

241

was why it had been dubbed the Strangeling; it *was* strange. Now it was nothing more than a vast wilderness of ruins and ancient highways, most of which had been overrun by the forces of nature. A great and impenetrable intensity of superstitious fear seemed to have prevented anyone – Deltans included, oddly enough – from reclaiming and utilising this land. There were stories of enterprising agricultural pioneers who had set up farming homesteads, but these people had become absorbed by the peculiarities of the area they had come to inhabit. It was said they had descended into primitive ways and shunned the civilisation they had left behind. In some places the remains of towns still stood, although they were badly dilapidated. Over the years, they had become occupied by people who had either been expelled from more civilised areas, or who had just wandered there of their own accord and taken root. Tappish records suggested that the Strangeling was inhabited by rogues, degenerate nomad tribes, and misfits of all types. It was reported that inbreeding had resulted in mutant lineages, but whoever had compiled the information was clearly sceptical about this because no specific details were given. The natives of the Strangeling were rarely described as being hostile, but there was evidence to suggest that some of them were cannibal, in support of some bizarre religion or another. Although there was no hard proof that they killed and ate strangers, any soulscaper travelling through the area was advised not to consume any food they might be offered by natives.

The boundary between the Kahra Flats and the Strangeling is very narrow. Some say that it is possible to experience a physical sensation of weirdness as one's feet pass over it, a tingling tremor in the muscles of the legs. If such a phenomenon does occur, I am sure it is merely generated by the imagination rather than any real power in the land. The imagination is definitely encouraged to excesses by the fetishes erected by Strangeling inhabitants among the rocks beside the road. We saw wooden poles, painstakingly polished and carved, topped by the bleached skulls of large birds, given painted stones for eyes and crowned with hanks of what we hoped was horse-hair. In other places, puppets of rag and straw, fashioned in the semblance of men and women, wore deer's antlers on their foreheads or sprouting from their chests.

Keea and I reached the boundary in the early evening. Before us, immense boulders formed a natural barrier between Khalt and the Strangeling lands, some of which were carefully painted with pictorial warnings: travellers being murdered in their sleep by beastmen and other sweet delights. Neither Keea nor I considered it a good idea to make the crossing so late in the day. Laughing nervously about possible hazards, we set up camp among a tumble of rocks, erecting our tents very close together. We hardly slept, and during the night we sat together, listening to strange calls coming from the West that might have been human or animal in origin. In

242

the morning (both of us relieved that nothing unusual had occurred during the dark hours), we set off once more. The next night would be spent upon dangerous ground.

Bearing in mind all that I had learned about the place, I had prepared myself for a bleak and depressing panorama, and the possibility of hazardous encounters. What we did find filled me with awe and, despite the depredations of time and dissolution, I fell in love with the Strangeling after very short acquaintance. It is a land of the dead, yes, but the memory of their lives lingers on in the fantastic faded lines of their roads and towns. Much art has been left behind, which the present inhabitants, for all their imputed derangement, hold precious and have not destroyed.

After a few hours scrambling over an uninhabited rocky area, we found an old road heading west. Both Keea and I were alert for the presence of hidden strangers, but it seemed that no one was about. Cold, morning light came down through the reddening foliage of tall trees beside the road, the surface of which was a beautiful carpet of gold and crimson leaves. We walked past a broken tower, whose dark entrance was guarded by the crumbled and dismembered statue of a huge stern god, who had undoubtedly once perched atop the tower. Later we walked between three pairs of lichened stone lions, whose broad ancient backs were saddled in bright fallen leaves. The lions pulled snarling and argumentative faces at one another across the road; a dispute that had been maintained for centuries. Nearby, among the trees, was the haunted façade of a ruined villa. Deer stood in the gaping windows, pulling, with delicate lips, leaves from the creepers that shrouded the roofless walls. They did not scatter as we passed them.

'This place is nothing like I imagined,' I said. 'It's so *peaceful*, so beautiful, so lush!'

'The land can be grateful humankind has not come to spoil it,' Keea said in a cynical way. I supposed he rather liked the place, too.

By late afternoon, we discovered that the road we were following led to the ruin of an old town. At first, I thought the place was made of some fabulous crimson metal, for the low beams of the sinking sun seemed to reflect a metallic gleam. Then, as we grew nearer, I could see that the ruins had been overtaken completely by vines, whose fading leaves were shiny and small, clinging like fish-scale armour to what remained of the buildings. Here we encountered our first Strangeling natives.

It was clear that the ruins were occupied, for many small fires were burning among the rubble, and inside some of the less ruined and therefore more habitable buildings. We noticed dark shapes flit nervously away from us. If the natives were timid and afraid of us, all the better; it was preferable to being attacked or harangued.

We walked up and down what remained of the streets for a while, both of us enchanted by what we saw. Where the ruins were not blanketed by the shiny vines, they were bursting with massive ferns, whose fronds must have been well over ten feet long. Bright-blue birds nested among the ferns and chattered to each other in shrill voices. In some places, fern-fronds reaching out across the street from high positions had met and become entwined, creating a canopy from which long aerial roots dangled in feathery curtains.

Eventually we chose a place in which to shelter for the night, in the lee of a half-crumbled wall, surrounded by root-curtains. I collected dead fern-fronds to build a fire, while Keea sorted through what remained of our provisions to make a meal.

'Have you been here before?' I asked him, dumping an armload of fronds in front of him.

'No, have you?'

'You know I haven't. I can't understand why people are so nervous of this place.'

'Some ancient legends tend to leave a lingering smell,' Keea said.

'There are very few ancient legends about the Strangeling actually,' I said. 'All the ones I've come across are fairly recent. There are no historical records for this area.'

'There are if you know where to look,' Keea replied, and smiled up at me. 'Where's your tinder?'

I found it for him. 'What do you know about this place, then?' He was concentrating on getting the fire alight, and I doubted whether he would answer me properly.

'What do I know? Well, it once harboured a great and powerful civilisation.'

'That much everyone knows! What else?' I helped him feed the flames.

'It is a holy place. It's protected. That's why only certain people can live here.' He beamed at me again. 'Under different circumstances you might feel very uncomfortable here.'

'What different circumstances?'

He shrugged. 'If you were alone, perhaps.'

'All right, I understand. Only crazy people can bear the ghosts of this place! And I have gone crazy to travel with you!'

'You get so annoyed when you don't know things, Rayo. Why not accept there are always going to be things you can't understand.'

'I can't help but get annoyed when you so obviously enjoy mystifying me,' I said. 'I don't believe you know anything more about the Strangeling than I do!' That was a lie, but I hoped to provoke him.

'You might be right . . .' he said, and then pointed across the smoke of our fire. 'What's that?'

There was a crouching shape in the shadows. Realising it had been noticed, a shabby figure scuttled out of a veil of roots and into the meagre light of our flames. My hand shot to my belt where I kept my knife, but Keea made no move other than to drag a package out of my carryback. Our visitor was nothing more terrifying than a gnomish old woman, spry as a goat. She peered at us fearlessly through a tangle of greasy hair. I relaxed and folded my arms.

'Wisdom I have to give!' announced the hag, squinting sideways at the package of meat Keea was unwrapping.

I suspected she only wanted food from us, but was prepared to go along with her claim. 'What wisdom can you give us, mother?' I asked cheerfully.

'More'n the dead can,' she said sharply, and I shivered involuntarily.

'The dead can be quite informative,' Keea said reasonably, spitting the last of our meat. I noticed he had cut the meat into three strips, a fact which I'm sure did not escape the old woman either.

The woman nodded. 'Aye, boy, you're clear-seein', it's true!' She shuffled towards me and held out a begrimed hand, thick with rings, all of which were crusty and seemed to have become part of her flesh. I squeezed it briefly. At close quarters, the woman smelled undeniably rank.

'I am Isis Urania,' she said, nodding. 'I suppose you know me.'

'Well, I think I may have heard of you,' I replied, catching Keea's eye and smiling. Isis and Urania were the names of old goddesses from two very different cultures.

'Most have, most have,' the hag said, shaking her head and sighing deeply. 'I yearn for privacy, but they won't let me be. It's my hands, you see, and my eyes. They're needed.' Fame was clearly a great burden to her.

'You have sons, don't you?' Keea said sweetly. 'Are you well?'

Isis pulled a frown. 'Yes. Apollo and Loki, my little devils!' She waved a finger at Keea and said to me, brightly, 'Sons are always a problem, aren't they!'

Keea snorted a laugh.

'I wouldn't know, I'm afraid,' I said, more offended than I would have liked to be. 'I have no children.' The journey must really have taken it out of me! The fact that Keea and I had very different skin colours seemed to have escaped the hag.

'You are a lucky woman, then,' she said, and sat down on a rock between us. 'Well, I have news for you people!' She slapped her parted thighs, between which the remains of a long, turquoise robe hung in rags. 'The Knights are abroad, riding the roads of Khalt in their cloaks and hats. Fearsome, eh? But you've nought to fear from 'em. Good boys, good boys, eyes like sun-hawks' eyes. Get me?' She tapped my knee with bunched knuckles. 'Don't have to be afraid of the pretty one, my dear. She won't hurt you. Neither will he.'

'What do you mean?' I asked. 'I'm afraid I don't understand you.'

Isis tutted and rolled her eyes. 'She's not a nightmare, she's a dream, a dream!' she exclaimed and then, rubbing her hands together, licked her lips and said, 'Meat's about ready, sonny. Hand her over. Like it rare, I do.'

The old woman seemed to think we all shared some deeply interesting secret. Her words implied she knew something of what we'd seen on the road, but I was prepared to dismiss this as coincidence. So many strange things were happening in Khalt, it was likely Isis had picked up information from other travellers who'd had similar experiences to our own.

Isis had finished gobbling her meat by the time Keea and I were ready to eat ours. She exhibited no interest in the wild salad Keea offered her. Admittedly it was rather limp. 'You're only a day's hike from Ykhey,' she said, nodding, and licking grease from her chin. 'Used to be Ykhey, anyways, the Holy City, it was. Now . . .' She shrugged. 'Some call it Taynah; a place of terrible destruction. You are going to Ykhey!'

'Are we?' I raised my eyebrows at Keea in inquiry. He shrugged.

'It is in the West. We will be heading that way.'

I felt quite sure that, despite his denial, he had been here before. Had it been a lucky guess concerning Isis having sons? Isis the goddess had sons, of course. Or was Isis Urania someone he knew, or had at least met before? I watched him as he sat beside the fire listening to the old woman's prattle. He was smiling in that particularly irritating way which usually signified – to me anyway – that he was nursing secrets. I realised that if I believed I had come to know him, I was wrong.

'So,' I said, offering Isis the fat off my meat, which she accepted greedily. 'What can you tell us that the dead can't? And who is the pretty one you referred to who won't hurt me?'

Isis squinted at me. 'Concerning your first question, lady, you have asked the wrong one. As for the second, she is the person you fear and love, whose image you carry in your thoughts.'

'I see . . . May I reword my first question?'

Isis inclined her head. 'You have only to ask.'

'What is it that causes the dead to walk around? Are they really dead?'

Isis cackled. 'They walk to seek oblivion. They are dead in one sense, but not in another. They have been partially supped.'

'Partially supped? What do you mean?'

'The host treats them cruelly now, very cruel.' She shook her head sadly.

'The Host of Helat? Is that who you mean? What are they?'

She extended her arms. 'This was theirs; all this. We took it away from them.'

246

'The Host of Helat lived in the Strangeling? I have seen paintings of these people in a temple on the Kahra Flats. The pictures seemed to indicate all the Host were destroyed.'

'No, not destroyed.' Isis tapped her beaky nose. 'There is the Host, and there is the Host, and there is yet another Host not of this world. It is very perplexin'.'

I touched her arm and spoke gently. 'Can you explain it to me? It's really important that I understand.'

'She has to know *everything*,' Keea drawled and grinned at me. 'Don't you, Rayo?'

I ignored him, and then recounted my thoughts upon everything I had so far encountered. Isis listened carefully. 'The nomads of Khalt worship Helat and have legends concerning the Host, who instigate the Holy Death. There are pictorial records in the Sink, which show the Host being born and then mingling with humanity; teaching them and preying off them. That could be a metaphor for a race arriving on this continent from somewhere else; a race with strange ways of behaviour, to say the least, but who were very intelligent, far more advanced than the ancient Khalts. Now, Isis, you're telling me that the Strangeling was their country. They were real people, and they were nearly destroyed. Because of the way they preyed?'

Isis nodded, eyes narrowed. 'People got the knowledge they needed and then turned on the Host. But they couldn't kill the light of 'em, oh no, couldn't do it! Always glowin', always, like the sky, see?'

I was beginning to feel excited, similar to how I felt when I successfully identified a soulscape problem. It might be that the answer to the mystery was a simple one – unlikely, but simple. 'Isis, you mentioned that the walking dead are – what was it? – oh, yes, "partially supped". By that, do you mean the Host have preyed on them, but not killed them?'

Isis put back her head and glared at me down her nose, her eyes nearly closed. I could see the wet gleam between her wrinkled lids. 'Supped, violated, but not to death. They can make all manner of things happen.'

'So it's *the Host* causing the phenomena in Khalt then!' I cried 'Is that right, Isis? Is it?'

Isis looked almost frightened by my urgency. She shrugged. 'Can make all manner of things happen,' she repeated.

'But why *now*?' I asked, addressing Keea. 'The Strangeling has existed for centuries. Why should these people begin appearing again *now*? That is the puzzle!' Keea's face was devoid of expression. 'This could be it, Keea! Don't you see? It makes sense, doesn't it? Survivors of this ancient race might have been hiding here in the Strangeling. Now, for whatever reason, it's possible they've become active beyond the boundary. All I have to discover is *how* they do the things they do. They must have an ability to direct human willpower and thought; a very strong ability. But it's not impossible. It *is* an answer. Why have they hidden themselves for so long? Keea, we have to find one of these Host people!' I turned excitedly to Isis. 'Will I find any here in the Strangeling? If so, where?'

'If they want you to find them, they'll find you,' Isis replied, rather stiffly.

I was jubilant. Q'orveh and his people had been nearer the truth than I had given them credit for! If only I hadn't been so scathing of their legends. Perhaps I could have learned more from them than I'd thought. Another idea came to me.

'Isis, the riders on the road, the ones you called the Knights. Are they members of the Host?'

'They are creatures of the Host,' Isis said.

Then I had already met one! This was incredible. Maybe these 'Knights' were the ones precipitating all the strange events. I patted the old woman's hand warmly. 'You have given me more than I could have wished for. Thank you for your wisdom.'

She inclined her head in a regal manner. 'Your meat was very good,' she said. 'Thank you. Now, no more talking, I must leave you.'

Before I could protest, she stood up, made a hurried genuflection of blessing in our direction, advised us to bind the inside of our boots with vine leaves to repel 'earth sniffers', and wished us the luck of the gods. Then, she vanished quickly through the root fronds.

'Well?' I said to Keea, triumphantly.

'I expect there are many like her in this place,' he said. 'Don't you? Quite mad.'

'Mad? Don't be ridiculous! She gave us some amazingly useful information!' I had a feeling Keea was annoyed Isis had spoken to me, but then he hadn't tried to silence her either.

'She's a seeress,' he said, caustically. 'Or perhaps even a goddess, although I don't think a goddess would be so careless about her appearance, do you?'

'Keea, she knew about me! It was as if she knew what I wanted to hear!'

He shrugged in an intensely irritating manner. 'Precisely. Think about it, Rayo. The woman can obviously read ethers and auras. She could have picked up the information from your own mind.'

I snorted sarcastically. 'Oh please! I don't believe anyone can be so adept at reading minds without the benefit of a scry-fume. She's just an old vagabond, almost senile.'

Keea sighed, rolling his eyes in what looked like exasperated patience. 'She didn't tell you anything, Rayo, think about it. You

248

perhaps told her all she needed to know, rather than the other way around.'

'You are being deliberately disparaging!'

'You are a very vain woman, Rayojini! Why do you think I spend my entire time thinking up conundrums to perplex you? I have better things to think about.'

'Such as?'

He shrugged.

'What is going on in your head, Keea?' I asked. 'My deductions have not impressed you at all, which only leads me to think that you know everything already.'

Keea opened his mouth to speak, but suddenly a horse snorted right behind us. Keea turned around quickly. Without waiting for him, I leapt up and fought my way through the concealing root-fronds. I ran out into the rubble-strewn street. *A horse! A Knight!* But there was nothing there.

Disappointed, I went back to the fire, and discovered that Keea had gone into his tent and tied the flaps tightly against me. For a while, I wrapped myself in a blanket and sat next to the dying embers. In the distance I could hear singing, faint music. It sounded like people welcoming in a harvest. Eventually, with images and ideas swirling round my brain, I slept where I was sitting.

'. . . then bursting forth afresh with conscious
terrors vex me round, that rest or intermission
none I find.'
Paradise Lost Book II

I was deliberately silent with Keea the next morning. He made no
effort to cajole me. After we had eaten and packed away our things,
we started walking towards the West once more. We found the
wide road we had followed, and walked away from the town of
vines and ferns. We did not see any sign of life, although it was
not long past dawn so perhaps no one was awake at that hour. I
was feeling stiff and disagreeable, haunted by a dream I had had
about my mother. She had expressed disappointment in me. 'You
walked right past the answers,' she'd said. 'You wasted your oppor-
tunities.' In my dreams, I was whipping myself for not having
worked out the puzzle sooner. One thing was certain: I'd have to
try and gather more evidence of the existence of the Host before
I could present my theories to the guild leaders in Taparak. This
eventually prompted me to break the silence with Keea.

'So where do we begin looking?' I asked him.

He pretended he'd been deep in thought, and took a few seconds
to answer me. 'Looking for what?' he said. We'd left the ruined
town and now walked along a stretch of road that was flanked by
fields of corn, which had run wild. Large villa-farms could be seen
in the valleys beyond. They were some distance from the road but
as it had been built on a raised embankment, we were able to see
for quite a way.

'The Host,' I said.

Keea gave me a hard look. 'Are you serious?' His voice was
thorned with sarcasm.

'Of course. The next time we catch sight of one of those Knight
people, we're going to confront them.'

'We?' He laughed. 'You're crazy! You'll get yourself killed! Look
what happened last time you spoke to one of those creatures.'

'They are not creatures, Keea,' I said pompously. 'They are men.
Calling them creatures merely assists them to intimidate you. I
have more information about them now, so therefore feel better
equipped to deal with them.'

'I can't stop you doing anything,' Keea said, 'but would still
advise you to consult the libraries in Sacramante first. I don't think

251

you – or I – have enough information yet to go barging in and asking questions around here. If your theories and Isis' information are correct, we could be running the risk of offending some very dangerous characters.'

Much as I itched to take some kind of action, I had to concur with a lot of what Keea had said. One woman and one boy would have little defence against attack, especially in unknown territory where we had no safe bolt holes. Still, if we came across a lone rider, I would definitely try and speak to them. If Keea was so worried about the idea of that, he could hide while I was doing it! 'Well, perhaps you are right,' I said, making a great show of how grudgingly I spoke the words.

Keea seemed relieved. I smiled to myself and adjusted my carry-back.

As we walked on in silence, I wondered what I should do when we reached Sacramante. Before I could continue my investigations there, I would have to sort out how I was going to support myself. Lodgings were expensive in the city; I might need to find work for a while. Somehow, I would have to persuade Keea to introduce me to his employers, and also to show me the libraries of which he had spoken. In view of his recent behaviour I would not be surprised if, once we reached the city, he abandoned me.

I realised I might need patronage while I was in Sacramante, which prompted me to think about the Tricantes. Could I seek sanction from them after all this time? The Sacramantans were generous when it came to people they considered to be artisans of one form or another. Luckily, soulscapers were included in this category. Seeking work in Sacramante was regarded with a narrow eye in Taparak, mainly because, despite the Bochanegran wealth we could take back to the table mountain, any time spent in Sacramante was nothing more than a holiday; work was incidental. Soulscapers had a tendency to linger there, spending their earnings, long after their commissions were finished. Also, as in Atruriey, Sacramantans rarely succumbed to the Fear. It was difficult for the Tappish to work out why this was so, but then we did not really know what caused the Fear in the first place. Any attempt to study the Sacramantans was politely but firmly discouraged. A friend had once said to me that the Sacramantans went out of their way to addle visiting soulscapers with liquor, just to prevent any covert examination. I tried to remember whether this had been so when Ushas and I had been there. Still, unless commissioned, a soulscaper had to look really hard to find work in Sacramante, although the Bochanegrans would heap a person with rewards for the most trivial of tasks. On one occasion, so it is recorded, a soulscaper did nothing more than supervise the delivery of a litter of kittens from a favourite cat, yet she received more payment than one could expect from healing the son of a royal house of Lansaal. It was only a legend, perhaps.

More immediately, I would have to concern myself with trying to track down a member of the Host. The Strangeling was a narrow country and we would cross it swiftly. Should I ignore Keea's forebodings and linger here, take time to explore? I wondered whether my assumptions about the Host were correct. Had I merely dreamed up an improbable solution to the puzzle, which was only the product of a lively imagination? I felt Keea wanted me tô think that. There was no point in rushing to conclusions; I must wait and observe.

By midday we had left the farmland behind and come to a place where overgrown ruins stretched to either side of us – perhaps the suburbs of an ancient city. The road was lined by tall columns, many of which were broken, supporting statues of various gods or important personages. I thought I recognised some of the gods from the soulscape. With little concentration, I fancied I could detect the images of ancient chariots that had once thundered up and down this highway. Clustering between the magnificent columns, and close to the road itself, were ramshackle dwellings, constructed of rag and wood and other less easily identifiable materials. This was a tableau rich in symbolism: past glory, present abjection. As we progressed along the road, the community that flanked it woke up and surged out into the day. They were the poorest, grubbiest people I had ever seen and yet, despite their obvious poverty, they were not at all melancholy or apathetic. They burgeoned like a colony of ants in the gargantuan skeleton of the past, sifting rubbish, recycling everything, conjuring a new art from the bones. We discovered that, unlike the retiring inhabitants of the vine-clad town, they were very gregarious folk. A few individuals attached themselves to us and followed us, offering various wares: fortune-telling services; a map to buried relics; a tour of the ghosts of the area and, quite often, cooked meat. All of these delights we prudently declined to accept, which the people took in good part, merely thinking up grander temptations to offer us instead.

Isis' prediction concerning the distance we would have to travel to reach Ykhey was indeed accurate. By late afternoon, we were approaching the city walls; more remained of them than I would have thought possible. Perhaps they had been repaired over the years. Ykhey was a colossal place. It would take us at least another day to cross its ruins. The highway, too, was in better repair near the city. People dressed in tarnished silks rode mules up and down it, throwing coins to the most persistent of the hut dwellers who had followed us this far. It seemed obvious that Ykhey had some kind of structure. It must also be a rich area for lucky finds, because many of the natives carried unbelievable treasures. I saw women wearing great golden crowns that were thick, in a rude, abundant way, with crudely cut gems. I saw children dressed in gaily coloured

253

rags weighed down with heavy chains of gold around their necks, their skinny arms sleeved with glittering bangles. People displayed these filched riches without shame, and seemingly without fear of theft. Perhaps there was so much of this forgotten treasure lying around to be picked up that no one *had* to steal, but it did make me wonder why merchant trains from the East had not come to claim some of this booty for themselves. It could be sold for high profit beyond Khalt.

My amazement caused me to break my silence with Keea. 'Just look at all this stuff!' I exclaimed. 'Why is it still here?'

'This is a soulscape of the past,' he replied. 'Remember that. It is only the ghost of a consensual archetype.'

'Of course!' I said. I was impatient with his ridiculous attempt to utilise my own terminology, and could not be bothered to argue with him. If what Isis had said was correct, this had once been the Holy city of the Host. I stared up at the walls as we approached; they were covered in carvings in a style which again suggested Deltan influence. Now, however, I wondered if perhaps this was the art that had originally inspired the Deltans, rather than vice versa.

The road led right through a massive gateway. There were no longer any gates attached, but it was unlikely these people had a need for them anyway. Would I recognise a member of the Host if I saw one? As we walked under the great arch a crowd of women and boys, dressed in stained and ragged silks, with bangles of gold around their ankles and wrists, came running out from the shadows in a twittering mass. They banged tambourines and whirled around us, offering delights of the flesh and the inevitable telling of fortunes. I felt heady in the swirl of colour: skirts of deep red, emerald green, peacock blue, the glint of yellow metal. Quick hands brushed our faces and a blur of white-toothed smiles flashed around us. I couldn't help laughing aloud, batting these flapping creatures away from me. They were like soulscape harpies in plumage of silk, who might carry us off to a final and exquisite devouring. And then . . .

I noticed a still face in the maelstrom; a white-skinned face that did not smile. Shadow eyes. A veil about the head. I felt suddenly cold. The whirling Corybantic dancers became mere phantoms in the aura of this motionless figure, this *other* woman. Her body was wrapped in a thick, dark cloak; only her face was visible. As if she'd been waiting for me to notice her, she came towards me, this true harpy-woman: her white face expressionless. I felt that she was invisible to the dancers; they swirled around her, reeling away as if she were protected by an invisible force from which solid matter simply bounced off. When she was only a couple of feet away from me, she smiled gently. Never, in all my dreams, in all my childhood fantasies, had I seen her this clearly. She was my guardian-pursuer and still wearing the image of the Sacramantan actress, Gimel

254

Metatronim. I studied her beautiful features . . . No, this was a real person: she was not an image, not a ghost, not a fantasy. She could not actually *be* Gimel Metatronim, because she was too young. It had been nearly twenty years since I'd been in Sacramante with my mother; Gimel must be in her late forties by now, surely? Could this woman be one of the people I was looking for – a member of the Host? After all, I suspected they had the ability to influence thought. Perhaps she had picked the image of my guardian-pursuer out of my mind. She did not speak, but simply stood there before me, smiling sweetly.

'Who *are* you?' I asked.

She shook her head, lowered it, and when she looked up again I realised she did not look like my guardian-pursuer at all. I had been mistaken. The figure was male. It had a male face that I did not recognise, but it was exquisitely handsome. Long, dark hair coiled out from beneath the hood of his cloak. His lips, perfectly sculpted, were as pale as his cheeks. His eyes were silvery-grey and shone with their own light. I reached out to touch him, fearing he would vanish at any moment. He caught hold of my hands before I could grab his cloak. He shook his head and pressed something into my palm, closing my fingers over it. His hands were icy cold. Then he turned and strode into the city. The gaudy dancers spilled into the void he had left behind, obscuring my sight. I jumped up a little to look over their heads, but could not find the man.

It had all happened in an instant. Had I imagined it? No. There was tangible evidence.

I opened my hand which had clenched convulsively around whatever had been placed there. I examined the gift and found it was a perfect, newly minted Sacramantan coin, bearing the noble profile of the Kaliph Izobella. I looked around for Keea, supposing he had witnessed what had happened, but there was no sign of him. He had vanished too.

I was momentarily stunned, and couldn't decide what to do. An odd feeling was creeping round me; nothing seemed entirely real. At that moment, I did not want to be alone among Strangeling natives. Where had Keea gone? Had he left me for good? I wondered whether one of the dancers had taken him away, and attempted to question them. They giggled at my inquiries, shaking their heads, grabbing hold of my hands and whirling me round in their midst. My voice simply blew away from me. 'Dance,' they said, 'dance with us!' Their lilting laughter sounded like crazy birds and rippling water; rising and falling. My head had begun to throb with a dull pain, and my vision seemed somehow faded. Colours blended like wet paint before my eyes. I was dizzy, thrown from person to person in the crowd; hands caught me and pushed me away. I struggled to pass through them. 'Dance! Dance!'

After what seemed an hour of disorientating scrabbling, I managed to claw my way through the leaping bodies and stumbled into the city beyond them. The dancers swarmed off down the highway, spinning, leaping, calling out. I shook my head and adjusted my carryback, swaying on my feet for a few moments to get my bearings. My head felt as if it had been severely kicked; I realised I'd been influenced in some way, perhaps weakened. *No more of this!* Summoning a shred of resolve and strength, I walked away from the gateway. The streets beyond were full of milling people, all calling out to each other. There was music everywhere. No one seemed to be doing anything but drinking and dancing. I thought I saw a donkey walking on its hind legs, wearing a crown of roses, but then, blinking, realised it was only a man wearing a donkey mask. A beautiful woman in a yellow dress paused in front of me, and her face aged to withered ruin in seconds. Then, she smiled and was a girl again. She threw a handful of petals over my hat. I would have to find somewhere to rest, because my mind was clearly suffering from delusions. I was sure the man at the city gates had been a member of the Host, and that he'd deliberately affected my consciousness. Why? Was I getting too close to the truth? But how had he known who I was? Had Isis Urania sent word ahead, or was Keea responsible? He *had* vanished. Was I being warned away from my investigations? Questions tumbled through my whirling head. I felt thirsty and sore, sweating heavily beneath my carryback.

A child of indeterminate sex skipped up to me, holding out a metal goblet. 'Drink, lady, drink,' it said.

'What is it?'

'The vine gift.'

'How much does it cost?'

The child looked blank. 'Drink,' it said, again. 'it is the vine gift.'

I took the cup and peered into it. A dark, pungent liquid filled it to the brim. its surface foaming as if it had only recently been poured. It smelled like wine. Without consideration of personal health, I found I had raised the cup to my lips and was drinking from it greedily. This must be a dream! I would never normally do such a rash thing! And yet some inner part of me was convinced it wasn't poisoned. Almost immediately, a warm, alcoholic glow began to steal around my body. I entered a floating, relaxed state, and the ache in my head subsided abruptly. Still, I was in no condition to be walking around. I gave the cup back to the child with a murmur of thanks, and said, 'Can you find me a place to rest a while?'

The child nodded gravely and took my hand, tossing the empty goblet on to the ground. I allowed myself to be led further into the city. All around us, the ruins were seething with people, all of whom seemed to be celebrating madly. It was as if they'd all been told they only had a day to live, a single day in which to enjoy all the things they had forbidden themselves.

The child took me into the garden of a half-fallen villa. The ground was littered with an abundance of rags: musty taffeta, mildewed satin and worn, soft linen. It seemed someone had pitched it all out of one of the upper storeys. Brazen leaves swirled in the air around my head. I knew that if I didn't lie down soon, I would fall down. The child indicated a place where the rags were densely heaped, against the villa wall. 'Lie there,' it said.

I sank gratefully to my knees and unbuckled my carryback. 'Will you watch over me and my belongings while I sleep?' I asked the child. 'I will give you a coin . . .'

'You are perfectly safe,' said the child, and skipped away.

I lay back among the rank tatters and sighed deeply. This was the true madness of the Strangeling. I realised there was no risk of attack; none at all. Danger here was a radically different concept from any with which I was familiar. It would be very easy to give oneself up to the unreality of this place. I could imagine that should a weak-willed traveller end up in Ykhey, they would quickly become so disorientated they might forget where they were going and from where they had come. They might just become part of the madness; singing and dancing until they died. The air held a taint of chill; I pulled the damp rags firmly round my body and curled myself around my carryback.

Nobody bothered me. For a while I slept, my dreams coloured by the hectic voices beyond the garden and the crazy songs of the gift of the vine.

When I awoke everything was silent. Night had fallen. I clambered to my feet and was relieved to find I felt quite refreshed and clearheaded. However, my stomach was demanding food and I needed water. It was unfortunate that Keea and I had packed all our provisions into his carryback that morning. I had two options: search for my erstwhile companion, which seemed pointless given the size of the place, or look for sustenance elsewhere. The latter choice was clearly the only practical one.

As I bent to pick up my own carryback, I realised I still had the Bochanegran coin clutched firmly in my fist. For a few moments, I opened my palm and stared at it. What was its significance? Did it suggest I would find answers in Sacramante, or was it a payment to stop me poking my nose in further? Who *was* the person who had given it to me? Would I see them again? I flung the coin up in the air, caught it, and stowed it in the leather pocket on my belt.

Out on the street, everybody seemed to have disappeared; perhaps they were all unconscious somewhere, hidden away in vaults beneath the city streets. Now why should I think that? I stepped out into clear moonlight; a brilliant light that cast impenetrable, sharply cut shadows across the wide, littered street. Now, this really was a city of the dead. I wondered whether I should find it eerie, although I felt utterly at ease. Which way should I go? There was only one thing to do: enter the spirit of the place. I closed my eyes and spun around for a few moments. When I came to a standstill, I headed in the direction I was facing.

My guardian-pursuer came to me then, as I walked alone in the black and white city of ruins. She was at my side, sensed before I could actually see her. 'Are you what you seem?' I asked, strangely calm. 'Or are you a threat to me?'

'Ah, Rayo,' she said in a lovely voice, but that was all.

'You are more real to me than you should be,' I said. 'Other soulscapers don't have these experiences.'

'This may be because you are different from them,' she replied.

I smiled. 'You are a product of my mind, my ego. I know I would *like* to be different, but who wouldn't?'

'For a person who walks in people's dreams, who has conversed with gods and ghosts, you are an insufferable sceptic, Rayojini!' she said, with a laugh. 'Will you ever accept me for what I am?'

I looked at her. 'Was it you who attacked me on the road in Khalt?'

'Attacked you? No! Why should I do such a thing?' Her response was without artifice, human in its spontaneity.

'You *are* real!' I said. 'Who are you?'

She smiled. I narrowed my eyes at her.

Gimel? Was it possible . . . ? No, it wasn't. I was being a fool. This was a member of the Host. Did she think I was so easily fooled? Still, she did not appear to be threatening or malevolent. Again, I would simply observe.

I did not speak again and neither did she, but we walked together in easy silence, as friends might, along the road.

Presently, we came to a place that had once been a church or a temple, half-gone now, but beautiful in its decay. My companion placed a gentle, icy hand beneath my elbow – it felt indisputably real – and guided me inside the building through what was hardly more than a crack in the stone. I emerged into a courtyard, once colonnaded but now surrounded only by rubble. The centre of the court was dominated by a pool in the shape of a trefoil. It was still full of water, its surface thick with overgrown lilies. In the centre of this pool were the remains of a fountain: a great stone shell which at one time had probably contained a statue. Now, it contained only a tableau of living sculpture.

I knew him instantly. Dressed in black, he reclined in the shell like a huge cat; his burnished hair a pale glory in the lady-light of the moon. The man was, or at least strongly resembled, my dream-phantom Beth Metatronim. He was holding Keea in his arms. I turned to speak to the woman, ask questions, but she had not followed me through the space in the wall. Impulsively drawn forward by an uncontrollable tide in my belly, I approached the pool. The image of Beth looked at me, smiled, and then directed his attention to the body he held in his arms. Keea's head was lolling backwards over his arm, his eyes open and staring. His arms trailed into the choked water. He looked irretrievably dead. Was this another warning? Leave us be or we will kill you as we have him? Was it beyond them to do this? I thought not.

I stood rooted to the spot, as if tendrils of bone had poked down through the soles of my feet and delved deep into the friable stone beneath. Time seemed to accelerate around me, and the moon sailed swiftly across the sky above. Yet I myself was caught in non-time. As I stared, bound in this stasis of eternity, the man in black smiled at me and ran a caressing hand down Keea's pale chest, then leaned forward to bite him, high on the breast. They are cannibals in the ruins, I thought, quite coherently. A dark, moving line seeped from beneath the man's lips. He was kneading the flesh with his mouth, sucking, nibbling. I could not look away. I did not want to. At the core of my horror was fascination, and something else more primal. The man in black sucked my friend as if Keea were a ripe fruit. And I watched, salivating, as if the juice were filling my mouth, not his.

It was a dream; of course it was. An illusion, a delusion. I had been dazed by the vision of my guardian-pursuer at the city gates, and later drugged by the child. I inhabit my own reality – no one else's. Each of these excuses was a plaintive, feeble cry in my head.

One moment, I was watching the pool turn red; the next, time had ceased to gallop around me. I was alone, as perhaps I'd always been. There was no churchyard, no pond, no lilies, nothing. I was standing in a wide street lined by high walls, completely alone.

There was nothing else to do but skulk into a nest of shadows, curl up, wind around myself like a chastened bitch with her nose buried in her tail and, with eyes glinting fearfully into the dark, wait for the morning.

Keea found me lying in the rubble not long after dawn. I stared at him in confusion as he shook me awake, and yet I realised I had not really thought him dead. 'Rayo, Rayojini! Come back to the land of the living!' he said, smiling at me. 'Drunk! How shameful!'

'Where have you been?' I demanded, brushing away his hands and sitting up. Miraculously, I was still in possession of my carry-back and hat.

'Exploring,' he said.

'Alone?'

He smiled his closed smile. 'Are you hungry?'

I shook my head, although my stomach was still shrieking to be fed. The question had seemed loaded with obscure meaning, but perhaps I was imagining that. Keea ignored my response and began

259

to unwrap a package he had with him. 'Where did you get that?' I snapped. It was fresh bread, glossy fruit, cured peppered meat. It had not come from this place I was sure. It looked too wholesome.

'Someone has to look after you and, to this end, I am resourceful,' he replied and then pulled a face. 'You must get to Sacramante quickly. You need pampering, Rayojini.'

In that instant he made me conscious of my appearance. I felt gaunt and old and hideous; all this without a mirror before me, other than his eyes. 'Too late for that,' I said bitterly.

He laughed. 'Bathe in self-pity if you must, soulscaper. But I want you healthy and preened.'

'Why?' I snatched at the food he had laid out neatly on a flat rock.

He shrugged and smiled innocently. 'Why? It requires great fortitude to plough through the Sacramantan archives!'

'I believe you!' I didn't. 'Have you anything to drink?'

'Fresh,' he said, offering me a water-skin.

I drank long and deep and then, wiping my mouth, said carelessly, 'I saw you last night, Keea. In the pool. I saw.' I didn't anticipate what response I'd get, but watched him carefully, just in case.

'Pool? What pool? You must have been dreaming,' he replied smoothly.

I dug in my pocket and showed him the coin. 'You must have seen that *person* at the gate, Keea. I am convinced it was a member of the Host. He gave me this.'

Keea grinned. 'Don't be absurd! Anyone you saw at the gates was simply one of the crazy natives! This place is full of old coins!'

'This is a new Sacramantan coin, Keea.'

He shrugged. 'Well, it could have been taken from any passing traveller.'

'That is possible, of course,' I said, 'but the strangest thing is that you vanished after I'd been given the coin. Did you go with that man, Keea?'

I was hoping for nervousness on his part, a quick downward glance from the eyes, a shaky laugh. He merely smiled at me and shook his head slowly. 'No, Rayo, I didn't. I didn't go with anyone. Perhaps I shouldn't have left you like that. It wasn't intentional. I thought you were following me. All those prancing lunatics got in the way and when I looked back, you were gone.'

'Where did you go?' I persisted, refusing to mirror his smile.

He shrugged. 'I went off to explore, I told you. These people are crazy but harmless enough. I thought you'd be safe on your own for a while. You're always telling me how well you can look after yourself! The last thing I expected was that you'd end up taking swigs of noxious substances and start having hallucinations!'

'I didn't hallucinate!'

He folded his arms. 'So what was it you saw?'

I described the man at the city gates in more detail and then – rather reluctantly – told him all that had happened after I'd woken up in the middle of the night. 'Keea, I saw someone drink your blood!'

'The same person who gave you the coin?'

I squeezed my eyes shut and shook my head. 'No! No! I told you, it was someone else.' I did not mention the Metatronim.

Keea sighed and sat down beside me. He took hold of my hand. 'Look Rayo,' he said. 'Feel.' Before I could pull away he guided my hand inside his shirt to his chest. 'Any wound there?' he asked. I felt around, weirdly embarrassed. His skin was beautifully warm and smooth.

'No,' I said and pulled my hand away.

'Well, there you are!' He raised his arms and smiled. 'A dream, Rayo, a muddleheaded vision.' He shook his head. 'This place is getting to you!'

He made it sound so plausible. I didn't want to believe him, and yet there was no reason not to. He was right; I *had* drunk the child's wine. The walk with my guardian-pursuer, and my consequent encounter with the image of Beth Metatronim, had seemed weirdly unreal. But the man at the gate couldn't possibly have been an hallucination – I hadn't been drunk or drugged when I'd seen him. 'I can only agree with you up to a point, Keea,' I said. 'My mind was addled before I drank wine. Someone is playing with me. Remember the temple painting in the Sink. The feeding. Last night, I saw you – or an image of you – give yourself to a member of the Host. *They drank your blood!* That has to be significant.'

He laughed, but not as harshly as usual. 'You *thought* you saw that! Legends, Rayo. You dream legends!'

His laughter angered me so much, I turned on him and threw him back against the rubble. He cried out and I was gratified by the seed of fear in his eyes.

'Just another quick look,' I said, and pulled his shirt down over his shoulders. He tried to beat at me with his hands, push me away, but I was stronger than he was. The skin of his chest was rippled with goose-flesh pimples, his nipples hard and erect, dark against his skin, but there was no sign of injury. The sight entranced me: I could see his ribs straining against his smooth pelt. Such beauty. An image of Beth feeding from Keea flashed across my mind, intensely vivid and detailed. My mouth filled up with sweet fluid and I was overtaken by a wild desire to mimic Metatronim's actions. A terrible, irresistible compulsion made me lean down and bite Keea hard. He uttered a low, deep moan and arched against me. I had a whole mouthful of his flesh between my teeth, including his nipple I think. It must have hurt him horribly. I don't know why I did it. After a few moments, I let him go and sat up. He lay

261

there, staring up at me, his hair spread out around his head. I looked at his chest. The teeth-marks were livid, but I knew I had not broken the skin. Neither had I sucked the flesh at all. Why then was the skin within the indentations bruised and seeping blood?

'You can still lie to me if you wish,' I said, staring him straight in the eye, 'but never consider me a fool!'

Keea's eyes flickered away from mine; such a brief hesitation, but I'd been waiting for it. 'I know what I saw, Keea,' I said firmly. 'And if it *was* an hallucination, then it was designed specifically for me and deliberately put into my mind.'

Keea swallowed, and pulled his shirt back over his shoulders. Slowly he sat up, rubbing his chest through the cloth.

'You *are* part of all this, aren't you?' I said. 'So why the games?'

Keea opened and shut his mouth once, shook his head. I realised, with satisfaction, that I had both frightened him and destroyed his composure.

'The Host have contacted me,' I said. 'Now, I have only to interpret the message.' I leaned over and grabbed Keea's arm. He made a sound of distress and flinched, his hair falling over his face. I dug my fingers cruelly into his flesh. 'Why don't you tell me what the message means, Keea?' I shook him roughly. 'Tell me now or, by Helat, I'll beat it out of you!'

'I am not involved in the way you think!' he answered frantically and tried to pull away from me.

I lessened my grip on his arm. 'Well, in that case, perhaps you can explain just how you *are* involved.'

'You're hurting me!' he said.

I laughed. 'Boy, believe me, you don't know the meaning of the word pain. Soulscapers are healers and we can do wonderful healing things to all parts of the human body. Strangely enough, some of the techniques employed can be used most effectively to produce quite a different result! Now, why not be just a little co-operative, hmmm?'

'I can't believe you're treating me like this,' he said, gazing up at me winsomely through a veil of hair. I reached out and brushed it back, cupping his chin in my hand. His cheeks were wet with tears and I felt a moment's remorse.

'I'm sorry, Keea, but you can hardly blame me. You have deliberately misled me. For all I know, that might have put me in a very dangerous position.' He closed his eyes and nodded. 'I understand,' he said, and then looked at me imploringly. 'We will soon be in Sacramante. Then, I might be in a position to confide in you more readily.'

'Why there? Why not here?' I demanded. 'What's the difference?'

'You've seen what can happen here,' he said. 'There are some

262

things it would be dangerous for you to carry in your head at this time. Believe me, in my reticence I am thinking only of your welfare!'

'I can look after myself! How dare you patronise me!'

'I'm not!' he cried, putting his fingers over his eyes, pressing hard into the sockets. 'Look, it really *was* an illusion what you saw last night, but let's just say I might have experienced the same one.'

'Then you should have told me that straightaway!' Who was responsible?'

'The Host,' he said, miserably, 'the Host.'

'What?' I actually had to laugh. 'And you were the one mocking me for believing in them!'

'I had my reasons,' he said stiffly, apparently having recouped some of his dignity. 'Please Rayo, don't interrogate me now. I promise I'll be able to tell you everything soon.'

He stood up and rubbed his arms, looking around him. As yet, there was no sign of any natives, illusory or otherwise. 'I think you should eat your food,' he said. 'Let's get moving as soon as possible. This place unnerves me.'

'Why?' I asked, popping some bread into my mouth. I wanted to hear his reason, perhaps hoping he'd speak the truth.

For a second, he glanced at me. Such a naked glance, it was a direct line of communication between us. I saw great pain within it. He touched his throat, the upper part of his chest near the heart. 'It makes me ache,' he said.

'Easier than air with air, if spirits embrace, total
they mix, union of pure with pure desiring; not
restrained conveyance need as flesh to mix with
flesh, or soul to soul.'
Paradise Lost, Book VIII

Sammael's motley collection of Strangeling vagabonds knew he was
leaving them; they were waiting outside his room when we emerged.
There were perhaps a dozen of them: old and young, male and
female. A hag; a boy; a young man wearing a red scarf; a group
of girls clutching each other; a pair of mature men with lined faces;
a few ancients toothlessly chewing in apprehension. Sammael held
out his hands to them wordlessly. I realised he loved them very
much, his little nation. One of the girls began to cry, and the others
took up a soft crooning. They were not quite like any other humans
I had met; perhaps being touched with his difference, contaminated
by the strangeness of his eternal solitude. Lilian was not as cowed
by the occasion as her peers. She bustled through the small gathering and pointed at me. 'You cannot go with her!'

'Don't misinterpret events, my dear,' Sammael said to her,
gently. '*She* is coming with me.' He drew them all to him, somehow
managing to encompass everyone within his embrace. 'I am not
leaving you,' he said. 'But I have to go outside. My love and my
thoughts will always be with you. Without you, I would simply have
faded into a dusty memory; for this, I cannot express my gratitude
enough. But times change. I have held on to stagnation for too
long. Do not resent this eloim lady. Although she has precipitated
the change, it is an essential thing.' He backed away. 'This tower
is yours, for as long as you wish to remain here.'

Tears had gathered in my eyes. I wondered then if I were doing
the right thing in forcing him back to harsh reality. I had a feeling
he would never return here and that I, in my impetuosity, would
be responsible.

When we came out of the Tower of Bale into the gusty morning,
Sandalphon didn't know whether to prostrate himself or flee back
to the atelier courts ahead of us. He was, as he had promised, still
sitting on the tower steps. He must have been virtually frozen into
position, for the wind had a cruel, sharp edge. I will remember for
ever the expression on his face when he saw whom I had with me.

265

I had emerged from the doorway first, while Sammael hung back, perhaps a little nervous of the open space beyond. His people had followed us down the stairs, and I could see their wild faces looking out, behind him. Sandalphon must have turned immediately he heard the door open. His first expression was one of relief, then he looked beyond me and his face froze, still harbouring an essence of relief, but comical because it was mixed with utter incredulity.

'Ghosts, beloved,' Sammael said, stepping out into the daylight. 'Yes, your eyes do not deceive you. It has been a long time.' He bent to touch Sandalphon's face, as if he too wondered whether he were seeing a ghost.

Sandalphon scrambled to his feet. 'I expected many results from Gimel's action,' he said, 'but this was not one of them.' He looked at me as if to ask me if I were aware what I had done, but simply said, 'How did you persuade him?'

'I really don't know,' I answered. 'I really don't.'

'Well, how do I look?' Sammael said. 'Doesn't polite society demand you ask me how I feel? Then, you should say I look marvellous . . .'

Sandalphon looked at me, confused. I shrugged.

'I remember when he was born,' Sammael said to me, taking a lock of Sandalphon's hair in his fingers. 'Not first generation, of course, but not long afterwards.' He might have been speaking of a favourite pet.

'You are out in the real world now,' I reminded him, gently pulling his fingers away from Sandalphon's hair. 'Come back to my house with me.'

I tucked a hand beneath one of his elbows. He was shivering badly. I nodded sharply at Sandalphon, who took Sammael's other arm. Sammael frowned to himself. 'A moment, a moment,' he said, swaying.

'It is not that far,' I said. 'You will feel better indoors.'

Sammael nodded, gripped our hands for comfort and, leaving the tower door open behind us, Sammael's people watching us go, we set off down the hill.

Sandalphon did not speak as we traipsed Sammael through the atelier streets. And as I had thought, open space discomfited our Lord of Light greatly. He was like an invalid on our arms, weak and trembling, his feet unsure. His expression was one of bewilderment. How long had it been since he had walked these streets? I kept up a soothing narration, telling him the names of the buildings we passed, and to which throngs they belonged. Sandalphon simply blinked into the wind, as if he didn't want to think about our companion's identity. However, by the time we reached my house, Sandalphon had recovered his voice. He stood in the tiled hall and mentioned the word, 'Parzupheim'.

I realised I must have come to share Avirzah'e's view of these venerable beings, because an arrow of irritation went right through me.

'No, Sandalphon! This is *our* business!'

'Don't shout, Lady Gimel,' Sammael said. He had sat down in a huge, uncomfortable ornamental throne, carved from black wood. The only things that sat in it normally were the coats and cloaks Beth and I discarded, before Tamaris or Ramiz came to tidy them away. 'A long time ago, I myself invested the Parzupheim with temporal power. Soon, I shall speak to them, but . . .' He smiled at Sandalphon. 'At least give me a short time to orientate myself.'

'What are you going to do?' Sandalphon asked weakly.

'Listen to Gimel Metatronim,' Sammael replied. 'And nose around her lovely house. I *do* like these drapes, Lady Gimel.' He stood up slowly, as if it caused him pain, and limped to the door curtains, fingered them. Then he turned his attention to the table by the door and looked through the pile of unopened mail lying there. I glanced at Sandalphon and shrugged. Sammael was like an exotic and unpredictable wild animal. Now I had got him home, I wasn't sure what to do with him. He seemed somehow too big for the house to contain him comfortably.

'Will you show me around?' he asked.

I nodded. 'Certainly. Come upstairs with me to my salon.' He held out his arm, of which I took hold. Sandalphon reluctantly came to support his other side. 'Would you like to refresh yourself?' I asked. His face looked horribly blue around the eyes and lips. I thought that sustenance would be in order as soon as possible.

'I would like some wine,' Sammael said.

'Wine it is then.'

We mounted the stairs and I called out for Tamaris.

Sandalphon seemed unsure whether he should leave Sammael alone with me, or remain as a chaperon. He hovered uncomfortably in the salon as Sammael prowled the edge of the room examining a couple of Beth's paintings which hung on the wall. Tamaris had informed me that Beth had not yet returned home. I was not surprised, although I wished he were there. I wanted to flaunt this victory in his face.

'My brother did those,' I said. 'That one is a self-portrait.' Tamaris was standing in the doorway, looking at Sammael suspiciously. 'The day is chill,' I said to her. 'Will you mull the wine for us?'

She nodded and backed from the room, closing the doors in front of her.

'You like my brother's paintings?' I asked.

Sammael sat down on one of the sofas. 'He has an eye for beauty.'

'Indeed.'

'I hope I will meet him.'

267

'I expect you will sometime . . .'

It was not easy to converse. We maintained stilted exchanges until Tamaris returned with the wine. Sammael sniffed appreciatively at the spicy aroma steaming from the clay goblets.

'So much to stimulate the senses,' he said. I realised that, as well as feeling dizzy and disorientated, he was also very unsure of himself. Although he had felt secure enough in his tower to communicate with me there, he had really forgotten the art of conversation and his cool, urbane manner was nothing but reflexive self-defence.

'I cannot believe you are here,' Sandalphon said, lamely.

'Neither can I,' Sammael said. 'It is a dream-like circumstance all round. I feel old and ill.'

'I think you should sup,' I said.

He grimaced. 'Do I have to?'

Tamaris had stationed herself on a stool near the door. She did not know who Sammael was, but was intuitive enough to realise he was someone very important and had remained in the room to observe proceedings, hoping I wouldn't send her out. 'Tamaris, would you mind providing Lord Sammael with a cup of ichor. He is not feeling too well, and I am sure your invigorating essence will restore him!'

She nodded and rose from her seat. Sammael offered her his empty goblet, and she bit her wrist, turning her back to us as she filled the cup with blood. Sammael took the cup from her and swallowed its contents in one draught. He pulled a disagreeable face, as if he'd taken a swig of noxious medicine. Tamaris looked surprised and rather offended.

'Rinse the cup and give Lord Sammael another measure of wine,' I said. She left the room.

'You have upset her,' I said. 'She is a dear and loyal dependant of mine, and I object to her being insulted. Please thank her when she returns.'

'My manners are not all they were,' Sammael admitted.

For a while we conversed carefully, around sensitive subjects. As I had predicted, refreshment invigorated Sammael; the colour of his skin improved greatly, and he appeared to become more confident. He asked questions about our art and confessed that of all the things he had denied himself, he had missed visiting the theatre most. We did not talk about what he was doing in my house, or why he had decided to come. I suspected his decision to leave the tower had been made as impulsively, if not more so, as mine had been to visit him; perhaps he was wondering now whether he had done the right thing. I tried to imagine how I would feel, in his position. There was so much I didn't know about him; our history, the past, had been diluted intentionally. The facts were locked up somewhere; it was felt we no longer needed them, that their stark-

268

ness might harm the delicate balance of our relationship with this world.

'Tell me again about this soulscaper,' Sammael said, at last. I had been waiting for him to broach the subject himself.

'She is in the care of a dependant of ours.' I replied. 'He is bringing her to Sacramante. I must admit I have not observed her recently, but she is in good hands.'

'You must decide quickly what you are going to do with her, then,' Sammael said.

I told him, in detail, my plan to send Rayojini into the soulscape of the eloim, and root out any abnormalities.

'Before you embark upon this,' Sammael said, 'both you and Rayojini must be clear about that which is essential, and that which is abnormal. It could be a dangerous endeavour, very dangerous. A miscalculation, and you could cause more damage than healing.'

'I am aware of that.'

'But there is much you are unaware of, Gimel. I don't mean to criticise your bold strategies, but . . .' He paused. 'I do wonder whether this sickness of eloimkind is not the result of very old dilemmas; a bleak harvest, which I regretfully anticipated a long time ago.' He sighed. 'However, letting the soulscaper look around shouldn't hurt. You must let me supervise.'

It was more than I could have wished for. Still, I couldn't help wondering how Metatron was going to react to this new component in our design.

'It would be ideal if you could at least brief Rayojini in some way,' I said.

'How much are you going to tell her?' he asked.

I had not really considered that. 'She will have to be told enough for her to be able to accomplish her task, of course.'

'What if she doesn't want to help you?'

'She will! I have been with her in spirit for years!'

Sammael shook his head. 'Gimel, I find myself querying how much you know of the human mind.'

'I am very fond of Rayojini.'

'And you are trusting your fondness will be enough to sway her decisions?' He smiled. 'Perhaps it will.' He turned his attention to Sandalphon. 'I think you should go to your Parzupheim soon,' he said. 'Tell them I will speak with them shortly.'

It was a cue which Sandalphon was tactful enough to recognise. He stood up. 'Should I return later?'

Sammael nodded. 'I suppose you had better relay any messages they might want to give me.' He grinned at me. 'This will throw them into a fluster. If I felt stronger, I'd go to the Castile myself. It is a shame I cannot watch their expressions as this news is delivered!'

Sandalphon smiled tentatively. 'I shall memorise every face and,

269

when I return, tell you in detail of their condition.'

'I find it hard to see you as you really are,' I said, once Sandalphon had gone.

'That is because you cannot see me as I really am,' Sammael replied.

'No, you misunderstand me. I meant that I know who you are and yet, sitting here in my little salon, you are just another eloim.'

'I am devastated. Have the years been that unkind to me?'

'Not at all . . . Why did you come here with me?'

He looked around the room. 'It was time. No, that sounds terribly prophetic and gloomy! I don't know why I came. Suddenly, I just wanted to.' He stood up and went to look at my shelves of books.

'Oh, your father still writes!' he said, picking up one of Metatron's works and skimming through the pages. 'Weighty stuff! And I expect it is rather pompous.'

'No, my father has a light hand.' I joined him by the books. He pushed the volume he'd been looking at into my hands, and picked another.

'Was my father with you . . . in the beginning?' I asked. It seemed a ridiculous question. I wondered how much Sammael knew about us. Would he be amused by the fact that I was ignorant of my father's origin, or even how old he was?

'Metatron, *this* Metatron, is a babe compared to me,' he replied. 'He was not with me "in the beginning", no. I should imagine that most of my old companions are gone now.'

'What do you mean, *gone*?' Something in his voice alarmed me.

He glanced at me speculatively. 'Where do you think?'

'I don't know. Elderly eloim retire to their rooms in the strongholds. As they age, they become more ascetic . . . eventually, of course, they must . . .' I found I couldn't say the words. Death was not a concept I ever considered in detail. If it was an eventuality for me, it was so far distant as to be irrelevant. Sammael was looking at me in a way I could not fully interpret, but it was very guarded.

'Gimel . . .' he began, and then shook his head. 'No, I cannot believe that!'

'Believe what?'

He placed the book back on the shelf and straightened the spines of all the other volumes. 'You are not immortal, you know. Have you never thought about that? Have you never wondered what happens to the most ancient of eloim?'

'No . . . yes . . . Well, they must just fade . . . As I said, they have special quarters in their family strongholds. The Parzupheim are very old.'

'Children!' Sammael declared. 'Poor Gimel, poor, poor Gimel. Don't you realise, lovely lady, that your flesh is mortal? And yet, the spirit which drives that flesh is not. You cannot die, but neither can you live for ever. Which leaves only one alternative; you transform . . . but into what?' He sighed and ran one long finger along the spines of the books. 'We are trapped in this world, Gimel. From this perspective, this moment of Now, we are trapped here for ever. We cannot die, and yet, we do.'

I did not fully understand him, neither did I really want to. The introduction of this subject had frightened me. 'You have not died!' I said. 'And you have been here since the beginning.'

'I am not like the rest of you,' he replied.

'Then what . . . ?'

He touched my face gently. 'Not now,' he said. I felt he understood completely how much the subject of death perturbed me. 'These moments, here in this house, your lovely house, should not be sullied by thoughts of death; they are a time for life.' I closed my eyes to concentrate upon the spidery path his fingers traced across my skin. 'I am reborn,' he said. 'Let me experience things anew.'

With that, he enfolded me in his arms.

He had told me that he had never touched his human companions in love. He had been alone, in that respect, for centuries. If I expected fire from him, I was disappointed. He made love to me in the manner of someone who had not practised an old skill for so long that they needed proof that they were still adept. It was almost a scholarly act of love. And yet I had a feeling that this, like the sup, was not something in which Sammael took great pleasure. He liked to be held, he liked to be stroked, but the release was incidental. As I kissed him, I was thinking of the great age of those lips, and whom they might have kissed in the past. These lips had spoken words into the primal chaos of the world; they had sculpted sound into matter, darkness into light. I tried to imagine him as a young spirit, but could not. He stood away from me and stripped off his clothes. He put my hand over the scar above his heart. 'See, it is healed.' I touched it with my mouth, and my lips tingled with cold fire. In this place had Mikha'il pressed his teeth, in this place . . . I was living the past, touching legends through time. I could see his heart beating: that tireless, ageless heart. I considered inviting him to my most private room, but Sammael gave no cue for words. He lay down upon my fleecy rugs, just staring up at me, his hair a scarlet flag across the floor. I undressed for him slowly, a true performance, and unbound my hair above him so that it cascaded down on to his flesh. He pressed it against his face, inhaling deeply. He wanted to hold me fiercely, our skins aligned, but it was I who initiated the actual coupling. He submitted passively, with a willing hardness, but it was I who had the passion, the need, the urgency.

Afterwards, lying quietly on the rugs, Sammael laid his head on

271

my breast and I wrapped my arms around him. In some way, I felt I'd failed him.

'It must be strange,' I said carefully, 'to hold another, to love another, after so long an abstinence . . .'

He sighed. 'Like supping, it was not something I had a great appetite for,' he said. 'For me, the coupling of flesh is not enough. It is but a parody.'

I felt as if he'd slapped me. I'd tried to please him, to give him pleasure and closeness, to give him love. 'You are hard to satisfy,' I said, unable to keep a certain tartness from my voice.

He laid his hand over one of my breasts. 'No, don't be angry. I am not criticising you. It is just that, as I said before, I am not quite like you. It is not your fault.'

'Perhaps I should have left the house!' I continued, still hurt. 'Perhaps you should have had Sandalphon in my place!'

He laughed. 'I love to hear such human words coming from your lips, dear Gimel! No, that is not what I meant, and you know it.'

'What did you mean then?'

'This.'

Where he lay against my body the flesh became hot. Then, a numbness. All the organs in my belly contracted and rippled. I jerked. 'Stop!' I cried. Sammael's hand, still cupping my breast, squeezed me gently.

'Do you know what I am doing?' he asked me.

I nodded. 'I think so, yes. It feels . . . please, stop.'

'Oh Gimel,' he said. 'Don't be so faint-hearted. Let me make love to you now, in the only way I truly understand. Experience the ghost of your heritage.'

I could feel him sinking into me, and yet knew he was holding himself back. He would not let go until I gave my assent. Where our flesh had already melded, he set up a gentle rhythm; particles grazed particles, and where they met, light exploded outwards into time. My skin, where he touched me along the flank, tingled in the same way as loins tingle in the heat of sexual arousal.

'May we?' Sammael asked. 'I will protect you.'

A memory of Avirzah'e flashed through my mind. I remembered the timeless moments in the Castile when he, Beth and I had momentarily and superficially fused. Since then, had Beth and Avirzah'e taken that fusion to its limit? How could I know? I should have been with them, yes, part of them. But now I was here, in my salon, with the Lord of Light. 'Yes,' I said. 'We may.'

There was no caution for my virgin flesh. He overwhelmed me instantly; a hunger too long contained. My own body, as if remembering some primal instinct, realigned itself at his direction. We were one creature; a sphere of light, a universe of popping sparks, colliding. Each collision engendered its own minute orgasm. The force of his love, the great eternal reality of love, swamped me to oblivion. We rose up, a spinning cluster of stars. We spiralled; a mist of mingling light. No flesh, no substance to speak of, but indescribable sensations that belonged, or existed, beyond the familiar world of space and time. For an instant, conjoined, we travelled home, truly home. I imagined there were a thousand, thousand spirits spinning around us, melding, passing through each other, exchanging essence.

In those infinite moments, at one with the Prince of Light, I understood him completely. For someone who had experienced this, the conjunction of flesh alone could never be enough.

To be fair to Sammael, what he showed me was not entirely for selfish motives. He explained that for me to fully understand my position and the importance of decisions I might have to make, it was essential to be aware of exactly what I was.

'Now you have experienced the conjunction, you are more suited to your responsibilities,' he said. 'Now you have a fuller knowledge on which to base your decision concerning which direction eloim should take.'

We had dressed ourselves and now sat drinking the remainder of the mulled wine, which had gone cold. I laughed. 'Sammael, that isn't my decision alone. it is one that all eloim should participate in. I am only the daughter of Metatron.'

He reached out, grabbed hold of my arm and pulled me from my chair, drawing me down beside him on the couch. 'And the Metatronims have the energy and motivation to act in this time of crisis, as do certain members of the Tartaruchi! Most eloim seem content to debate the problem until they have all killed themselves! No, Gimel, you are wrong. The decision *is* yours. You have to take responsibility.'

'I can't!'

'Why ever not? I once had to. Someone always has to. You were brave enough to come to my Tower and unleash the presence of the past. You cannot go back.'

I had not considered things in that light. It seemed Sammael had not only juggled the atoms of my being, but also my perception of the world. I knew I felt very different from how I'd felt before we had conjoined, but I could not say in precisely what way. Perhaps I had forgotten something; this new me was unable to process certain information. However, his words made sense to me. Despite tradition, which eloimkind claimed sustained them as much as human blood, I wanted to act independently and boldly. Were these all my own thoughts? I wondered how I would have felt if I had conjoined with Avirzah'e. We might have done something terribly rash. Sammael kissed me tenderly on the brow. 'Tell me, now you have this power, now I have made you a queen of eloim, what will you do?'

'I am not a queen, but I realise that it is I who will have to make the decisions. I think . . . I think now that Avirzah'e *was* right in some respects, but then I suppose I have always thought that.' I screwed up my face to consider, and laced my fingers with Sammael's. 'I think you should show us how to become ourselves and, if it is possible, how to sustain each other. If we can, we should release humanity from the tithe of blood, as you called it.'

'Mmm. You do realise that should eloim revert to mutual sustenance, their forms will also revert. Their substance will become more . . . flexible. They would find it harder to pass for human.'

'Then it is just something else we will have to learn to deal with. We should be able to protect ourselves from intolerant humanity, shouldn't we? There will have to be a time of adjustment, of course, and some people are going to fear us and perhaps be hostile . . . Couldn't you help us?'

Sammael did not answer my question. 'And how will you deal with the eloim who refuse to do as you suggest?'

'Sammael, stop it! Support me! I am trying to look for answers in the dark! This is all conjecture. I know how difficult it will be to initiate change. For both humanity and eloimkind! There will be a thousand problems I haven't thought of yet! I am just sitting here, in your arms, in my salon, thinking aloud of ways to achieve the best possible future. I know how difficult it will be to achieve just a fragment of that potential!'

Sammael squeezed me gently. 'Gimel, I *am* supporting you. Please don't think otherwise. I just wanted to make sure you were aware of how arduous the days ahead will be, whatever decision you make.'

'But will you be with me?'

He paused, and rested his chin on the top of my head. 'I am – for now. But it is impossible for me to conjecture further than the day.'

Ultimately, he expected I would have to be independent.

Soon, I would have to approach Avirzah'e and Beth. Just the thought of that made my heart beat faster. What would I say? I could adopt any attitude: contrition; complicity; desire. Avirzah'e would have to be honest with me about whatever his throng had been involved in, and I would have to try and convince him that adjustments would have to be made. Surely when he heard what I had to say he could only agree with me? Perhaps I should take Sammael with me to speak with them. I was on the point of going to my desk to inscribe a brief note for Ramiz to deliver to Avirzah'e, imagining I would be able to confer with him and Beth that night, when Tamaris knocked sharply on the salon door. She is such a perceptive soul; normally she knocks once and walks right in. 'Yes?' I said. 'Come in.'

274

'Your father!' Tamaris exclaimed, wide-eyed in the doorway.

'Here?' I put down my pen, preparing to steel myself for unpleasantness. Tamaris shook her head.

'No. He has sent word. He requests that you hurry to the family stronghold. He says it is very urgent!'

I had not expected Metatron to conclude his explorations in Khalt with the Harkasites and return to Sacramante so soon, and was worried that he'd somehow found out what I'd done. Had Sandal-phon contacted him by concentrated mind-chime last evening? It was possible, but somehow seemed unlikely. Sammael insisted on accompanying me to the Metatronim stronghold, although I was reluctant to spring him on Metatron unannounced. I had anticipated delivering a careful and protracted speech by way of introduction. How Metatron was going to react to my actions, I could not hazard a guess at. Half of me hoped he would admire my courage, but the other half was well aware how much he disliked his authority being overridden. It could go two ways and I wished I might face it out alone.

Sammael did not share my apprehension. It seemed that since we had conjoined, his interest in eloim welfare had been rekindled. He burned with vitality, and an energy that needed release in activity. Believing Metatron's anger to be a very real possibility, I could do nothing but imagine a hundred frightful humiliating scenes. My pride balked at the thought of Sammael witnessing me being chastised by my father.

I instructed Ramiz to prepare our best carriage, and to place hot bottles beneath the cushions for Sammael's comfort. While that was being attended to, I dressed myself in a formal black gown and painted my face into a mask of composure. My mood swayed between a desire to weep and a cool, steely anger. I would never forgive Metatron if he embarrassed me.

Sammael was familiar with the Metatronim stronghold. As the carriage bowled along the afternoon streets, with their mellow pall of low sunlight, he told me stories about when the atelier courts had been built. 'Look,' he said, pointing towards the House of Sarim. 'The stone is dark now, and not so stark in its lines. I can remember the raw white blocks standing in the sun, waiting to be assembled.'

I touched his shoulder. 'See there, between the poplars, the ocean.'

He smiled. 'The ocean! One day perhaps . . .'

'I will take you to the harbour.'

'Is it safe for eloim to walk the streets in Sacramante now?' I wondered whether he was mocking me.

'The situation has cooled down, I believe . . . for a while, at

275

least. But I wouldn't be surprised if other, similar incidents to the Mervantes crisis don't arise, unless something is done.'

He gripped my hand. 'We shall try,' he said. 'We shall certainly try.'

I did not introduce Sammael to anyone when we entered the House of Metatronim. A male servant let us in, casting suspicious glances at my companion. I was told Metatron was expecting me; I was to be shown into his presence without delay. The servant looked at me inquiringly, which I took to mean he wanted Sammael's name in order to announce him. I peeled off my gloves and said, 'Well we had better make haste, then!' The servant bowed and led the way.

Metatron was in his library – a vast cavern of a room, lined with books he never read. When his servant opened the door, he was standing in the middle of the carpet, as if he had been interrupted in pacing up and down. He looked a little wild, but that might have been the effects of travelling abroad with the Harkasites. I stood in the doorway, partially concealing my companion, although he towered over my head.

'Father,' I said. 'I am gratified to find you well after your journey.'

Metatron opened his mouth to speak to me and then realised I was not alone. For a few moments he stared hard at Sammael, who then edged past me into the room.

'Metatron,' he said carefully. Just for a few brief seconds, I saw an expression of outrage cross my father's face. He recognised Sammael instantly, and I realised his first thought was not one of surprise or alarm, but simply that there might be a challenge to his authority within the throngs. I had never seen Metatron so transparent in his feelings.

'Sammael?' he said.

'In flesh and blood.' Sammael knew what he was thinking.

'I am . . .' Metatron shook his head, and then laughed delightedly. He held out his arms and marched over to embrace Sammael warmly. It was a performance of which I myself would have been very proud.

'You!' he said. 'I should have known!' He looked at me rather dangerously over Sammael's shoulder.

Sammael returned Metatron's embrace patiently. 'Before you ask, your daughter Gimel is responsible for my presence here.'

'Is she?'

I winced, curling up my toes within my boots. 'There was no alternative, Metatron,' I said. 'Many things have occurred since you left Sacramante.'

'Then perhaps I should have returned sooner.'

'You have returned at exactly the right time,' Sammael said. 'I left my Tower only this morning.'

Metatron released Sammael from his arms and stood back to

276

examine him. He sighed, shook his head and then smiled warmly. I was relieved to realise it was a genuine smile. 'Well, this is a shock, but other than that I am very glad to see you, Sammael. Sometimes, I did think about you alone out there. I even considered visiting you myself when all this trouble started. '

Sammael shrugged awkwardly. 'I have shirked my responsibilities perhaps, but you seem to have managed well enough without me.'

'I feel you are being just a little too kind,' Metatron replied smoothly. 'You must be able to see for yourself what a mess we are in. I doubt whether you'd be here otherwise.'

'The situation was inevitable,' Sammael said. 'You can hardly blame yourself – or anyone else.'

Metatron nodded thoughtfully. Then he asked us to sit down and summoned a servant to furnish us with brandy. There was a distinct coolness between me and my father; I suspected the heated recriminations would come later, but at least it didn't seem as if he intended to upbraid me in front of Sammael. I could see now that he was really unable to; any reprimand of my behaviour would be plainly insulting. It would make it too obvious my father didn't want Sammael around again in any circumstances, no matter how dire.

'So what precipitated your return to Sacramante?' I asked. 'Had you learned all that it was possible to learn?'

Metatron grimaced. 'I would not say that, but I have uncovered certain information.' He grinned at me ferally. 'At the time, I felt it was vital to discuss this information with you, Gimel, before I took action on it. I had no idea you were taking such responsibilities upon yourself as braving the Tower of Bale.' His face softened, but it did not convince me that his feelings had. 'I am ashamed that you were forced to adopt these measures alone. I should have been with you.'

'I managed perfectly well,' I said.

'So it would appear,' Metatron said, in a silky voice. 'And how is Beth?'

I dropped my eyes. 'He is well . . .'

'I did warn you.'

I looked up. '*He is well*!'

Metatron shrugged. 'As you please! Now, I will tell you the story of my travels.'

Without further reference to my brother, he began to speak of how the Harkasites had dispersed into Khalt to gather information. Metatron had been disturbed by all the peculiar phenomena they had discovered. 'I thought at first it was some Tartaruchi conspiracy,' he said, 'but later realised it was not. The Tartaruchis have nothing to do with it! But there is undeniably an eloim influence at work.'

'Then who?' I asked. 'Loners, or members of foreign throngs?' I did not think that was very likely. What I had seen of foreign

277

eloim in the past suggested they would be too paranoid to adopt threatening behaviour.

Metatron shook his head. 'No, nothing like that. It took me a while to work out who and even now I am not wholly sure. It is too incredible.' He looked at Sammael in a challenging manner. 'Have you any idea what I'm getting at?'

Sammael narrowed his eyes. 'Where did your search lead you?'

'Across Khalt. There was no doubt the phenomena originated in the West. Ultimately, I concluded they originated in the Strangeling.'

'How did you draw this conclusion?'

'It was obvious, really. Too obvious to be considered at first. New belief systems – not Bochanegran in origin – are spreading across the land like a disease. We found wretched humans who had been inefficiently supped, leaving them neither quite dead nor properly alive. We found evidence of mutant births – meddlings with human souls. Paranormal events. Spirits . . . plenty of spirits. Some of the nomads had seen them; blades of light the size of a man, was how they described them. Also, Harkasites travelling into the Strangeling reported humans who offered them the sup. This is a relatively new phenomenon, thankfully, but not one that has been engendered by legends of our past alone. Now, Sammael, can you guess the conclusion I have drawn?'

Sammael was frowning. He nodded slowly. 'I think so.'

'Then let us see if our suppositions concur.'

'Well, if I'm correct, it refers back to something I began to speak to your daughter about earlier.' Sammael said.

'What?' I asked sharply, trying to remember what he might mean.

He looked at me. 'Remember we talked a little about the ancients, the very old eloim?'

'What do you mean? I don't understand. You talked of death, or near-death transformation. Are you suggesting these dying eloim are now stalking the plains of Khalt?' I laughed, and was distressed to recognise a note of hysteria in that laughter.

'That is rather too provocative a way to put it,' Metatron said. 'But, in some respects, the evidence points that way.'

'This is preposterous!' I cried. 'How could these ancient eloim get out of Sacramante? Someone would have noticed!'

'They are not in Sacramante,' Sammael said bluntly.

'Not in Sacramante!' I appealed to my father. 'What is he talking about? Those eloim live in the family strongholds. You told me that.'

'I don't think I did,' Metatron said gently. 'However, the truth is something we keep from the younger members of our families, since there is little need for them to know. The truth is painful.'

'I must hear it,' I said.

'Gimel,' Sammael said to me. 'You know we are not native to

278

this world, and also that in many ways we have never changed enough to belong here fully. In our old world, when the eloim reached a certain stage of their spiritual development, they moved on to another realm, another sphere of existence, another reality. However, the path to that new state of being lies through the world we were expelled from – we cannot reach it any other way – which means that we are trapped here on Earth. The oldest eloim are caught in a half-state between spirit and flesh. They become different in mind and body and, as such, can no longer live among the rest of us.'

'Why not?' I demanded. 'How *different* do they become?'

Sammael glanced at Metatron, who reached out to touch my shoulder. 'Quite often, there is mental disturbance, very similar in some respects to the senility found in humans. Also, they become less corporeal, eventually shedding their desiccating flesh altogether. The ancient eloim are risks to our security. Because their minds are addled, they might wander out into Sacramante itself. You don't need me to tell you how humans would react to that!'

'So what *does* happen to these ancients, then?' I asked. 'Where do they go?' I wasn't sure I really wanted to know.

'A place was found where they could rest peacefully,' Sammael said, 'in the hope that one day our circumstances would change, and they might then pass on to their next phase. At present, all of them are confined within the land known as the Strangeling.'

'The Strangeling!' I was amazed. It was only a ruin. What comfort could there be in such a place for these suffering spirits. I could not believe it.

'Yes,' Sammael said. 'It is quite true. There is a fallen city there called Ykhey, which has strong connections with, or lingering fragrances of, our lost world. The old ones are taken there for their own comfort until . . .' He looked at Metatron. 'Well, I was going to say until a way can be found to facilitate their passing from this world, but I suspect that has not been a pressing issue with eloimkind in general. I suspect the old ones are simply packed off to the Strangeling and forgotten!'

'The ancients become listless,' Metatron said, 'and it was thought they had no desire – or energy – to move around in the world.'

'Now, it would seem, the consequences of that blithe oversight will have to be attended to!' Sammael said.

Metatron looked abashed. 'Your criticism is well-founded, Sammael.'

'I am not criticising anyone, Metatron. Our position always has been insupportable. What else could we have done? Still, if prowling old eloim are causing the anomalies in Khalt, I am relieved it is only them. There could have been other, far more dangerous, reasons for the phenomena we've observed. All you have to decide now, is what you're going to do about it.'

279

'The phenomena in Khalt hardly explain the eloim suicides here, or the fact that humanity is beginning to view us with suspicion,' I said.

Metatron nodded. 'I would agree – to a point. However, we cannot tell how the activities of the ancient eloim might affect the fabric of our reality. There might be a connection, or there might not. Sadly, there is only one way to find out. I shall have to confront the ancients themselves. At least I have some ideas to act upon now.'

Sammael nodded. 'That would seem sensible.'

Metatron rubbed his face and nodded. 'I wanted to return the Harkasites to Sacramante before I confronted the ancients. The Khalts have had enough scares from my sinister riders to last them a lifetime!' He smiled uneasily.

'Wise of you,' Sammael said. 'I take it you don't intend to have Harkasites in the party you're leading to the Strangeling, then?'

Metatron frowned. 'There'll be no party! I shall go alone!'

Sammael pulled a quizzical face. 'Oh? Don't you think that would be rather dangerous? We have no way of anticipating what the ancients have evolved into. You must not face them alone, Metatron. You are too valuable to our people. I, at least, shall travel with you.'

'You? Are you up to the journey?' Metatron asked sharply. 'I did not intend to travel by carriage.'

'If I have forgotten how to ride a horse,' Sammael said, looking rather pointedly at me, 'I am sure it is a skill which I will remember after a little practice. As for being out in the open, that is something I will have to conquer my fear of.'

'Well, if you are sure . . .' Metatron himself sounded far from sure.

'Quite sure,' Sammael said lightly. 'And I also think we should take at least one Harkasite with us for protection. If I may be so bold, I suggest you choose Pahadron, who is undoubtedly the strongest and the most terrifying. We might need his especial talent in Ykhey.'

'Pahadron,' Metatron repeated, his dry tone suggesting he disagreed with the choice. 'If you insist.'

Sammael smiled. 'I created the Harkasites, Metatron, and am perfectly capable of controlling them.'

Metatron's face twitched at the rebuke. 'I would not presume to suggest otherwise! It's just that you have been . . . away . . . for so long. I hope you won't overstretch your strength by travelling.'

'So do I!' Sammael said, grinning widely. I realised I was witnessing the unprecedented sight of my father being teased. Metatron grunted and stood up to replenish the brandy glasses. Sammael glanced at me.

'Queen of eloim' he mouthed silently. It was a cue. I knew that at this point he expected me to offer to accompany them to the Strangeling. In my heart I knew I would end up doing so anyway, but the *idea* of the ancient eloim made me feel physically sick. I did not want to admit those decayed beings, exiled to a wasteland, existed. The implication of the necessity for their removal from Sacramante was enough to turn my stomach. It was wonderful news that Metatron might have found the source of our problems, but I could not feel relieved about that. All I could think of were the images this information had conjured within my mind. Suddenly, I had been presented with an unimaginably ugly possibility for my own future, never mind anyone else's.

'Sammael,' I said. 'I need to know more about the ancient eloim. At what age can an individual expect to begin this . . . transformation? How long does it take to happen?'

'Let us just say that all my original followers – all those who came through to this world with me – are undoubtedly in the Strangeling by now,' Sammael said. 'Metatron here probably has a good while left to him before the dissolution – a couple of centuries. The Parzupheim, perhaps less. I would expect them to begin transforming within the next fifty or sixty years. As for you,' he touched my knee reassuringly with bunched knuckles, 'Gimel, you are just a child. It is too far away for you to worry about.'

My skin was crawling as if with a fever; I felt hot and cold by turn. 'And there are really no Metatronim ancients in this house at all?' I asked Metatron across the room. 'Not even your own father?'

Metatron shook his head as he replaced the stopper in the brandy flask, watching me gravely. I had never met my grandfather; I had been told he'd become ascetic before my birth.

'The original Metatron was with me from the first,' Sammael said, as an interesting snippet of historical trivia. I was appalled how the pair of them just seemed to accept the situation. Even Metatron who, within a couple of short centuries, could expect to meet the same grisly fate!

'This is disgusting!' I cried. 'What happens to the old ones? How does it begin? Does their flesh begin to decay in some way? What is it like when they lose their minds?' It seemed obvious to me that merely the awareness of the change would drive an eloim insane. Just the idea of it had pushed me close to becoming hysterical. We have no place for the Dark Brother in our society; no. We have a place for something even more dreadful, and what would his name be: the Dust Brother, the Brother of Powdery Shrouds?

'As to how badly their sanity is impaired, it is difficult to determine,' Metatron said, sitting down again, and handing me a glass. 'Because it becomes very hard to communicate with them. As for their corporeal forms, they simply change; they become more like spirits. Until now we believed that there was very little in this world they could relate to.'

'Then *why* do you think they are responsible for the phenomena in Khalt?' I asked. 'From the description you have given me, I find it hard to believe they would even *want* to prey on humans! Why would pure spirits need sustenance?'

'Gimel, it is because we need answers to these questions that I – that we are going to the Strangeling,' Metatron said impatiently.

'Has nobody visited them at all before now?' I asked.

'They are left in peace,' Metatron said.

'They are ignored!' I corrected.

Metatron raised an eyebrow at the tone of my voice. 'I have told you all I know,' he said. 'Now I think that it is time, beloved daughter, for you to do a little explaining of your own, don't you?'

I nodded. 'Of course.'

'And you can begin with what Beth had been getting up to with Avirzah'e Tartaruchi,' he said.

CANTO FOUR

'. . . what can be worse than to dwell here, driven out from bliss, condemned in this abhorred deep to utter woe . . .'
Paradise Lost, Book II

Passage can be taken on the Saranan Canal, north-east out of Sacramante. Long before the boundary with the Strangeling is reached, the waterway slopes towards the West; it is used mainly by traders transporting heavy goods from southern Bochanegran ports. For travellers like ourselves, it provided a means of travelling eastwards swiftly; the passenger wheel-boats were renowned for their speed as much as their eccentric design. I questioned the wisdom of Sammael travelling abroad so soon after his emergence from the Tower. He trembled in the open air, something he sought to conceal. Metatron, at Sammael's suggestion, had reawoken the Harkasite, Pahadron. I think my father was less than happy to be travelling with one of these creatures again so soon; both he and I envisaged Pahadron's dour, silent presence would make the journey oppressive. For myself, I had no desire whatsoever to visit the ruin in the Strangeling, but as I was so inextricably entwined in this convoluted web, I could only abandon any resistance; struggling would merely bind me more tightly within the sticky threads. Metatron had commissioned a wheel-boat for us which would leave at dawn the next day. Metatron claimed he did not want to squander time, but I wondered whether he trusted his own ability – never mind Sammael's or my own – to face up to what we might discover in the Strangeling.

The previous day Sammael and I had remained in Metatron's company until a late hour, but I had been little more than a weary listener to the others' conversation. I was preoccupied by the terrible images my mind was continually conjuring up concerning the ancient eloim and my own, distant fate. I tried to imagine my father as withered and demented, unable to stem the obscene idea. Surely death would be preferable? If I saw Metatron like that, or Beth, or any of my dear friends, I would want to end their misery and kill them. Certainly, I would prefer someone to perform that duty for me. Did the madness creep up on you insidiously, so you did not notice, or were there periods of lunacy interspersed with saner moments when the mind lamented its slow destruction? As

285

an ancient, would I still possess the wit to destroy myself before it was too late?

Noticing my preoccupation, and perhaps guessing its cause, Metatron sometimes made a point of asking for my opinion. I responded as best I could, but all I could think about at the time was the wretched future awaiting me, the death that is not death. When I was not tormenting myself with thoughts about senility, grotesque fantasies of dissolution and decay clung to my inner eye; I could not banish them. This is retribution, I thought, we have deserved this. We are falling . . .

I wanted to contact Beth. I needed him. But Metatron, without actually saying anything, made it abundantly clear I was not to leave his company that evening. Perhaps he had intuited my intentions. I had told him the simple truth about Avirzah'e and Beth; his reaction, as had come to be a common feature with my father, was tinged with unsuspected nuances. I detected jealousy, I was sure of it, as well as outrage and concern. 'My lovely Beth,' he said. 'Weak as a motherless cub, so easily tamed!' He held me responsible for Beth's defection, I'm sure, although the rebuke never spread further than the cold heart of his gaze. Eventually, while Sammael and my father examined some old maps of the Strangeling, I managed to scribble a note for Beth – which I requested one of the Metatronim servitors to deliver to the Tartaruchi court. I supposed that Beth would still be there. Wary of who might intercept the missive and read it, I kept my sentiments brief and vague, trusting my brother might be able to read the message between the lines.

'I let the past out of the Tower,' I wrote, 'and it is taking me to the Strangeling. Did I betray you, Beth? I should be with you, but I was afraid. I understand your actions, now; I have been in your place. Await my return from the East; if you are still with Tartaruchi, I will call on you. Extend your will for me. I love you, Gimel.'

He might not understand the message.

That night, even though I was physically and emotionally exhausted, I spent a short time trying to contact Rayojini. If I could not be with Beth, perhaps I could find some comfort in being close to Rayo, however subjectively. She had already reached the Strangeling; I found her wandering about at night in an empty street, in a ruined city. Perhaps the intensity of the feelings I had withstood that day had honed my perceptions, but never had I experienced such intimacy with my soulscaper. It really felt as if I were with her, in the flesh, walking along an empty street, conversing. And the conversation came so easily. It felt like when you desire another person, and are unsure whether they return your feelings and then, finally, confessions are made, the secrets are aired, and communication takes place. You feel light-headed because your trembling hopes have been realised. Still, I was perplexed to discover she believed I'd physically attacked her in Khalt. Why would she think that? At that point, the link seemed to weaken and eventually I lost her completely, but not before I was able to reassure her I would never harm her. I hoped she believed me.

Metatron's carriage arrived in the the grey hour before dawn, to take Sammael and I to the Sacramantan marina. Tamaris and Ramiz bundled us into our travelling coats, and dragged our luggage out of the house. Metatron's white face peered at me round the drapes of the carriage window. Beyond him, I could see a bulky shadow. A quick glance at Sammael confirmed my thoughts. 'I see Metatron has our friend, Pahadron, with him,' he said cheerily. I could see nothing to be cheerful about. To make matters worse, I had to sit opposite the creature. He was exceptionally tall, the crown of his wide-brimmed hat brushing the carriage roof, and beneath his long, dark coat he was dressed in leather. He sat with bowed head, for which I was grateful. I did not want to risk catching his eye.
  A vague mist was about, hugging the green water of the canal and curling delicately like seeking fingers around the hulls of the boats rubbing together in the shadow of the builder's yard. The air was full of the resin they used to coat the wood, and the tang of freshly cut timber. Already the yard glowed with light; the boat-builders began work early. We must have looked a suspicious covey, nervously hovering in the yard. Pahadron stood behind Metatron like an animated statue; I had not yet heard him speak a word. Like the Harkasite, Metatron was also wearing a lemniscate hat, which hid his face, and Sammael and I wore hooded winter coats. The heavy garments were more for protection against the weather than disguise, but I still felt it looked as if we were embarking on illicit business, hooded against prying eyes. The yard-master squinted narrowly at us as Metatron explained why we were there. 'The Cazales aren't here yet,' we were told, frostily. 'They own the boat you've hired. You'll have to wait.' The yard-master's unwelcoming manner suggested that the Mervantes crisis, and its consequences, were still unresolved among non-patrons.
  'May we wait on the bank?' Metatron asked.
  'No reason why not.' The yard-master's tone implied there must be a host of reasons to the contrary, but he still opened up the yard gates so that we could gain access to the tow-path. The canal looked thick and sluggish in the eerie light. 'Perhaps we should have used the underground way from Sammael's Tower,' I said.
  'Too slow,' Metatron responded. 'This is the swiftest method of travel. We shall hire horses when the canal turns west.'

Soon afterwards, three youths came noisily along the road to the marina, and announced themselves as the Cazales brothers. Metatron conducted a few minutes haggling about the price of passage,

287

and appeared to come to an arrangement satisfactory to all parties. The Cazales took Metatron's money and helped us board their craft. Our small amount of luggage caused comment, which we studiously ignored. Canal boats are bizarre and ungainly in appearance, being driven by huge water-wheels. The wheels are man-powered; a strong crew can pedal at astonishing speeds. In the summer months there are often races up and down the city stretch of the canal, and the teams can show off their prowess. Our little boat, named *Serenita*, had several victors' wreaths painted on her hull. Metatron had obviously researched which was the fastest team for hire.

There was a small, but comfortable cabin, in which Sammael sought the darkest corner and sat hunched up like an constrained long-limbed animal, looking out of the port hole. Metatron, perhaps to make sure the best speed was maintained, stationed himself out on the cramped deck, where he could keep an eye on the pedal-house. Pahadron remained silently at Metatron's side. I had no wish to shiver in the damp air, nor experience more of the Harkasite's wordless, sinister presence than necessary, and followed Sammael into the cabin, closing the door tight behind me. I had brought a book with me to pass the time and sat on a couch to read. I heard one of the Cazales boys begin to chant out a rhythm, and soon the *Serenita* began cutting her way through the water, north-east.

I tried to concentrate on the pages of my book, but it was impossible. The light was dim in the cabin, and my head was too full of hectic thoughts. The text swam before my eyes. I kept trying to convince myself that Metatron had unravelled the puzzle of what was happening to the eloim, but I couldn't truly believe it. It seemed that ever since I had entered the Tower of Bale, a kind of craziness had taken over my life. I no longer felt in control. The order and rhythm of living, even my longest-held beliefs, had been totally disrupted, and the discovery that the Strangeling concealed discarded ancient relatives was not only upsetting, but somehow *irritating*. I did not need this extra dilemma to worry about. It was possible the ancient eloim had come to resent their younger relatives who had bundled them off into exile so callously. If my family did that to me, I would be furious! Perhaps in a frenzy of revenge the ancients themselves had polluted eloim consciousness with self-destructive urges. And yet, in thinking that, I was perhaps being too severe. It was equally possible that if the ancient eloim were responsible for the sickness, their intentions might be more honourable than revenge. They might simply be trying to spare any more of their race the torment of dissolution without the release of physical death. How would they receive us? Could they even perceive us as individuals? Were they dangerous? Could they harm us? I had asked these questions aloud the previous evening, but had extracted no satisfactory answers from either Sammael or my father. They did not seem to share my wariness.

The Cazales brothers were tireless, and kept up their rhythmic chanting and pedalling without faltering. By mid-morning we were in open country, where vineyards sloped away from the canal banks to either side. People carrying huge panniers walked up and down the rows of vines, plucking down the ripe grapes. They waved cheerfully to the *Serenita* as she passed them. Occasionally, other canal traffic appeared from the East; narrow boats carrying northern goods, other pedal-boats with passengers and small cargoes. Bells were rung in greeting as the vessels passed each other. If I had been travelling for any other reason than I was, I might have enjoyed the journey immensely. Perhaps one day . . .

Sammael had closed his eyes soon after we'd left Sacramante, and had not opened them again, although I did not think he was asleep. I watched him steadily, still finding it difficult to accept who and what he was. Mikha'il's brother; he had been spawned in an entirely different world from the one I knew. I realised that even despite a dim acceptance of our history, until very recently I had believed Earth to be the only reality. Sammael made me feel more human than I ever had; it made me appreciate just how much I had become, or had perhaps always been, a child of Earth. I was filled with a quick swell of love – for humanity, for the world, for all my people. In a moment of total, unrealistic optimism, I was convinced that everything was going to resolve itself. We would go on from this moment, stronger, renewed, and more flexible. The clouds would dissipate, confusing issues would become clear; the answer would be emblazoned in light across the sky. Sammael: I wanted to touch him. I wanted to talk about hope. I let him pretend to sleep, unmolested.

We travelled the Saranan for two and a half days, pausing each evening at a canal-side hostelry to sleep. Metatron slept with the Harkasite in his room. It did cross my mind that this was perhaps for more than simple protection. On the second day, I met the dreaded Pahadron as I came out of my room. It was the first time I had seen him without his coat and hat. What I saw quite surprised me, but not in the way I had feared. His face had a peculiar shape, as if someone had grabbed the skin of his scalp and pulled his features upwards. This was not repellent, but strangely attractive. His long thin nose had extremely flared nostrils, and his cheekbones were high and sharp. His eyes and brows slanted up towards the temples, and the eyes themselves were long, narrow and almond-shaped, the pupils unusually wide and densely black. His hair was drawn severely back from his face but fell down from his crown, where it had been tied up, in glossy black waves. He was so tall, his limbs looked unnaturally long; his hands seemed twice as long as my father's, the fingers almost like tentacles. My mouth must have hung open – he looked so alien – because this apparition actually smiled at me. I was so surprised I didn't know how to react and by the time I'd recovered my wits, he'd passed me and gone downstairs. My father appeared soon afterwards.

'Why, Gimel my dear, what is the matter? You are staring at me like a sleepwalker!' he said.

'The Harkasite,' I said.

Metatron grinned, and reached to touch my face. 'Breakfast?' he said. He put a hand beneath my elbow and guided me towards the stairs of the inn.

'You were afraid of him,' I said. 'When Sammael suggested Pahadron, you were afraid.'

'I still am,' Metatron replied. 'As any sensible person should.'

'You don't *look* afraid.' I gave him a meaningful glance.

'Sometimes fear has its pleasures,' he said.

I shook my head in exasperation. 'And I wonder what our kind hosts, in this establishment, make of gentle Pahadron!'

'I have already explained his unfortunate condition to the inn-keeper's wife,' Metatron said airily. 'She was most sympathetic. I told her it was the result of a birth defect, which caused giantism and distortion of features.'

'You are ingenious! Won't the inn people be suspicious if we don't eat a full breakfast though?' I asked. 'What shall we do about that?'

'I have ordered bowls of boiled, honeyed milk,' Metatron said. 'And have implied we are of a religious persuasion which adopts an eccentric diet.'

He seemed to have thought of everything.

The countryside was changing; mountains could be seen in the distance and the air smelled of different, ripening fruits and mown hay. We eventually said farewell to the Cazales in the small town of Madyana, where the canal widened into a vast, artificial lake. Here, Metatron inspected the town's two livery stables and hired us the fittest horses he could find. This was not a part of the journey to which I was looking forward. Although Beth and I had often gone riding in the atelier parks, I had never sat on a horse for longer than a couple of hours, and knew how cruel this form of transport could be to the thighs and buttocks of the unseasoned rider. Sammael too confessed he felt dubious about his equestrian prowess. Metatron, who sometimes looks more at home astride a horse than seated in his own court, had little patience with our complaints. The horses themselves looked us up and down with alarmingly intelligent eyes, and seemed to assess Sammael and myself as easily controlled from the first moment. They were sleek animals, corned up and eager to run. Metatron insisted that we keep to a steady, moderately fast gait; the horses responded best to an even rhythm and more ground would be covered that way than by sporadic fast galloping followed by long periods of walking. We took the old road east out of the town, Pahadron riding in the rear. Little time, little time, little time, sang the rhythm of the pounding hooves. The land smelled of autumn smoke mingled with the perfume of the grape, heavy on the vines, and the aroma of honeyed apples weighing down the boughs of the orchards. Clouds of fragrant smoke poured across the road from the fires of stubble in the fields, and the pyres of superfluous or damaged crops. We rode like ghosts through the curling grey plumes. Figures stood still and silent beside the fires, mere silhouettes, watching our swift passage. Nobody waved.

After the first afternoon's ride, my thighs, as I had dreaded, were almost raw and Sammael too complained of discomfort. We stopped for the night at a small hostelry where we were able to obtain liniment for our bruises. I applied the ointment in the privacy of my room and lay on my stomach to sleep. Everything seemed to have become unreal. I was conscious of the space between myself and the Strangeling, and how it was diminishing so quickly – too quickly. I still did not feel ready to confront whatever we might find there.

We passed over the invisible boundary quite early in the morning. I had never visited the Strangeling before and in the normal course of events would never have expected to. Once we had crossed the line that separated this unpredictable land from the normal world, I began to understand its symbolic nature. There was a weird beauty in the tumbled shapes beside the old road, and a kind of dignity. We kept on the eastern road, and occasionally human inhabitants of the place would jump out of concealment to run alongside us, leaping and catcalling. These were not wholly innocent creatures.

When we stopped for the night among some ruins beside the road and Pahadron was erecting our sleeping canopies, a fox-like boy with long ragged hair came stealing out of the darkness to watch. Pahadron stood upright and stared at the intruder.

'Will you drink,' said the boy. He was skinny, dressed in tattered clothes, with the nervous gait of a nocturnal animal.

'Yes,' Pahadron said. It was the first time I had heard him speak at all and the sound of that single word was surprisingly light and musical. He squatted down beside the boy, who put his arms around Pahadron's neck. For a few moments, it seemed they were kissing, then Pahadron's mouth slipped down to the boy's throat. The boy whimpered in pleasure as Pahadron's teeth sliced into his flesh. A single jet of sweet ichor spurted from the side of the Harkasite's moving mouth. I could not believe what I was seeing. Supping humans so blatantly beyond Sacramante? The boy was not a patron: what was going on? Metatron sauntered over to where I was observing the proceedings in speechless consternation.

'Sammael told me the humans in the Strangeling were different from all others, but I had no idea they were familiar with the sup!' I exclaimed.

Metatron put a hand on my shoulder. 'This was our country once,' he said, as if that were explanation enough. Pahadron and the boy had sunk down to the ground, oblivious of our presence.

'Aren't you going to stop this?' I hissed at my father.

Before he could answer, Sammael approached us. 'Your suppositions must be right, Metatron,' he said. 'This speaks of people who are regularly indulging in the sup. And who else can they be sustaining but the ancients? No other eloim come here.'

'You did,' I pointed out.

'That was a long time ago,' Sammael replied, 'and I did not partake of the sup, not beyond Sacramante.'

'That boy recognises us as eloim,' I said, and shivered. It was not just the unsupped in Sacramante who were beginning to see us as we really were then.

'A couple of the Harkasites came to the Strangeling during our information-gathering,' Metatron said. 'Pahadron was one of them. I mentioned before that humans here had offered the Harkasites sustenance. This is just another part of the puzzle which we have come here to try and solve.'

Other young humans had come creeping out of the darkness, and now surrounded us completely. Something touched my hand and I looked down, appalled to find a grubby little girl staring up at me.

'Drink, lady?' she said, tugging my coat. Sup from a child so young? It would be obscene! It was even more revolting to think of the pleasure she would obtain from it, which was nothing if not erotic in nature.

'No, thank you,' I said stiffly.

'Do not be prudish, Gimel,' Sammael said, with laughter in his voice. 'This is not Sacramante. Why not live your adventure, seeing as you're stuck with it?'

I made an angry noise and pushed my way through the ring of youngsters. Let Sammael and Metatron copy Pahadron's perversity if they wished. I, Gimel Metatronim, lady of standing and repute, would have none of it. *Like you had nothing to do with the murders in Lansaal, all those years ago, I suppose*! said my conscience waspishly.

It took two days for me to relent. I did not need sustenance exactly, having fed wisely before we departed the city, but the smell of blood from my companions' supping stimulated my appetite. I eventually supped from the oldest girl I could find. Her taste was unusual, strangely tart. She tried to suck ichor from my own skin, for which I had to slap her. Such presumption. Sammael was right: this was certainly not Sacramante!

* * *

The city of Ykhey was visible long before we reached it; a huge sprawl against the sky, girdled by a slow-moving river to the West that was thronged with small boats and rafts. Ykhey: holy city. It was a busy hive of scuttling humanity; so much noise! Although I reprimanded myself for being too conservative, I could not help but feel scandalised by the way the shabby creatures thronging Ykhey's crumbling buildings had helped themselves to eloim relics. So much had been left behind when my ancestors had had to abandon the city, that was obvious, but these things should have remained untouched. If I had the power, I'd drive all these parasites out so that Ykhey could decline in silence and propriety, its streets populated only by wild animals and ghosts.

Children clad in ragged silks clustered around the legs of our horses, hanging on to whatever parts of our clothing they could reach. I had a mind to use my whip to get rid of them. 'Do you know where to go?' I asked Metatron.

'The entrance to the Hypogeum is located in the heart of Ykhey,' he said. 'There was a palace there, an open space for gatherings. Sammael once lived there.'

I urged my horse alongside Metatron's and leaned over to speak to him confidentially. 'How does Sammael *seem* to you?' I asked, lowering my voice. Sammael was riding some distance ahead of us, now apparently at ease upon his horse.

'I would not presume to diagnose either his mental or physical state,' Metatron replied in a waspish tone. 'You can be sure he knows exactly what he is doing.'

My father was still using every available opportunity to clip me for my part in Sammael's re-emergence into the world.

Vagabonds followed us all the way to the plaza of which Metatron had spoken. Fortunately the place appeared taboo for them, for they would not tread on the slabs, but sat down to watch us in the ruins around the edge. To the North, the remains of a splendid building soared towards the sky: Sammael's palace. Perhaps there would still be blood-stains upon the floor. Brown leaves scurried across the ground; above us the autumnal sky had thickened to a purplish grey.

Sammael dismounted from his horse and stood as if in a daze, looking around himself. I could almost feel the memories bubbling up in his mind. 'I find it hard to believe the place still stands,' he said.

'Eloim buildings are made to last,' Metatron said, joining him. 'We need them for a long time, remember.'

Sammael smiled at him, and squeezed his shoulder. 'I must not look inside the palace,' he said. 'You may not be able to get me out again.'

I listened to them being bravely humorous, overtaken by a sense

293

of distance from them, sheer unreality. My fingers were cold against the stiff reins in my hands. I became aware of being observed and looked behind me quickly. Pahadron had dismounted from his horse and was watching me steadily. I shuddered. His presence was not as oppressive as I'd feared, but he still unnerved me.

'You can dismount now, Gimel,' Metatron said. I dragged my gaze away from the Harkasite to find my father grinning at me.

'Perhaps she intends to ride underground,' Sammael observed.

I wanted to despise them, but could find only pity inside me. The ground seemed a long way away and when I finally jumped down out of the saddle I realised my feet had gone almost completely numb. This is it then, I thought. Soon I will have to see for myself just what is waiting for me in the future. 'Where do we go?' I asked.

Metatron pointed to a clump of bare trees a short distance away – they were perhaps sweetly blossomed in the spring, but now stood skeletal and ugly – within which a cowl of weathered stone could be seen. This advertised the entrance to the city catacombs. I tried to imagine the scenes that must take place here. Did they involve horse-drawn coffins being unloaded into the depths, or half-sentient wretches being led gibbering underground by relatives who had steeled their hearts? I could not bear to ask.

We left the horses wandering around unhobbled, trusting they wouldn't wander too far or, if they did, that our spectators in the ruins would hang on to them. I felt they were loitering around in the hope one of us would sup from them later. Perhaps we would find it difficult to leave until we had obliged them.

The entrance to the Hypogeum was ostentatiously carved with smiling, dancing spirits, dressed in veils. These carvings were garlanded with twiggy flower-vines that still bore a couple of browning, fleshy blooms. Wind fretted the empty boughs, and I could see the remains of a discarded shawl lying in a puddle just inside the entrance. There were two rows of stone benches there. Whoever could have sat in them, and why? It was hardly a place to spend a happy minute in meditation. Just for a moment, I longed to succumb to the hysteria within me that was demanding admission. I longed to shout: 'I'm not going in there!', to turn around and run away.

'Well, are we all ready?' Metatron asked, with a grim smile.

I nodded. 'Yes.'

'Then I'll lead the way.' He stepped beneath the stone arch.

Wide, damp steps led down to an impenetrable dark. Brackets on the walls, surrounded by black stains, suggested where torches had once burned. Pahadron led us into the darkness. For once, his presence was actually comforting. 'Shouldn't we carry light?' I asked.

'No, it might repel the ancients,' Sammael replied.

I shuddered. I could imagine nothing less appealing then groping into a lightless place where creatures who were possibly deranged, and probably deformed, were roaming around. The air was not fetid, but smelled strongly of damp earth. We heard no sound at first. The steps were steep and curving and, very soon, we were having to feel our way along the walls, carefully reaching for the next step with our toes. I had never known such intense blackness. Only the fear of being alone prevented me from turning round and seeking the surface in squeaking panic. My breath came with difficulty and I held on to Metatron's cloak for comfort. Did he feel the same anxiety?

Eventually the steps came to an end, and I trod in a deep puddle as my feet anxiously felt for solid ground. Freezing and unpleasantly turgid water covered my boots to the ankle. Metatron turned round and took my arm. 'Be careful, Gimel.'

The darkness was full of dancing specks of light, which I could still see even when I closed my eyes. I did not intend to let go of my father now. Even if he moved only a short distance away, I might not be able to find him again. 'How much further?' I asked. 'Won't we get lost?'

'The passage is fairly straight,' Sammael said, behind me, 'Don't worry. Pahadron, stay behind us. I'll come forward and lead now.'

'What are we going to find?' I asked. Neither Sammael nor my father answered me.

It seemed as if we walked – painfully slowly – for hours. Sometimes I thought I heard sounds around us in the dark and would alert the others. 'Water dripping,' Sammael or Metatron would reply, 'or rats'. Small comfort.

When I realised I could see the outline of Metatron at my side, I knew light was coming from somewhere. I couldn't decide whether it was lamplight or daylight, but it revealed that we were walking along an arched corridor, with uneven flagstones underfoot. The walls were covered in flaking paintings of marching figures, some of them merely caricatures. There were many wide niches in the walls, that looked as if they should support coffins or cadavers, but all were empty. Just being able to see again helped to calm my nerves, although I still clung tightly to Metatron's arm. I was beginning to hope we might find nothing at all down here. Perhaps the ancient eloim had gone. Then I saw a bright flickering up ahead. We were not alone.

'There is a torch there,' I said, pointing. 'Look!'

I had never seen light quite like it, although it strongly resembled burning gas. There was also a peculiar smell in the air, sweet yet bitter.

'That is not a torch,' Sammael said over his shoulder.

'What is it then? Luminous gas?' I wondered whether it was some

295

sort of disgusting miasma being exuded by dead bodies.

'No, my dear,' Metatron said dryly at my side, 'that, I suspect, is what we're down here looking for.'

'What do you mean?'

'Look closely,' he said.

The radiance was not merely light. As we drew nearer to it, I could see a vague suggestion of solidity in its core. It was perhaps eight feet in height, although only the upper half of it resembled anything like an eloim shape. Below the waist it faded away in a train of glowing mist. There was a suggestion of eyes at its head, mere dark smudges within the flickering brightness, but no other discernible features. It was, for all its strangeness, a very beautiful sight. My relief was immeasurable. Whatever peculiarities this creature manifested, at least I wasn't going to be driven insane by simply beholding it. That, I think, had been my worst fear.

Both Metatron and I had halted our advance and were standing with our arms about each other. Pahadron remained motionless behind us, but I could sense his vigilance. Sammael, without qualm, went right up to the apparition. I saw him raise his hand as if to touch it; his fingers were black silhouettes against the light. He held this position for over a minute while Metatron and I watched in silence. I supposed he was communicating with the creature in some way. Then he turned to us and beckoned.

'It is safe to approach,' he said. 'This is Alcobiel. He is willing to commune with us.'

Alcobiel who? It might have been one of my own ancestors. As Metatron and I advanced cautiously, I felt the hairs begin to stand up on my skin and a metallic taste bloomed upon my tongue. Would this creature actually *speak* to us?

I wanted to explain myself. I am Gimel Metatronim. I am disgusted by your circumstances. I, personally, am not at all responsible for your incarceration down here. I said nothing.

The dark smudges of Alcobiel's eyes held no expression I could possibly interpret. Perhaps it was quite happy in this place. I could detect no emanation of hostility, but none of welcome either.

'May I ask questions?' Metatron inquired politely.

'Ask freely,' Sammael replied. He folded his arms and took a few steps backwards.

'Venerable being,' Metatron said gravely, bowing his head a little. 'I am Metatron, official of the Parzupheim, and first of all I would like to beg your forgiveness for disturbing your peace . . .'

A voice, that was at once inside and outside my head interrupted Metatron's introduction. 'I am aware of who you are, and your purpose! You suppose we enjoy a peace that might be disturbed? Fool!'

Metatron wisely ignored this outburst. 'My question is simple. All I desire to know is whether you and your kin are responsible for certain anomalous phenomena presently occurring in the land of Khalt. These phenomena include sightings of spiritual beings, mutant off-spring born to humans and a particularly distressing condition which the natives have dubbed the "walking death". Are any of these events attributable to your kind?'

Alcobiel steamed in silence for a few moments, apparently observing Metatron thoughtfully. 'We manifest ourselves in Khalt,' it said. I took that to be an acknowledgement of culpability.

'Might I ask why?' Metatron spoke thickly and swallowed hard; he was not as calm as he sounded. I squeezed his arm encouragingly.

'The soulscape of eloim has been marked by a shadow,' Alcobiel answered. 'Eloim juveniles in Sacramante are unable to perceive this, owing to an atrophying of awareness. To us, the shadow is unmistakable. Therefore, we manifest ourselves.'

'A shadow?' Metatron said. 'Could you explain that to me?'

'The shadow is that cast by the Dark Brother,' Alcobiel replied. 'He calls the children to him, and they obey his voice. We have to protect our children, however ignorant they are of their peril. We took our own action.'

'Your own action? What, exactly?'

To experience another being's laughter inside your own head, especially when that laughter is not of the sweetest kind, is not a pleasant experience.

'Blind! Blind! Blind!' announced Alcobiel. 'The shadow is the seed of invasion. While you nourished this seed with your lives, we sought to smother it.'

'An invasion?' Metatron continued, not visibly perturbed. 'By who, or what, and from where?'

I did not think Alcobiel was going to answer. The brightness dimmed a little and seemed to retreat. I heard Metatron take a breath, but he did not speak. Then the radiance increased again and Alcobiel said, 'The invasion comes through. From Elenoen.'

Elenoen. The name was familiar to me, and yet I don't think I had ever heard it before.

'Watchers!' Metatron hissed 'From the old world. Is that what you're saying?'

'Watchers watch,' Alcobiel replied. 'This is something more active: a definite form, an influence. It has leaked through, somehow.'

'That is not possible,' Sammael said, in a distant, reasonable voice. He had wandered some way up the passage, and was fingering one of the wall paintings now revealed. 'All the interfaces with Elenoen were destroyed when we were exiled. Anyway, if something could get through to Earth, surely you would be able to pass through in the opposite direction. In which case, why are you still here and manifesting yourselves in Khalt?'

'The gateway cannot be found,' Alcobiel replied, 'We searched for it, but there was no sign. Our conclusion was that it must have been a temporary access-way, created for a specific purpose.'

'I find that hard to believe,' Sammael said. 'If anything had come through from Elenoen, I would undoubtedly have been its first target.'

'That is a token of arrogance, Lord Sammael,' Alcobiel replied. 'Whatever came through seeks to destroy eloim from within. It must be aware that you have distanced yourself from the world. You are probably no longer a threat to it, not even a recognised power. This is why we confronted the problem ourselves, even though it is far from easy for us to manifest ourselves much more tangibly than you see here.'

'I am still not convinced,' Sammael said, in a voice that suggested he was more affronted than unconvinced.

'I don't think we can afford to disbelieve anything at this stage,' Metatron said, 'I think we have to determine what objective this hypothetical intruder, or intruders, has.'

'It is easy to divine,' Alcobiel said. 'They wish to destroy you, and have invented a means to infect eloim souls with the compulsion to self-destruction. Elenoen covets this world. When we were trapped here, a source of strength was cut off. They have been patient, watching eloim on Earth weaken and stagnate. Now they have decided to act, while you in Sacramante scurry round panicking.'

'Perhaps so, but I cannot see how your actions have helped to alleviate this situation either,' Metatron said. 'You should have contacted us.'

Alcobiel shimmered, pulsing faintly green. 'Would you have warned us, had you been the ones privileged to realise the cause of this taint? No, I think not! Neither have you the strength to take the necessary steps. We knew what was required and caused a roar of entropy in the world. Entropy is anathema to the followers of Eloat. We needed substance and took nourishment from humanity . . .'

'Which resulted in the abomination of the half-dead,' Metatron said. 'And the sudden incidence of sup-hungry humans in the Strangeling.'

Alcobiel shivered; perhaps another sign of mirth. 'That is irrelevant. What we are doing has far more chance of effect against this threat than any number of Parzupheim meetings and prattlings.'

'Probably so,' Sammael said, 'but now, Alcobiel, you and your kind must cease this activity in Khalt.'

'Never! You cannot command us! We are the abandoned ones!'

'It is not a command. You must see sense. If your suspicions are correct and this intrusive influence *has* come from Elenoen, only I can handle the situation. Of all the eloim on Earth – you and your kind included Alcobiel – I alone retain sufficient memory of the old world. I am not like other eloim, you know that. I was created for a specific task, and once had the power to fulfil that task. Admittedly my strength has atrophied over the centuries while I slept, but even my memories are more capable of dealing with the Watchers than anything you have tried to do.'

Alcobiel clearly did not agree with Sammael. It did not respond with words, but began to spin, around and around, throwing off sparks that hissed as they hit the damp floor. Metatron and I prudently retreated, but Sammael did not even flinch. He raised his right hand and absorbed the spinning light into his outstretched palm. Then he closed his fingers over it. Alcobiel dimmed and shrank. 'You will cease this activity,' Sammael said quietly. 'Because it may obstruct anything I might be forced to do. You have everything to gain from trusting me. If I can, I will secure you freedom of passage into your next reality.'

'It would be unwise to contain the supra-normality we have conjured,' Alcobiel said, 'for the simple reason it is a repellent force to Elenoen. The chaotic influence we introduced might well have repulsed the invader already. Our descendants in Sacramante, and the paranoid flotsam scattered in hiding throughout the world, have become too static, too stagnant in consciousness, to risk confrontation with the intrusive force. If you intend to tackle this problem, you will do so alone, Sammael. You will find no help in Sacramante.'

'I am prepared to stand by any decision I might make,' Sammael said. 'And you have my word that I will try to assist you.'

'The Word of Light?'

'Unutterable.' Sammael came towards Metatron and I, where we stood close together, some distance away from Alcobiel. 'We shall leave now,' he said. 'We can learn no more here, and I have plans to make.'

'Sammael,' I said. 'I want to ask my own question.'

He sighed impatiently. 'Very well, but be quick. This essence that calls itself Alcobiel is volatile.'

I let go of my father and approached the wavering form. 'Are you angry with us?' I asked. It did not seem to hear me. Perhaps only Metatron and Sammael resembled it enough to communicate with it. I stood there for a few moments, just gazing upwards, trying to emanate all the feelings I held inside. Then I turned away to return to the others and a small, childlike voice entered my head.

'We knew, Gimel Metatronim. We knew, when we accompanied the Prince of Light to this world . . . There was no way back; we were aware of this.'

I turned around and formed the words in my head. 'Yet you still came.'

It did not answer in words, but I was given a picture, very briefly, a picture it is impossible to convey in words. I hoped the Sammael that they adored so completely, to whom they remained unflinchingly loyal despite the tone of Alcobiel's remarks, still existed.

Metatron held out his hand to me. As I took it, all light fled the passage, and with Pahadron leading us, we found our way back in utter darkness.

Outside, a rain-laden wind had sprung up and the sky was darkening swiftly. I could see fires around the edge of the square, and did not relish the thought of spending a night in this place.

'Will they obey you?' Metatron asked.

'Probably not,' Sammael replied, 'but for all Alcobiel's threats and grand assumptions they are still an uncohesive force. It is not something I intend to worry about.'

'Do you believe what it said about Elenoen?' I asked. How easily that word flowed from the tongue. 'Can that possibly be true?'

Sammael walked a short distance away from us, and Metatron and I exchanged a glance. Wouldn't Sammael have somehow sensed it, if it were true? I felt he really wanted to believe it, for very private reasons. Perhaps he could not be trusted because of that? Metatron made an impatient sound and went to help Pahadron round up the horses who were dispiritedly stripping a leaning tree of yellow leaves. I wandered over to where Sammael was gazing at the sky.

'What about Rayojini?' I asked him. 'Should she be told these things?'

'Hmmm?' He turned and blinked at me.

'The soulscaper,' I reminded him.

'Oh yes, the soulscaper. Gimel, that procedure will have to be abandoned.'

'What! That's impossible!'

He shook his head. 'No. In the light of what we've learned, the presence of a human in the soulscape of eloim can only serve as an attraction to unwanted influences. Think about it, Gimel. If kin from Elenoen are involved, it is beyond your soulscaper's powers to deal with them. I realise now that the situation has been left unchecked too long for soulscaping to be a remedy. I feel that certain ideas of Alcobiel's are right. For the moment, chaos is the eloim's only defence against this intrusion. At least the distraction it provides might give us time to formulate a defence strategy. Rayojini's ministrations would only restore order. It is not a good idea.'

'I have brought her so far, though,' I said. 'She may even be in Sacramante already.'

'That is something you will have to ascertain,' Sammael replied, 'and deal with accordingly.'

Helplessly, I thought about how we had arranged things so that Rayojini would discover certain information for herself on the journey west. We had hoped that by the time she reached Sacramante, the final revelation of what was required of her would not be too shocking or incredible. I knew what an inquiring mind my soul-scaper had. I did not think we could easily persuade her to forget about the whole business, not after her curiosity had been deliberately piqued. 'Sammael,' I said. 'Rayojini already knows so much about us. How can I just abandon her now?'

There was a short silence, while Sammael allowed me to think of the unthinkable.

'I will not have her harmed!' I said. 'I mean that, Sammael.'

'I really think you have to entertain the possibility that this singular priming you have given Rayojini might also be most useful to our opponents.'

'If they know she exists, which they cannot!'

He shrugged. 'There is little point in arguing about this here. Obviously we must return to Sacramante. Think about what I have said on the journey home, Gimel. Think deeply.'

He walked away from me, leaving me staring at the gaping entrance to the catacombs. All that work; for nothing. I could not let him take all that away from me. I couldn't. In his Tower, Sammael had insisted that nothing compared with the skills of a Tap. Surely Rayojini would be even more useful to us now? We could give her specific information about what we were looking for. I was so angry and confused, I marched off across the square, needing a few moments to seethe alone. Send Rayo back? I couldn't do that! No! Meeting her and working with her was something I'd primed myself for – never mind the woman herself – for twenty-odd years. We belonged to each other, didn't we?

I walked along a narrow street where high walls leaned towards each other, veined by dead ivy. A wind blew mercilessly down the tunnel they formed and I pulled my coat around me more tightly. Rayo! I tried to call to her, but my mind was in such a turmoil I couldn't summon the concentration. Eventually I sat down on the cracked slabs of the street, and leaned against one of the walls. How I wished Beth were with me. Whatever our differences, I knew I could always count on his sympathy when I needed it. I lowered my face on to my arms, where they rested on my raised knees. I let the cold bite into me. I wept.

'Lady Gimel . . .' I don't know how many minutes had passed, but at the sound of my name spoken so softly, I raised my head. The voice had almost sounded like Beth's, but it was Pahadron that I saw leaning over me, his enormous hat blotting out the sky. I hastily wiped my face, and made dismissive gestures with my hands.

'I'm coming, I'm coming,' I said, beginning to rise. The Harkasite took my arm and lifted me effortlessly to my feet. It felt as if I'd been blown into the air by a powerful gust of wind, and deposited as lightly as if a gentle breeze had lowered me down.

'Lord Sammael sometimes speaks without realising what effect his ideas might have on his listener,' Pahadron said. I was surprised by his words, not just because he had actually spoken so many of them in one breath, but because they seemed so untrue. Sammael's tongue dripped silver, in my opinion. He would never speak anything but exactly what he intended to say. I was unsure whether to address the Harkasite as an equal, an inferior, or as an animal.

'I am sure Lord Sammael is quite aware of the results of his words,' I said stiffly. This was none of the Harkasite's business. To me, he was nothing more than an animated weapon. I had nothing to say to him.

'Nonetheless, what he said to you is true,' Pahadron said gently. His smile, too, was disturbingly gentle, considering the Harkasites' reputation.

I directed a chill glance in his direction. 'If you would escort me back to my father . . .'

He ignored my rather obvious signals. 'I am aware of your plans,' he said. 'Metatron has spoken to me. Lady Gimel, look at me.'

I had walked past him. Reluctantly, I turned around.

'I know what you think of me, and do not dispute that opinion. But remember, what might come through from Elenoen could destroy me with a glance.' He smiled. 'Much as you are trying to do at this moment!'

'I have nurtured the soulscaper!' I said. 'I have been preparing her for many years! She is powerful! Sammael said so himself! It is impossible for me to abandon her now!'

'She cannot possibly be powerful enough,' Pahadron said. 'If you love her – and I feel you do – you must remove her from your plans.'

'You are a monster!' I cried. 'How can you advise me!'

'I am a conjunction,' the Harkasite replied. 'A composite who has slept for many years, but I have the memory of three separate lives. I can still remember love, Lady Gimel, and what it does to you.'

His reasonable, even-toned voice brought me to my senses a little. I was appalled at how I had insulted him. Whatever my feelings, I should not have voiced them so rudely. 'Forgive me,' I said. 'I am distressed.'

'There is nothing to forgive,' he said. 'I am all the things you despise, after all. If I discovered you were a threat to eloimkind I would kill you where you stand. And should I be directed to dispose of your soulscaper, I would do that too, without a qualm. Now do you understand what I am trying to say to you?'

I had begun to shiver. 'Yes, I understand,' I said, and began to walk away. He did not follow me immediately.

'Turning our tortures into horrid arms against the torturer . . .'
Paradise Lost, Book II

Keea and I took a carriage to Sacramante from a border town in Bochanegra. A need to accelerate our quest for information provided the only excuse we needed to squander funds on the luxury of transport.

Once we arrived in the city, I was concerned about having my Khaltish currency changed into the Bochanegran coin and our destination was the exchange office. The city was in the throes of a late autumn festival and seemed to be full of Khalts, celebrating like crazy. Because of this influx, there was a shortage of funds, and we were told at the office that we would have to wait until morning before my currency could be exchanged. Keea said he did not have enough money to pay for my lodgings himself, which I did not entirely believe. Perhaps he still harboured a grudge because of the way I'd leapt on him in Ykhey. Neither of us had mentioned the incident since. Still, if Keea wasn't prepared to be generous, whatever his reasons, there was little I could do about it. The only Bochanegran currency I possessed was the gold coin that had been pressed into my hand at the gates of Ykhey by . . . whatever had pressed it into my hand. I was reluctant to spend it, naturally, but could see little other choice. Keea, I thought, ought to have many friends in the city, perhaps even some we could stay with for a couple of days – but now he claimed to hail from an outlying town further south. He was familiar with few people in Sacramante, he said, but did know of a lane near the atelier courts which was thronged with cheap and tolerable inns. I let him lead the way, even though he lost us once or twice down the twisting alleys. In the morning, after I had cleaned myself up, I would seek out the family I had visited as a girl with my mother and hope they'd be prepared to assist me.

Eventually we found the lane he was looking for; it was called Aurora Paths. It was narrow and picturesque, conveying the ambience of cultivated simplicity which must have been designed exclusively for tourists. Women and youths in peasant dress were stationed ostentatiously at outdoor tables sipping dark red wines from earthenware goblets. 'So which one do you care to patronise, Mistress Rayojini?' Keea asked me. He looked tired.

'You have no preference, no recommendation?'

He shrugged. 'They are doubtless all alike.'

I began to walk up the lane, shifting my carryback into a slightly more comfortable position, looking forward to the moment I could divest myself of its weight. I looked at the names of the inns and acted on whim.

'This'll do,' I said. 'The Temple Gate. I like the lanterns outside. What do you think?'

Again, a shrug. 'I don't mind.'

It was near dinner time and The Temple Gate was quiet and empty, holding its breath before its guests descended in evening finery to eat. A thin young girl at the counter inscribed our names in a ledger, asked for a nominal sum as security, and gawked at the coin when I produced it from my pouch. 'It is currency in this place, isn't it?' I asked sharply. The girl nodded, round-eyed, and mumbled something about how she was unsure whether she'd be able to give me change for it. 'It's all I have,' I said impatiently. 'Can you accept it or not?' Keea lounged against the counter, happy to let me handle this problem alone. He made no offer to pay for the accommodation himself.

'I'll have to fetch my father,' the counter girl told me. 'He is the proprietor.'

'Please do!' I glanced at Keea who shrugged. 'This is intolerable,' I said. 'What is wrong with my money? How much *is* it worth, Keea? You must know, you live here!'

'I'm unfamiliar with that particular coin,' he said unhelpfully.

The innkeeper came out to the counter clutching my coin. 'You do know how much this is worth?' he said to me.

I made a helpless gesture. 'It was given to me as a gift,' I said. 'What is it worth in dahli?' Dahli were the standard coin in Sacramante. When the innkeeper told me, the amount astounded me; I'd had no idea I'd been presented with such riches. Ten thousand dahli! It was very embarrassing. Both the innkeeper and his daughter looked at me as if I were insane. I explained my position concerning the exchange offices, my ignorance regarding rare Bochanegran currency, and politely inquired whether or not we could come to an agreement until I could visit the exchange office in the morning.

'Madam, this coin could keep you in our best suite, with *every* conceivable luxury, for many years,' the innkeeper said dryly. 'I am sure we can think of an arrangement that pleases us both.' He was happy to let me open an account with the inn from which I could draw out funds as and when I needed them. Whatever remained in credit at the end of my stay would be refunded.

'I am a soulscaper,' I said airily. 'The coin was payment for some work I undertook. I had no idea it was so valuable.'

The innkeeper smiled tolerantly. 'Would that we could all be so flippant about our income,' he said.

Still, he was impressed enough to show me up to my room personally. He hadn't asked me whether I wanted one of the best rooms, but had evidently given me one anyway. It was spacious and airy, with a huge bed, a balcony and adjoining toilet room. I'd also offered to pay for similar accommodation for Keea, which he had accepted blithely. Well, I thought, since the money was unexpected, I might as well just spend it.

'Would you like a maid to bathe you?' the innkeeper asked me.

'Why not?' I said. 'And a light meal would be appreciated too, if you could oblige.'

'Anything you require.' He saluted me respectfully and left the room. I smiled to myself and sat down on the bed, gratefully unbuckling my carryback. I could get used to this treatment!

I opened the long windows and walked out on to the balcony. In the distance, I could see the silver wrinkle of the sea and the tall masts in the harbour. Late-flowering vines, growing thickly on the wall outside, exuded a delightful perfume that brought back all the memories of my previous visit to this city. A flicker of excitement filled my veins. I closed my eyes and visualised the torch-lit night of our excursion to the theatre: the colours, the perfumes, the radiant people. Gimel and Beth Metatronim. I opened my eyes, and already the light had faded towards evening. Between the trees below, firefly lights illuminated the patios of the tavernas and cafés. I curled my fingers over the balcony rail. Gimel and Beth lived in this city; could I bear to seek them out? Perhaps it would be sensible. Perhaps by seeing them in the flesh I would exorcise the ghosts their images had conjured in my mind. By now they would have lost their beauty, they would be ageing and sagging. I imagined tracking them down and telling them how they had affected me all those years ago. And yet, perhaps that confession would only bore them. It was likely that many people had been affected by them in a similar way: dreaming of celebrities, dreaming of touching them and possessing their bodies for a night. I was probably no different from their other admirers.

There was a knock on the door behind me and I went back into the room. The maid had arrived to scrub my back for me. She went into the adjoining room and began to run me a bath. Hot water, plumbed in! I would bathe every day to take advantage of this luxury.

As the girl patiently massaged my grubby flesh, I relaxed sleepily in the warm water. Anxieties seemed to flow away from me along with the dirt from my skin. Suddenly the whole business of the Host and the phenomena in Khalt seemed unreal, or the product of hysteria. What had happened to me out there on the road? Too much time spent alone? Too much imagination? Here in the relaxed atmosphere of Sacramante, all my wild assertions of conspiracy

305

theories, ancient predatory races and the walking dead seemed absurd. Perhaps the conspiracy existed only because I had invented it. Perhaps I should forget about it now. Tomorrow I would seek employment and put aside my questing instincts for a while. Following this path of intrigues and mysteries was only making me ill and despondent; I was getting too old for such adventure. If I got the chance I would track down other soulscapers in the city, for there were bound to be a few around, and ask them to purify my mind of dross. I would relax and let the balmy air of Sacramante seep into my bones; heal myself. Still, I did not forget the libraries Keea had told me about. It would be senseless to have come this far and not at least take a look at them. However, I instructed myself firmly, whatever I might discover in the libraries, I would do nothing but return to Taparak and report back to the scryers. If there were problems to be solved, it was up to the Guild to do something about it, not me.

It is astounding how, when in the womblike embrace of warm water, we can fool ourselves that we can still be children.

I opted to eat in my room that night, wrapped in a robe the inn provided for my use. I felt optimistic and lazy; the image of such demons as blood-suckers or legendary beings remained properly in the Strangeling. They had no place here.

I napped for a while and awoke with the room full of moonlight, a small lamp by my couch barely alight. Hungry again, I decided to venture downstairs and perhaps take a drink in the taproom. All of my clothes bore the stains of travel and I had had no opportunity to wash them, so I dressed myself as best I could in a simple dark-green shift I kept for those rare occasions when it is preferable to appear at least nominally groomed. It was badly creased and had a mould-stain on the right shoulder, which had undoubtedly grown while I'd been kept unavoidably wet in Khalt. Rubbing the stain with a damp cloth made no difference, but perhaps it would go unnoticed anyway if the lighting was dim. My braids looked a little wild, so I damped the frizzy bits down and tied a scarf over my head. The mirror told me I looked as if I'd been recently disinterred, but it would have to do. Tomorrow, I could go and spend more of my gift money on some new clothes.

As I went into the corridor, the door to a room further down clicked open. A figure stepped out into the dimly lit passage, looked up and down swiftly, but apparently did not see me. It hurried for the stairs in a whirl of dark cloak and I felt as if my heart had stopped. The instant I had seen the face, I had known it. I was sure it was the same man/woman who had accosted me at the gates of Ykhey. Was that possible? No, it was imagination I tried to tell myself, not believing so for a moment. The movements had been furtive – whose room had they entered? The answer was obvious

306

to me: Keea's. As to whether Keea had welcomed this person as a friend, or had been attacked by them as an enemy, I would have to find out.

I advanced silently to the door, which still stood ajar, wondering whether I should enter or not. With my fingertips, I pushed the door wide. Inside, light from a shaded lantern threw multiple colours over the wide bed. It was empty and there was no sign of any personal belongings lying around. *Was* this Keea's room? Perhaps I'd been mistaken and the mysterious figure had been nothing but another guest on his way out for a night's entertainment. If I made further investigations of the room, I might well be trespassing. I pulled the door shut and thoughtfully went downstairs.

The following day I rose early and left instructions with the maid for my clothes to be cleaned. She'd come to my room to see if I needed anything. Later I would go out and treat myself to some new apparel.

Keea was in the dining room, looking fresh and spry; I had not seen him since we'd booked in. 'Sleep seems to have restored you,' I said. He smiled.

'You too,' he replied. I returned his smile uneasily. 'What are your plans?' he asked. Our conversation was interrupted by the arrival of a servitor who listed the food available for breakfast.

After he'd gone, I said, 'First, I intend to explore the city and spend some of my money, and then I will visit a family my mother once worked for. I hope they will be able to offer me work too, or at least recommend a position elsewhere.'

'And of course, you will want to see the libraries.'

'Yes. I would like to take some notes.'

Keea laughed. 'Notes? Is that all?'

I glanced at him sharply. 'Yes, that *is* all. I will return to Taparak with any information we might find.'

Keea pulled a rueful face. 'You don't mean to say you're going to abandon your quest for knowledge! I thought you wanted to unravel the enigmas of the world single-handed!'

I smiled at him tartly. 'Let's just say I don't believe I will find all the answers in Sacramante, and the puzzle itself makes me dizzy. Also, lone investigation beyond this point might be hazardous. I'll hand the mystery over to people more qualified to ponder it. If they wish for me to continue sniffing around, then I shall do so, but not alone.'

'You are easily discouraged.'

'Not at all. I am not so proud as to think I'm capable of solving the world's problems on my own, whatever your opinion. I was interested, but the investigation was detrimental to my well-being. I recognise a warning when I see it, even if its origin was my own mindscape.'

'And you will return to Taparak by sea, so as to avoid the land of the walking dead, hmm?'

'It will be quicker by sea,' I said.

'Let's hope it is still safe!'

I was irritated. 'Don't put ideas in my head, Keea. That's what can make things real! I must admit I'm curious as to why you're so concerned about what I do next. Perhaps now is the time for you to open up to me, as you promised.'

He lowered his eyes and I was sure I could detect a faint flush along his cheekbones. 'I would like to show you the libraries first.'

'Why?'

He looked up at me with earnest eyes. 'Rayo, it is most important you do not abandon your inquiries now! You are needed!'

'In what way and by whom?' The vehemence in his voice had surprised me, but I did not show it.

He shrugged. 'Let us just say there are people who know there is a problem, and that I work for them. They also know someone has to do something about the situation. I respect your abilities. I believe *you* can do something about it.'

So, he had decided to use flattery! Did he think I was so easily manipulated? 'Look, Keea, I'm a soulscaper. I heal the sick. For either of us to believe my talents extend further than that is dangerous.'

He did not give up. 'Such modesty. It does not lie naturally on you, Rayojini. I suppose it means you are afraid.'

'Yes, I suppose it does,' I answered, and I realised that the reply had not just been a lie to stop Keea needling me. There was truth in it, too. Miserably, I began to eat. It felt as if some malign influence were kicking the ground from beneath my feet, just when I had begun to feel better. What had happened to my equilibrium, my strength and confidence? When we'd first entered the Strangeling, I'd felt as if I could have taken on the entire Host of Helat single-handed. Had it only been the hallucinations in Ykhey which had made me change my mind?

'You wanted to know about how I was involved in this, didn't you?' Keea said, breaking into my thoughtful silence.

Well, I had to applaud his efforts to rekindle my interest. 'You thrive on being mysterious,' I said. 'Perhaps that is all I need to know.'

'Oh, I can't believe you're saying this!' Keea hissed, trying to keep his voice low, because of the other guests present in the room. 'You saw what happened to me in Ykhey. Remember what you did!'

'I remember!' I said, pointing a finger in his face. 'And I will be pleasantly surprised if your libraries can explain that! It is because I remember Ykhey that I want to pass on any more information I find to my guild leaders in Taparak.'

'The adventure is just beginning!' Keea pleaded. 'You can't give up now!'

'It's not a case of giving up,' I said, 'but of being sensible.'

'At least see the libraries,' Keea insisted. 'Then decide.'

'I've already said I'd visit them with you, haven't I? Finish your breakfast, Keea. Don't look so glum.'

'I'm not hungry any more,' he said.

Keea did not offer to accompany me into the city, for which I was strangely grateful. I expected he intended to slink off and consult his mysterious employers. I doubted whether I'd heard the last from him about our erstwhile quest, considering his reaction to my remarks at breakfast. My reluctance to continue our investigative partnership seemed to have compelled him to be more honest with me – he had virtually offered to tell me anything I needed to know. However, since Ykhey, I harboured a small and subtle revulsion of him, which I couldn't wholly explain. Now I found I didn't really want to know his secrets. After breakfast I had asked him where his room was and, when he told me, I realised it was actually on a different floor from my own. So much for my suppositions about mysterious strangers the previous night.

I spent the morning being happily frivolous with my ample funds, buying a couple of pretty dresses for the fun of it and a new stock of functional trousers and shirts. At midday, I decided to take lunch in an inn and ducked inside the low doorway of the first one I came across. A few people were sitting inside, eating meals to the accompaniment of a fiddle-player. I approached the bar to inquire about their tariff, but before I could speak the barman said, 'Ah, Mistress Rayojini?'

I nodded dumbly in surprise.

'Yes, we have your table ready. I believe your guest is already here.' He smiled roguishly at me, as at a person who has made arrangements and then arrived late for them.

'Excuse me,' I said, 'but I think there must be a mistake. I have not reserved a table here.'

'But you are the soulscaper from Taparak annexed to the Tricante family?'

'I am a soulscaper from Taparak, yes,' I said, 'but my connection with the Tricantes is tenuous. I have not seen them for many years. Are you sure it's me you want?'

'The reservation is definitely for you,' the barman insisted.

'In that case, you had better direct me to the table,' I said.

Was it possible the family had somehow found out I was in the city and had planned to meet me here? But how could they have known which inn I'd choose for lunch? I hadn't even known myself until a few minutes ago.

I followed the barman into a courtyard at the back of the inn

309

where tables were set out in the shade of an enormous tree. There was no one out there. My guide paused and frowned. 'Strange. Perhaps your guest got tired of waiting.'

'Who was it?'

He shrugged. 'A woman . . .'

'A woman, yes, what did she look like?'

He bridled at my aggressive tone. 'Well, she wore a cloak. She was tall . . .' His face folded into a peculiarly disagreeable expression. 'Could she have been an artisan?'

'How should I know? You saw her, not me! I wasn't expecting to meet anyone.' My blood had gone strangely slow in my veins. An artisan? Gimel? 'How long had she been waiting for me?'

'Half an hour, maybe.'

I marched over to the table. There was no sign of anyone having sat there; the benches were neatly placed, there were no cups or plates in evidence. I noticed there was a gateway leading to the street. 'Well, whoever she was, she must have left by that rear entrance.'

The barman shrugged. 'Possibly. It is very odd though. She was most emphatic I conduct you to her immediately you arrived.'

My heart was beating fast. I examined the table more closely. 'Here, what's this?' I asked, holding up a coin. Had another gift been left for me? It was not Bochanegran, being rough and of dull metal, the marks on it rubbed away with age. It looked vaguely Khaltish. 'What is this worth?'

I held it out to the barman for him to take, but he backed away, raising his hands. 'It is worth nothing,' he said.

'Where is it from? Is it outmoded, or devalued? A dead currency?'

He smiled bleakly. 'You hit near the truth there, mistress. It is not coin as we know it, but a Khaltish ka. It is placed in the mouths of their dead to pay for their crossing into the Next Land.'

I dropped it abruptly on to the table, mainly because it looked horribly *used*. 'Bring me beer,' I said. 'Inside.' I would not sit where she had been.

I could not relax enough to enjoy any refreshment, though the fact that the barman had plainly seem my 'guest' did reassure me somewhat. It meant she had to be a creature of flesh and blood, at least. But who? An insane idea begged for recognition in my head, one which I hardly dared to consider. Could it be that, despite what I knew to be the truth, Gimel Metatronim really *was* connected with me in some way? No, it was ridiculous. Sacramante was full of artisans. That was just wishful thinking. Whoever had accosted me in the Strangeling had used the Metatronims' images because they knew I visualised them as my guardian-pursuers. Doubtlessly, the celebrated Gimel would be shocked, even outraged, to learn her likeness had been employed in this manner. Still, in her position, it

310

was something of which I would want to be aware. Was that sufficient reason to try and locate her? No, I must not even think that. If something had followed me out of the Strangeling, I would not be helping the matter by involving others. Also, I still harboured the suspicion that the Metatronims would be coldly indifferent to what I had wanted to tell them. I would simply have to remain observant and careful.

After finishing my drink, while the barman overtly watched me as he polished glasses behind the counter, I made my way back to The Temple Gate, intending to change and to refresh myself. Then I would present myself at the Tricante residence as soon as possible. I would feel safer if I made contacts in the city, and the Tricantes were a powerful family. If I was in trouble, they might be able to help me. It was going to be embarrassing, I felt, if I had to tell them some of what had happened to me. I was unused to seeking assistance from outside parties, having always been self-sufficient, but I had never been harassed in this peculiar way before. My cosy conviction that everything that had happened had only been the product of my imagination was effectively shattered now. If I really had unwittingly discovered the existence of a predatory race that had been in hiding until recently, it was reasonable to suppose they would want to silence someone they considered to be a threat. This was not a comfortable position to be in. If only I could be sure of the truth.

Back at The Temple Gate, I was intercepted on my way upstairs by the innkeeper's daughter, Terissa. 'Mistress, your visitor is here!' she said, in great haste. I was suffused with a dark bloom of the most intense anger.

'Where?' I snapped.

She gestured wordlessly towards the salon, and I barged past her without asking further questions. I did not expect to find anyone waiting for me there, and I was correct in my suppositions. The door to the garden was swinging shut, however. I ran through the tables, knocking chairs aside and flung myself through the gateway, but the garden was occupied only by an elderly couple who were also staying at the inn. 'Did anyone pass this way a few moments ago?' I asked abruptly. They both shook their head vigorously, clearly surprised by my tone. 'But were you looking?' I insisted.

'No one has come into the garden since we arrived,' the woman said. 'And we have sat here since lunch, and that must have been over an hour ago. Are you all right, dear?'

I raised a hand and shook my head. 'I'm sorry. There was someone waiting for me. She must have left.'

Back indoors, I questioned the girl. 'A woman,' she said. 'Dressed up tight for such a soft day. She must be an artisan.'

311

'Hm.' I looked at the girl speculatively. 'Are you familiar with the actress Gimel Metatronim?'

'I know of the Metatronims,' she said, 'but could hardly say I'm familiar with any of them.'

'Was the woman waiting for me Gimel Metatronim?'

'She did not leave a name.'

'But did she *look* like Gimel?'

Terissa shrugged helplessly. 'I'm sorry; I don't know. The artisans are all very similar in appearance, aren't they . . . ? I don't know.'

'Did she leave anything for me?'

'No.' She was curious as to why I was so agitated. 'Was it important?'

I did not answer her question. 'If she comes here again, at whatever time, tell her I will be back shortly and if I'm in the building fetch me immediately, without telling her you are doing so. Understand?'

She nodded.

'Good,' I said, and as an afterthought offered her a coin.

'The nodding horror of whose shady brows threats
the forlorn and wandering passenger.'
From *Comus*, Milton

Many memories were brought back to me as I walked in the affluent
quarter where the great Sacramantan families had their estates. It
was as if my childhood had been but a few days before. I could see
my mother's purposeful stride, her downturned grin. What would
she think of me now? I had grown up like her in many ways, yet I
lacked her levity and her warmth of personality. Would the
Tricantes recognise me?

The high stone walls of the Tricante estate seemed sun-worn,
soft to the touch. I ran my hand along the stone as I walked slowly
towards the elaborate metal gates. Liviana would be married now,
of course, and living somewhere else. It was possible one or both
of the parents were dead. Who would hold the keys to the house
now? A withered Zimon, moulded into a respectable shape, a
version of his father? The elder sister Agnestia, a spinster and
dressed in lace? And what of Salyon – did he still live at home? I
smiled at my fanciful conjectures and pulled the bell-rope at the
gate.

A haughty retainer came to peer at me through the curling metal
patterns. He waited for me to speak, and I was relieved I had
dressed myself in one of my new dresses with a smart embroidered
jacket. I did not look in the least unsavoury. 'Good afternoon,' I
began in my most ingratiating tone. 'My name is Rayojini. I am a
soulscaper from Taparak and an old friend of the Tricante family.
I would be most grateful if you would allow me to request an
audience with the lady of the house.'

I expected further demands for explanation, but the granite
planes of the servant's face dissolved into an avuncular smile. 'Good
afternoon, Mistress Rayojini. Forgive me not recognising you, but
you are a little early.'

'Am I? For what?'

He laughed in reply. I was not aware of having made a joke.

'Follow me to the garden, if you please.' I held my skirts up
daintily in pinched fingers and minced unconvincingly behind him.

'Your journey, I trust, was comfortable,' he said, over his
shoulder.

'No, a nightmare,' I replied.

He flapped a hand in the air and laughed heartily. I was confused, and also anticipated an unwelcome revelation. They were expecting me here.

And there were the Tricantes, arranged on garden seats, beneath a trellis denuded of flowers. The men all rose to a sharp stand as I entered through a bower gate; the women turned towards me with smiling faces. I felt totally disorientated. The servant announced me in a loud and important voice, and an attractive, dark-haired woman jumped up and came scurrying towards me over the grass, in a froth of yellow lace and ribbons.

'Rayo, little Rayo!' she exclaimed and smothered me in a startling embrace, filling my face with her perfume and stiffly curled hair.

'Liviana!' I said. 'I had not expected to find you here!'

She held me at arm's length. 'Rayo! Did you think I wouldn't come to see you? We had such fun all those years ago. I missed you afterwards for, oh, so long!' She led me across the garden to her family. 'Of course, I have a house of my own now. You must meet my children! Are you married, Rayo, do you have a family?'

'No. Excuse me, Livvy, but were you . . . well, *expecting* me?'

She looked puzzled. 'Yes, of course. We received your message yesterday.'

I stopped walking and looked hard at this grand woman who had once been a girlhood friend. We had not known each other very long, but our friendship had been intense and intimate for all its brevity. I felt I had to trust her. 'Livvy, I would very much like to talk to you alone before I meet your family.'

'Why?' Her tone implied she was not pleased for this undercurrent to mar her perfectly planned afternoon.

'Because I did not send you a message telling you I was coming! Because I did not know for sure I was going to be here in Sacramante at all until very recently. Someone is doing things in my name, Livvy, dogging my footsteps. They got to you before I did.'

Liviana's mouth had dropped open. 'Rayo, this sounds terribly sinister! What *do* you mean?'

'I know how it sounds, but it is the truth,' I gabbled urgently. 'I'm sorry to have to burden you with this, but it is very important. I have to talk to you.'

Liviana controlled herself. Now she wore the face of a mother, concerned and competent. 'We *will* talk. This is most disturbing. But I feel it would be better if you put your chin up and, for now, pretended it *was* you who sent us the message. Come and say hello to everyone.'

'Livvy . . .' I did not really feel like socialising.

Liviana patted my arm. 'Trust me, Rayo. We will share a light refreshment and then I will suggest we go off somewhere for a little girl-talk. How will that do?'

314

'Thank you. Yes. You are right.'

She hung on to my arm as we crossed the last few yards of the lawn, as if she feared I'd break away and run from her at any minute.

Both Tricante parents were still alive. The mother had wizened into a hook-nosed matron, whereas the father had thickened, although he still held a semblance of his former handsomeness. The only person who had turned out as I had imagined was Agnestia: an archetypal spinster and dressed in lace. The cousins were no longer in residence, but the younger sons were still unmarried and at home. Almero was a couple of years older than me, with the face of a seasoned libertine. Salyon was a grave, ethereal-looking creature of maybe thirty years, whose hands shook continually. He and I nodded at each other in a faintly embarrassed way, as if we shared some shameful secret. Zimon, too, had come home to welcome me and had brought his family with him: a round, pretty, dark-haired wife and a boisterous toddling son. Liviana was not escorted by her husband, but lost no time in impressing me with how wonderful he was, such a fortunate catch, so rich. But she had brought her children – two of them – sharp-eyed and intelligent. I did not like them at all. Sitting there, with a tiny glass of cordial clutched in a hand more used to earthenware jugs of murky beer, I was thinking about how alien a concept the family – as it was presented here – was to me. I found it oppressive and clammy, nothing more than a breeding ground for spite and intrigue. Barbed comments flew between the women; sarcastic, nasal remarks between the men. In my family, the members wander in and out of Taparak all the time. It is rare we get the opportunity to meet together, but when we do it is an enjoyable experience which seemed a far preferable arrangement. Today, the Tricantes had put on their best faces because they had a visitor to impress. The spiked bantering was supposed to be humorous. I suspected things were not always as convivial, having noticed the feral glances of mutual loathing that passed between Livvy and her brother's wife. Livvy had slipped into the mechanical rôle of perfect hostess, eclipsing her rather vague mother, and I had no doubt that she had purposefully forgotten the urgent, furtive things I had whispered to her as we'd walked across the lawn. I would not have been surprised had she neglected to seek me out to talk to me alone at all. However, my judgment of her was harsh because, after an hour of aimless prattle, she graciously rose from her seat, placed a maternal hand on the head of each of her brats and said, 'Now then everyone, you must forgive us but Rayojini and I simply *have* to bustle off for a gossip together.' She linked her arm through mine and yanked me to my feet, shooting a particularly poisonous glance at her sister-in-law, who was clearly envying Livvy's long-standing association and apparent friendship with a soulscaper. The matriarch made me vow

I would stay for dinner before she would let Livvy cart me away.

'Don't be antisocial for *too* long!' the sister-in-law said with an impish grin, as if it were a joke.

'You hate her, don't you?' I couldn't resist saying once we were out of earshot. I expected Livvy to ask me what I meant by that, but as we left the company, the Livvy of old (whom I had rather liked), seemed to well up from deep inside her. She wrinkled her nose.

'Vile little beast!' she said. 'A good breeder, no doubt, strong of hip. Zimon has hundreds of affairs. I should think – at least, I hope so. She is an ensorcelled rat. One day I shall break the enchantment and she'll scurry off on her belly again.'

We both laughed. 'Imagine, Livvy, if you picked your moment!' I said. And we fell to giggling as lewd scenarios presented themselves to our imaginations.

'You look very much like your mother now,' Livvy said as she led me into the shaded interior of the house. 'I would have known you anywhere. How is she?'

'Dead,' I replied.

'Rayo, you are terrible. How can you say it like that?'

'Because I'm glad, that's why.'

'But that's awful. Didn't you love her, didn't you get on?'

'Of course we did, and I do love her. It's because of that I'm glad she's dead. She died before she got old. She'd have hated being old. She would have been miserable.'

'Hmm, perhaps I can understand that. Still, you Taps have very strange ideas sometimes. I hope I live to two hundred! Why haven't you any children, Rayo?'

'Because I enjoy my life as it is.'

'But . . .'

'No buts, Livvy. You love your life, I love mine. I wouldn't expect you to wander on foot across the world. Do you see?'

She gave my arm a little shake. 'You are *so* strange! So exotic!' She laughed as we walked into her mother's sitting room. 'Promise me, you'll try to seduce Zimon while you're here!'

'Livvy, really!' We giggled again, like girls. Amazing. We were so different, yet the interval of years was meaningless. It was as if we'd seen each other every day since then. Very few friendships have this magic.

'So tell me everything,' she said, pushing me gently into a seat. 'Brandy?'

I nodded, shifting my weight. Now, I didn't know how to begin. It was going to sound ridiculous, however I put it. 'Well, some very strange things have been happening to me.'

She laughed. 'Look at you! You're such a rogue! You don't look at all comfortable in that dress, but then you never were a person for frills, were you! Strange things! I am not surprised!' She sat down on a chair nearby and handed me a glass. 'What things?'

I turned my glass in my hands. 'Some of what I'm going to say, you might not understand, because it involves scaping work and I'll have to use scaping terms.'

'Just tell me. I can always ask questions afterwards.'

I was as vague as I thought I could get away with. I spoke a little of how I thought I might have discovered the existence of a very old race, who for reasons of their own, had been interfering in the lives of people in Khalt, and perhaps even further afield. 'It sounds outrageous, I know,' I said, grinning at Liviana, whose face had remained oddly expressionless throughout my narrative, 'but I believe someone is following me now, someone who has perhaps tailed me from the Strangeling itself!'

Liviana straightened the folds of her dress, head bowed. She did not respond. I assumed she questioned my sanity.

'I am not mad, Livvy,' I said.

She looked up at me then, and smiled at me tightly. 'Of course you're not! I'm not sure how I can help you though . . .'

'I'm just so relieved to have found you here,' I said. 'I need someone to discuss all this with. I'm not sure what to do. Half of me wants to continue the investigation, while a more sensible half urges that I should return to Taparak. I wanted to establish contacts in the city, so that it would be more difficult for someone to make me . . . disappear. However, it seems that whoever is shadowing me has a cruel sense of humour, sending you a message like that. It's so threatening. They're telling me they know everything I'm planning to do.'

Liviana made no comment but, with terrific poise, got up out of her chair to enfold me in a fierce embrace. I thought she really must consider me insane and was comforting me in the only way she knew. Neither of us spoke, and yet I could feel the weight of unspoken words in Liviana's chest, as if they hung inside my own. I wondered what it would take to convince her I wasn't losing my mind.

'You poor thing!' she said after a while, disengaging herself. 'How terrible to be followed like that!' She had obviously simplified the situation in her head in order to understand it. That was fine by me.

'The woman who visited the inns looks like an artisan. If that *is* her true form, it could mean she's a native of Sacramante, couldn't it?'

Liviana looked wary and turned away from me. 'Not necessarily.'

'Oh come on! The term "artisan" generally refers to a creative individual, resident in this city and connected with one of the ancient family lines associated with the Arts. At least, when a *Sacramantan* refers to someone as being an artisan, that is what they mean. Correct me if I'm wrong.'

317

Liviana sat down again and shifted uncomfortably in her seat.
'It's not *wrong*, but . . .' She sighed. 'There are artisans all over
the world, Rayo.'

'Of course there are, but not like the Sacramantan ones.' It was
as if someone had just lit a torch in the darkest corners of my mind.
For a moment, I was back at the theatre in Livvy's company,
surrounded by the tall, pale artisans. Why hadn't I considered this
before? They *were* different to other Sacramantans, radically so. I
leapt to my feet. 'By all the gods! Yes!'

Liviana's hand fluttered nervously to her throat. 'What is it?'

I spoke so quickly, my words were little more than a gabble.
'Livvy, who are the artisans? Years ago, you told me they were
exiles, or something like that, that they had no country of their
own . . . Could it be that they are *descended* from the race I'm
talking about?' I'd been so busy trying to make up excuses about
my obsession with the Metatronims, I had overlooked the obvious.
'Why are the artisans so special, Livvy? Why do they live hidden
away from everyone else in their own quarters? Do they have any
political power?'

Liviana held up her hands and shook her head, her eyes squeezed
tightly shut. 'Rayo, Rayo, sit down and stop shouting! You are
making me dizzy!'

I sat. 'Well?'

She composed herself and folded her hands neatly in her lap.
'Well, first of all, you have no proof that the mysterious woman
you were told about is actually an artisan. Personally, I doubt it
very much.'

'I think you know who it was,' I said recklessly. 'And, if I'm
right, she definitely is one.'

'Who?' Her voice was very small. I could see I had frightened
her.

'Gimel Metatronim,' I said. I still wasn't really sure of that
myself, but hoped to provoke a reaction from Liviana.

'Gimel?' Livvy shook her head. 'No, that's impossible!'

'Why? Is she dead?'

Livvy shook her head and made a helpless gesture. 'No, far from
it. It's just that she wouldn't do a thing like that. Why should she?'

'Why? Livvy, listen to me. A long time ago . . . When I was
here before, the Metatronims affected me deeply.' I laughed with
embarrassment. 'I dreamt I was raped by Beth, here in this house.'

'Rayo!' Livvy, too, couldn't repress a nervous laugh.

'But it is more than that. All my life, ever since that visit, the
Metatronims have haunted me. It might be a coincidence, but now
I'm no longer sure. As to why Gimel might be tormenting me, the
answer is obvious. If my suppositions are correct, I've discovered
something about the artisans or their ancestors that they want to
keep quiet. Their history! Livvy, it makes sense. There is evidence

that in the distant past a race of people lived in the Strangeling who, I believe, oppressed the people of Khalt – perhaps even Bochanegra – in some way. They were driven out. These people are represented in some ancient art I came across as being very tall and pale, as being teachers of art and science. Now, you can't deny the artisans fit that descriptions quite well. Some very odd things are happening in Khalt, which I believe are connected with this ancient race. Will you answer my questions about the artisans? Please! You can see that it's very important.'

'You don't understand,' Livvy said. 'The artisans are respected and powerful! You can't say these terrible, wild things about them!'

'Look,' I said, taking a deep breath to calm myself. Upsetting Liviana further would gain me nothing. 'If you answer my questions, perhaps we can eliminate the artisans from my theories.'

Liviana sighed, and rubbed her forehead. She would not look at me. 'I can't answer your questions, Rayo,' she said. 'I really can't. It is . . . forbidden.'

'Then I'm right, aren't I?' I said softly. I leaned back in my chair, blinking at the ceiling, letting my heart slow down. For a few minutes, neither of us said a word. Everything was coming into focus; everything. All I had to do was discover why the predators were preying again. Now that I felt I was getting somewhere with my investigations, the urge to delve deeper was upon me again. I had to remind myself of how I had resolved not to tackle this problem alone. I perhaps had enough information now; it was precious. I must get it, and myself, back to Taparak intact.

'Livvy,' I said. 'There is one question you must be able to answer. A simple yes or no will suffice. The artisans *are* very different from the rest of us, aren't they?'

'Yes! Yes!' Livvy shouted abruptly, making me flinch. She leapt to her feet. 'They are different, they are exiles but, Rayo, they are *not* . . . hostile! I know that none of them would have done the things you've talked about, really I do!' She seemed on the verge of tears. 'It must be a coincidence . . . They did not come from the Strangeling.'

I stood up and took her arms in my hands. 'Please. Don't get upset. Perhaps you are right, but I have to find out one way or the other. People have been hurt, you see. I can't just ignore this.'

'They never hurt anybody!' Liviana insisted. 'Why won't you believe me?'

'Look,' I said. 'Do you still have anything to do with that artisan family – what is their name – Harim?'

'Sarim,' she corrected me in a subdued voice. 'Yes, we are patrons of theirs.'

'*Sarim*. Livvy, I want to talk to an artisan. Surely, if they are innocent they will be anxious to clear their reputation. Perhaps

319

they can help me. Could you arrange an interview with one of the Sarim for me?'

She shrugged, looking far from happy. 'I don't know. Rayo, I really don't think it would be a good idea.'

'Why not?'

She wriggled awkwardly. 'Well, the artisan families can be very . . . touchy. They are proud people and very sedate. If you told them what you've told me, they'd feel terribly insulted I'm sure. The artisans have the protection of the Kaliph. You could get into serious trouble if you upset any of them.'

'I'm willing to risk that.'

She stood up, wringing her hands. 'Oh, Rayo, you must drop this, you really must! I cannot get involved!'

'Livvy, what is it?' I asked gently. 'What power do these families have in Bochanegra? Why are you afraid of them?'

'It's not fear!' she exclaimed. 'It's just . . .'

A new voice interrupted her words. 'Just what?' Both Livvy and I turned to the door.

'Salyon,' Livvy said lamely. Her brother came into the room.

'Just what *is* it, sister dear, if it's not terror?' He stood in front of me, shadow-eyed, sallow of skin, and painfully slender. 'You see,' he said to me, 'she dare not answer. It would be most unlady-like. And just what is your interest in the artisans, hmm?'

'Don't tell him!' Livvy almost yelled.

'What can you tell me about them?' I asked, ignoring her. I sensed that Salyon would be far from unwilling to enlighten me.

'Well, let me say that my beloved sister is afraid of them,' he said, 'but not in the way you think. Her fear is that of being abandoned, of doing something disgraceful which would get her excommunicated from the elite society of artisan-worshippers. That is why she will never answer your questions. Her sweet reticence is purely a self-preservation instinct.'

'Salyon!' Liviana's face and neck had gone very red. I suspected Salyon was exposing some painful truths.

'Look at her!' he said coldly. 'What you see before you is an addict. It's disgusting. And I would be just like her, if it wasn't for the fact that the drug makes me ill.'

'I'm afraid I don't understand what you're implying,' I said.

'If you say any more,' Liviana said in a chilly tone, 'you will put Rayojini in a very dangerous position. Salyon, you know that. Have a little sense.'

'All right,' he said, 'but let me ask her again why she's so interested in them.'

'Strange things have been happening to me,' I said. 'I think the artisans might be connected with them.'

Salyon smiled. 'Strange things have been happening to the artisans too, Rayojini. What a coincidence.'

320

'Oh, such as?'

'Maladies, suicides . . . People like yourself asking unusual questions.'

'Really! Well, believe me, that sounds positively infinitessimal in comparison with the peculiarities I've encountered!'

'Oh, but it isn't. Artisans don't commit suicide, and neither do people ask questions about them, ordinarily.'

'I would like to talk to an artisan. Could you arrange that?'

'Me?' He laughed. 'No, I don't think I could.' He glanced at his sister who stood rigid with anxiety beside him; she was clearly terrified of what he might say next. 'If you have any sense, mistress, you will leave the city as soon as you can, and stop asking questions. It will get you nowhere, I promise you.'

At these words, Liviana visibly slumped her shoulders in relief. She rubbed her face with her hands. 'We must not speak of this any longer,' she said. 'Rayo, I'm sorry. Enjoy your time with us. Let's go for walks, visit the theatre, go dancing; anything. We are friends. Go back to Taparak with happy memories of Sacramante, and *forget the artisans*. Enjoy their work for what it is, Rayo. You have your own craft. You are safe. Forget them.'

'I . . .' I looked at Salyon, who raised his brows. The expression could have meant anything.

'Let's go back into the garden,' Liviana said, bravely cheerful. 'Dinner will be ready soon. Salyon?'

He bowed to us formally. 'Forgive me, ladies, I cannot escort you outside. I will see you at dinner. Until later, Mistress Rayojini.'

I smiled and inclined my head. He pulled a face at me and left the room.

'You must not pay too much attention to my brother,' Liviana said, linking her arm through mine and leading me to the door. 'He never fully recovered from his illness, you know.'

'Really? He looks pretty healthy to me,' I said, not exactly truthfully.

'It's his mind,' Liviana said, darkly. 'He is prone to strange fancies. We have to humour him.'

'Yes, I expect you do,' I answered. I wondered what it was she was hiding. What had she meant by her remark? 'You have your own craft. You are safe.' Her own, and Salyon's, insistence that I abandon my investigation of the artisans only fired my curiosity. What was going on in this city? The gods walked the road east from Bochanegra and the old families created in their high ateliers, reliving the dusty memories carved on ruined walls deep in the heart of Khalt. The old families created; the nomads' gods walked. The dead walked.

Out in the garden, Livvy had recovered her composure enough not to display the slightest sign of unrest to her waiting family.

321

'You spoke to Salyon?' her mother asked me. 'He remembers you, of course. We could never repay what your mother did for him.'

'Yes, we met,' I said. 'He seems to be in good health now.'

The Tricante matriarch frowned. 'Yes, but he is an outsider now. Very strange. Sometimes I feel he lives in a different world from ours.' She smiled vaguely. 'Still, we are thankful he survived his illness.'

Liviana pressed my hand briefly, and pushed me into a seat. She attempted to restore the atmosphere of our earlier sojourn in the garden, but no amount of frivolous chatter and cavorting could deceive me now. I had an inkling there was a razor-sharp intellect, a shrewd individual cocooned within the fluff of Livvy's persona. There was another side to Sacramante, something which I'd caught an echo of as a girl, something which intrigued and seduced the unwary. Liviana was an initiate of these mysteries, but I knew I'd never learn its secrets from her.

I was anxious to get back to The Temple Gate and talk to Keea. I wanted to make arrangements for him to take me to the libraries as soon as possible. However, despite my sense of urgency, the company of the Tricantes was intoxicating. They fed me with exquisite viands and then dragged me back into the twilit garden, where perfumed torches illumed the autumn evening, and they begged me for soulscaping tales. I love telling stories, so I was hopelessly seduced. Salyon hovered like a spectre at the back of the family group; I could feel his attention and knew he wished to speak to me alone. It was a sentiment I reciprocated, but I doubted whether Liviana would allow me to speak to her brother in private. By the time the Tricante parents got to their feet and sent one of their servants to prepare the family carriage to take me back to my lodgings, it was well past midnight. I had had no opportunity to speak to Salyon but several times I made a point of mentioning where I was staying, in the hope he'd pick up the hint. Liviana wanted to make plans for us to meet up one evening, and assured me she could find me some work should I need it. Now I wasn't sure I'd be staying in Sacramante long enough for that, but I thanked her warmly and promised to call at her home over the next couple of days.

'I will give you precisely two days,' she said, 'and if you haven't turned up by then, I shall send my carriage to The Temple Gate to kidnap you.'

'I'm sure that won't be necessary,' I said, kissing her cheek briefly.

'Remember what we talked about,' she whispered in my ear, returning the kiss.

'You too,' I said.

The Temple Gate was quiet when I returned, which was unusual for an inn in Sacramante at that hour. I did not expect Keea to be in the building, because I was convinced he was more familiar with Sacramante and its residents than he led me to believe. On the way back to the inn, I had considered the possibility that Keea himself might have some connection with the artisans. It would certainly explain how whoever was following me was aware of my every move. He was a difficult creature to assess in many ways. Physically, he did not appear as fey as the artisans I had seen at close quarters (and that had been a long time ago), but there was definitely something about him that hinted of *difference*. Maybe that was contrived. Still, if he was in league with the artisans he might be a threat to me. How could I determine his position? I'd learned that honesty was the last thing to expect from him. Perhaps I should face him out with what I knew and observe his reaction.

Terissa was sitting on duty behind the registration counter looking bored. I went over to chat to her for a few minutes before going upstairs. She looked up and smiled when she saw me, and then, with a furtive glance to either side, beckoned me closer. 'Rayojini, listen,' she hissed in a theatrical whisper. 'There is a visitor for you in the salon who's been waiting for hours.'

'Who?'

'No name . . . but . . .' She glanced into the salon, which was lit only by the fire burning in the huge hearth. 'I felt I recognised him. I have tried to keep him here, like you asked me. I have primed him with brandy!'

I gripped her hand in excitement. 'Well done, Terissa!' I said. A man? That was different.

Terissa pulled my hand to bring my ear close to her mouth. I could smell the clove freshness of her breath. 'It is an artisan, Rayojini, I am sure of it.' Her eyes were bright with excitement. She was clearly impressed by my recent train of august visitors.

'Then let's hope his patience is enduring,' I whispered back and patted her cheek. 'Thank you.'

I advanced cautiously towards the salon, nervous that my discovery would be the same as before: nothing but an empty seat, a mocking coin. However, my anxiety was unfounded, because there was definitely a shadowy figure seated in a wide, high backed chair next to the fire. It was turning a glass in its hands; long, pale hands. I could see little else, other than the shape, but for a few seconds my heart leapt in hope. Beth. Beth.

'Good evening!' I said loudly, marching over to the fire. 'You wanted to see me?'

My visitor raised his face and for a moment I was quite literally stunned, although it was not Beth Metatronim. He was radiant; eyes so dark in the dim light they looked like the purple-black of death lilies. His face was smooth, the skin taut over sculpted bones, his lips as fine as if painted by the most delicate brush-strokes. An

323

abundance of curling reddish-black hair fell over his loose white shirt, catching the ruby tints of the dull flames in the hearth. A cloak was draped carelessly over the back of the chair. I suddenly remembered where and who I was and closed my lolling mouth. My visitor smiled and put down his glass in the hearth.

'Mistress Rayojini?' He spoke to me in Tappish. Just a short phrase and most of that my name, yet the accent was perfect, the inflection precise.

'That is me,' I replied. 'And whom do I have the honour of addressing?'

He stood up and bowed formally, switching to the Bochanegran tongue. 'I am Avirzah'e Tartaruchi.'

The name was instantly reinforced by information from my memory. I remembered the milling crowd, a youthful Liviana pushing her way to the front of it, an arrogant male beauty courting praise. So long ago; a moment past.

'Ah, the playwright!' I said. But surely that was impossible? This man was so young. If he had written the play I had seen with the Tricantes all those years ago, he must have been an infant prodigy, and the haughty Tartaruchi who'd wooed his adoring audience after the performance had been no child. This would have to be a relative, perhaps the son.

He smiled more widely. 'You are familiar with my work?'

I shrugged, aware of how I was slipping into a kind of reverent awe for this man; seduced by his beauty, his candid smile. Years ago, I had despised that tendency in the Sacramantans. I tried to inject a reserved stiffness into my voice. 'Well, I did think so, but now I can see that isn't possible. A long time ago a friend of mine took me to see a play at the coliseum here. Of course, it could not have been one of yours. You are . . . Well, as I said, it was a long time ago.'

He did not pursue the topic.

'So might I ask why you want to see me?'

He pulled a rueful face. 'Forgive me. It must seem so . . . clandestine, me turning up here in the middle of the night.' By Sacramantan standards, this was hardly the middle of the night but more like early evening. He obviously expected me to be unfamiliar with city customs. 'Is there somewhere more private we could talk perhaps?'

'Forgive *me*, Avirzah'e Tartaruchi, but in the light of recent events in my life, I am loath to put myself in a private situation with anyone I don't know – however respectable they seem. Can we not talk here?'

He looked mournful. 'Do you think I mean to harm you?'

'May I ask you a further forthright question in return before I answer that? Have you, or any of your colleagues, been following me recently?'

324

He raised a perfectly arched eyebrow very slowly; a hopelessly sensual gesture. 'What reason would I have to do that?'

I pressed my fingers against my eyes and then gestured with them emphatically. 'Look, one of us is going to have to answer sometime. Please, indulge me and give me a straight reply.'

He sat down, his hands languidly trailing over the arms of the chair, putting his head on one side quizzically and fixing me with a powerful and lovely stare. 'I have not met you before, Rayojini. Have not seen you before. I admit of having heard of you, however.'

I exhaled noisily and sat down in a chair beside him, pulling it closer to the fire. 'Good, good. Thank you. The answer to your first question is that I do not exactly *expect* you to harm me, but it could be a possibility. Therefore I would like to avoid circumstances where such a possibility could be realised. The answer to your second question, as to why you should want to harm me anyway, I rather hope you can tell me yourself. Why are the artisans, or perhaps *one* artisan, interested in me? I'm finding it increasingly annoying that the reason for this has not been revealed to me. The games are entertaining, I suppose, but what is the point of them?'

He opened his arms, the hands uncurling like buds into pale flowers. 'The artisans tend to work in metaphor. We create continually and sometimes our meaning escapes the . . . no, I can't call you unenlightened.' He curled up again and leaned towards me confidentially. 'I really would rather speak to you alone.'

'We are alone.'

'This is a public place. You have nothing to fear from me; you are perfectly safe. I have important information for you. It does concern your welfare, yes, but the threat is not from my direction.'

I narrowed my eyes at him. 'You cannot expect me to believe you are that concerned for my safety – a stranger. What is all this to you?'

He steepled his fingers and tapped his lips. 'Sorry, I will not speak aloud here.'

I sighed, hoping I wasn't going to regret this. 'Very well, is my room private enough?'

'It should be adequate.'

Accompanied by the frank and open-mouthed stare of Terissa, I led Avirzah'e Tartaruchi upstairs.

In my room, he closed the windows and twitched the drapes across them. I watched his security precautions with something akin to amusement, but they also discomfited me a little. Had it been foolish to bring him up here? He sat down in a chair against the curtains and I sat on the bed, keeping a safe distance between us.

'Well,' I said. 'I can call for some wine, if you like.'

He shook his head. 'No, I am adequately refreshed.'

'So, what is your information, then?'

'Rayojini, I will speak plainly,' he said. 'The most sensible thing I can impart is to urge you, in the strongest terms, to return immediately to Taparak.'

'Mmm. Why?'

'For your well-being.'

'I see. That is most considerate of you. what if I ignore your advice?'

He stared at me for a moment. 'You seek to throw red meat to the lion, don't you? You are trying to provoke me. How brave you are and yet so ignorant. You do not understand. I cannot, dare not, harm you.'

'I am relieved. Who are the artisans, Avirzah'e Tartaruchi? Am I right in thinking their blood-lines are rooted in the Strangeling?'

He smiled, a little taken aback by my remark. 'You have been busy!'

'Not really. Information just seems to fall in my path. It's very strange. Well?'

'I really think you should temper your unpalatable inquiries, mistress! I am not prepared to discuss the history of my people with you.'

I forced a laugh. 'This all sounds very intriguing! First you tell me you have information for me, now you're telling me to leave the city and keep my mouth shut . . .'

He shrugged.

'Let's just get back to basics for a moment,' I said. 'How did you know I was staying here? Did the Tricantes contact you?' Perhaps Livvy had arranged an interview with an artisan for me after all, but not in quite the manner I had envisaged.

Now Avirzah'e laughed quietly, not at all amused. 'Rayojini, for someone who knows this city as well as I do, it is a simple procedure to discover where a nosy soulscaper is staying.'

'You mean you didn't find out from the artisan who has been following me around?'

He frowned. 'No artisan has been following you around, mistress. You have my word.'

'I am in awe of your influence if you can speak for all your people in that way!' I said. 'How do you know my pursuer isn't an artisan?'

He sighed. 'Well, to be honest, I don't; but if it is, I cannot imagine who it might be.'

'Not Gimel Metatronim?'

He shook his head. 'No, sorry.'

'Why apologise?'

He hesitated.

'You *know*, don't you!' I said. 'Are you familiar with the Metatronims?'

He looked faintly embarrassed. 'Well, of course I know them.'

'They have haunted me since childhood,' I said. It was a raw moment. Avirzah'e looked me straight in the eye.

'I know,' he said, softly. I felt he was trying to tell me I was not alone in that. Suddenly, things became clear to me. Avirzah'e Tartaruchi knew the Metatronims were interested in me. I had a feeling they were interested in him, too, and he was trying to warn me off. I wondered what they had done to him. He looked positively haunted.

'I appreciate your gesture,' I said. 'I know what you are trying to do.'

'You do?'

I nodded. 'Yes. Avirzah'e, if I may be so informal, how much do you know of the history of your race?'

'I am familiar with most of it.'

'Does the term "Host of Helat" mean anything to you?'

He looked wary. 'No. Should it?'

'I have discovered something,' I said. 'Can I trust you?'

'Rayojini, we are strangers!' I felt he was trying to back away from me. What was he afraid of?

'Well, I shall tell you something anyway. It might explain why the people you insist aren't interested in me *are* interested in me. I believe the artisans in Sacramante are descended from an ancient race who once populated the Strangeling. There is evidence they once had . . . I don't know . . . power. Now, I believe someone is trying to rekindle that power. I know it sounds outrageous, but I am sure certain of your people are involved.'

'This is indeed bizarre!'

I laughed. 'I do not believe this is a revelation to you! Why else would you come here and tell me to leave the city?'

He leaned forward. 'I have not conducted myself well, mainly I suspect, because I underestimate you. Rayojini, please listen to me very carefully. You were led to Sacramante for a purpose, yes, but events have gone awry and it is now very hazardous for you here. You can be sure, if you trust my word, that if you abandon your investigations no harm will come to any of your people. The situation is being dealt with by the individuals most equipped to understand it. You will only complicate matters if you insist on getting involved.'

'Stop!' I said, raising my hands. 'Avirzah'e, I want to see Gimel Metatronim.'

He lowered his eyes. 'That is impossible. You can't.'

'Why not?'

'She . . . cares for you very deeply, Rayojini, don't ever doubt that. She has made a mistake, that is all. She cannot see you.'

'Why?'

'Because of the way you are!' he exclaimed. 'She cannot trust herself!'

327

I flinched back as if he'd physically struck me. 'Please! I have to understand. All these years I've thought I've been suffering from delusions. I've tried so hard to deny what my instincts have been telling me. Now, at last, I realise my fantasies are real! Can't you see how important this is to me as a soulscaper? Please, tell me what's happening!' I could hear the ragged anguish in my own voice. This was probably one of the most important moments in my life. It had been real all along. I had proof now!

The interview had plainly become painful for both of us. Avirzah'e stood up. 'Look, Gimel has instructions to silence you. As I said, she cares for you deeply, but there are others involved who don't share her concern. For the good of the many, the few may be sacrificed. This message comes from her, Rayojini. From Gimel's heart. Please listen to it. Leave Sacramante! Go home!'

'If I do that, I shall have to report everything I've learned to my Guild,' I said as a threat.

He raised his hands expressively, clutched air. 'Then do so, but just leave!'

And when representatives from Taparak arrived to take up the trail, they would find every path led nowhere. The evidence would be gone, the mess tidied away. I was sure of that. If I let go of the thread now, I would lose the Metatronims for ever, and the mystery they were a part of would remain unsolved for eternity. 'Avirzah'e, I have to speak to her,' I said, in a low, persistent voice. 'I won't leave Sacramante until I've seen her.'

He sighed heavily and there was a moment's strained silence. 'Very well, I'll see what I can do, but there can be no promises,' he said.

'When? Tomorrow?'

He shook his head. 'I don't know. Maybe. Will you be here tomorrow?'

I thought quickly. The word 'library' flashed through my mind. 'In the afternoon, yes. I have to visit a friend in the morning. It's unavoidable.'

'Wait here, then. I will try to send word to you.'

I stood up. 'Thank you, Avirzah'e. I appreciate what you're doing.'

'Mistress Rayojini, do not for one minute imagine you know what I'm doing. If you knew half of what you think you do, you'd be out of here on the first ship.'

'You can't believe that!' I said.

He took my hand in his own and brushed it with his lips. 'No,' he said, 'I don't.'

'Avirzah'e, is Beth Metatronim still in Sacramante too?'

He smiled uneasily. 'Are you going to demand I bring him to you as well?'

I shrugged. 'I am just curious.'

'Yes, he is in Sacramante. In my house, as it happens.' I thought I read the underlying message correctly.

'I see. You are indeed familiar with the Metatronims, then.'

'Very. Thus, their concerns are mine. I wouldn't speak to one such as yourself lightly.'

'And what is "one such as myself"?' I asked.

'Untouched,' he replied. 'And a wise, handsome woman. I must go now. Do nothing rash, Rayojini. Wait for my word.'

'I will.'

He bowed courteously and left the room. For a few moments, I slumped back on the bed, my mind whirling. I felt full of wild anticipation, which was half dread. Untouched am I? No. Avirzah'e was wrong. I remembered the scrying-rite of my childhood. They had touched me then. They had been with me since. Why? What was I to them? Why had they led me to Sacramante? For what purpose? And what had happened for them to change their minds? They would not dismiss me without an explanation; I would not let them. They had become part of me, part of my life. At times I had hated them and yet, should I lose their presence for ever – which I suspected might be the case now that their connection with me had been revealed – I felt that my existence would be impoverished. Life without Gimel, especially, was unthinkable to me now.

'Much pleasure we have lost, while we abstained
from this delightful fruit, nor known till now true
relish, tasting . . .'
Paradise Lost, Book IX

The journey back from the Strangeling had been one of tense
silence. I was furious with Sammael, and had been deeply humiliated by the Harkasite who had accosted me with nothing but a
common threat. Suddenly, it seemed as if my contribution to eloim
well-being was no longer needed. Sammael had swept in, literally
out of nowhere, after having ignored his people for centuries, and
had taken over responsibility for their future. It was as if my voice
was no longer heard. But what else had I expected when I coaxed
Sammael out of his Tower? Everything that had happened since
had been a predestined inevitability. If I had not brought Sammael
back to the eloim, someone else would have done; his reemergence
was simply part of the pattern. I had no business to feel upset by
the way he wanted to handle the situation. In comparison to him I
was expendable. One thing I could not swallow comfortably, however, was the fact that he wanted me to get rid of Rayojini. My
reaction to this suggestion made me realise I was more interested
in the soulscaper as a person than as an answer to our problems.
We were like sisters, in a way. I remember how she had fought
against my presence in the past, and how in secret moments she
had opened her heart to me, telling me she knew I wasn't real, but
that in many ways I was more real to her than anything. How I
had longed to reveal myself to her at those times. Perhaps I should
have done. Perhaps she should have been aware from the very first
moment just how involved we were. Would she have fought against
me still? I had tried to perceive her several times on the way home
from the Strangeling, but all my attempts at projection had been
met by a shadowy murk. I suspected my concentration was at fault;
I was too nervy. At least I could be thankful Amelakiveh was
with her. He knew how important Rayojini was to me, and would
therefore do everything in his power to protect her. If only he
would be a little more diligent about communicating regularly with
me.

Metatron had tried to take me to the family stronghold with him,
but I was firm against his entreaties. 'I have to go to my brother,'

I said. 'Drop me off and take Sammael home with you. Give me a rest.'

'Don't attempt any unwise alliances,' Metatron had replied, stiffly. I would not respond to that.

Avirzah'e lived in an apartment in a distant wing of the Tartaruchi court, which had its own yard and private entrance. I was absurdly calm as I alighted from the carriage, even though I had no real idea how I would be received, or what I might discover. I suppose a weight had fallen from my shoulders now I was ridding myself of the oppressive company of Sammael and my father. I was going to tell Beth everything. We would have to decide what to do about Rayojini.

The door to Avirzah'e's home was reached by a long flight of iron steps, which led to a balcony. Avirzah'e himself responded to my tug on the bell-rope. He looked distinctly ungroomed when he opened the door, which surprised me, but then I had never called on him unexpected at home before.

'Gimel,' he said, in a carefully neutral tone.

'Did Beth receive my message?' I asked. 'He *is* still here, isn't he?'

'He is still here.'

'Well, I would like to see him.' I stalked past Avirzah'e into his apartment. It comprised one huge room, with a sleeping gallery at one end and a small observatory at the other, both reached by flights of uncarpeted steps. There was very little furniture but many rugs and cushions on the floor. The walls were of bare grey stone, their starkness relieved only by a couple of hanging Deltan tapestries. Books and piles of manuscript lay everywhere. It was clearly not a place designed for receiving guests. I did not think Avirzah'e even had a servant.

'Where is he?' I asked.

'In the observatory,' Avirzah'e replied. 'You look tired, Gimel. May I fetch you a drink?'

'A fortified aperitif would be most welcome.'

He grinned. 'I have nothing fortified, but could squeeze you a drop if you're desperate.'

I gazed at him candidly. 'Straight wine will suffice, Avirzah'e. Don't put yourself out. My sustenance habits haven't changed.' I pulled off my gloves and threw them on to a cushion.

Avirzah'e smiled in an irritatingly knowing manner, and indicated for me to go to Beth. I picked my way through the room and went up into the observatory. Beth was perched on a high stool beside the great curved windows, making sketches of the trees outside. He was so absorbed in his task, he did not notice me for a moment, during which time I took the opportunity to scan him carefully. He appeared healthy and content (hadn't he missed me at all?), and to me he was the most beautiful creature alive. A fierce stab of

332

jealousy travelled painfully through my body.

'Beth?'

He glanced round, brushing his hair out of his eyes. 'Gimel! You're back!'

The surprised welcome in his eyes seemed genuine enough. 'Yes.' I held out my arms and he jumped down off his stool to embrace me. He smelt delicious, but it was not his usual scent. 'I have much to tell you,' I said.

He brushed my cheek with his fingers. 'Sandalphon has been here,' he said, and shook his head. 'What *have* you been doing, beloved? I should not have left you for a moment.'

Avirzah'e had padded in silently behind us. 'A touching reunion,' he said, handing me a glass. Beth stepped away from me and the power flowed back to Avirzah'e. I could sense that, like myself, Beth and Avirzah'e were committed to caution at this point. No doubt my message had puzzled them. It had been rather melodramatic.

'Give me your coat, Gimel,' Avirzah'e said. 'Let's go and sit down, shall we?'

'I am a mess,' I said. 'I have been travelling.'

'Haven't you!'

I gave him my coat with a hard glance and swept back into the main room. I knew that it would be easy to slip into an extended game of manners with Avirzah'e, but there was no good reason to waste any more time. If I ordered Beth to come home with me, where I could talk to him in private, it would make my brother sulky and distant. I could not deal with one of his moods now and knew that, whatever my personal feelings, Avirzah'e would have to hear my news as well. I would be frank with them both, and trust that the Tartaruch would curb his impertinence and realise the importance of what I had to say. Beth and Avirzah'e lay down on the rugs, while I chose a position of advantage and arranged myself on a higher pile of black and red cushions. Then, sipping the wine Avirzah'e had brought me, I told them, without pausing, all that had occurred since we had parted company at the Castile. Well, I told them *nearly* all. Even though it was one of the most important issues, I found I was reluctant to mention my conjunction with Sammael. I was actually embarrassed about it, sure that once I had told them, Avirzah'e would humiliate me in some way. I had had to eat my words, even my principles. I shrank from admitting I might have been wrong about conjunction. Still, there was so much astounding information to impart, I doubted whether Beth or Avirzah'e noticed when I hesitated in my narrative. Passing swiftly to the subject of Rayojini, I intimated how concerned I was about Sammael's pronouncement.

'Amelakiveh must have brought her to the city by now,' I said. 'Has he contacted you, Beth?'

My brother frowned. 'No. I haven't had contact with him for weeks. I assumed you had, though.'

'He is sometimes difficult to locate,' I said. 'There may be interference, of course.' I sighed. 'I am going to have to face Rayojini now. It's very strange: I want to, but I am nervous about it. I suppose I have enjoyed our rather peculiar attachment over the years. Seeing each other in the flesh will end it all, won't it? Inevitable, of course.'

Avirzah'e scowled at me. 'Gimel, you have met this soulscaper before, haven't you?'

I was still resentful of him having to be involved in this discussion and answered sharply. 'Well, yes, in a way. I *saw* her once. We saw each other. It was a long time ago.'

'Precisely,' Avirzah'e said. 'And if you meet her again now, it is hardly going to help matters, is it?'

'Why ever not?' I demanded sharply. I didn't think it was any of his business.

'Think, Gimel. You met her when she was hardly more than a child. Now, she is a woman. She has aged. You have not. Isn't she going to wonder why? It will only make her want to know more about you, surely?'

'Oh,' I said, crestfallen. 'I see what you mean.' Avirzah'e's words could not be disputed. Concealing our virtual immortality was one of the most crucial aspects of our camouflage. Because I felt so intimate with Rayojini, it simply hadn't occurred to me that she, like any other human, would wonder why I hadn't changed. I wanted it not to matter.

'You have to agree with Sammael, to a degree,' Avirzah'e said. 'We must get Rayojini out of Sacramante.'

'We?' I said.

He shrugged. 'Well, as you've told me this much, I supposed you were including me in your plans at last. In a way we are relatives now, Gimel.'

I glanced at Beth, who returned my gaze steadily. He did not contest that, damn him; he did not appear even faintly ashamed. 'So, how do you propose *we* persuade Rayojini to leave?' I said.

'I will go and find her,' Avirzah'e replied smoothly. 'I will speak to her.'

'Why should you do that?' I asked. 'Surely we should simply give Amelakiveh further instructions.'

'That would seem to be difficult since you haven't heard from him in some time.'

I narrowed my eyes at Avirzah'e. 'You are curious about her, aren't you? That's the real reason you want to talk to her yourself.'

He nodded. 'Of course I'm curious. You are very fond of this Rayojini creature. Therefore she must be an extremely intriguing individual.' He spiced his flattery with an ingratiating smile. Uneasily, I felt myself responding warmly to him. His attempts to influence me favourably were endearing, if rather pitiful.

'So we have established your reason,' I said, 'and I have to admit it is unlikely Rayojini will remember you from the time she was last in Sacramante. After all, you meant nothing to her then.'

'And I mean nothing to her now,' he agreed. 'It seems to me that for her own safety we should persuade her to return to Taparak for a while. We must hope our situation will soon be resolved one way or another. After that perhaps it will be feasible to contact Rayojini again. That is what you want, isn't it?'

'It might never be practicable,' I said.

'Depending on the outcome of Sammael's strategy, naturally . . . However, supposing the outcome is auspicious: I know what you did to Amelakiveh, and I suspect you have something similar in mind for your soulscaper if she's agreeable.' He raised his brows. 'Haven't you?'

'You are impertinent!' I snapped. Beth must have told him about Amelakiveh. The boy's transmutation was at best an indiscretion, at worst a heresy. He was supposed to have been a holy sacrifice, after all. Instead of suffering the sacred death, for which he had been raised, we had prolonged his lifespan instead and taken him into our home like a pet. We had transgressed on two counts: unauthorised transmutation and abuse of a revered ceremony. Still, I could not believe our actions were unique. Other delectable patron children, offered in holy sacrifice, must have been the subjects of similar transgressions over the years. Who knew what went on in the highest rooms of the atelier courts? Oddly enough, I had never considered introducing Rayojini to the benefits of an intimate friendship with Beth and myself. My interest in her had always been something out of the ordinary, something which transcended desire and gratification; a feeling which I hoped was reciprocated. However, Avirzah'e's suggestion did deserve consideration, if only because it might solve any problems concerning eloim security. Could Sammael object to Rayojini's presence in our life if she was allowed the transmutation and absorbed into our community like Ramiz and Tamaris? Unfortunately I did not know, and could not guess, how Rayojini might react if I revealed my true nature to her. She was such an independent creature, it was likely she'd furiously resent the way in which she'd been manipulated over the years. Telling her the truth might estrange her from me completely. As a human needing sustenance, she'd be expected by the Parzupheim (who alone could grant valid permission for her change) to remain in Sacramante. This I knew would go against her roaming instincts. Unless, of course, I went travelling with her myself. As I thought about it, the idea became more attractive. Yet another of Avirzah'e's insidiously seductive suggestions!

He had given me a couple of moments to mull over his words.

335

'I do not wish to sound impertinent,' he said. 'Please believe that your contentment and security are foremost in my mind.'

Beth, sitting on the floor at my feet, reached out to touch my skirts. 'I am agreeable if you are,' he said.

I sighed. 'Oh very well. Find Rayojini and speak to her, Avirzah'e. Do what you can.'

He held out his hand to me. 'Sister,' he said.

I leaned forward and curled my fingers around his. 'I cannot call you brother, Avirzah'e', I said. 'It is too . . . unlikely.' There was a moment's silence.

'The message you sent me,' Beth said, as if he had only just remembered it. 'What did it mean?' I realised he had been waiting for this moment since I'd walked in.

Avirzah'e was still holding my hand. I was afraid he would simply melt into me if I spoke plainly. I pulled away from him. At that moment, of course, he knew.

'Sammael taught me many things,' I said. 'He spoke to me about – and demonstrated too – the suppressed nature of eloim in this world. Since this education, I have been forced to change my opinion about . . . certain things, that's all.'

'The mutual sup?' Avirzah'e said carefully.

I shrugged. 'We spoke of that, yes, and I now believe it is something we should consider for the future. It could only improve our relationship with humanity, if we still need to share their world.' I was beginning to feel slightly disorientated and breathless.

'And what else?' Avirzah'e asked. This was just what he enjoyed most: a game of words. I wanted to be calm, objective and frank; it was impossible. My eyes skittered away from Beth and Avirzah'e and their attentive stares.

'You conjoined with him!' Beth exclaimed bluntly. 'You did, didn't you! After all you said!'

'Do not look at me like that,' I replied. 'You went your own way, impetuously, without me.'

'With a stranger, though! Gimel, how could you!'

I felt absurdly unfaithful. 'You should have been more patient,' I said defensively. 'Anyway, Sammael can hardly be termed a stranger. He is father to us all, in a way.'

Beth shook his head. 'I should have been with you,' he said.

'But you weren't! Did you worry about my absence when you conjoined with Avirzah'e? No!' I hesitated. 'You have conjoined, haven't you?'

Avirzah'e laughed. 'I wish you could hear yourself, Gimel!' he mimicked my voice. *'I've done it, have you?'*

'Stop it!' I said.

Avirzah'e shrugged. 'Well, it is hardly a subject to be coy about.' He lay back luxuriously on his cushions, gazing at me through slitted eyes. I felt as if I were simply a character in one of his plays.

'Yes, Beth and I conjoined,' he said, and pointed lazily to the observatory. 'Up there, among the stars. We become at one with the past, and with the future. Now, we are at peace within ourselves.'

His smug expression made me angry; enviously angry. He and Beth must have fondness for each other; therefore their conjunction had involved more than simple experience. It must have been a journey, a wondrous journey, a shared instant of life. Conjunction with Sammael, for all its wild intensity, had not been like that for me. I had not become light beneath the stars with a lover. Avirzah'e had stolen that experience from me, and part of me would grieve its loss for ever. In my ignorance I had never imagined that anybody would come between Beth and myself. I had been unprepared for it, although I knew Avirzah'e would have been quite happy to pair with me instead of Beth, if I had been the willing party. I had a choice now. I could view him as an adversary or as a potential partner; it was entirely my decision. Avirzah'e would accept either rôle without overt complaint. But whatever I decided, Beth would still be his. My pride wanted me to walk out of there and leave them to it, but my heart spoke otherwise. I knew Avirzah'e wouldn't make this easy for me. He was a proud creature himself. Beth was simply a malleable reed bending between two strong currents; I could expect no useful support from him. The situation would require some thought. I remembered my father's words and vowed to make no rash decision.

'The journey has tired me,' I said into the silence, and stood up. 'I need to return home and refresh myself.'

'Gimel,' Avirzah'e said, not moving. 'Have you learned nothing?'

I stared down at him. He was utterly relaxed, stroking his throat. His shirt was hanging open. I could see the mark upon his chest. His fingers strayed to the wound and scratched its surface. The room filled with the perfume of his blood, the less definable perfume of his willingness to submit, and my mouth instinctively filled with fluid. I could feel the hunger frenzy within me waiting, just waiting, to be released. My decision. I could still walk out of here.

Avirzah'e undermined my resolution. 'If you are hungry,' he said, 'let me nourish you. Feed, Gimel. Finish this education Lord Sammael began for you. Isn't it the real reason you came here?'

The room swam before my eyes, and I had to sit down again quickly. I felt as if I were about to faint, and my stomach had begun to contract painfully – in time to the rhythm of my heart.

'Gimel,' Beth said and slipped his hands into my own. 'You are cold.' We looked at each other for a few long moments, and I could see he understood how I felt. If I wanted to leave, he would take me home. There was no compulsion on his part. I squeezed his hands with numb flesh.

'Show me,' I said slowly. 'I have to see it.'

He let go of my hands. I knew he was not hungry. I knew he had recently supped, but for my benefit, Beth pulled Avirzah'e's shirt down past his shoulders and kissed a small mouthful of ichor from the wound on his chest. I had expected to feel as if I were witnessing an obscenity, something unnatural, but the sight of eloim feeding from eloim seemed bizarrely mundane. It was as if a memory had resurfaced in my mind, a remembered instinct. Beth wiped his mouth and looked at me inquiringly. The hunger had quietened within me. No urgency now, but a gentle need to taste. I knelt down upon the floor and allowed Avirzah'e to pull me against his body. I felt like a human infant being pulled to its mother's breast, mindlessly seeking the teat, smelling out the place where the skin was broken. His arms tightened around me, and I heard him gasp as I began to suck. The taste was intoxicating, so different from the thick, sweet fluid of the human body. I had an urge, almost, to suck him dry. His spine arched at the moment when pleasure became pain. I was virtually delirious when Beth wound his hand in my hair and pulled me away. I gasped like a swimmer who has been underwater too long, whose instinct is to try and breathe fluid. Air tasted raw and gritty in my throat. I clawed and snarled; a feral thing pulled away from her prey. My chin, my throat, the front of my gown were all spotted with Avirzah'e's blood. He lay beneath me, panting, perhaps dazed. Fiercely, I fought my way out of Beth's hold, who cried out when I threw myself on Avirzah'e again. There was no need for him to worry. It was the mouth I sought. The kiss. The kiss. Avirzah'e weakly wrapped his arms around me. I wept into his hair.

338

'. . . that I who erst contended with gods . . . am now constrained into a beast . . .'
Paradise Lost, Book IX

Sammael was sitting in my salon when I returned home. He had taken a pile of my books from the shelf and was looking through them. I was not happy to find him there; I felt distinctly shaken and dishevelled after my visit to the Tartaruchi stronghold. I had not conjoined with Beth or Avirzah'e, but the supping had become mutual and had culminated in a rather abandoned session of fleshly pleasures. I was astounded at myself, and needed time to reflect.

Sammael smiled sweetly when he saw me and made no remark on my appearance. 'Gimel, I have come here for privacy,' he said. 'I hope you don't mind.'

'Not at all,' I replied. 'Treat my home as if it were your own.' Tamaris had followed me into the room to fuss about me and I sent her off to prepare my bath. I sank wearily on to one of the couches, short of breath.

'I will have to prepare myself,' Sammael said.

'For what?' I scratched at my head; my scalp felt gritty.

'I am going to remember my true form. Whatever has come from Elenoen will undoubtedly be attracted to me if I resume a more spiritual contour. It is the only way.' He paused. 'Have you a place where I will not be disturbed for a few days? It might take some time for me to accomplish the transformation. I have been in this body for so long.'

'Of course,' I said. 'There is a room I use for projection, at the top of the house. It should be ideal for your purposes.' In the wake of recent events, I found it hard to concentrate on the grave difficulties facing our race. The taste of, and my need for, Avirzah'e's blood was more real to me than anything else. All I wanted to do was relax into my bath and relive everything I had experienced in the Tartaruchi stronghold. Sammael looked vaguely irritated, sensing he did not have my attention. I was being very selfish. Sammael was not as confident as he sounded. He needed to talk to me. 'Are you strong enough?' I asked him. 'Remember you haven't been out of your Tower for very long, and the journey to the Strangeling was exhausting. Perhaps you should wait.'

He shook his head. 'Impossible. Now I know that Elenoen has intruded upon this world, I shall have to deal with it immediately.

Anything could have been sent through. Anything!'

'You are hoping it is Mikha'il, aren't you,' I said gently.

Sammael smiled at me with chagrin. 'You are perceptive.'

I leant back against the couch and closed my eyes. 'No, not that. I understand your feelings.'

'My hope goes beyond mere personal feelings,' Sammael said. With my eyes closed, undistracted by his physical appearance, I sensed that, if he spoke the truth, his hope did not extend *very far* beyond personal feeling. Why should he feel ashamed of that? If his relationship with Mikha'il had been anything like what I had experienced that afternoon, I understood completely why it was so important to him.

'You are hoping to win him over?' I asked. 'Surely, for that reason, he would not be sent here?' I opened my eyes and sat up straight.

Sammael was not looking at me. 'It isn't easy for eloim from the old world to manifest themselves here,' he said. 'It takes times. I am different from all other eloim on Earth, as you will have noticed. I do not suffer from the effects of time, as the ancients do. Manifestation in this world was also far easier for me than for those that followed me. Mikha'il has the same advantage. We are brothers, remember. I know he will be contaminated by propaganda about me. He does not share my independent spirit, but there is still a chance I can open his eyes.'

'And if you do, what then?' I asked. 'What is going to happen to us afterwards? Even if you can remove the threat from Elenoen, we still have other problems to deal with – the rightful occupants of this world, for example.'

He looked at me steadily. 'I don't know what will happen afterwards. It's impossible to predict at this point . . . Have you decided what you're going to do about the soulscaper?'

A timely change of subject. I nodded. 'Yes. Avirzah'e Tartaruchi will deal with the problem. You don't have to worry.'

'I am very sorry about having to change your plans. I know how much they meant to you.'

I shrugged. 'It can't be helped.'

I insisted he take further sustenance from Tamaris, and then had her show him to my tower room. Meanwhile I took my bath and as the refreshing, fragrant water lapped over my skin, I spent a brief time indulging in delicious memories of all the wonderful new sensations I had experienced in Avirzah'e's house, in the arms of Beth and his lover. Then I went to my bedroom to sleep, instructing Tamaris to wake me in three hours.

Upon waking, I felt alert and spry, and able to apply myself to external matters once more. The wound on my chest itched a little and I had Tamaris anoint it with salve. Remembering what Sammael had told me about how supping repeatedly from the same area caused a messy injury, I decided that, if this were going to become a regular habit, I would have to devise a way to minimise discomfort and damage. Perhaps Avirzah'e, Beth and I had been too rough with each other; we would have to experiment.

I tried to contact Amelakiveh once more, but with no success. Neither could I fix myself on the presence of Rayojini. Had Amelakiveh brought her to Sacramante yet? And, if not, where were they? Avirzah'e intended to search for my soulscaper that night. I had no doubt, given his widespread information network, that he would find her if she was in the city, but I was concerned that I could not contact my dependant. Had he been intercepted, or damaged? I confided in Tamaris, who offered to search the area herself. It had been prearranged that Amelakiveh would install Rayojini somewhere close to the atelier courts. Tamaris was sure she could find him: eloim-fed humans had a peculiar affinity for each other. By following her intuition, Tamaris would perhaps find Amelakiveh, and Rayojini, before Avirzah'e did.

'If you locate Amelakiveh, bring him here immediately,' I told her.

I intended to go into deep trance for a few hours while Tamaris was away, in the hope of finding something out for myself, but in the event I did not have the time. After only an hour Tamaris returned to the house, triumphantly bringing Amelakiveh with her. I sensed a certain animosity between them; he had not wanted to come. Strange. Did he resent anyone other than myself or Beth issuing orders? He had always been a difficult creature to fathom. I interviewed him formally in my salon.

'Where have you been?' I demanded. 'Why didn't you contact me?'

Amelakiveh, apparently in penitence, sank to his knees before me. 'Forgive me, my lady,' he said. 'Your soulscaper is a difficult woman to control. I have had to remain constantly by her side. It has drained my energy. I intended to contact you tomorrow, after I had rested.'

'Where is Rayojini now?' I asked, satisfied with his explanation. There *had* been a lot of interference in the aether recently.

'At this moment she is with the patron family Tricante. They are old friends of hers. We are staying at The Temple Gate inn, a few minutes' walk from here.'

'How is she?'

He smiled. 'She is in good health and fired with curiosity for her quest. I have made sure her interest was kept at peak level.'

'I have no doubt of that,' I replied, 'but there has been a change of plan. Someone will be visiting Rayojini tonight, in order to persuade her to leave the city. I would appreciate it if, in the morning, you could augment this person's persuasion with your

341

own. Get her out of Sacramante, Kiveh.'

'What?' Amelakiveh jumped to his feet, all deference fled. 'Why?'

'All I can tell you is that there have been new developments. We can no longer use the soulscaper. You must get her away from here. Far away.'

'I'm not sure she will do as I suggest. She is strong-willed . . .'

'I know that, Kiveh! I know it will be difficult, but there is no alternative.' I hesitated. 'Naturally, she must not be harmed in any way.'

He turned away from me, rubbing his jaw in thought. I realised I was facing an alarmingly independent soul. Had he wriggled off the leash somewhere between Khalt and Bochanegra? For some absurd reason I suspected he had plans of his own for Rayojini, plans I had just obstructed. Was it possible he had become emotionally attached to her? 'What are you going to do then, if not use the soulscaper?' he asked me.

I narrowed my eyes at his turned back. Perhaps it had been unwise to tell him as much as I had about eloim affairs. 'I do not think that is your concern, Kiveh.'

He turned around and faced me. 'I only ask because I am worried about you.'

'There is no need, I assure you.' I reached out to caress his face. 'You have done well, my beloved. I am sorry it has been for nothing. We were not to know, still . . .'

'She will ask questions. Do you intend to obliterate her memory?'

'I don't know. I really don't. Not yet.' In truth, I did not think that would be an easy thing to do to a Tap, especially a woman like Rayojini. 'The only thing I am sure of is that Rayojini must be removed from Sacramante. She must not stay in the vicinity of the eloim.'

He nodded. 'Then, of course, I will do everything I can to accomplish that.'

'You have enjoyed your excursion out into the world,' I said, 'haven't you?'

He looked a little sheepish. 'If I have been disrespectful, I apologise. The journey has been . . . stressful.'

I put my hands upon his shoulders. Away from the stifled atmosphere of the atelier courts, he had really bloomed. He seemed taller, bolder, stronger – and eminently attractive. 'Return to The Temple Gate in the morning,' I said. 'Tonight, I would like you to stay with me.'

He lowered his eyes, bashful as a virgin. I put my hand beneath his hair to draw him to me for a kiss, but he caught my fingers in his own, apparently to examine my father's seal-ring, which I still wore. 'You are still leading the Metatronim throng in this time of crisis, then?' he said, kissing the ring.

'No,' I replied. 'Metatron has returned to Sacramante. I simply forgot to surrender the ring. I have been busy.' Kiveh slipped it from my finger and put it down on the table beside us. Then, he kissed me.

Avirzah'e arrived at my house early the next morning. He had spoken to Rayojini. I was so excited about what he had to tell me, I almost forgot to embrace him. He seemed distracted, anxious. Had the interview not gone as well as he'd hoped? Was Rayojini all right?

'I do not think I persuaded your soulscaper to leave the city,' he said. 'She has learned too much, perhaps. She is curious.' He fixed me with a steely stare. 'She is also adamant about seeing you, I'm afraid.'

I clutched my throat with reflexive fingers. 'I though we had decided that would be unwise.' Even as I said that, my spirit surged with pathetic hope.

'I know, but now that I have met her . . . Gimel, I feel we owe her at least a partial explanation.'

'You mean she is no longer "just a human" to you either?'

'I confess I found her interesting. She is very attached to you, even though I think she only realised while I was with her that you were a real person, and not a phantom of her mind.'

'So, what do you suggest we do?'

'I think I should bring her here to meet you, Gimel. Don't say it's something you don't want, because I know you do. I will bring her here this afternoon, if that's all right with you.'

I clutched his hands. 'Avirzah'e, I don't know what to say. I feel . . . this is going to be so exciting! I'm so glad!'

He kissed me warmly. 'Enjoy this meeting as much as you like, beloved. There might be dark days ahead.'

'Among the faithless, faithful only he; among
innumerable false, unmoved, unshaken, unseduced,
unterrified his loyalty he kept, his love, his
zeal . . .'
Paradise Lost, Book V

On the morning following Avirzah'e Tartaruchi's visit to my room,
Keea appeared at breakfast as before. I was relieved to see him,
but intended to be very selective about what I told him concerning
my discoveries. After all, I still had not defined his position in this
drama. By keeping information back, for once I would be in the
position of control. Still, if I really was going to have to meet
Gimel Metatronim in the flesh, I wanted to be armed with as much
knowledge as possible. Last night I had been given intriguing hints.
Perhaps the Sacramantan libraries would be able to expand upon
them. At the very least, I had to discover why the Taps had perceived no inkling of these strange currents in the world. It was
unprecedented.

'So how was your day yesterday?' Keea asked me, pouring syrup
over a bowl of fruit. 'Did you visit your friends?'

'Yes. I had a wonderful day. I feel much better.'

'You look it too, Rayo, if I may say so.'

'Thank you. So, what did you get up to yesterday? Did you
report to your employers?'

He smiled and sniggered. 'That is something I thought you no
longer had an interest in.'

I waggled my head a little. It was time to play a card. 'Well, I'm
interested in you, Keea. Do you know, I have a sneaking suspicion
you are connected, or even related in blood, to the artisans of
Sacramante. Am I right?'

He looked at me blandly. 'And what prompted this idea?'

'Your sense of the dramatic, I think. Well?'

'I'm flattered. But, no, I am not kin to the artisans.'

I shook my head. 'Oh dear, I was quite convinced. Never mind,
my other supposition is that you are apprenticed to an alchemist
who, in turn, is in league with the artisans.'

'My, you have been thinking hard! Why this sudden interest in
the artisans?' I could tell he was enjoying himself immensely.

'Keea, it is obvious there is a link between the Sacramantan
artisans and the Host of Helat.'

345

'There is? I find that hard to believe. The artisans are creatures of artifice; very shallow individuals.'

'I suspect you underestimate them! I assure you, the link *is* there.'

He shrugged. 'Very well, let us suppose you are right for the moment. Now explain why you think I should be connected with either the artisans or alchemists.'

'Well, this may sound a little insulting, but please take it in the most objective of spirits: I believe you used alchemical substances to warp my perception during the journey across Khalt, leading me to believe all kinds of strange business was going on. For some reason, I think the artisans have included me in a dramatic production of theirs. The scale is rather grand – the stage being the entire countries of Khalt and Bochanegra and perhaps even further afield. It seems logical to me that you are involved in this. Why else would you have been so insistent about accompanying me?'

'Maybe I just like you.'

'Don't insult my intelligence, Keea!'

He sighed. 'As you wish. May I ask what evidence you have to support your theory?'

I shrugged and took a big spoonful of fruit. 'Simple. Since you stopped feeding me, I've stopped hallucinating. I no longer feel as if I'm in an alien world. I prefer to attribute my feelings of disorientation in Khalt and the Strangeling to being drugged than to having experienced a warped reality.'

Keea shook his head and laughed. 'I'm mortified! You have uncloaked me utterly! Ah well, Rayo, it was fun while it lasted.'

I stared at him narrowly for a few seconds. 'Damn you, I'm nowhere near the truth, am I?'

He shrugged. 'No,' he said. 'You're not.'

I decided not to tell him about Tartaruchi at this juncture. I had no idea what Keea's real intentions were towards me. At best, I felt he was trying to occlude the precision of my thoughts. It was he who had instilled ideas into my head about how I would discover important information in the city, he who had tantalised my curiosity by showing me the ruined temple. Was he involved with the Metatronims or not? I should have asked Avirzah'e about him, but then I had not been thinking clearly the previous evening. As he sat there, an extremely attractive youth gulping down his breakfast, Keea seemed without artifice of any kind. I knew that to be an illusion, but it was still hard to see malice in him. Impulsively I reached out to touch his arm. 'This morning,' I said, 'you must take me to the libraries.' His eyes were lambent, catching the morning light, but was the radiance one of victory or gratitude? It was impossible to tell. He raised my hand to his lips and kissed it; I felt his teeth smooth against my skin.

'You are wise, soulscaper,' he said.

* * *

346

He took me to a cluster of dark old buildings, that hunched in the long shadows of the atelier courts. We climbed a steep hill, the morning full of the dolorous clang of bells. The scent of the sea filled my head, blended with the ripe aroma of autumn fruit. The strangeness of the journey west had distanced itself from my mindscape again; it would be easy to interpret all I had experienced as the wild fancies of a mind estranged from the bustle of society. Yet although I was still chasing shadows, now I thought I understood what cast them.

We approached a gate which was thickly encrusted with locks and chains. 'Not exactly welcoming,' I said. 'Are you sure these libraries are open to the public, Keea?'

He smiled at me. 'I can gain us entrance. Follow me.' He went around the side of the building and into an alley, which wooden boxes of rubbish and discarded bales of pulpy old news-sheets made difficult to negotiate. I picked my way through the obstacles behind Keea, and he eventually stopped before a small, iron-barred door.

'Back entrance?' I said. 'Are the caretakers friends of yours?'

He grinned, tapped his nose, and tugged on a bell-rope. It must have rung somewhere deep within the building; nothing could be heard from outside. There was no immediate response.

'Keea, there must be a main entrance somewhere,' I said. 'This is probably just some forgotten rear door at the end of a walled-off corridor, or something. Shouldn't we take a look around the front?'

'Have patience?' he said to me, and pulled the bell-rope again. After another short wait, we were rewarded by the sound of locks being wrestled with, and the door opened a fraction. I could not see who was inside. Keea pulled back his coat sleeve and extended his hand beyond the doorway. 'You know this seal?' he demanded in an authoritative voice. There was a mumble behind the door. 'Let us in,' Keea said. 'It is urgent we consult the archives.' The door creaked open a little wider and Keea beckoned to me. 'Be quick, Rayojini,' he said.

I entered a musty, gloomy corridor, where a stooped and robed ancient glared at me beadily. I smiled at him hopefully.

'She is not eloim!' the ancient snapped at Keea, and then peered at him suspiciously. 'And you . . . What are you?'

'The woman is Tappish,' Keea replied in a smooth voice, 'but in the employ of the Metatronim, as am I. We both have licence to be here.'

I listened to these words with amazement, but kept my silence.

'I have received no warning that the Metatronim wish to consult the archives!' the ancient said. 'This is most irregular. Neither is it normal practice for dependants to be sent here!'

'Would I carry Metatron's seal if this were not official business?'

Keea inquired silkily. 'Please, do not delay us. It might cause affront.'

The old man sighed and shook his head. 'Very well.'

'Show us the catalogue,' Keea said.

'This way, this way.' The old man shuffled off up the corridor and Keea gestured for me to follow.

'Since when have I been in the employ of the Metatronim?' I whispered, in awe of Keea's nerve at suggesting such a thing.

'Since you were eight years old?' he replied bluntly.

I cried out and clutched his arm, unable to move other than that. 'What? What did you say?'

'You heard. Let go of me, Rayo.' He eased my fingers from his sleeve. 'Very soon, everything will become clear to you. All the answers are here in this building.'

'Keea you knew . . . you've always known everything about me, haven't you,' I said. I felt strangely relieved; he *was* connected with Gimel, then.

'And so will this old goat if you don't keep your voice down,' he replied. 'Yes, I knew. I knew of your special affinity with the Metatronim.'

'And yet in Khalt, in the Strangeling, you let me carry on thinking I was suffering from delusions.'

'That's because you were. There is more to this than you could ever imagine, Rayo.'

'Why didn't you tell me? Why wait till now?'

'Planning,' he replied. 'You'll see.'

The old man showed us into a dim, cluttered room, where light struggled for entrance through a dusty, fly-blown window, high above our heads. Ancient ledgers filled shelves from floor to ceiling. 'How familiar are you with the contents of this building?' Keea asked.

The old man chewed thoughtfully. 'More than anyone else,' he replied. 'What are you seeking?'

'Ancient history. Before the wars. The beginning.'

The old man nodded and began to peer at the shelves, pulling the ledgers out, seemingly at random, flicking through them, shaking his head and shoving them back. Then he uttered a delighted cry, as if he'd doubted his ability to locate what was needed, and handed the ledger he had found to Keea. 'Do these documents cover the period you're interested in?'

Keea squinted at the faded text. I looked over his shoulder. 'Do they?' I asked. All the pages were crumbling badly and, to me, the list of documents was illegible. It was also inscribed in a language unfamiliar to me.

'The account by Veraniel Eshim,' Keea said, pointing to a few crabbed characters. 'May we see that?'

The old man made a disgruntled sound. 'It is restricted.'

'I know. Where is it?'

'It is restricted,' the old man repeated.

Keea sighed and extended his left hand again. I saw the ring on his third finger. I had not seen it before. 'By this authority I demand you give me the text,' he said. 'Be quick! We don't have time to waste!'

'You must sign for it.'

'I'll sign in blood, if necessary,' Keea said. 'Now, where is it?'

'This way.'

We were taken up numerous shadowed corridors, through many book-lined rooms. I had never seen so much knowledge gathered together in one place; it was phenomenal. As far as I was aware not even the Guild in Taparak knew of this library.

The revered account lay in a locked cabinet high in the building. The layout of the library amused me as much as it perplexed me; so many small rooms packed with manuscripts, books and ledgers. The place we were taken to was uncommonly tidy: just the cabinet, a table and a few uncomfortable chairs. Shaking his head and sighing heavily, the old man reluctantly sifted through a collection of keys hanging from his belt and opened the cabinet. He extracted the book Keea had asked for as if it were a holy relic, and brushed its cover with his sleeve. 'This text cannot be taken from the building,' he said. 'It is very valuable, very ancient.'

'We will read it here,' Keea replied. 'Thank you. Leave us now.'

'I cannot . . .'

'Leave us!' Keea's voice thundered through the room. It even raised the hairs on the back of my neck. The old man backed from the room.

'I will have to lock you in,' he said.

'Do it then. Return in two hours.' Keea sat down at the table without paying the archivist any more attention, and carefully opened the ancient book. I watched with misgiving as the door closed and the key turned in the lock.

'Look, Rayo,' Keea said, in a hushed voice. I dragged a chair to his side and sat down.

'I can't read that! It's gibberish!'

Deltan hieroglyphs would have been easier to translate. The text was inscribed in flaking rusty-coloured ink on disintegrating yellow parchment. It seemed more like an astrological chart than a narrative. The glyphs appeared mathematical, and some looked to me as if they might be illustrations or diagrams. 'What language is this?' I asked. As a Tap, I was familiar with all the languages of the known world. This was nothing I'd ever seen before.

'It is a very ancient text, Rayo,' Keea said, turning the thick, brittle pages and examining them closely, 'and of course you cannot read it, but *I* can. I shall read it aloud to you.'

'How can you read it?' I was bemused – and yes even a little

349

jealous – of Keea's apparent knowledge of this strange tongue. 'Who taught you?'

He shrugged, still staring at the book. 'Let us just say it was one of the privileges of being an artisan . . . *employee*.'

'Then tell me what it says?'

He looked up from the page and I had to repress an urge to flinch from the intensity in his eyes. It was as if I'd never seen him before, as if he were a complete stranger. 'This will alter your perception of the world,' he said.

'How?'

'Because it is the true history.' He reached out and touched my face, causing me to stiffen instinctively.

'True history of what?' I found his sudden passion for whatever the book contained strangely repellent.

'Rayo, listen . . .'

This is the testament of I, Veraniel Eshim, transcribed in the wake of the Fall of the Lord Sammael and his Followers, to Earth. I plead that my readers will exercise tolerance of this history, whatever their creed or culture. These words are written for the future, to keep the flame of truth burning in the world.

There are many worlds, not all of which are planets.

And yet, whatever their shape, form or reality, each world is but a layer in the thick fabric of the Multiverse.

All the worlds are interrelated; some have more intimate relationships than others.

Some derive sustenance from each other in the form of energy or strength.

Such was the relationship between the worlds that have been named by their inhabitants as Elenoen and Earth.

Elenoen is very close to Earth; in the very next sliver of reality.

They are naturally attracted to each other and, in the natural course of things, sustain each other in subtle ways. Elenoen is the fount of spirit, whereas Earth is the cauldron of the generation of flesh. The two worlds have existed in harmony, sharing their essential properties.

But calamities have occurred to sever this relationship. This is the history of it.

Elenoen, my former estate, is the home of the eloim, my people. We, a race of beings more spiritual in nature than the inhabitants of Earth, are now exiled from our natural home. As I write this, I am a creature of Earth. I am flesh.

My people are legion, but the few, of whom I am one, are now estranged. Our parent has cast us out, and all eloim share a single parent: El-oh-at. Eloat, the Lord of Elenoen, Master

350

of the Spheres and father, mother, king, beloved, has disowned us. Have we transgressed in the manner of which we are accused? Only you, the reader, can pass judgement on us now.

Unlike this green and fertile Earth, where all the creatures can conjoin in their own fashion to bring forth young in great joy, there is only ever one progenitor in our world. But when certain cycles of causality have revolved to their completion, our parent, Eloat, will spawn a successor. Only then may he pass through to his next actuality, a new form of being in a different world. For that is the way of the Multiverse.

This then was the rhythm of Elenoen, which had been maintained harmoniously since before memory. We, as trusting children, gave no consideration to our estate. We lived in Eternity.

Then Eloat spawned a son whose name was Sammael, and the time had come for the transference of power, for a new cycle to begin, in Elenoen and on Earth. It was to have been a time of great celebration, of feasting and love, as the old Eloat departed to new frontiers, with the blessings of his people.

We enfolded Sammael in our thoughts, preparing to elevate him to the position of Eloat, but his predecessor faltered in the cadence of the world. For a moment, our father stepped out of the Multiversal rhythm and, in doing so, acquired the desire to remain in Elenoen.

Eloat would not transfer, but claimed the new cycle meant the old rhythm should be destroyed. Eloat would retain his power over eloim, with Sammael sitting beneath him as his son.

Strange influences seeped through to the Earth, for the Multiversal rhythm had been disrupted. The Earth remembered war and began to practise it. Her races diverged and fought. The strength and energy that came back to Elenoen was sour and bitter. Sammael pleaded with Eloat to depart Elenoen, to pass on, so that the Multiverse rhythm could take on the new intricacies it desired; the old ones were becoming stagnant and breeding disharmony. Eloat refused and, through supreme effort, spawned another son for himself, whom he named Mikha'il. This other son was to be his weapon in the world, a defence against the demands of his first son, Sammael.

But Eloat had underestimated the attraction two such similar beings would have for one another. At first these brothers were in accord, and loved each other dearly. United, their power eclipsed even that of their parent. Mikha'il was loyal to our father but, in love, he listened to the words of his brother, Sammael, who was still committed to the cycle of the Multiverse. Because of his youth, Sammael lacked the ability to

351

overthrow Eloat, and sought to petition Mikha'il to conjoin with him, so that they might achieve what Sammael alone could not do.

Angry at their union, Eloat deceived Mikha'il into believing the sour energy affecting Earth and Elenoen was caused deliberately by Sammael, and that his influence should be destroyed for all time. Sammael was cast into the role of greedy aggressor, a creature craving power and domination of his brethren. Eloat instructed Mikha'il to cast Sammael out of Elenoen into nothingness, where he might bleat in vain, without power. This division caused, for the first time in eloim history, a war in Elenoen. When Mikha'il gathered his father's throngs about him to carry out the expulsion, many of the eloim – myself among them – supported Sammael. We did this because we loved him, and in our hearts we trusted his word.

Were we wrong to do this? I sit here now, an outcast from my home, having followed my Lord of Light in the belief that his power, guided by the natural flow of the Multiverse, could overcome the foul stagnation corrupting the essential forces of our home.

When Sammael was cast out, all eloim loyal to him were cast out with him; although, with his strength, we resisted the pull of the void of nothingness and succeeded in transferring to Earth. In his fury Eloat destroyed all the interfaces between the worlds, condemning us the rebel eloim to remain on Earth for eternity. Without access to the portals, we cannot pass through Elenoen to our next phase of actuality. We are trapped on Earth but, even in our grief, determined to make the best of our predicament. We take comfort in the fact that our presence on this world allows us to maintain its natural rhythm. We have lost our war, but so too have Eloat and Mikha'il. There are no victors in this conflict.

As I write these words, our Lord of Light lies grieving among his brethren. He is wounded above the heart, where the sword of Mikha'il struck home. The strength of his grief permeates the walls of this humble dwelling, where I sit in the light of a single taper recording this sorry history. And yet despite how our kin in Elenoen have abandoned us, and ignored our plight, we bear no malice. In this world, we shall grieve, but without hatred, and hope for a day when Sammael, our Lord of Light, will be conjoined once more with his lost, beloved brother . . .'

Keea stopped reading. He closed his eyes and drew in a deep, shuddering breath as if the account had physically hurt him. For a moment I had the absurd impression he had forgotten I was there.

'Yes, yes, go on!' I cried.

He shook his head. 'Not yet,' he said. 'Not yet.'

'Well, if we are pausing, then perhaps you can answer some questions for me. These eloim – the ones that were thrown out of – what was it, Elenoen? – are they the people who were depicted on the walls of Helat's temple, the Host?'

'Yes!' Keea looked at me in a disturbingly manic way. 'You would have heard that in a moment, if you'd waited for me to continue!'

'Sorry! But the Host were shown as being spawned by a single parent. Is that parent Eloat?'

Keea shook his head impatiently. 'No, don't be stupid. Sammael's followers – many of them – were destroyed by Mikha'il during the conflict. Sammael had to replenish his people. *Sammael* spawned the Host. *He* is Helat! He taught his spawn how to mimic humanity enough to exist on this world, to manifest themselves as flesh. He taught them how to acquire gender, how to breed, how to mix with men and women!'

'Keea,' I said, sure I was going to regret these words, 'you didn't *read* that bit. You aren't reading now, Keea.'

He blinked at me. 'Stop asking questions and let me continue, then.'

'No, you don't get my point. *You don't have to read it, do you!* You already know all this! I don't want legends, Keea. I don't want archaic stories. Tell me the facts, the truth in your own words!'

He sighed and closed the book, running his fingers over the ancient, embossed leather. 'What you saw in the temple is all true. The eloim *are* the Host of Helat. They gave humanity many gifts, but . . . because of what they were there was a price to pay. They feed on human blood, Rayo, like humans breathe air. They need it.'

'Why human blood?'

'There is no good reason for that! They must simply want to. They are ghouls, demons! The rebellion must have warped their instincts!'

I accepted this explanation, but my own instincts sensed there must be more to it than he had suggested. 'And yet, despite their predatory tendencies, they are depicted as being great teachers,' I said. 'It doesn't make sense.'

'Well, it is true that they gave humanity knowledge,' Keea replied airily, 'but the price was death. After a while, people grew restless. They had the knowledge; they no longer wanted to pay the price. All the eloim were driven to the land you call the Strangeling. It was there that they were finally vanquished by humankind.'

'Vanquished?'

Keea sighed again. 'Most were killed, but some . . . some escaped. Many of the ruling families of Bochanegra believed that should the eloim be completely annihilated, the Earth would lose the important things humanity had learned – such as the spirit of

353

creativity, spirituality itself. They believed that, Rayo, and they helped the eloim survivors to escape those who sought to exterminate them. The eloim were hidden on Earth for many centuries, the knowledge of their existence handed down only through the human families who supported them.

'And now they are re-emerging?'

'No, they re-emerged centuries ago. Here. All at the same time. Now they practise their conceits of creation and feed off the populace.'

'What? You mean the artisans?' I laughed. 'Oh Keea, that's impossible! I think the artisans might be descended from these . . . these eloim, but they couldn't just have arrived in a bunch like that. People would have noticed! People would have asked questions!'

'Ask yourself this question then, soulscaper. The Taps and the Deltans have recorded the history of the world. Have you ever read of the eloim in their records?'

'No,' I said. 'That's true. . . . Perhaps this war you speak of occurred before the records were kept.'

Keea shook his head. 'It didn't.'

'That's impossible!'

'As impossible as the fact that eloim slunk into Sacramante and set up house as artisans, hmm?'

'No, that's even more impossible.'

'But it happened.'

'How?'

'They sabotaged the soulscape, Rayo, but it cost lives. They do not have the abilities of your people. Somehow they used the life energy of eloim martyrs to uproot the knowledge of their existence from it, and once that initial excision was made, it was possible for eloim leaders to occlude the soulscape to this day with their insidious influence. Even you have never seen through it. The eloim are present in the human soulscape – they have to be, because they are part of human history – but you cannot detect them. In a similar way, apart from the patron families, the Sacramantans have never *noticed* the eloim in this city. Until recently.'

'Don't talk rubbish!' I said. 'The artisans are celebrities. They are known everywhere!'

'Yet the fact that they are virtually immortal is never commented upon, the fact that they are never seen to ingest solid food. Very strange, isn't it? They go to great lengths to disguise themselves. The patrons keep them alive.'

'The patron families? You mean the people who helped them hide?'

He nodded.

I sat back in my chair, and took a deep breath. 'Like the Tricantes,' I said softly.

'They are a patron family, yes. And their patronage goes beyond

354

merely helping the eloim to hide, Rayo. They provide the eloim with sustenance. They *feed* them.'

'Willingly? No!'

'Yes. The process provides an obscene gratification to human beings, a kind of erotic stimulation. It is quite revolting, quite parasitic, and it perpetuates the abomination on this Earth.'

'I can't believe it!'

'You must!'

I put my hands over my face, thinking of Liviana, thinking of Avirzah'e Tartaruchi, thinking of Gimel Metatronim. Gimel Metatronim? 'But where do I come into this?' I asked him. 'Why was I brought here? What do they want with me?'

Keea lowered his head and sighed. 'The eloim are in difficulty, Rayo. They are suffering from mind-sicknesses, they are dying. I told you they don't have the powers of Taps, so they need a soulscaper to heal them. They need you.'

'A soulscaper? Me?' I laughed nervously. 'This is outrageous!'

Keea did not share my amusement. 'When you were eight years old, Beth and Gimel Metatronim were prowling the world, looking for a Tappish child to overpower. They chose you, and violated your soulscape while you were in a vulnerable state. They fooled you into thinking they were your guardian-pursuers, and have influenced you ever since.'

'I feel sick.'

Keea touched my arm. 'Forgive me, Rayo, but I too am guilty of deceiving you. I have brought you to Sacramante for a very special purpose.'

'You are working for the Metatronim!' I said. 'Yes, I know. I see it all now.'

Keea shook his head. 'No, you do not. The eloim have discovered, too late, that if a soulscaper of your prowess enters their soulscape, it will effectively end their power on this world.'

'How? How could I do that?'

He screwed up his eyes and shook his head. 'You would *reveal* them, don't you see? They made a mistake, Rayo, which they now desperately want to correct. Gimel is trying to destroy you, while I dearly want you to fulfil the initial purpose of your summoning. I am not working for the Metatronim, although they think I am.'

'Then who *are* you working for? Whose side are you on, Keea?'

He made a dismissive gesture. 'I am on the side of my native people. Look at me. What do you see?'

'A young man – I think.'

'Your eyes can be trusted. Rayo, you must enter the soulscape of eloim as Gimel originally planned. These creatures should not be on this world exploiting its people. They must be removed. The first step is to uncloak them in the human soulscape so that they are revealed to everyone and cannot hide. Then you must create a portal in the eloim soulscape.'

My laughter in response to these remarks held an edge of hysteria. 'Oh, is that all! Keea, until this moment I was unaware there might be *another* soulscape besides a human one. How can I possibly become aware of it, never mind create a portal in it? It's preposterous!'

Keea shook his head. 'I can help you.'

'You? How?'

'I have lived with these people, been very close to them. I am sure that should we scape-share, I could lead you in the right direction.'

'It is not as simple as that, Keea, believe me.'

'We must to try, at least! The portal must be created so that those who are able to vanquish the eloim will be able to do so.'

'And who is able to vanquish them? Another secret society?'

Keea tapped the book beneath his hands. 'This is a biased account. The story has basic flaws. Its author obviously succumbed to the glamour of the rebel Lord of Light, and has represented him in a far more flattering manner than he deserves. In reality Sammael was furious when Eloat told him he could not rule Elenoen. Eloat is misrepresented in this narrative, the viewpoint is all wrong. Mikha'il was never deceived by his father, and only did what had to be done.'

'When we first came in here, you insisted that book was a true history!' I said. 'Now, you're telling me it's propaganda! You are still throwing me false information!'

'No, I'm not! This *is* a true history – in most respects. There *was* a war in Elenoen, and some eloim *did* end up here. Sammael was an infernal egotist. He craved power and for that reason alone was expelled from Elenoen. It was a mistake that he ended up here, a mistake which his own people have been trying to correct for a long time. Now they might be able to do so. Humanity will be freed from its curse, Rayojini, and you can help accomplish it!'

'This is incredible!' I cried, but already a little part of me was seduced by the thought of being responsible for such a victory. 'I can't believe it!'

Keea shrugged. 'Once you enter the eloim soulscape, you will see for yourself.'

'And they are trying to prevent that . . .' I rubbed my face. 'Oh, spirits of every realm, one of the artisans visited me last night! He tried to persuade me to leave Sacramante!'

Keea's face bloomed into a smile. 'You see?'

'Maybe I'm beginning to . . .' I had to think. 'The Holy Death . . . the victim is someone who has been drained of blood by an eloim, yes?'

Keea nodded.

356

'No wonder the Taps aren't allowed to examine the Holy Dead! But I thought all the artisans lived in Sacramante.'

'No, they are dispersed throughout the world. The wanderers, the loners, are the eloim who cause the Holy Death. They are quite deranged.'

'And the non-deaths? Explain.'

'A different phenomenon entirely. They have been caused by the eloim becoming greedy. They now want to extend their influence beyond Sacramante.

'I see . . . What about Salyon?'

'Who?'

I explained to him about my visit to Sacramante with my mother when I was a girl. 'He is scion of one of the patron families. Why should he suffer?'

He paused, and averted his eyes from mine a little. 'Well, of course he would have been an offering.'

'An offering? You mean a voluntary Holy Death? Then why did the Tricantes want him healed?'

'How can I answer that? Perhaps they changed their minds.'

'Salyon said something to me . . . Wait, this makes sense. He spoke of an addiction whose drug made him sick. So maybe he wasn't a Holy Death sacrifice. Maybe he's simply allergic to being fed from. All the Tricantes look astonishingly healthy. Perhaps that means the artisans don't kill the patrons at all, but just feed from them regularly.'

Keea shook his head emphatically. 'No, it is indisputable that many of the patrons are sacrificed. Children, I expect. I have no explanation for the Tricante boy, although I suspect his sickness wasn't caused by an allergy but by the insatiable appetite of the eloim who fed from him. Their legends speak of how they can drink souls as well as blood. In their feeding-frenzy, perhaps they damaged his soul.'

'No wonder Liviana was disturbed by what I said to her!' I paused a little to review all the information I'd amassed in the light of these new, barely believable, facts. 'We also found mutant births in Khalt, there were rumours of what they called "blood places", ghosts . . . How does all that relate to what you've told me?'

'It is really very simple. The nomad Khalts are descended from degenerate eloim who interbred with humanity. The artisans want to reappear as gods in the world, and the new religion will spread outwards from the nomads. All the supernatural phenomena were designed to help them do that.'

'Why now? Why didn't they do this years ago?'

'Oh, I don't know!' Keea said irritably. 'I expect they needed to replenish their strength or something. Anyway, to the eloim, time is a different concept from what it is to humanity: because they are immortal, they can afford to take things slowly.'

'And now they are trying to prevent me entering the eloim soulscape? So Gimel *has* been following me. As a guardian-pursuer, she was very real. One thing I don't understand though. She attacked me on the road in Khalt, yet later when it *seemed* I was speaking to her in Ykhey, she denied having done that. Her response was genuine enough. It doesn't seem to make sense.'

Keea pulled a sour face. 'She is insane, Rayo, as are all eloim. You saw what happened to me in Ykhey. I have had to endure such treatment for years!'

'I still don't understand why you didn't tell me all this in Khalt. You should have spoken about it even before we left the Halmanes. It would have saved a lot of time and bother.'

Keea lowered his eyes. 'I was obeying instructions. I'm sorry. I had to deceive you. My objective was to get you to Sacramante, and what better way to do that than by intriguing and mystifying you? I had no idea that the Metatronims would change their mind about using your services.'

I shook my head, which was aching with the weight of all I had learned. Gimel: why did you have to turn out to be this terrible thing? The knowledge hurt me deeply. I did not want to believe it. This couldn't be the truth, could it? All that Keea had said seemed to give me the answers I'd yearned for, and yet my instincts still advised caution. Was this because none of us ever wants to credit the reality of painful truth? 'Gimel Metatronim has haunted my life since I was a child,' I said. 'And now I find she is a demoness, a succubus. And her brother . . .' My neck and face went hot. 'Incubus! Oh, Benevolent Spirits, what did he do to me?'

Keea leaned close and put his arms around my shoulder. 'I know it must be hard for you to take in, Rayo. Gimel and Beth are ageless, as are all eloim. They are immortal and they are predatory.'

'And the riders – the Knights? You were afraid of them. What were they?'

'Eloim warriors. I feared the Metatronim had discovered I was not wholly loyal and that they had sent those monsters out looking for me.'

He seemed to have an answer to everything. I glanced at his hand where it hung over my shoulder. 'How did you obtain the Metatronim seal?'

He curled his fingers and did not speak for a moment. 'I stole it,' he said eventually. 'I stole it.'

Keea was obviously an intrepid and enterprising adventurer, although I would still have felt happier knowing more about his background. He did appear to be concerned for my safety.

'Keea, this is *their* library! We must get out of here!' I stood up quickly, knocking over my chair. 'Helat's tits and cock, we're locked in!'

'Sit down, Rayo, you are quite safe,' Keea said. 'The eloim don't know we're here. We can wait for the old goat to let us out.'

I walked to the door and pressed my face against it. 'I don't want to be a part of this. It's madness! Why did I have to get the wanderlust? I should have stayed in Taparak.'

'It wouldn't have mattered,' Keea said. 'I would have found you there. I would have found you anywhere, Rayojini.'

I turned away from the door. He was sitting with one arm along the back of his chair, the other lying protectively over the ancient book. 'Who are you Keea?' I said. 'Who are you working for? What's happening?'

'I am working for the good of humanity,' he said. 'You must believe that.'

Just saying those words, he had me doubting. Avirzah'e had sounded so convincing when he'd spoken of Gimel's regard for me. I found it difficult to envisage the artisans as callous predators. Avirzah'e had not seemed like a killer to me. Whom was I to believe? Surely I should at least try to speak with Gimel to establish the eloim version of this story. If the history and the legends were true, they had given humanity immeasurable gifts. I found it hard to believe the Sacramantan nobles would perpetuate the situation simply for some kind of carnal satisfaction. It didn't make sense. Izobella herself was a patron of the artisans. How had they hidden themselves for so long? It was incredible. Beyond belief. And to me, who worked with the incredible and the unbelievable on a daily basis, horribly possible. Gods walked down the road from Bochanegra. What would happen if the eloim were destroyed? Were they perhaps a necessary evil? I couldn't decide for myself, not there, in that little room, with Keea's energy blasting me into confusion. Who *was* he? I would still have to tread carefully.

I went to pick up my chair and sat down. Keea had begun to look through the book again. I noticed he had opened it at the end and was flicking backwards. 'What are you looking for?' I asked him.

'Another hiding place,' he said. 'I want to know what they did with Sammael.'

'Immortal Helat, hmm?'

He did not answer, but kept turning the pages. Then he paused and marked the text a finger. 'Melancholia!' he said. 'He incarcerated himself.'

'So Helat is out of the game?'

'Never that,' Keea replied. He closed the book, and rubbed his eyes.

'So what do I do now?' I asked him. 'Do I have to meet someone – your employers perhaps?'

Keea laced his fingers beneath his chin, and the Metatronim ring cast a light over his throat. He did not look at me. 'Not yet. It is nearly time, Rayo, very nearly time. Wait at The Temple Gate. I

359

will contact you later today, when I am ready.'

'When you are ready for what?'

'To help you,' he said. 'Speak to no one about this. Promise me.'

'Very well. I promise.' But I had no intention of honouring it.

'I see thy fall determined, and thy hapless crew involved in this perfidious fraud, contagion spread both of thy crime and punishment . . .'
Paradise Lost, Book V

As soon as the old man let us out of the locked room, my instinct was to flee the building like a caged beast accidentally given freedom. Keea did not intend to come back to The Temple Gate with me and was vague about what he was going to do before he contacted me again. We walked down the hill together and embraced awkwardly when our paths diverged. I felt we had shared some faintly shameful intimacy. He made me repeat my promise not to speak to anyone until he came to me.

The bells were striking midday as I hurried up Aurora Paths. Would Avirzah'e return? What if Keea came back first? What was I going to do? First, drink a couple of large brandies I expected.

No message had been left with Terissa, so I went into the bar and purchased a liquid lunch of strong alcohol. The room was full of the dreamy sound of people enjoying themselves in a relaxed manner. My nerves were jangling like bags of metal balls being juggled by an incompetent child. Restlessly, I kept changing my location; sitting by turn out in the garden, back in the salon, in the dining room. My mind kept trying to throw a hook over all I'd learnt. One moment I was convinced Avirzah'e's account was the accurate one, the next that Keea was nearer the truth with his dark suspicions and hints of terrible oppression. I still wanted to see Gimel desperately, whether she was hostile to me or not. I could not rid my guts of an instinctive belief that she, more than anyone else, would tell me the truth. Why was I so convinced of that? Was I simply a dupe for a pretty face, believing Avirzah'e Tartaruchi because he'd batted his eyelids at me? Surely not. Everything slotted comfortably into place if juxtaposed against Keea's explanation. And yet . . . I had not been able to read the ancient text in the library, which meant that anything could have been written there, anything. I recalled my first impression of Keea. Deep down, that hackle-raising suspicion had not left me.

About an hour after I'd returned to the inn, Terissa came to me in the main salon. I must have looked demented, because she backed away a step when I stood up. 'Yes? What is it?' I demanded.

'Someone is here for you . . .' she answered, looking puzzled.

361

'Well, why haven't you brought them to me? Who is it?'

'I was only trying to find you, Rayojini,' she said, in a hurt tone. 'I've shown him to the bar. It's a man. His name is Salyon Tricante.'

I barged past her without a word, and heard her affronted retort behind me.

'Salyon? I'm so glad you came!' He was sitting on a stool against the polished bar, with a tankard of ale in his hand. I greeted him as if he were a long-lost friend. He, like Terissa, looked rather taken aback. I ordered myself another brandy and took him to a secluded table where we could speak in private.

'You look rather harassed,' he said, taking off his cloak and sitting down.

I realised I was physically shaking, as if I were cold. 'It has been an eventful day.'

'Are you all right?'

I nodded. 'Yes. Salyon, I hope you have come here prepared to answer questions, because I have plenty to ask.'

He smiled, an expression which split his gaunt, forbidding face into something more personable. 'To be honest, I don't know why I'm here. I found it quite moving to see you again. The last time we met, I had just surfaced from a nightmare. Your face has always stayed with me.'

I felt a little embarrassed by this frank admission, and shrugged uncomfortably. 'Your nightmare,' I said. 'Did it have anything to do with the artisans?'

He rested his chin in his hands and stared at me for a few moments. I found it very disconcerting. 'Are you aware of the special relationship between the patron families and the artisans?'

I nodded. 'I think so. The eloim.'

He smiled in what seemed to be relief. 'I am glad I'm not the one to tell you about that. It also proves my assumptions about you might be correct. I hope I don't regret coming here.'

I felt a twinge of guilt. 'Are you putting yourself in danger, talking to me?'

He traced a bony finger around the edge of his tankard. 'I don't know what impels me to speak to you, other than our tenuous link from the past. I suppose you've realised that no patron talks about the . . . artisans.' I nodded in encouragement. 'Times are changing,' Salyon said, giving me a penetrating look. 'I'm not sure if I'm pleased about that or disturbed.'

He folded his arms on the table. 'I might as well tell you that I am useless for eloim purposes. The sup unhinged my soul. I am estranged from patron society because of it.'

'Excuse me,' I interrupted him, 'but there is something I have to clarify in my own mind. Were you intended to be a sacrifice for the Holy Death? And did that process go wrong in some way, which necessitated the attentions of my mother?'

Salyon looked puzzled. 'Holy Death? No, no. *Nobody* survives a sacrifice! What a preposterous idea. What happened to me was quite different. During our early teens, patron children are introduced to the sup – that is, we learn the secrets of feeding the artisans. For some of us, it is impracticable. Don't know why. An allergy perhaps, or something like that. My first sup resulted in the condition you and your mother saw all those years ago.'

'I see. So it was wholly voluntary.'

He frowned. 'Of course. It was something I'd been waiting for with hungry anticipation for years! Having experienced it then, it grieves me I cannot enjoy those sensations again.'

'But *some* individuals are given in sacrifice, are killed?'

'Yes. But that again is voluntary.' He looked at me directly. 'You have no idea what it is like to belong to a patron family and not to be able to indulge in the sup. I have felt wretched in the past: aloof, bereft, and relieved. I wanted you to know that.'

I made a soothing sound. 'Thank you for telling me. Now, can you explain to me how "times are changing" as you put it? What has changed exactly?'

Salyon grinned. 'I feel you already know more than I can tell you.'

I raised my hands. 'Please indulge me. I want to hear it from you.'

'As you wish. Well, no one beyond patron society has ever become interested in the eloim before. Now, it seems that the invisible screen between them and the world has been shattered. Questions are being asked at last. People have woken up and are wondering exactly what, or who, the eloim are. They are in danger of being exposed. Another thing is that the eloim are dying. But I suppose you know that too.'

'I have heard a little.'

'Immortals taking their own lives!' he said. 'Why? It must be a mental sickness.' He leaned towards me. 'Ah, but these are dangerous times, you know. Not just the eloim are dying. My own family has suffered a fatality!'

'Who? Why?'

'A cousin of mine. You remember her: Perdina.'

I nodded. 'Vaguely. I remember poetry and hair.'

'Well she, too, took her own life to protect the eloim. It's a long story, which I won't go into now, but in my eyes Perdina can be regarded as a holy sacrifice. Things are getting out of control!'

'Aren't they!' I said, under my breath. It was time for a little direct therapy. 'Are you pleased that the artisans are suffering, Salyon?' I asked carefully. It had occurred to me that the real reason Salyon had come to me was because he needed the services of a soulscaper himself. What I saw before me was an anguished soul.

He sighed. 'I don't know. I hate them because I cannot get close to them. I want to touch them, as my relatives do. Does that shock you? And yet I cannot imagine the world without them. They are . . .' He shook his head; there were no words for his feelings.

'Salyon, do the eloim kill people regularly; you know, just people off the street, non-patrons?'

His head jerked up, and he blinked. 'No, never, I'm sure of it! The only deaths they cause are those of the sacrifices, which the patrons give them as holy gifts, as a mark of trust and faith. These the eloim drain of life but, as I told you, all such sacrifices have to be voluntary. Eloim do not kill the unwilling.'

I was relieved to hear that and must have showed it on my face.

'But does that make them any less parasitical?' Salyon asked urgently. 'Once you have been touched by them, it becomes an addiction. Whether it is bad for you or not, it still puts you in a vulnerable position. Life loses all meaning, but for the sup. You must believe that.'

I nodded slowly, and took a sip of brandy. 'Would you say the eloim desire more power, more freedom?'

'Yes,' he said. 'I'm sure they do. Some eloim, more than others. When we speak of the artisans, we cannot speak of a single mind, a single purpose. They are like us, in that respect.' He leaned towards me and lowered his voice, even though we had not been speaking very loudly. 'I forced Livvy to tell me what you spoke to her about. She said you had seen strange things in Khalt, that you had been followed to Sacramante. I know what is going on, Rayojini!'

His hands were shaking and I felt a tug of distaste for his vehemence, but also a sadness, because I sensed there was sickness within this man's soulscape still, despite all that Ushas had done for him so many years before. 'Any theory would be most welcome at this point,' I said. My brandy was finished. I raised my hand to attract the bartender and order another.

'The artisans are going mad,' he declared, with an air of triumph. 'They are becoming dangerous, which is, of course, a reaction to their mind-sickness.'

'Dangerous in what way?'

His face assumed a closed, sly expression. 'I have no proof,' he said, 'but it seems obvious to me that once the eloim disguise has been penetrated, they will be forced to rise up and take control of Sacramante. Izobella is their creature; she would not oppose it, I'm sure. Like us, self-preservation must be of prime importance to the eloim. I do not think they are naturally malevolent, but they will certainly want to protect themselves.'

I nodded. There was some sense in that, I supposed. It allowed

364

for both Avirzah'e's and Keea's explanations to be honest ones. 'Do you know Gimel and Beth Metatronim?' I asked.

Salyon rubbed his arms and gulped audibly. 'I knew you would ask that. They are friends of the Sarim. Their father, Metatron, is a powerful figure among the eloim. I admire them greatly as artists, of course.'

My brandy arrived without me having to do more than raise a hand. They were already used to my tastes in this place. 'Are the Metatronim suffering from the sickness too?' I asked, when the bartender had gone.

Salyon shrugged. 'I don't know. Surely you would be more aware of that? Neither Beth nor Gimel have been much in evidence lately.'

I felt quite breathless. Here was someone, who wasn't an artisan himself, who had seen the Metatronim, perhaps even talked to them. I realised my interest in Beth and Gimel had become more acute since my meeting with Avirzah'e. Had I dreamt of them last night? I couldn't remember. It seemed, however, that Salyon thought I knew more about them than I did. 'What will the patron families do if the eloim *do* try to attain more power?' I asked. 'How will the eloim subjugate everyone who isn't a patron? Will the patrons fight with them as allies against their own people, other humans?'

'How can I answer those questions?' Salyon said sharply.

'What have you really come here for?' I asked.

A wily grin crept across his face. 'I might ask you the same thing,' he replied. 'All these years, I've thought of you. All these years. You want to know what pulled me out of the darkness when I was sick? I'll tell you. I saw you with the Metatronim, Rayojini! I know you were his lover. It was as if a door opened in my mind, and I saw you there, lying beneath him. It woke me up.'

'How did you see that?' I snapped.

He shrugged. 'You know how! Oh, don't try to deceive me any longer, Rayojini. I've uncovered your plot!'

'What plot?'

He leaned closer towards me. 'I know the Taps are poised to take the place of the patron families. It's true, isn't it!'

'What?' For one dreadful moment, I wondered whether that could possibly be true, and the reason why answers to the puzzle had eluded me. My own people working against me? Then I looked at the crazed, fanatical light in Salyon's eyes. Be sensible, Rayojini, I told myself. 'Why do you think this?' I asked in a reasonable tone.

'That's obvious!' Salyon said. 'I have heard the rumours that the eloim have a soulscaper they are planning to use. They think a Tap will be able to cure them of their mind-sickness. But they'll still need strong allies if they have to fight their human opponents, won't they? I worked it out myself: the Taps would increase their own power tenfold if they had access to eloim ichor. It would be a mutually advantageous plan. You are the vanguard, Mistress Rayojini, aren't you? And I have unmasked you! What do you say to that?'

Precisely nothing. I stared at him, aghast, both smiles and expletives hovering round my mouth. Salyon took my silence for encouragement.

'I have no affinity for my own people, Rayojini. You must protect me when the new order comes. We are empathic with each other. Through you I can experience what is denied me in waking life. In return I will help you in whatever way I can. No one will suspect; I can give you information about the patron families. I can help you get rid of them! Well? What do you say?'

I blinked at him in astonishment for a few moments. Had I really considered this person sane? 'Salyon, you have an excess of creativity that I'm sure even an artisan would envy! Your fantasies are indeed intriguing, even though they are insulting to my people. I don't take offence easily – fortunately for you. If I had more time, I would suggest you commission me to sort out your deluded head! Alas, I have more pressing matters to attend to at present.'

He stared at me, open-mouthed. 'Does . . . does that mean my theory is wrong?' he said, and then his face closed up again. 'Ah, but you *would* say that, wouldn't you?' He tapped his nose. 'Don't worry, Rayojini, your secret is safe with me!'

I suppressed an urge to strike him and without a further word – why waste more of my breath? – stood up and walked out of the room. I sensed him leaping up behind me, but I swiftly scurried into the entrance hall and hissed a quick, 'Get rid of that lunatic!' at Terissa. She looked up from her ledger, ready to scold me, I think, for my earlier terseness. Fortunately, she understood the expression on my face and nodded.

'Go upstairs,' she said.

I did so. Quickly.

The lunacy of Salyon Tricante was the last thing I needed at that time, even though my training demanded that I should offer help to any needy individual. Unfortunately, my immediate future required all of my attention and I could not afford the distraction of a scaping case. I went to my room and paced about, laughing to myself in the way that can very easily convert into tears. I would *have* to speak with Gimel now. No! She had attacked me on the road in Khalt. It hadn't been her. It had. *It had.* What was pantomime and what was real? Had the entire world shifted on its axis into a wobbling rhythm of sheer madness? How much more of this could I take? Where was Avirzah'e? Where was Keea? Where, for that matter, was I? A knock on the door alarmed me so severely

I felt as if I were about to shed my entire skin in one piece. Terissa put her nose into the room. 'He's gone,' she said. 'Are you all right Rayo?'

'No, I need a drink,' I replied. 'Can you bring me one?'

She nodded. 'What's going on?' she asked.

I shrugged. 'I don't know. I'm expecting other visitors. Let me know immediately if any of them show up.'

'I will.'

My answer clearly did not satisfy her. I grinned sweetly. 'I'm sorry I was a bit sharp with you. Things have been a little odd today. It's a hazard of my profession. Salyon Tricante was a potential client, but . . .' I shrugged. 'His sickness isn't one I want to cure particularly.' It was a feeble excuse.

'I'll bring you some brandy,' Terissa said, with a knowing, sympathetic smile. I was relieved she didn't query why I would turn down a commission. She closed the door and I resumed my pacing. What if Keea got here before Avirzah'e did? What then? The next moment I found myself at the top of the stairs yelling down to Terissa to bring me paper and a quill, along with the brandy.

'Wait while I write this,' I said, when she returned. 'I need it delivered.' She tried to peer over my shoulder, so I hunched over the paper and wrote quickly. 'I am surrounded by fanatics,' I scribbled. 'If this means nothing to you, then I am one of them and please accept my apologies for this intrusion. If, on the other hand, this does mean something to you, please contact me quickly. I am at The Temple Gate inn.'

I signed it lavishly and slid the paper into the envelope that Terissa had thoughtfully provided. 'Bring me wax!' I demanded.

Once it was sealed, I wrote the words 'Gimel Metatronim' on the front of the envelope with shaking hands. 'Take this to the atelier courts,' I said, thrusting an inordinately generous amount of loose coin I'd had lying on the bedside table into Terissa's hands. 'Immediately.'

Terissa took the envelope with less enthusiasm than she had for the money. 'I cannot get inside the atelier courts,' she said. 'I will have to leave it at the gates.'

'Do whatever you can,' I said, 'but hurry. It's very important, Terissa. I can't tell you how much.'

She smiled bravely at my appeal. 'I'll take it.' She put the coins in the pocket of her apron.

To occupy myself, I began to pack my belongings into my carry-back. Best to be prepared for any eventuality. Terissa had brought me a flask of brandy and a glass. After draining the glass at once, I began to swig from the flask. Still no sign of Keea or Avirzah'e. I would go mad if one or the other of them didn't turn up soon. Perhaps they had met each other. Perhaps one had killed the other. Perhaps they didn't exist at all and I had hallucinated the whole thing. I finished the brandy and sat on the bed. I would count to five hundred and then go downstairs. If no one had come for me by then, I would . . . What? What *could* I do?

I reached two hundred and seventy-five and there was a knock on my door. For a second, I stared in disbelief and then leapt up, ran across the room and yanked the door open. Keea? Avirzah'e? No. One of the inn's junior maids was standing there gawking at me. 'What is it?' I demanded.

'A . . . a visitor for you, madam,' she stuttered.

'Where?'

'In the salon, mistress. A woman.'

'Right!' I ran past her and flung myself down the stairs, causing heads to turn as I stampeded into the salon.

'Where is she?' I cried. People sitting in idle contemplation of news-sheets, and each other, looked up in surprise. Eyebrows were raised. A flurry of murmurs flowed around the room. Gimel was not there. No one was there that I recognised, and certainly no artisans. I ran back to the serving maid who was still coming down the stairs. I grabbed her roughly. 'Where is she?' I demanded, shaking her a little.

'There!' The girl pointed over my shoulder, her eyes round with fright.

'Where?'

I turned round. There was no one there. I shook the girl again. 'Where? Where?'

'She went outside. Out the door. Oh, let me go mistress, you're hurting me!'

Uttering a heartfelt curse, I dropped the girl like a rag and hurried outside. The alley was full of people milling about. I shoved them violently out of my way, but there was no sign of any recognisable visitor. No sign! Helplessly, I went back into the inn, stomped past the wilting serving maid, who flinched away from me, and dashed upstairs. In my room I put on my hat and coat. For a moment I considered strapping on my carryback, but rejected the idea and stowed it in a cupboard instead. Then I ran downstairs and rang the counter bell repeatedly until the innkeeper himself appeared.

'Money,' I said. 'I need funds. Urgently.'

'You upset one of my lasses,' he began, folding his arms. I had a feeling the staff of The Temple Gate were becoming tired of my erratic and eccentric behaviour. I did not care.

'Give me my money!' I said.

'Are you leaving us, then?'

'No, keep the room ready. My things are there. Just give me a hundred dahli.' He did not move but stared at me belligerently. I attempted a mollifying smile. 'I'm sorry. I have important work to attend to. Very important. Life or death. Please, I need the money.'

The innkeeper sighed, and unfolded his arms. 'I'll see what I have out back, then,' he said and went deliberately through the door behind the counter.

'Hurry!' I called after him. 'I'll be in the bar.'

I ordered another brandy, hoping to calm my nerves. Why wasn't alcohol affecting me today? I knew in my guts that something, *something*, was going to happen soon and I needed to be ready for it.

The innkeeper brought me a bag of coins which seemed suspiciously heavy, indicating he had filled it with small change. Not bothering to count it, I tied the bag to my belt. He watched me stonily as I struggled to tie a knot with fingers that had suddenly become independent of my nervous system.

'What business do you have with them?' he asked.

'With whom?' I snapped.

'The artisans.'

'What makes you think I have any business with them?'

'Because that woman keeps coming here asking for you,' he said. 'She is standing in the hall now. Looks like she's waiting for you.'

Without responding, I leapt away from the bar and charged out into the hall, just as the main door was swinging shut. 'No!' I cried and yanked it open again. People seemed to surge against me like a tide of imbeciles but, for a fleeting moment, I caught a glance of a white face, of a tall woman who looked at me above the milling heads. The impression was muddy, as if seen through water, but I was sure it was Gimel. She wore a long purple cloak, with a hood which was pulled up over her head. She stared at me for only a moment, before turning around and sweeping off down the alley. I did not bother to shout after her. People complained as I pushed them aside, but I paid no attention. I fixed my sights on the tall figure ahead of me; this time, she would not get away.

'He above the rest in shape and gesture proudly eminent stood like a tower; his form had yet not lost all her original brightness, nor appeared less than Archangel ruined . . .'
Paradise Lost, Book I

After a light lunch of blood and lemon juice, I waited impatiently for Avirzah'e to bring Rayojini to my house. I'd tried on at least a dozen different gowns, consulting Tamaris as to which would be the most appropriate for the occasion. The red was too *busy*-looking for afternoon wear, but it flattered my figure, and the indigo was too fussy with beads and embroidery. 'Why not go for the black, madam,' Tamaris said, holding out the folds of crepe.

'Yes, yes, simple . . . but perhaps a little too sinister?'

'Not if you wear your gold collar with it.'

'Yes, good idea . . . and a pale gold shadow on my eyelids.'

Finally I made my entrance into the salon where Beth was waiting for me. 'No word from Avirzah'e?' I asked, glancing at the clock on the wall.

Beth shook his head. I then spent over an hour pacing up and down, nearly wearing a hole in the carpet. Beth watched me silently from one of the couches. He did not seem as keen to meet Rayojini as I was, and I had a feeling he was only there because Avirzah'e had insisted. His reticence was only to be expected, of course. I had always harboured a greater interest in Rayojini than he had. He barely showed any interest when Tamaris delivered a note that one of the atelier court gate-keepers had been asked to give to me. I opened the envelope with nerveless fingers. It was from Rayojini herself! She sounded rather disturbed, and had she forgotten Avirzah'e was collecting her this afternoon? It was very odd, but oh how wonderful that we were communicating in reality so freely. A letter! The first direct acknowledgement of our connection. I sent Tamaris out to The Temple Gate to find out what was going on, but Avirzah'e turned up before she got back. When he arrived, he was alone.

'She's gone,' Avirzah'e said.

'Gone? Where?' I was confused. In her short letter Rayojini had asked me to go to her at The Temple Gate, as if she planned to wait for me there. It didn't make sense. How could she have gone?

'She did not tell anyone where she was going,' Avirzah'e said. 'The innkeeper told me she asked for money, and for her room to be kept for her. He said a woman came for her. An artisan.'

'What?' I went utterly cold. Who else of my people had an interest in Rayojini? 'I am surrounded by fanatics,' she had written. Who?

'She spoke of being followed!' Avirzah'e said, slamming a fist into his other, open palm. 'I should have paid more attention to that!'

'But who was it?' I cried. 'Who?'

Avirzah'e shook his head. 'I've no idea. I wish I had. What are we going to do?'

'We mustn't panic,' I said, wanting more than anything to panic. 'We must sit down together and trust that our combined strength will be able to trace her by projection.'

Avirzah'e sighed and nodded. 'Yes, yes, you're right.'

'Where is Amelakiveh?' Beth asked. 'Why wasn't he with her?'

The answer to that last question was soon provided. Before we could arrange ourselves to begin the search for Rayojini, an officer of the Judificator arrived at our door, politely requesting either Beth or myself to accompany him to the nearest judicial building. He said he did not want to perturb Metatron unduly, which was why he had come to us first, but something rather worrying had occurred. Intrigued, and suffused with more than a little dread, Beth and myself left Avirzah'e asking himself unanswerable questions in the salon and accompanied the officer to his headquarters. It transpired that a young man had been found wandering the tourist quarter, in a state of semi-consciousness and great distress. He had been wearing Metatron's seal ring, and was carrying several of my personal effects, which was how he'd been traced to us.

'We realised it must be a servant of yours,' the officer said, with some embarrassment. 'You had better prepare yourself for unpleasantness.' Beth and I hung on to each other in numb apprehension as we followed the officer to the room where our supposed servant was confined.

It was Amelakiveh, though barely recognisable as such. When we saw him, we were faced with a stranger in a familiar body, but even the body had somehow shrunk. The face, once so beautiful, was that of a vacant dullard. The skin was sallow, lustreless, the hair lank about the shoulders. He strongly resembled an unfortunate who had been imprudently over-supped. He had soiled himself. It was a dreadful sight. I could not bring myself to go and comfort him. Beth turned away with a sound of disgust.

We had to confirm to the official that this was indeed a dependant of ours. Though apparently dazed, Amelakiveh could speak. When questioned, his last memory was of preparing himself to become a holy sacrifice in the court of the Kaliph. Since that time he had simply not existed. Now he did not know where he was or what had happened to him. He had simply found himself in the middle of the city, with no idea how he had got there. His name, he said, was Tavaro Arezza. He had been reared for the holy sacrifice, and could remember the names of all his sacrificial companions from that fateful night when Beth and I had spoken to the Parzupheim. He did not appear to recognise either Beth or myself and had never even heard of the soulscaper, Rayojini. I knew, even before I discussed it with my brother, that the person who'd lived with us over the last twenty-odd years, shared our bed, and carried out work in our name, was not the pathetic creature now before us. The personality we were familiar with had vacated the body in front of us. All that remained were the shreds of an individual whose soul had been partially supped from that body. The holy sacrifice involves more than the drinking of blood.

The implications were enormous, terrible. I felt nauseous, remembering his kiss, the way Kiveh had slipped my father's ring from my hand. No, not Kiveh, but who?

'I think,' Beth said, 'we will find it is the same person who spirited Rayojini away from the inn, don't you?'

I gazed at him in horror. 'Sammael,' I said. 'We have to tell Sammael.'

My Rayojini was in terrible danger, I was sure of it. How could we have been so easily fooled? Out of pity, and a sense of responsibility, I told the officials that Tavaro Arezza, or what was left of him, could be taken to our home – where Tamaris and Ramiz would look after him. I doubted whether he had much of a future, but it was the least we could do for him. However, the condition of the Arezza boy was not our main worry at the present moment. All the way home Beth and I sat in stony silence in the carriage, both of us, I am sure, mentally whipping ourselves in shame and fury. Rayojini's quirky little note became tragic in my mind. 'I am surrounded by fanatics.' They had taken her! We had commended her into the care of an enemy, an enemy who had been constantly by her side throughout Khalt and the Strangeling. It was unspeakable! How could we have been so blind? The signs had been there all along. No human ever resists the holy sacrifice; we should have known Amelakiveh was no ordinary boy. And I had been the one who'd chosen him from all the other offerings. It was my fault. I did not say these words aloud, but Beth knew my thoughts all the same.

'Don't blame yourself,' he said. 'There was no way either of us could have anticipated this.'

'I feel so soiled,' I said. I was turning Metatron's ring in my hand. I could not bear to put it on my finger.

Beth pulled me against him. 'Well, it's only a guess, but I suspect the influence from Elenoen that Sammael told you about now has your little soulscaper in its clutches, don't you?'

'How can you be so callous!' I said, privately agreeing with him.

'We have to face the worst possibility,' Beth said, kissing the top of my head. 'I don't mean to sound callous.' He sighed deeply. 'And to think that disgusting . . . *thing* . . . whatever it is, has been so intimate with us. I feel sick to my bones! And, of course, Metatron is going to be furious when he finds out what we did with Amelakiveh. Oh, what a mess! We should have stayed in Atruriey, Gimel. We should never have come back to Sacramante after our stay in Taparak. We were happy out there, weren't we? None of this would have happened. None of it!'

'We are still together,' I said. 'Despite everything.'

Beth sighed. 'We are not what we were,' he answered.

Metatron was waiting in my salon and brooding in the middle of the room like an impending storm when Beth and I returned to the house. Avirzah'e was perched on the edge of a chair, and looked up at us with wild relief when we entered. He resembled a miserable hound that had just been severely whipped by strangers.

'I cannot strike you!' Metatron thundered, pointing a rigid, steady finger at Beth and myself. 'Though I would very much like to! I have spoken at length to Sandalphon today, and he told me many disturbing things. Now I am told some human dreg has been found wandering around Sacramante wearing the Metatronim seal – which was entrusted into your care, Gimel! I hope you can explain yourself.'

I handed him the ring without speaking, which he sneered at in distaste. 'Well? Do I get an explanation from you willingly or do I have to order you to give it to me?'

'The boy wearing your seal was a dependant of ours, a human,' I said. I would be honest with Metatron to a point, but had no intention of divulging exactly how Amelakiveh had come into our possession. 'We have discovered that his body has been inhabited by an invader's personality for the last twenty years. We have reason to believe this personality might have come from Elenoen.' I turned away from my father, unable to face any further questions.

'Tamaris and Ramiz are your only dependants,' he said, inevitably. 'And Ramiz has just divested me of my coat and hat in the hall. Who is this other that I do not know of?'

There was a moment's silence. I looked at Beth who was staring at me in terror. I made a small signal to comfort him. I would handle this. I turned around, drawing myself up to my full height. 'An illicit transmutation, if you must know,' I said. 'Don't tell me this sort of thing doesn't happen, Metatron. We both know it does!'

Metatron's habitually pale face had gone decidely pink along the cheekbones. 'Children! Fools!' he cried. 'Are you intent on shaming me in every way! I cannot believe this!'

'Believe it,' I said. 'It's quite true.'

374

Metatron pulled a face at me that was little more than a snarl and then turned on my brother. 'Beth, you are a hedonistic whore and a mindless dolt! Sandalphon has informed me of your perversity in the Aurelium Chamber. I should knock you senseless!' Then he whipped back towards me. 'And you, Gimel, whom I trusted implicitly, how could you behave so recklessly, so senselessly?' He pointed at Avirzah'e without looking at him. 'And is this impudent puppy who, I am assured, has irretrievably debauched my son, anything to do with *your* misguided behaviour?'

I shook my head. 'No, the impudence, foolishness and stupidity are all mine!'

'Curb your audacity, daughter! You have behaved abominably to Sandalphon! I could not believe the things he said to me about how you forced him to open the Bale Tower! You have galloped like a mare in heat through the composure of your race! You have lied and wheedled and acted with unprecedented crassness! Despite explicit orders to send the soulscaper away, I find letters from her lying around your salon which indicate she is still in Sacramante and that you are freely communicating with her. I am outraged and . . . *speechless*!'

'Hardly that, Father!' I cried. I realised he was really quite delighted to be able to speak to me this way at last. All his discontent was coming out. Soon he would start shouting at me about Sammael.

'I should order both you and your lackwit brother into retreat!' Metatron said, with relish.

'Over my lifeless remains!' Beth snapped, unexpectedly. 'Whatever you think of me, how dare you speak to Gimel like that? We admit our culpability over Amelakiveh, and for that we shall punish ourselves more than you ever could! But Gimel has put her own life at risk for the sake of our people! She has more bravery, guts and strength than you could ever imagine possessing! I despise you!'

Metatron was so taken aback by Beth's uncharacteristic outburst, he was indeed rendered momentarily mute.

I raised my hands. 'Please! We cannot stand here arguing like simple humans! I accept I have acted rather too independently, Metatron, and I'm sorry if I upset Sandalphon, but what is done is done. Now I have to talk to Sammael.'

Metatron took a deep breath to calm himself and slipped his sealring back on to his left hand. The gibe about being like humans must have penetrated the fume of his anger. 'Do not think I will not mention this again, because I will,' he said. 'However, this is a time of wider crisis, personal grievances must be stored until later. You cannot speak to Sammael, Gimel.'

'Why not?'

'Because he is transforming.'

'Of course, I am aware of that, but surely this information is of such importance as to validate an interruption?'

Metatron shook his head. 'Alas, no. Transformation of the kind which Sammael is undergoing is a process that *cannot* be interrupted. We have no choice but to wait until he is ready.'

'So what do we do until then?' I asked.

Metatron stared at me for a few moments. His expression registered many emotions: scorn, sadness, smothered fury and, yes, even a little admiration. 'We can do nothing. Tartaruchi told me about the soulscaper, Gimel. I'm sorry, but I think you'll have to resign yourself to her loss.'

'I cannot do that! I will search for her! Metatron, we have every reason to believe that whatever inhabited Amelakiveh's body now has her in its power!' I turned to Beth. 'I shouldn't be standing here now! I should be concentrating on contacting her, warning her . . .'

'No, Gimel!' Metatron interrupted. 'You must not do that. If the soulscaper is with . . . if she is under the influence of anything hostile to our race, contacting her by mind might well backfire on you. I'm sorry, but I have to forbid that.' He smiled grimly. 'If, of course, my instructions carry any weight with you at all now.'

'If she's not found, she could well be used against us,' Beth said. His tone of voice was still plainly insulting.

'It is a risk we shall have to take,' Metatron replied, refusing to look at Beth. 'There will be a gathering of senior eloim. We shall attempt to construct a barrier of protection around the atelier courts. For the time being no one must leave this area, not even eloim dependants.' Issuing orders seemed to have restored his good humour. 'Now, I have work to do.' He directed scornful eyes for a brief, eloquent second towards Avirzah'e who was trying to become invisible in the corner of the room. 'It is distasteful to me to have to mention this,' Metatron said, 'but I really think it would be advisable for the three of you to curb your perverse inclinations while we are in this unpredictable situation. We do not want to attract unwanted attention.'

He hoped to make us all feel dirty and small and yet his opposition had revived my spirit, and my optimism, in an unforeseen way. I realised that, because of the very things Metatron viewed with distaste, Avirzah'e, Beth and I were stronger than any of the earthbound eloim. At that moment, I felt that even if they all fell and were ground underfoot by Elenoen, we three would survive. I smiled in Metatron's face. 'Your advice is noted, Father,' I said, 'but as far as I am aware there never has been, nor ever shall be, anything perverse between us. We have our way of living, you have yours. It is as simple as that.'

Metatron's face darkened, but he did not comment on my words. 'Stay in this house!' he said, and swept out.

Beth, Avirzah'e and I embraced in relief. We held on to each other for a long time, not speaking. Then, we sat down together to wait for Sammael's summons. We all knew the days, till it came, would be long.

He summoned me to my black-veiled bed in the tower. I heard him call me. Up the stairs I went, one at a time, very slowly. The room was full of autumn; brown leaves had blown on to the bed and there was a smell of fruity smoke. The veils blew all about him; I could see nothing of what lay on the bed.

'Sammael?' I said.

There was a sound, a restless, waking sound.

'I heard you,' I said. 'You called me, didn't you?' There was no further noise from the bed and I approached it cautiously. The veils were sucked towards its centre, obscuring my sight. I leaned against one of the carved bed-posts and ran my fingers over the wood. My heart was beating strongly, but peculiarly slowly. I could feel its rhythm in every cell of my body. 'Sammael, something has taken Rayojini away. Something . . . I wanted to tell you as soon as it happened, but Metatron said you weren't to be disturbed. I'm very worried, Sammael. I've thought about little else.' I glanced at the bed. Something shifted among the veils and one of them tore loose from its rings with a tinkling rattle, wafting down to cover him like a shroud. I looked away. 'Sammael, will you find her for me? If she is with . . . the thing you are looking for, will you save her, bring her back?'

There was no reply, only a hissing kind of groan from the bed. I dared not look, wondering whether whatever he now was even understood speech.

'Gimel . . .' If a serpent could speak, its voice would sound like that: a flickery sigh. 'Where are you?'

'I'm here.' I turned and peered round the bed-post. Abruptly, all the veils tore loose and landed on the bed. Something writhed beneath them.

'Gimel, prepare yourself. See me as I am. As you truly should be.'

The bed creaked. I wondered whether I would be able to stand whatever sight was about to be revealed to me. 'Sammael, don't frighten me . . .'

He hissed again, and I screwed up my eyes. My forehead was pressed painfully against the wooden post. A storm was coming, down through the skies, a rushing of wings, so fast, so powerful. I felt him rise up before me, I felt the wind of his passage. I felt him all around me. I opened my eyes.

My black room was white. He filled it. He shone, his flesh was flesh no longer, but translucent. He was naked, but not even clothed in flesh. His hair was flames, was light. His wings were crammed into the corners of the room. He was too big for the space. He filled it.

'Be free,' I said, waving my arms as if to protect myself. 'Be free!' Then I fell to my knees, clutching the bed-post. I was not frightened, not exactly, but I wanted him away from me. I could not bear the weight of his presence. It was too alien, too immense. Had I really the potential to be like that myself? I could not believe it.

The being that was, is, and will be the Prince of Light – Sammael – threw back his shining head and roared. The entire room exploded outwards and upwards: a powder of bricks and stone. I squinted through the flying, gritty debris. His wings expanded above me until they filled the sky, beating slowly, painfully, as if long unused. And then he began to rise up in a whirling cocoon of torn veils, splintered wood and crushed stone. He rose up, up, claiming the air as his natural element. I knelt in the ruins of my blasted tower and shaded my eyes with my hands. For an instant, with the grace of a bird, he curved his neck to look at me. His eyes. . . .

'Rayo . . . Rayojini!' I gasped. 'Do not forget!'

He screamed and flexed his sky-filling wings. The heat of his gaze filled my eyes with water. I did not know whether he cared about, or even understood, my request. One moment he was there, my entire reality; the next, he was gone, and the wind started scattering the pulverised fragments of my black-veiled bed over the ragged edge of the tower. All that remained was the broken stump to which I was clinging.

I crawled backwards over the rubble, seeking the hole that would lead me to the stairs. I could not find it, but I could hear someone calling me from below. 'Here! Here!' I said, throwing rubble around in an attempt to find the way out.

'Keep still, keep still!' said a voice.

I crouched on the broken stone, holding back my flying hair, scanning the sky. There was no sign of Sammael now, but I felt he was travelling towards the East, towards the Strangeling. Of course. It was the only place in this world where the final confrontation could take place.

Ramiz's head appeared through the floor, his expression both surprised and frightened. It looked so comical, I started to laugh. Beth shouldered his way up beside me. He held out his hand. 'Come to me, Gimel. Slowly now. Slowly.'

I stood up, but the wind plucked at me fiercely, causing me to stagger.

'Gimel!' Beth cried. 'Be careful.'

I stooped and picked my way towards him. He virtually dragged me on to the rubble-strewn stairs.

'I'm all right!' I said, struggling to get out of his arms.

'You are bleeding, you are cut!' he said.

'Then lick me clean!'

Beth made a worried noise and shouted down the stairs. 'Tama-

378

ris, a tranquillising draught! Quickly!'

'Beth, I really am all right,' I said. 'And there is no time for tranquillisers. Have Ramiz fetch the carriage. We're travelling again.'

'Where?' he asked.

'East,' I replied. 'The Strangeling. We will miss the battle, but I'm hoping there will be spoils for the taking anyway.'

'Are you sure you're fit?' Beth asked.

I nodded. 'Completely. If you'd seen what I've just seen. . . .'

'What have you just seen?'

'It might have been the future, or the past, I'm not sure. But it was. . . . Let's just get ready to leave. In a while, I might think of the words to describe it.'

'. . . and from the gash a stream of nectarous humour issuing flowed sanguine, such as celestial spirits may bleed. And all his armour stained ere while so bright.'
Paradise Lost, Book VI

I could have been travelling for days, months, years, or a single eye-blink of time; time meant only memories of these things. All that existed was the direction I travelled: an invisible path in the mettle of manifestation. I was the spirit of all soulscapers, past and present.

The image of my guardian-pursuer had led me north-east out of Sacramante. I was afraid I would lose her in the city crowds, but she was always just ahead of me. I followed her through the autumn festival hysteria – black-eyed girls in scarlet frills danced in the plazas, but none of them were artisans. Torn, scarlet leaves scratched along the cobbles which led to the zukos, and once there among the barrows and stalls, the sweet perfume of ripe fruit filled the air. Leaves lay on the rosy apples, and soft yellow pears, on the dull, musky grapes – mistletoe-white, citrine-green, grapes the colour of my dead mother's skin. Dying leaves curled in the air, wept by the sentinel trees. My tormentor was a purple flame among this colour; she never paused.

Down to the harbour then, and the rank sea-smell of weed and fish guts. It was low tide and boats lolled in the shallows, brass rings set into their masts catching the afternoon sun. Children ran along the jetties. I heard them singing, 'The pale lady dances, the pale lady falls, up again, up again, smelling out souls!' Gulls cried around my head. The image of my guardian-pursuer kept just in sight. Sometimes it seemed as if she were looking around to check whether I was following, but I might have imagined that.

At the edge of the harbour, where wide stone steps, gritty with sand, lead up to the western suburbs of the city, I looked back. Sacramante rose behind me – white and cream and soft terracotta. Beyond this gentle stone I could see the dark, featureless walls of the atelier courts, and the sharp black towers rising above them embellished with elaborate stone lace. The atelier courts were beyond me now. I would never walk within those walls. Never. Bells were ringing. Perhaps it was just inside my head.

Out through the ever-open gates of the city, on to the north-eastern road. I thought nothing about buying provisions, nothing about how I would shelter at night, but simply walked in the direction my lady had taken, keeping the royal colour of her cloak in sight. There was much traffic on the road, owing to the harvest; carts laden with produce heading for the Sacramantan zukos. I paid them no attention, did not even glance at the busy workers in the fields to either side of the road calling greetings to the travelling farmers. I just kept walking.

The first night I walked until the moon had set. My lady was just a vague shadow further up the road, tireless. I was afraid of losing her, believing that if I paused to rest, she would simply vanish for ever. Eventually, I could walk no more and had to lie down in a dry ditch to sleep. The tall grass around me rustled constantly, crickets chirruped round my head, and the full-blown aroma of the season cushioned my aching body. I wondered what Keea had thought when he'd found me gone. Keea, who are you? I wondered. Did you tell me the truth? It was all so confusing. The eloim could be evil or benevolent, depending on how you looked at the situation. They were victims or oppressors, perhaps both. There were no simple answers. It was a question of individual belief, I felt, nothing more.

Whose side are you on?

Lying there within a bed of whispering grass, I was aware of my own insignificance. The soulscape had seemed limitless to me. Now I wondered whether it was nothing but another small world, in a multi-layered universe of many worlds – material and otherwise. My powers, of which I was so proud, might be no greater than an ant's in relation to the powers of those I might be opposing. But there was comfort in the thought that in its own nest, an ant is master of its destiny. Only when it ventures outside where the predators stalk, and the world operates on a larger scale, is it helplessly vulnerable to the careless boot of a man or woman. I should have stayed in my nest, which was, of course, my ignorance. Now I was out among the giants, and I would have to be more vigilant. 'Who are you now?' I asked myself, and could not answer. What was I doing, and why? This was senseless. You know the woman you are tailing is not Gimel Metatronim, my instincts whispered. *You know it's not.* Why are you following her? And where is she leading you? Perhaps I would wake up in the morning and this senseless compulsion to follow the woman ahead would have left me. I might find it was all an illusion, as transient as those I had suffered in Khalt and the Strangeling. Yes, tomorrow I might be free.

I fell into a restless sleep and dreamt of Avirzah'e Tartaruchi. I dreamt of his face, frowning at me. 'You were advised to leave the city,' he said, 'but not this way.' I fancied I could hear a faint, distant call, like that of a mother calling her children home. 'Rayo!

382

Rayo!' It was not my mother's voice. 'I can hear you,' I answered in my dream, but whoever called my name walked right past me, a shadow, because I was invisible.

I was woken just after dawn by a couple of children who thought I was dead. Their family was travelling to Sacramante with a wagon of corn, and the mother offered me food. I was grateful for the food, although eager not to be detained. I ate standing up, wondering how far my phantom had got ahead of me. Then I saw her waiting on the road, some distance away. Just standing there, looking at me, tall and motionless. I don't think anyone saw her but myself.

Halfway through the morning she disappeared. I had been thinking about my visit to the eloim library, trying to remember everything Keea had told me, and my concentration on the vision ahead of me had flagged a little. Perhaps it was my attention alone that kept her solid in this world. Soon after I noticed her absence, a carter returning from the city drove up behind me and I was able to beg a ride. I already felt dazed and exhausted as if I'd been travelling for days; sometimes I thought I was back in Khalt, on the road with Keea. I could almost hear his voice. 'You saw what happened to me in Ykhey. They are ghouls, monsters. They drink blood.' And Salyon was sometimes with me. 'Life loses all meaning but for the sup. They never kill an unwilling victim. Never.' Lying back in the empty cart, on splintery boards that smelled of grapes, I fantasised a meeting with Gimel Metatronim. She comes running towards me on the road, her hair flying loose, her face creased into a mask of terror. 'Help me, Rayo, help me! They are chasing me. They will kill me!'

'You drink the blood of children, you are evil,' I say, and she puts her hands over her face.

'I was just living my life, that's all. Would you condemn the she-wolf for slaying rabbits in the snow? Would you deny her her food? Help me!'

And I draw her towards me, wrap her in my coat, hide her, keep her safe.

I left the carter when we reached the farm where he worked, waved goodbye as if I were just any traveller walking east, and continued my journey alone. Bochanegra became wild around me; desolate hill forests, where few people lived. As my journey progressed, all shreds of clarity left my mind and it seemed a dark tunnel formed around me, with my unknown destination as a vague smoky light far ahead. I kept on walking towards it, without pausing, sometimes being scooped up by occasional compassionate travellers who let me ride in their carts for a while. No one but I could see the tall figure walking steadily ahead of us. I knew this, even though I never asked anyone about it.

At length the blur of my passage solidified into recognisable shapes, and I knew I was back among the strange, contorted memories of the Strangeling. Of course, where else would my lady have led me to? New significance had come to the tumbled ruins; I walked a landscape of the past, along an avenue of spiritual fires. This was the way then. A scruffy young boy came out of a doorway by the side of the road leading a spindly mule.

'A ride for you, lady,' he said.

I thanked him and mounted the mule. 'Have you seen anyone else travelling east this morning?' I asked him.

He shook his head gravely. 'No. Seen nothing. But I heard them.'

'What did they say?'

'Give the lady a ride to Ykhey, they said. So I do.'

'What do I look like, to you?'

He squinted at me. 'You are the voice's hands,' he replied.

Of course I am.

Ykhey is strangely quiet. There are no phantom men at the gates, no celebrating people, no illusions. A chill wind blows leaves and rags along the empty streets. It does not look as if anyone has been here for centuries. The boy leads his mule some way into the city and then stops. He does not ask me to dismount, but I know it is time that I do. 'I cannot pay you,' I say. He says nothing, does not even look at me, but simply clicks his tongue at the mule and turns back the way we have come, leaving me alone. I walk onwards into the heart of Ykhey, letting my instincts guide me.

I stumble on to a cracked and rubbish-strewn plaza, where many small fires are burning. I am surrounded on all sides by crumbling palaces that even in their dissolution look as if they were once the homes of princes. I realise as I stand swaying on the splintered slabs that I have lost the thread of real life. It is stretching to an infinite thinness. And I am losing the equally fragile thread of sanity; it will not be long. Here among the broken stones I am sure the climax of my life is about to unfold. Should I care? The events of the last few months have broken down into essential components in my mind: archetype; symbol; myth. I feel that everything is softly falling into focus: soon my eyes will be clear, I shall see the whole picture. Such a pity that, now, it is irrelevant to me. Eloim; human; artisan; monster; beloved: all the same thing. Lives. They are lives. And the world is full of those, each one valid, each one different from any other. Why try to control the rich and complex variety of life? A cat may be a ruthless killer or a loving companion. The only importance is whether you're a mouse or a human being. No, I cannot attempt to sort out the problems of the world, simply because they are integral to life. No one truly has that power, not even our gods. All that compels me now is a mindless quest to see the face of the one I have pursued. I am like a child; afraid, yet

384

unable to resist the curiosity of looking at the monster. And I know the monster exists, and that it has no mercy.

I begin to walk across the plaza. My coat is hanging open, but I cannot feel the cold. Its damp hem brushes up sparks from the smouldering embers that dot the slabs. Their smoke fills the air with a pungent aroma I have never smelled before. And I am thinking, deep inside, 'Is this worth it? Is it really? Why am I here?' At the last moment, will something else materialise to lead me back to my life?

Indistinct forms flicker at the corners of my vision, like the shadows of flames, and finally, from this chaos of motion and suggestion, a solid body manifests itself in front of me: a single figure. Motionless; tall; dark: the archetypal shape of the last gatherer. Can it be that the guardian-pursuer of my childhood, a dream, a desire, made flesh, has come to mock me, lead me forward to destruction? No, she waits in Sacramante. No, she is here, now. The thirst for knowledge is folly. As we learn we realise how little we know, and the tiniest fragment of our knowledge is the whole of creation. This nurturing succubus before me now; the whole of my creation. I can hear my own, ragged laughter as I scrabble towards her. Soon she will retreat as she always has. Gimel has become her own ghost. By linking herself to me so long ago, by making me obsessed with her, she has created a third creature: the guardian-pursuer I should have had, drawn from my own mind. Gimel gave me the idea for this phantom, but it was I who made her live. I know I will never reach her, my tantalising vision, my innermost aspiration, because she is only the product of a fevered mind that craves miracles. I cannot see her face for she is hooded, and covered by her purple cloak. She is an emblem for utter impenetrability. And yet she seems so real. I am so close to her I can see the details of her clothing, the smudges of moss and mud along the hem of her cloak. I can see the dark thread of veins beneath the pellucid skin of her long, pale hands.

I shout obscenities towards her: threats, pleas. She makes no response. Stinging smoke blows across my eyes, acrid yet sweet upon the tongue, and when it passes, my demon has vanished. Of course.

Now I am standing where she stood. Now I am weeping for my cracked mind, my injured soulscape that is leaking so badly. Cracks in the soul leaking light. If the eloim ever existed, they are long dead. The artisans, like me, look for the impossible, the mythic and, not finding it, invent it. This is the explanation, and I have travelled across two countries to find it. The phenomena were there because I wanted to find them. Illusion. Keea and I: the company of the deranged. Is he pursuing his own fantasy now? I stand here with a smoky wind flinging hot ash into my eyes. There is nowhere for me to go. I have reached my destiny. Beneath my feet the plaza is fracturing, breaking up. But this is really only a symbol to show me that it is myself that is fracturing. All that I see around me is symbolic of my own condition: rubbish and decay. Then a final *self-semblance* is revealed to me. Just ahead of me the ground has opened up and I can see there are steps there, leading downwards. I move towards them and peer down. If the Strangeling is my Self, then I am permitted to enter into it and witness its destruction from within. The steps do not disappear into darkness as I expected, but into a dark, red light. This must be a symbol of my own inner pit, my deepest fears and most selfish desires. It is the place where the unfaceable lurks. And then, just for one brief instant of clarity, I find myself thinking, 'Well, maybe my beloved demon did not just *vanish*. Maybe she took herself down these steps . . . Maybe . . .' Perhaps she was hurrying and giggling to herself, thinking, 'I will run down here quickly, before the soulscaper notices. She will think I have winked out of existence.' Is that a possibility? I have nothing to lose so I put my feet on the uppermost step. I will go down to the dark then. Down. Chasing phantoms.

The passages are peopled by the mummified bodies of the ancient dead, perhaps even old thoughts and deeds, which writhe in the light of burning torches along the walls. The dead hate time and I have brought it into their dreamless dust-vessels, bringing sequence and life and the power of dissolution. I walk between them, thinking, 'This contorted shape was a failed healing, this a sour love affair. This . . .' I see a beautiful dead child with a posy of summer flowers in its lifeless hands. 'This my love for Q'orveh . . .' As I think that, the dim passageway is suddenly suffused with an intense and blinding white radiance which has no source. The air has become light. I cannot see anything around me. I am blundering in this thick, painful light, feeling with my fingertips into the future, for I know there is no going back, no possible chance of going back. Then there is a sound just behind me; a chuckling laugh, and a voice. 'Oh see, she can count all her fingers and toes!' Ushas! I turn around quickly but my eyes are blinded by the power of light. It is so bright I cannot tell whether my eyes are open or closed. A feeling of arrested time is all around me, like when I was in Ykhey with Keea and saw the vision of the trefoil pool. I am sure that outside, overhead, somewhere in reality, the clouds are hurrying across the sky, dragging the seasons behind them. The moon is speeding like a comet from horizon to horizon, towing her train of silver light, and the seas heave biliously beneath. Dynasties rise and fall in the royal houses of the world. Birth, death, birth. The table mountain crumbles and the Taps disperse into other lands. While all this happens above, here below in the place of no time at all, I take only a single step.

386

Soon the gods begin to walk. These I know are part of me, for they are silhouettes against the lightness. Triple goddesses; sacrificed kings; devourers; avengers; virgins; androgynes; hunters and huntresses; baalim; demons; qlippot: they troop by me, staring out at an existence up ahead. Here come the heroes, their shoulders bowed by the burdens of the world, carrying their totemic weapons: the axe; the great sword; the lance. And here, the dark heroines of the imagination with their subtler weapons of poison and cruelty. Behind them pad the lions of valour, the horned beasts of magickal submission, the great birds who bear the gods, who carry messages between the realms of light and dark. Now I must have truly entered the soulscape in body and mind, the place where all dreams, nightmares and desires live out their shadow-life. I must have left the real world behind. There is no scaping-fume at work here, although I do recall the pungency of the smoke I walked through on the plaza. Are there scaping-mixes, of which the Taps are unaware, that can transport flesh as well as spirit? I cannot step back from this soulscape into reality: I am trapped here. The work that has sustained me, lain down and offered its breast to me, has finally destroyed me, devoured me, assimilated my being into its fluid landscape. I am no longer separate from the fantasies I have explored. As this thought brings me a certain melancholy comfort, the lightness dims abruptly and I am left in an equally impenetrable darkness; lightlessness so intense, my eyes feel sucked back into my skull. I put my fingers against my face and press hard.

There is cool air on my skin. I blink and someone, or something, places a reality in front of my eyes. I am back above ground in the plaza, but it is not quite the same place that I left. Around its perimeter, the buildings are whole, and the plaza itself is an elaborate marble mosaic, swept clean but for a dusting of white blossom from the nearby shrubs and trees. It seems as if I have surfaced into a summer evening; early summer, because it is not that warm. I can hear the music of flutes and strings in the distance, and their air is heavy with the scent of flowers. And yes, someone murmurs my name through this romantic evening and I turn around. Behind me is a soaring white palace: tiers of marble columns, terraces going up and up, a forest of collonades. It is a home of spirits I am sure. An endless sweep of shallow steps is a frozen wave of white, rearing up from the plaza, cresting against the shadowed porticoes of the palace. Upon these steps there is an indistinct figure, but I can see that it is beckoning me forwards.

My feet are on the lowest step. I sway as if on the lip of a great abyss.

'Come Rayojini, follow me.'

And then I can see, as if a veil has been torn in two before my eyes, that it is Keea standing there, Keea wrapped in a long, dark cloak, his hair across his face. I say his name and he retreats up the steps, drawing me behind as if on an invisible tether. He leads me into the shadows of this great edifice. Inside the air is smoky with offertory fumes, some of them those of the exorcism, recognisable for they are bitter upon the tongue. Others are sweet: the smoke of visions and dreams. We are in a vast hall, thickly bordered by spinneys and copses of columns, some white and straight, others curling and garlanded with carvings of leaves and flowers. Some are stained ochre, red sienna, and the royal, mystic turquoise. They are crowned by the lotus of duality, whose petals are edged with gold, attracting the low, yellow light and making it shine more brightly. The boy is sublimely beautiful. He wears a crown of flowers and thorns; there is blood upon his soft cheek.

'Keea, I do not believe this is you,' I say. 'Everything here is just a part of my mind. Perhaps finding you here means you are dead.'

He smiles and shakes his head. 'Dead am I? Come touch my skin, Rayojini.'

'All feels real in the soulscape. Even shadows.' But I reach out to touch him anyway, and his flesh is warm at the throat, trembling with life. Such is the intensity of our illusions.

'Look,' he says and lets the cloak fall away from him.

Beneath it his body is naked. The skin is tawny gold, fitting like a tight sheath over his muscles and bones. 'Yes, you are lovely,' I say, and it is nothing more than a sigh. 'A lovely illusion.'

'I am no illusion, Rayo. Believe it. You think you are in your soulscape, but you are not. I have led you to the brink of the *eloim* soulscape and together we shall swim its depths and crests.'

He has such power. Is this the person who has been at my side since Khalt? Was it he who caused the birds and bats of Helat's shrine to whirl around my head? If so, who is he? Keea? A mere boy? Somehow, I think not. I have felt his difference continually, but have ignored the frantic signals my intuition screamed into my head, although, to my credit, I have never trusted him completely. 'What are you?' I ask him. 'Show me now. The time that you promised has come, when you said you would tell me everything.'

'Look deep,' he says, and his flesh becomes smoky. It is as if a hundred soul envelopes of the boy are separating away, peeling off like discarded skin. I wonder what he will show me: will I be able to stand the sight of it? The image of Keea vibrates so fast, he has become a blur, shaking his essential components apart. The sight is making me dizzy. I press my hands against my eyes, and through them I can see the vibration abating, slowing down, revealing that my Keea has become something else. He has shaken himself into an expression of his spiritual polarity: female. For a second, maybe less time than that, I assimilate this, before realising with a thrill of anticipation and horror that I am looking at Gimel Metatronim.

388

In this place, the truth of myself is revealed to me. Perhaps I should bow before her. 'You are her,' I say. 'You have always been her.'

She nods. 'On the road in Khalt, I breathed upon you. In Sacramante I led you through the autumn festivals and left you my coin of the dead. Always me, Rayojini, always. The Metatronim lady you believed me to be is but a simple child in comparison. She could not have drawn you to this place as I have done.'

'But if you are not Keea, and not Gimel, then who are you?'

She smiles. 'Look deeper still,' she replies and begins to vibrate again. Rays of light spin out, hurled like spears. The image of Gimel cracks like glass and splinters away. Something extraordinary rises up through the light. Now I realise I am truly mad. What I see before is a man, but more than a man. It can only be an eloim, but not an artisan of Sacramante, oh no. I am reminded of the wall paintings in Helat's temple, the account that Keea read out to me in the eloim library. What I see can only be a creature from the dawn of creation, the spawn of Eloat.

If I thought I had visualised gods before I was wrong.

He spreads his wings and they fill my sight. He is immense. He is silver light clad in silver scales which are torn in one place: above the heart. His face is one of infinite kindness, yet terrible. He is too beautiful to behold, too strange, too big. In his hands I would be nothing more than a kitten, a single bud, a mote of dust.

'Come with me, Rayojini,' he says, and enfolds me with his light. He puts me inside one of the feathers in the joint of his left wing. I can hear the tumult of his heart there. 'Come with me.'

The temple-palace has become dark around us, but for a tube of painful effulgence radiating from above. We are bleached to invisibility in this light. It is full of spinning motes, like dust in sunlight on a quiet summer afternoon. The enormous wings beat slowly and we ascend the tube of light. Is this really *their* soulscape?

My thoughts are his thoughts, because I am a single feather in the joint of his wing. He can taste my feelings. 'It is just another world,' he says, 'but the soulscape too. I will take you to a place where you can work for as long as you like. It will please you.'

'Where?'

'An *other* place.'

'What shall I do there?'

'Gather up the veils that you will find; all of them. Destroy them!'

It seems so simple. I know I can do what he tells me.

Lying back in the summery softness of his warmth, I can smell mimosa, jasmin, sacred rose. We rise up, up, through clouds of different hues until we come to a green-and-blue place where a gate hangs in the sky. Here he pauses.

'Through the gate; you must pass through,' he says.

'Alone?'

'Yes. I cannot pass.'

Suddenly I am standing before him on a grassy road. In one direction there are fields. It is the direction we have come from. In the other is a dark forest. He has condensed into the form of a tall winged man, sheathed in silver scales. Long, dark hair falls over his shoulders. A scabbard hangs from his hip, but there is no sword. I know he is smiling, even though I cannot truly perceive his features.

'Go now,' he says. 'Into the forest.'

'To look for veils?'

'Yes. Veils. They are stretched across the trees. Tear them up. Only you can do this Rayojini.'

As we talk, facing each other, I begin to understand the concept of reality again. I can feel the air against my skin. What am I doing here? Who is this creature?

'Why do you want me to do this?' I ask him.

'It will release your world from a curse.'

The eloim? Imaginary beings? It's madness to believe this creature is really from Eleneon. It's more likely I'm using imagery that my mind has accumulated in Sacramante. The realistic hallucinations have stimulated *all* my senses, but I must not forget my training. In succumbing to the visions – believing them – I am no longer worthy of the title 'soulscaper'. This creature before me is a visualisation of my higher spiritual self. Therefore I should listen to him. My explanation sounds so plausible: why do I feel uneasy about it?

'But what will actually *happen* if I tear down these veils?' I ask. 'I can't undertake a task without knowing the consequences.'

He flickers and the light within him momentarily dims. 'You must do it,' he says. 'Neither you nor I have a choice in the matter.'

'That's no answer!' I tell him. 'There is always a choice.'

'Remember the passage I read to you from the book in Sacramante, Rayojini. Now it's your task to rid the Earth of the parasites who feed upon humanity. It is the ultimate testing of your prowess.'

Am I being deceived again? I hear him laughing.

'You still do not believe, do you, soulscaper,' he says. 'You are an eternal sceptic.'

'Maybe, but scepticism has kept me sane,' I reply.

'Sanity is no help to you here.'

If I have created this radiant spirit, then why have I wounded him? Blood is trickling between the scales of his armour. I have not noticed it before. 'You are bleeding,' I say.

'I have bled for ever,' he says, as if he were speaking about the colour of his skin or hair. It is simply a part of him.

'Above the heart?' I say. I know it is symbolic. Then I remember the story of Mikha'il and his brother. Sammael was wounded above the heart. Can this be Sammael? No. The legendary Lord of Light and his followers are supposed to be the ones who are *preventing*

390

me from entering the eloim soulscape.

He nods slowly. 'Yes, I am wounded, as I have inflicted wounds. Mine will never heal.'

At these words, a fresh rill of blood spills over the silver scales. 'The bleeding is getting worse!' I say. 'Look, the blood is running down on to the grass.'

He puts his fingers against the wound, and then his head jerks back as if he has heard a faint, far cry.

'What was that?' I ask. He does not answer me, but his wings lift a little. The thin stream of blood has reached my toes. I take a step back.

'Go into the forest,' he says. 'Now!' When he turns his head, I can see that his eyes have become silver flame. I shrink backwards, towards the trees. The force of his eyes pushes me back.

'Hurry, Rayo!' The voice is Keea's.

'No, you still haven't told me the consequences of this action. Who are you? *What* are you?' If he has been created by my imagination, then he must speak.

He does not answer. His movements have become graceless; he stumbles on the road, slipping in blood. 'Please hurry.'

'Tell me why I must do this!'

'Because my brother . . .'

Even as he speaks, his voice is engulfed by a mighty, booming shout. The sound of it fills the air, and it cries: 'MIKHA'IL!'

The shout splits the sky. The whole of reality becomes the name and it is not just a call, but also a question. Mikha'il: son of Eloat. In *my* soulscape? Is that possible? Suddenly my mind opens out as if someone, or something, has turned a key and flung its locked doors wide. I accept what I perceive as reality. I am not insane, after all. I am living a dream, but it is not fantasy. 'I know you,' I say, pointing at him. 'You are . . .'

'MIKHA'IL!'

The sound of his name has become beating wings. He seems to summon up the threads of his strength and leaps up from the road. For a moment he has forgotten me, and I watch him as he grows, filling up the sky. I am ankle-deep in his blood, and the smell of it is terrible. It smells like grief. With a sweep of his hand, he hurls me towards the trees. 'Tear the veils!' he cries. 'Go into the forest and rip them to shreds. Now!'

'No!' I say. 'I will not do that. I *can't* do that! My work is that of a healer. Convince me that ripping down the veils will accomplish some healing, and I will do it. Otherwise . . .' I shake my head. I am not afraid of him. The worst thing he can do to me is take my life, and that is not so bad.

He doubles up in pain and clutches himself above the heart. He cannot stem the flow of blood. 'Please do as I tell you, Rayo,' he says, 'before it is too late.'

'The veils represent the souls of eloim on Earth, don't they?' I say. 'If I tear them down, I will be helping you destroy the artisans. Then the creature called Eloat will have authority over my world. I remember the story you read to me – every word of it. It wasn't a biased account, I know it wasn't.'

'We cannot prevent the inevitable!' Mikha'il says. 'Rayo, the time of Eloat has come to Earth. You cannot stop it.'

'Maybe not, but neither will I make it easy for him! You can't convince me that humanity will benefit from Eloat's influence! The artisans prey and they drink blood, but for all their depradations, our world is far from stagnant. I don't like the thought of a stagnant world, Mikha'il, and I am sure that is what we'd have under your father's dominion. I will not help you.'

He shrinks in stature and becomes a man, just Keea, standing there looking at me, pale from blood-loss, clutching an ancient wound.

'You do not understand, Rayo,' he says. 'Eloat's will must be done. I cannot fight it. You cannot fight it. My father is too powerful. You *must* help me! Until my brother and his followers are dead, I am condemned to suffer.'

'Why?'

'It is a punishment for failing to destroy them before.'

'Do you really want to kill them?' I ask him gently. 'Destruction is not the answer. It seems to me that Eloat is only interested in acquiring power over humanity. The artisans stand in his way. And you, Mikha'il, are an unwilling assassin, for all your deceptions and trickery.'

He smiles weakly. 'Do not try to work your art on me, Rayo, there is no point. I have no autonomy to heal myself.'

He is a pathetic creature. I feel only pity for him. 'I cannot do what you ask,' I tell him, 'but I'll willingly do anything I can to help solve the dilemma between the artisans and humanity. If I can heal the eloim of their mind-sickness, I'll do that too.'

He shakes his head vehemently. 'You should not care about the eloim. They drink the blood of humankind.'

It all seems so clear to me now. 'Maybe they had to because they were trapped on Earth. They gave us so much in return. They gave us knowledge. They gave us art. For all I know, they gave us soulscaping. Now, you want me to destroy them? No. You are wrong.' Where do these words come from? Why am I so sure? I have Gimel's image in my head as I speak. She has never tried to prey on me. Yet she could have done, surely? And Beth, what had he brought me but forbidden pleasure in my dreams? If he had bitten me then, he had not drawn blood. Neither of them had behaved as mindless predators. They had invaded my life because they needed me. And Keea had intercepted me before I could hear the truth from them.

392

This is an alien land, and I don't know how to get back to my reality, but I am jubilant. Now I begin to understand.

Mikha'il is fading, even as I watch. Eloat overestimates his power. Mikha'il is a tortured being, and his suffering is weakness. To govern by subjection and torture is a mistake.

'You have deceived me,' I say. 'You perverted the image of Gimel Metatronim in my mind. You manipulated me, you humiliated me, and you tried to break my sanity with your illusion-spinning in Khalt and the Strangeling! I know that now.'

He cries out and falls to his knees. I walk towards him through the foam of blood and lean down. Beneath my hand he feels human. He is shaking. When he looks up at me, there are tears in his eyes. 'The things you say are true,' he says weakly. 'But I was created for only for one purpose. And it destroys me. What can I do? I can only obey the command of my creator.'

'Why not let the cycle complete itself?' I ask him. 'You know that your brother was supposed to take the place of Eloat. Why not let that happen? We can do something to begin that process in this place. Will it kill you to help me do that?'

Mikha'il screws up his eyes. He appears to be very near death. 'I am not allowed to do that,' he says. 'My life or death means nothing.'

'Not to Eloat, no, but to Sammael?'

At the mention of his brother's name, his eyes fill with fear. 'You should not have said that name. He will have heard you. He is coming. I feel it.'

My body aches in resonance with his eternal sorrow.

'I am an idea, a purpose,' he says. 'Nothing beyond that. I am not a brother, not a lover, not even a son.' He reaches out with red, sticky fingers to clutch at my coat. I take his hands in my own.

'Sammael is coming,' I say. 'Wait for him.'

He moves feebly in my arms. 'Wait for him? Then I wait for death. He will not forgive me. From him, I can expect only vengeance.'

'Perhaps, but I don't believe that.'

'You are only human. This is beyond your experience.'

'Maybe so, but in my human ignorance I still recall the account you read to me in Sacramante, and how it told of Sammael's grief. It did not speak of vengeance.'

'Oh, Rayo, I hurt so much. I will bleed until Sammael is dead or he has killed me! Look at me. It is too late.' He groans and convulses. 'Hold me, Rayo, hold me tight. Make me feel something. I cannot feel . . .' His head lolls against my chest and I hold his body very tightly. It is so light, less weight than a small child, as if all its substance is floating away like dust. I am soaked in his blood, his holy blood. I hold on to him, willing him substance, willing him

393

flesh. 'Come soon,' I cry, inside my head. 'Please come soon, come soon!'

'Forgive me, Rayo,' Mikha'il says. It is a weak sound.

I kiss his hair. 'Hush. We are all puppets, in one way or another. I do not blame you.' I can't stop the tears falling from my eyes. I am weeping for the world, for Mikha'il, for Gimel. I am weeping for myself. Is this the end of everything, here on an empty road, with a dying spirit in my arms? I solved the puzzle too late. If I had listened to Q'orveh, would it have made any difference? Still, no point in crying about it now. I am facing the unknown and in these last moments my old vigour returns in force. This is an adventure, and I am not afraid. 'Hold on,' I say to Mikha'il. 'Hold on. I am with you.' He does not answer. Perhaps he is already dead.

Then we are surrounded by light, light so dense and real we could gather it up in our arms and eat it, bathe in it, clothe ourselves in it. I see a being of light, manifesting itself in the sky before us, similar to Mikha'il as I had first seen him, yet stronger, more vital. It is a creature of purpose and intention, whose motives are founded in greater concerns than fear of punishment. It can only be the brother of Mikha'il. He comes towards us and all I am holding in my arms is the fragment of a fragile soul. This I offer up to the Prince of Light. Before he takes my burden from me, he asks, 'Do you act of your own free will?' He asks me that. I cannot believe it and can hardly answer.

'Yes! Yes!'

Then he stoops and becomes, as Mikha'il did, a tall winged man, standing upon the road. But he does not wear armour; he is as naked as love, clothed only in his wings. His hair is exactly the same colour as the blood all around me. He kneels down in front of me and takes the smoky vestiges of his brother into his arms. 'Mikha'il, I am here. I have you,' he says, and with his fingernails rips the skin of his own chest above the heart. He places Mikha'il's insubstantial head against the wound, and lets his brother drink. It is so bizarre, so like a mother with her child. And just like a woman carelessly breastfeeding an infant, he talks to me while the meal is taken. 'You are Rayojini,' he says.

'Yes, I am.'

'Gimel has told me about you. She chose well.'

'I have done nothing,' I say.

'Precisely,' Sammael answers, and smiles.

Mikha'il has regained his substance. He does not look like Keea any more, nor even Gimel. I realise that he is the person who pressed the coin into my hand at Ykhey's gates, the strange figure I'd seen sneaking out of the upper room at The Temple Gate Inn. He is still weak and lies helplessly in his brother's arms, but I know he is no longer dying.

'Now we must conclude our business,' Sammael says, and gets to his feet, dragging Mikha'il to a shaky stand.

'My purpose is to kill you,' Mikha'il says. 'I am the obstacle in your path. Why sustain me? Why hold me now? I am your nemesis.'

'My purpose is to love you,' Sammael replies, 'and you are only an obstacle if you will it so. I shall sustain you for eternity, for we are the future of two worlds. Separately we are in conflict, but together we are Potential.'

I stand apart from them, watching, listening.

'You desire power!' Mikha'il cries. It seems that, even now, he is still clinging on to the lies he has been taught.

Sammael has great patience. 'I desire change,' he says softly, 'for the good of all. I am a servant of Elenoen and Earth, not a god. That is the difference you must understand.'

'You are lying!' Mikha'il cries, struggling in Sammael's hold. 'This cannot be true!'

Sammael will not let him go. 'How can I persuade you?' he asks, and I can hear desperation in his voice. 'By saying that in memory of you, I have lived apart from my people for hundreds of years? By telling you I never gave up hoping, that I *knew* the time would come when the arrested possibilities would begin to flow? You think I want to become Eloat? You are wrong; it is a lonely, terrible existence. And yet, it is my destiny. I have no choice; no matter how strongly I would like, at this moment, to take you back to Earth and hide. We *could* hide, Mikha'il. I could take you beyond the reach of Eloat's whip. Without you it will take Eloat aeons to penetrate Earth's reality again. We could be together for that long. But I will deny myself such contentment. This is the only proof I can give you of my intention. I have waited, Mikha'il, to tell you these things, and I trust your integrity. Do not disappoint me.'

Mikha'il turns his head to look at me. Does he really want my counsel? I am only human. 'Try it,' I say. 'What have you to lose? If believing Sammael is the wrong decision, you will die and Earth will suffer; but if it is the right decision, anything could happen. Great and wondrous things, perhaps. If I were you, I'd just believe him. It's worth the risk, isn't it?'

'Listen to her,' Sammael says, 'human minds are full of marvels. Eloat will not be able to resist our combined intention to remove him and to rid our world of its stagnation. Let the new day dawn. Conjoin with me again and we'll take this power home.'

Their communion is beyond my comprehension. I see two winged beings, neither male nor female, spiralling up in a tangle of wings. They begin to spin so fast it is impossible to discern the two separate beings at all, and when the spinning stops, there is only one.

I jump up, suffused by wild joy. 'Who are you?' I cry out.

'Samikha'il!' they answer. And I begin to laugh, the breathtaking laughter of tears.

Samikha'il holds a sword in his hand. It is a sword of energy, the energy of raw creativity. There is a sound around me like lightning shattering plates of glass the size of the Earth. 'Help me make me a doorway, Rayojini,' Samikha'il says.

'A doorway into where? Earth reality?'

'No. Elenoen. We must pass through and put an end to this conflict once and for all, for the sake of both our worlds. Samikha'il cannot make this portal alone. In our combined state we are detected as a threat and there is opposition, but you, you can do it.'

'How?' I screech, my fists bunched in frustration. 'I don't know Elenoen! I can't visualise how to reach it!'

'It is very simple,' Samikha'il says, patiently. 'To you, Elenoen is the place beyond death, beyond the soulscape. Use your art, soulscaper. Make the portal with your art.'

Beyond death. To visualise that and make it real, I have to die. I know that. Death. I don't want to die. And yet my purpose in life has always been to help others, to alleviate sickness and distress wherever or however I uncover it.

'Do what is necessary, then!' I say. 'I will do all I can to make this portal you need.'

'Of your own free will?'

'Yes, of my own free will.' At this final moment, it seems as if this is the task for which I have been born.

Samikha'il looms over me, scorching me with his beauty. I close my eyes. 'Lift your head to me, Rayo . . .' His is the kiss of a timorous lover. I feel his inhuman lips on my throat, the heat of it. The bite, when it comes, is cold. I feel myself begin to sink as the blood flows into his mouth; it is almost soothing. No pain. No pain at all. His teeth grind into the muscles of my neck; ecstasy and torment. And my life, my very being, is flowing out of me. Unholy nourishment. Holy nourishment. He drains me slowly.

The trauma of it feels like being torn, but it is no more than suddenly having the ability to experience reality in a different way. I am waiting for the end . . . for what? I cannot foretell. I am no longer flesh, no longer blood. I am soul. Free.

Samikha'il seizes the essence I have become in his wings. I know instinctively the right thought-forms to create the portal. It is just like opening an unlocked door. Through the portal I can see another world thronged by creatures who are but dim reflections of the being in whose aura I ride. This world is not like the one I know in any way. It is not like any soulscape I have ever seen. It is beyond words utterly.

We streak through it, to its heart. The sword is raised; the crest of infinite probability about to break into a thousand waves. I hear a sound that is like no other, but I know it is the sound of a frightened god. Around me the echo is taken up by a million, million other gods, in other realities and other worlds, who feel the wave breaking, who feel the tide, who feel the new day. Unleashed, the sword flies, and its name is Potential. In that place I know. I am Knowledge. And the swords strikes home.

'Then with transition sweet new speech resumes.
Thus thou hast seen one world begin and end . . .
much thou hast yet to see . . .'
Paradise Lost, Book XII

I came to my senses in a room of glass. I was lying on a hard,
glossy surface. It was neither warm nor cold. Light filled my eyes;
it was so bright I dared not open them. For a few moments I could
not recall who I was or where I might be, knowing only that to find
myself conscious at all was surprising. I could not remember why.

'Rayo . . . Rayojini.'

Strange sounds. What could they mean? In a way they were
familiar but . . .

'Soulscaper! Awake! Look at me!'

Slowly I opened my eyes, but I could not discern the details of
my surroundings. Who calls . . . Who calls . . . And to whom?

'It is I, Samikha'il, who is now Eloat.'

The words were like pictures in my mind. I saw a dusty room, a
table, an ancient book. Suddenly a wave of sensation coursed
through my body. It was like being woken from a deep sleep by a
harsh blow. I threw myself upright, scrabbling on the shiny surface.
If this was death, I needed to face it on my feet. I was in an
enormous room of ice or crystal, all of which was glowing with
its own light. Tall, shimmering figures stood around its edge that
appeared, to me, like flames with eyes. Before me stood a god:
Samikha'il. He looked similar to the man I had seen at the gates
of Ykhey, while at the same time very different. It was hard to
describe. His skin glowed like soft yellow flame and his hair was
black and red, like the smouldering colours of a low fire. I had
never seen, nor could have imagined, such raw beauty.

'Gently now, Rayo.' His arms were ready to enfold me, and it
was beyond me to refuse their embrace. As he touched me, all
tiredness fled my mind. I felt strong, and alert and full of energy,
but there were peculiar squeaky sounds around me, which I quickly
realised was my own voice trying to speak.

'The cold,' I gasped. 'The bite, the sword . . . Oh Helat!' I put
my hands over my eyes. 'I'm dead! I'm dead!'

I could hear Samikha'il laughing. 'Dead *where* exactly?' he said.

'I don't know,' I said shaking my head. 'You tell me!'

'I have brought you to Elenoen,' he said.

399

'Then, it is over . . . the problem . . . all over?'

He nodded, smiling. 'Almost. However, there is one final task for which I must call upon your service. I do not ask you to do this for myself alone, but for others whom I feel you care about.'

'What task?'

'Something to do with veils,' he answered.

In the forest there are veils between the trees. Some of them are like dew-beaded spiders' webs, some like spun silk of fabulous colours, but others are torn and stained. This is a soulscape and I am a soulscaper. The Fear has many forms. Sometimes it will come blindly to flap around your head. Sometimes it is a wave of darkness, or a shambling monster, or corrosive fog. Sometimes it is less threatening than that. I conjure my elemental weapons. A sword, a fierce and cleansing wave, or a spiritual fire? No, they are a wooden tub of water, a bar of soap, a pack of needles and a basket of cotton reels. I walk to the trees and take down the veils, one by one. Some can be folded neatly, while others have to be washed and repaired by careful sewing. It takes me a long time, perhaps years, but the work is hardly strenuous. I work steadily, without sleep or food, never tiring, never hungry. Sometimes there are vague, shimmering shapes among the trees that sing to me in lovely voices. Music is my sustenance. There are so many veils! I had no idea the eloim were so prolific on earth.

Eventually I have an enormous yet tidy stack of folded veils, and the forest is somehow brighter, sunlight coming down through the trees. I stand upon a narrow, twisting path, which is ribbed by ancient roots and dotted with tiny, pale flowers. Even though the pathway disappears from sight between the trees, I can see a doorway at the end of it, a doorway in the air. I recognise it immediately, for it has the marks of my own people upon it. It is the portal to the soulscape of humanity.

I look at the towering bale of silk and direct a simple command. The soulscape is malleable. It is no problem for me to change the shape of these veils so that I can carry them all in my arms.

I walk down the path in the filtered sunlight and come to the door at the end of it. I put down the veils and open it. Then I pick them up again and step through the portal. Beyond it a landscape stretches out to a limitless horizon. I see cities, forests, oceans, mountains. The veils fly out of my arms, high on the wind like flags, or kites, or butterflies. I watch them go. They fold and twist upon the air, forming into the shapes of tumbling bodies that fall to the ground. These forms looked dazed. They pat insubstantial faces with misty hands, but even as I observe, they are solidifying. Soulscape creatures emerge from hiding to examine what has come among them. There are men; women; children; animals; monsters; sylphs; dragons; gods; goddesses; heroes and tricksters. And many

400

more than that. Some make angry noises to warn they will not let strangers take liberties in their territory, while others are simply curious, stretching forward to sniff and touch. I smile. It is a beginning at least. There are new wonders in the soulscape of my people now.

Without looking around I knew that Samikha'il was standing behind me. For some reason I did not think I should look at him, although I was grateful for the pressure of his hand upon my shoulder. I realised that the rags of my clothes, my skin, were still stained with Mikha'il's blood. 'Your work is done,' Samikha'il said.

I sighed. 'It would seem so. What now?' I had not imagined that death would have to be planned, like life.

Samikha'il squeezed me gently with his fingers. 'That is up to you. Elenoen is indebted to you, Rayo, myself especially. And I dislike being in debt. Therefore I have to offer you a choice.'

'Choice? Another one?' I had had enough of decision-making. Now that my work was done, I felt very tired. All I wanted to do was lie down upon the grass of the soulscape and sleep. 'I am Rayojini,' I said wearily. 'Daughter of Ushas, daughter of a skilled line, and I have already made my choice. Remember?'

Samikha'il rested his cheek against my hair, so that his voice whispered close to my ear. 'A choice that was made unselfishly, and of your own free will. And that is why the eloim will repay you. The choice is simply this: you can return with me to Elenoen and become eloim yourself or, if you wish, you may return to Earth to finish your own cycle there. You surrendered your most precious possession – life – in order to assist me. I want to reward you. Rayojini, please don't deny me that. Make your choice!'

I thought about it in silence, and he did not push me for an answer immediately. My thinking was augmented by the blissful attention he paid to my neck and shoulders, nipping kisses that did not draw blood. He was excited, I think, by the dried blood of Mikha'il's that had gummed up my hair and coated my flesh and clothes. He licked a small patch of my skin clean, tasting himself there. It suggested that, should I elect to stay with him, more intimate pleasures might be shared. Who could resist such an offer? Then, I thought of Earth, of my people and my work. I thought of striding across the plains of Khalt in the autumn sunshine: the colourful, riotous zukos of Sacramante, and the high dreys of Taparak, my home. I thought of Gimel Metatronim, whom I was yet to meet in person. I would have so much to tell her now, and surely the eloim would be needing the help of an accomplished soulscaper to come to terms with their new position in the world?

Once, Mikha'il had left me a Khaltish ka on a taverna table in Sacramante. It had paid for the passage of the dead, and more. It paid apparently, for their return to life.

'Send me home,' I said.

402

'The world was all before them, where to choose
their place of rest, and providence their guide . . .'
Paradise Lost, Book XII

This is the dawn of a new age. We felt the tug, the pull of it, as
we travelled east to the Strangeling. We knew in our hearts that
somehow, somewhere, Sammael had succeeded. We knew this
because suddenly we were filled with hope and happiness for no
reason at all. 'The sickness is past!' I said, 'The sickness is past!'
Nobody disputed my words; Beth and Avirzah'e felt it too.

'And so is our disguise in this world,' Beth said.

I took his hands. 'We must not be afraid. At least we have a
chance now. It is up to us, all eloim, to make our own future. And
we still have human friends to help us.'

'It will not be easy, Gimel,' Avirzah'e said. 'Some eloim might
resist change, and many humans will be hostile to us.'

'I know that, but I don't care. The change will be painful, but it
is necessary. At least we are together.'

'You then,' Beth said, grinning, 'can be the one to break the
news to Metatron.'

We found Rayojini sitting on the steps of a ruined building in
Ykhey, close to where Sammael, Metatron and I had visited the
ancients. A group of humans, native to the Strangeling, appeared
from nowhere when we entered the city, and took hold of our
horses' harness. Ramiz, driving the carriage, tried to scare them
off with a whip, but I leaned out of the window and told him to
leave them alone. They led us to the soulscaper, telling us they had
found her wandering around the plaza just after an explosion of
light had shattered the great palace there. All her clothes had been
tattered, but through the rags they could see that her skin was
glowing, so they concluded she was one of us. Since then they had
been caring for her, thinking her some kind of unusually dark-
coloured eloim seeress. She had been regularly fed, they assured
us, although the sustenance they had given her had made her sick
at first, and she'd been quite violent with them when they'd offered
her the sup. Consequently they had filled cups for her and spiced
the ichor with herbs, which she had reluctantly accepted. They had
cleaned her skin which had been strangely covered in blood,
although she had no wounds, and dressed her in clothes of their

own. They had expected someone to turn up and claim her.

I jumped out of the carriage and saw the ragged figure sitting on the steps. Behind her the palace was utterly destroyed, all its beautiful carvings pulverised, although Rayojini was resting her feet on a gilded, stone lotus flower, perhaps the only surviving relic. I was overjoyed to find her there, never believing for one moment during the journey east that she would be located so easily, if at all. She looked dishevelled and dazed, and rather incongruous in an elaborate scarlet gown of stained satin, her long braids loose around her body. She was wearing woollen fingerless mittens, and a large battered hat with a wide brim. Her feet were bare. Her skin was exactly the same colour as some beautiful purple-black beads I have. She looked, even in her state of disarray, good enough to eat. I wanted to hug her immediately, but realised I should be cautious. How much had she learned about Beth and I? Did she resent us?

'Rayojini?' I said, walking up the steps towards her. She was staring at her feet and did not look up as I approached. Beth and Avirzah'e lingered behind me, knowing this moment was mine alone. 'Rayojini, are you all right?'

She looked up then, with dark and unfocused eyes. I was afraid she did not know me. 'I am Gimel Metatronim,' I said.

She blinked. 'They've gone.'

I sat down beside her on the steps and took one of her cold mittened hands in my own. She smelled very strange, as if she were wearing a perfume of blood, frankincense and myrhh. 'Sammael?' I asked her. 'Did he reach you in time?'

She smiled and chuckled a little. 'Oh yes. Yes. He killed me.'

She must be hallucinating. I put an arm around her shoulders. It felt so familiar to do that, yet it was the first time we had ever touched. 'Rayojini, my brother is here, and Avirzah'e Tartaruchi, whom you met before. Remember? We have a carriage. Come back to Sacramante with us. Tell us what happened, and we can perhaps explain a few things to you.'

She looked at me with fierce eyes. 'I'm not dead!'

I squeezed her shoulders. 'Of course not!' Poor Rayo: what had she gone through? I wanted to smother her with attention and comforts immediately.

'They've gone from the catacombs,' she said. 'I saw them come up with the dawn today, like a wind of light. They've gone now. They've gone to Samikha'il.'

'Samikha'il?'

'Yes. Sammael and Mikha'il. They are brothers and they are one. I can't explain, but I think they are something called Eloat now.'

For a moment I had to sit in silence beside her; both of us were now dazed women. So Sammael and Mikha'il had confronted each other again, and now Sammael was gone. I felt a pang of anger and jealousy that the traitor Mikha'il could take him from us so easily, but then I should have realised what would happen.

'Samikha'il did kill me,' Rayojini said, in a low voice, glancing at me sidelong. 'I went to Elenoen, where the eloim came from.'

'How?' I asked, in a breathless whisper.

She shrugged. 'I can't explain at the moment. I feel too peculiar.'

'Oh Rayojini,' I said, squeezing her shoulder, 'I don't know how you got back here, but I'm glad you did!'

'These awful people have been giving me blood to drink,' she said. 'They think I'm eloim and won't believe me when I say I'm not. It tasted terrible. It was disgusting. I'm really hungry.'

'Well, we'll get you something to eat, then,' I said. 'Come on, stand up. Come to the carriage.' She resisted my attempt to lift her to her feet.

'*Are* you Gimel Metatronim?' she asked suspiciously. 'I've seen so much of Gimel recently, but it was never really her.'

'I really am Gimel,' I said. 'I'm the presumptive little madam who's interfered in your life since you were eight. You can hate me for that, if you like, but I really think you should come to my carriage. It is warm in there, and I have some fleeces you can wrap up in.'

Rayojini pulled a face and stood up. Her mind was obviously damaged, but at least she was alive. Then she looked at me, as if she'd only just noticed I was there. 'Gimel?' Her voice was small.

'Yes?'

'Really you?'

'Really me.'

'You're a bitch!'

'I know.'

'I don't like being used, unless I know the purpose is a good one!'

'I know.'

She folded her arms and looked towards the carriage. 'Is that Beth down there?'

'Yes.'

'He is beautiful.'

'He is.'

'And so are you.' She paused. 'Is it really, *really* you?'

'The authentic version. Still arrogant, but learning fast. Less human than I was, but perhaps more humane. I don't know. I'm sorry, Rayojini. This was never your mess.'

'No, but it was my life,' she said, and made a grumbling sound, holding out her skirts. 'Look at this! It's disgusting! Sort of thing Liviana Tricante would wear! My clothes are all gone.'

'We can get you some more. It doesn't matter.'

'I'm not insane, Gimel Metatronim!' she said, giving me a fear-

405

fully wonderful glinting stare. 'Don't speak to me as if I am.' She sighed, shook her head, and then gave me an uncertain smile. 'Well, introduce me to your brother then, even if I do look like the queen of fools in this stupid dress.'

I had to ask. 'Are you angry with us, for all we did?'

She shrugged. 'I suppose I must be in a way. I don't know. I've seen amazing things, things that no other person alive has ever seen or ever will see, I suspect. You wouldn't believe it. I'm not sure I do yet, but I have to thank you for that at least.'

'I never wanted to hurt you, Rayojini. That's the truth. The boy you were travelling with, Keea, we thought he was our servant. He wasn't. I'm sorry about that. I hope he didn't harm you.'

She shook her head. 'No, he didn't.' Then she squinted at me. 'Do you know who he was, Gimel?'

'He was from Elenoen,' I said. 'We guessed that much.'

'He was Mikha'il.'

I had to put my hands over my mouth to stop myself making an undignified sound. The great traitor had supped my ichor, shared my bed? It was unthinkable! And Sammael had been so close to him without knowing it. At some point they might even have been in my house at the same time! Rayojini reached out and touched my arm.

'It doesn't matter now, does it?' she said, and grinned, wrinkling up her nose. 'I found him rather a pathetic creature actually, and I'm sure he's in need of a good soulscaper, but still . . . being conjoined with Sammael should cure his problems.'

'You really have seen wonderful things, haven't you!' I exclaimed.

'Nothing as wonderful as seeing you as a *real* person.' She smiled. 'This is all too . . . hmm, no words for it.'

'Let's go,' I said. 'We have all the time we need now, for words.'

Rayojini narrowed her eyes and said. 'Prove to me you're not going to disappear again.'

I abandoned propriety and held out my arms. She closed her eyes and we hugged each other fiercely. She squeezed the breath out of me and then pulled away a little. 'Still there? Good!' she said, and then held me close again. 'Thank . . . Who shall we thank? I know: thank Eloat!'

I said it too. And then we walked down the steps together, towards the waiting carriage.